SAVAGE
AWAKENING

Rosalind Haggard had been born and raised on Barbados. Never had she felt a moment's danger on this seething island paradise. But now, suddenly, the men she knew as faithful servants were fearful strangers. She could see their skins glistening with the heat of desire as they looked down at her stripped naked figure on the ground.

"Please, please. No more. Please . . ." she began.

Then she felt their hands. So many hands, exploring her breasts and buttocks and between her thighs, her mouth and her ears and her eyes and her nose and her hair. And then she felt the swelling flesh that filled her again and again and endlessly again.

These men were doing what none had ever done to her before—not even her husband. They were giving her a lesson in lust that no later lover would ever make her forget. . . .

THE INHERITORS
The HAGGARD Chronicles #2

Great Reading from SIGNET

The INHERITORS

The HAGGARD Chronicles # II

By
Christopher Nicole

A SIGNET BOOK
NEW AMERICAN LIBRARY
TIMES MIRROR

PUBLISHER'S NOTE

This novel is a work of fiction. Names, characters, places, and incidents are either the product of the author's imagination or are used fictitiously, and any resemblance to actual persons, living or dead, events, or locales is entirely coincidental.

COPYRIGHT © 1981 BY CHRISTOPHER NICOLE

All rights reserved

SIGNET TRADEMARK REG. U.S. PAT. OFF. AND FOREIGN COUNTRIES
REGISTERED TRADEMARK—MARCA REGISTRADA
HECHO EN CHICAGO, U.S.A.

SIGNET, SIGNET CLASSICS, MENTOR, PLUME, MERIDIAN AND NAL BOOKS are published by The New American Library, Inc., 1633 Broadway, New York, New York 10019

FIRST PRINTING, MAY, 1981

1 2 3 4 5 6 7 8 9

PRINTED IN THE UNITED STATES OF AMERICA

THE HAGGARD FAMILY

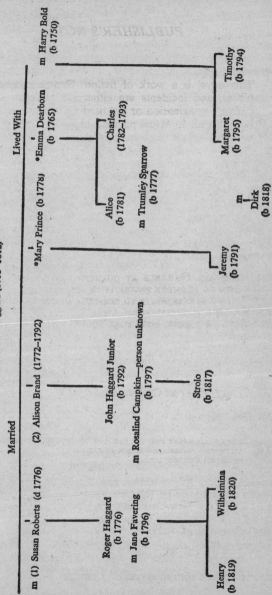

The
INHERITORS

PART ONE

THE TORY

Chapter 1

The Squire

The door of the bedroom opened, and Roger Haggard sat up. He had not slept, had made himself remain lying down, to obtain what rest he could; this was going to be a long day. And there had been a great deal to think about.

"Dawn, Captain Haggard," Corcoran said, and drew the draperies.

Roger got out of bed, splashed water on his face, cleaned his teeth, sat down for the batman to shave him.

"Not much cloud," Corcoran said. "It should be a good day, sir. Later."

Later, Roger thought, and inspected himself in the mirror. The features were all Haggard, aquiline, dominated by the long nose and jutting chin, rendered attractive by the high forehead and the wide mouth, the gleam of the pale blue eyes. He realized that he looked very like his father, a resemblance extending to the tall, spare frame, the square shoulders. It was not a comparison he had ever made before, consciously. Today it was very necessary.

Corcoran, small and busy, fussed as he dressed his master in the red jacket and gray trousers of his regiment, the Worcestershires, fastening the buttons and giving a last buff to the brasswork, holding out the shako as he might have held out a crown. "You'll do, Captain," he said as he always said, waiting with the sword belt.

Roger Haggard slowly opened and closed the fingers of his right hand, several times. The tendons, slashed during the assault on Badajoz six months before, were the sole reasons for his being here, at such a time and on such an occasion. But now they were healed. He could handle a sword again. And

3

therefore he must rejoin his men, and Wellington, in their long, slow push across Spain.

And leave Derleth behind. If he could. If he dared, now.

"Then let's go," he said.

Corcoran opened the door, Haggard stepped into the hall. At the bottom of the stairs several other people were gathered, turning to face him as he approached.

MacGuinness, the bailiff, big and bluff, and distinctly nervous this morning, raised his hat. "All ready, Mr. Haggard."

"Thank you, MacGuinness." Roger nodded to the butler and the footmen who also waited, dressed for outdoors, shuffling their feet. Corcoran had already opened the door to the huge withdrawing room. Roger hesitated for a moment and then went inside.

The furniture had been pushed back against the walls, as it had been when Alison Haggard had been mistress of Derleth and entertained the Derbyshire gentry. But today the very center of the room was occupied by the trestle table and the coffin. Roger slowed even more as he approached it. He had been a soldier since 1793, had seen death in all its many horrible and horrifying guises, had supposed himself immune. But this corpse was that of his own father, and besides, he was not going to *see* death today; John Haggard had put the muzzle of the pistol into his mouth before squeezing the trigger.

"Close it up, MacGuinness," Roger said.

"Yes, sir, Mr. Haggard." MacGuinness beckoned the two carpenters.

"Wait."

Their heads turned to look at the doorway, and Emma Bold. Amazing to suppose, Roger thought, that Emma was forty-seven. But equally amazing was it, for him, to realize that she was *only* forty-seven. If she had hardly changed since he could first remember her, she seemed to have been there forever. He had been four years old, a barefoot West Indian boy, when John Haggard had brought home his beautiful red-haired indentured servant. It had been the day Father had shot down Malcolm Bolton in the duel that had rocked Barbadian society to its core. Already a widower, with but the one young son, John Haggard had changed from the handsome and dashing darling of the island into an angry misanthrope, finding his only pleasure in bedding the transported thief who many said was a witch. Until he had

come to England and quarreled even with her, and driven her
out to become the wife of a tinker. But now she was back, at
the very end, and with her her daughter Meg. Meg had slept
under this roof last night, for the first time. But not for the
last. Roger's heart began to pound as he thought of it.

"You'll not want to look at him, Emma," he said.

She glanced at him, stood beside the coffin, peered inside.
Roger watched the gaminelike face, as pretty as it had been
when she had acted his foster mother amid the rolling canefields of Haggard's Penn, or here on Derleth during that first
year, before her quarrel with Father, when there had been so
much to explore, so much to learn. It had not changed, and
neither did her expression, now. A slight flaring of the nostrils, nothing more. That faceless corpse had taken her virgin-
ity, made her a mother and then robbed her of her children,
inflicted countless other injuries upon her. Yet Roger had no
doubt that, despite all, she loved him. Whatever his crimes,
John Haggard had been that sort of a man.

Emma turned away from the coffin, herself looked at
the door, where her daughters had also taken their positions.
Alice was her firstborn, only five years younger than Roger
himself, conceived on those hot Barbados nights when Emma
had lain in John Haggard's arms. Here the Haggard height
was tempered by the petiteness of her mother, the forceful
Haggard features softened by the tiny curves which were
Emma's beauty. But here too was the Haggard personality,
capable of hatred on a scale Emma had never found possible.

"I'll bury him," Alice said. "I'll not look on him."

"Close it up," Emma said.

Meg Bold stared at Roger, a faint flush filling her cheeks.
Perhaps she felt as unreal as himself. No Haggard here;
Harry Bold was very little larger than his wife, and Meg was
a tiny bundle of delight, her face peering wonderingly from
within her poke bonnet, brown as a berry and even prettier
than her mother's. All was on a similar minute scale, and the
more delicious for that. A tinker's daughter, by the cast-off
mistress of the wealthiest man in England. A tortured child,
set upon and raped by John Haggard's gamekeepers, on his
orders, to break up her budding romance with his younger
son, now knowing that her erstwhile lover lay under sentence
of death while her father and brother fled for their lives, and
yet, recovered, able to live, able to love. As Roger had discovered. And able to be loved?

Something else to be accomplished, if he could. If he dared.

"What of Master John, Mr. Haggard?" MacGuinness asked. He had the sense to know that things were different, with old John Haggard dead. Things could never be the same again, and for him as well, as he had for so many years carried out the dread bidding of his master.

Roger shook his head. "I doubt he'd wish to come. Leave him be." He took Emma's arm, knew that Alice and Meg walked behind, in front of MacGuinness, and then the servants carrying the coffin.

"What will you do?" Emma asked softly.

Do, Roger thought. Johnnie Haggard had led the Luddites against his own father's cotton mill, driven by anger and despair at the years of misunderstanding and festering hatred. The Bolds had escaped, but Johnnie had been taken, and frame-breaking was a capital offense, made so by an act of Parliament only months before. But there was more involved. Peter Wring, the head gamekeeper, had been shot. So the evidence suggested that Wring had led the assault on Meg Bold, but it was nonetheless murder, and John Haggard had promised his people of Derleth vengeance, be the culprit even his own son. Johnnie Haggard, manacled in the back room of the inn until a gallows could be constructed, was his most pressing problem.

"He'll not hang, Emma," he said softly. "I swear it. I'll not hang my own brother."

Her grip tightened on his, and they stepped outside. As Corcoran had said, it was going to be a good day. Only fleecy white clouds marked the early-morning sky, and the summer breeze was already warming. Derleth people claimed their valley was the most beautiful in all Derbyshire, even in winter, when the snow coated the surrounding peaks and the rain dripped damply into the duck pond; on a good summer's day there could be little argument, for this gentle zephyr did no more than ruffle the leaves in Haggard's game park, flutter a bow here, a cravat' tail there—the hideous scar that was the coal mine, and the ugly, square airless monolith that was the mill, were both hidden beyond the hills. As the turnpike followed the other side of the valley, only Derleth people knew the monstrosities which provided their daily bread were there at all, and this morning it did not matter. The villagers of

Derleth, men and women and children, were gathered on the road which crossed the manor-house drive, a vast mass, watching the house, watching the end of the man they had come to know, and fear, and respect, over the past twenty years.

Had they ever loved him? Roger doubted that. But would they ever love their new squire, either?

The procession from the house turned to the right, down a path which led by the lawns and the flower garden, parallel with the road, so that the crowd could move along with them. At the end of the path there was a wicket gate, and here a yardboy had been stationed to open it for the master, and the late master's body. It was scarce wide enough for two people to pass together, and Roger stood back to allow Emma first. Behind him the manor house towered, gray and green, stone and ivy, dominated by the turret room which John Nash had designed for John Haggard, and in which he had always slept, and in which he had killed himself. This house had stood for more than twenty years, yet was it still referred to as the New House. The Old House, the original manor, had been farther down the valley, in the direction the procession was now moving, following the path which had been the old driveway. John Haggard had torn that house down, replanted the site with poplars, and in the center of it had built the family vault. There were only two bodies in that vault, to this day. Alison Haggard lay there with her second child. She had died, so it was said, screaming curses against the man whose lust had destroyed her; Johnnie Haggard's mother, she had looked to him to avenge her.

And had she not won in the end? Had not Johnnie Haggard been, after all, her instrument of vengeance?

The crowd halted on the road above them, looking down on the little procession as it approached the gray mausoleum. There was less respect now than anticipation. Roger sucked air into his lungs and felt Emma's fingers again tighten on his as they saw the small black-clad figure waiting for them.

"That is my family vault you protect, Mr. Malling," he said.

The Reverend Malling drew himself up, arm outflung, finger pointing. "This is consecrated ground, Captain Haggard," he said. "Consecrated ground. That cadaver is a suicide. He'll not enter here."

"I'd not expect you to say a prayer for him, Mr. Malling,"

Roger said. "But you'll not stop me burying my father where he intended. Step aside."

"You'll be damned," Malling said, and threw out his other arm as well. "Every one of you. Damned."

Feet shuffled behind Roger. But he was not afraid of being deserted. The Derleth domestics feared the name of Haggard far more than they feared the name of God.

"I'll take the responsibility for that," Roger said. "Step aside."

"I'll have the law on you," Malling said, descending to practicalities.

"I *am* the law on Derleth, Mr. Malling," Roger said. Now, how often had he heard those words uttered by his father, as the prelude to some act of tyranny or self-indulgence? "Corcoran."

The soldier left the procession and went forward, his red jacket glimmering amid the green of the trees. "No trouble now, parson," he said. "No trouble."

"The law," Malling growled. "The law of God and the law of England. You'd set them both aside, Roger Haggard. Like father, like son. Aye, and your end will be no better."

Roger waited. It was not a point he felt able to debate this morning. But the parson had walked to one side, Corcoran at his elbow. Roger unlocked the great wooden door, peered inside. Alison Haggard had lain in here alone, for twenty years, and she had been no more than twenty when she had died. She would still be a beautiful woman had she lived. And suppose she had? Suppose she were standing there, to look at him, as she had looked at him on that never-to-be-forgotten night when he had held her in his arms, his father's wife, and understood that he was the victim of as perverted a plot as he could ever have thought of. Twenty years, and he could remember her face as if he had seen it yesterday.

But she was dead. Her coffin lay neatly on its plinth, the only coffin, because her babe had been buried with her. She was dead, and the tragedy which had split the family was finally complete, as John Haggard's coffin was laid beside her.

Behind Roger the vault was full, the servants pressing forward to peer into this hallowed place. The only sound was that of breathing.

"May your soul rest in peace, Father," Roger said. "At last."

He turned, and the crowd hastily backed out.

"Why?" Emma asked. "I can't believe it. Why?"

"He was evil," Meg said. No doubt, Roger supposed, as she had never met his father, only encountered his works, she was quoting.

"He sometimes acted hastily or irresponsibly," Emma said. "But he was strong, and powerful, and bold. He feared no man. And no demon, either."

"He had just condemned his son to death," Roger said. "Simply because he did not know how to stop the proceedings once they began."

"I can't believe that," Emma declared. "Just as I can't believe he really meant Johnnie to hang. I know he didn't."

"You did not know him." Alice Haggard spoke quietly, as she always spoke quietly. "I lived with him for all of my life. You came and went. He killed himself because he was alone. Because no one would understand him."

They gazed at her.

"He killed himself because of me," she said. "When he returned from court yesterday, he came to my room. He told me what he'd done, and how he felt. He told me that there was no one in the world, not even you, Roger, knew how he felt. Only me. Because we had lived together for so long. He asked me to go back to Barbados with him. He said he had been happy, on Barbados with Emma. He would be happy there again. He was going to place Derleth on the market and go home. He asked me to go with him." She sighed. "And I refused."

Roger followed them outside. "He was Haggard," he said. "He set himself certain goals, certain ideals, and lived by them. Then he died by them."

The door clanged shut, and the key rasped in the lock. The crowd still waited, to watch the family return.

"And now *you* are Haggard," Alice said softly.

"What will you do?" Emma had asked. But he was Haggard. He could do anything, defy church and law, here in Derleth. He could even marry Meg now. If he chose. If he dared. Because church and law were not so severe enemies as society.

The crowd had thinned, and Alice walked beside her mother. Whether by accident or design, Meg was next to him, and a moment later her hand stole into his. They had loved but once, wildly and tumultuously, and for him, unbelievably.

He had known, he had *supposed* he had known, why, at least on her part. She had loved his brother until the dreadful night John Haggard, learning of his younger son's liaison with a tinker's daughter, had sent Wring and the gamekeepers to teach her a lesson. That was the night Johnnie Haggard had run away, and learned to hate. But what had Meg learned? Hate as well, certainly, but fear, of so many things, even of herself. Until she had met a stranger, big and bluff and apparently so sure of himself, who had also borne the name of Haggard, and who was everything his brother was not. To give herself to him must have been almost a necessity, he supposed, to prove herself a woman still, to prove that she could feel still—and perhaps to avenge her wrongs.

At seventeen, Meg Bold knew so much about men. At thirty-six, Roger Haggard knew so little about women. He had known nothing of women that night he had so carelessly drifted into the orbit of his stepmother and her sister. Even after only a year of marriage, Alison had already learned to hate John Haggard, already yearned to avenge *her*self on the arrogant, self-sufficient millionaire her father's ambitions had driven her to marry. And how better to achieve that revenge than by seducing her sixteen-year-old stepson, newly commissioned into the Royal Artillery, about to depart with the army for a campaign in Holland—and already also estranged from his father? When he had understood what was happening, what had happened, she had laughed at him, in that ringing peal that would haunt him for the rest of his days. That laugh had driven him to desert his regiment and his commission, and then had driven him to reenlist, under a false name, and spend the best part of his life as a private soldier, following the fortunes of the British army from Walcheren to Alexandria, and then from Lisbon to Badajoz. He had sought nothing more, had earned himself a reputation as a silent, morose, womanless man. The very thought of the sex had been anathema to him.

That he was a born soldier, that he had risen to be a company sergeant major, that his act of heroism at Talavera should have brought him to the attention of Wellington, and that his delirium following his wound on that occasion should have betrayed his secret had made no difference to the essential personality. Even the reconciliation with his father—who had long known of Alison's crime while supposing his eldest son dead—had broken through none of his reserve. And the

looming domestic crisis to which he had returned had not encouraged him to throw himself into the arms of his family,
after so long. That he had been restored to his inheritance,
that he would one day be Haggard, had seemed less important than the war to which he ached to return; Father had
still been a comparatively young man, and a remarkably fit
man—there had seemed time enough for acclimatization to
the world he had abandoned nineteen years before.

Until he had so strangely wandered into the ken of this
marvelous Gypsy. As her mother had been for so long his father's mistress, his own foster mother when he had been a
boy, they could share almost as brother and sister. As there
was no blood between them, they could share as no brother
and sister would ever dare. He had been appalled at what
had happened, afraid to look on her face, afraid of her
hatred and her disgust. And she had laughed her pleasure.
And so he had promised her anything and everything she
might ever want. How his brother officers would laugh were
they to hear that.

He had always intended them to hear that. Meg Bold was
only the second woman he had ever known; he wished to
know no others. But even there, he had supposed time was on
his side. Meg might not yet know which fork to use, what to
do with her napkin, but Emma had once known those things,
and Emma could teach her daughter. There had been time.

Until last night, there had been time. But he was Haggard,
and he had things to do. There would be time again.

They walked up the path. The servants had hurried on
ahead. Only MacGuinness hovered. Time had run out for
MacGuinness as well. He would be remembering all of
twenty years ago, when he had been sent to evict the tinker
Bold from Derleth, and been opposed by the young master,
and Alice, and poor Charlie, Alice's younger brother, for
nineteen years now drifting around the Mediterranean Sea,
his bones picked clean by the fish. Now the young master,
and Miss Alice, were the heirs to Derleth. MacGuinness
would be wondering how much *they* remembered.

"You'll come to the study, MacGuinness," Roger said, and
climbed the stairs. Emma and Alice watched him go. They
knew better than to interfere with the squire's thoughts. But
he needed Alice. He paused, looked down. "You too, Alice."

Meg climbed beside him; she was afraid to let him out of
her sight for a moment. What will you *do*?

But he was Haggard. He could do anything.

They entered the study, and he put his arm around her shoulders. Instantly she had turned against him, her gown and single petticoat nothing more than an extra layer of skin as she moved her groin against his.

"Oh, Captain Haggard," she whispered. "Oh, Roger, if you knew how I *want* you."

Haggard gazed over her head at MacGuinness, face scarlet with embarrassment, twisting his hat between his hands.

"We'll talk in a moment," Roger said to the girl, gently disengaging himself. "But don't go. Sit over there."

She gazed at him, bit her lip, and then backed across the room and sat down. She was flushed and breathing heavily, and looked lovelier than ever. Was she angry? But the first thing she would have to learn, if she would ever be the mistress of Derleth, was that their love must be kept for their bedchamber.

Their love. He could feel his own cheeks filling with blood at the thought.

"Are you a Derleth man, MacGuinness?" he asked.

"In a manner of speaking, Mr. Haggard. I've lived here for twenty-five years. Before your dad, God rest his soul, came."

"I remember, MacGuinness. What did my father pay you?"

"Well, sir, Mr. Haggard, he paid me five pounds a week. And the house, you understand."

Roger nodded. "Well, I think you have served your time, MacGuinness. You were a faithful servant of my father's, and I'll not hold it against you that you carried out his bidding." He opened his drawer, took out a sheet of headed notepaper, wrote quickly and neatly. "Here is an order on my bank for three hundred pounds. That is a year's wages plus something for the house."

MacGuinness took the paper slowly, stared at it. "What am I to do?"

"You are to retire, MacGuinness. Three hundred pounds. There's a fortune. It'll set you up somewhere, if you've any sense. But not on Derleth."

MacGuinness' head came up. "You'll be your own bailiff?" His gaze drifted over Roger's uniform. "You'll be giving up the army, then. Again."

He was so angry he did not care that an insulted Haggard might well stop payment on the order.

But Roger merely leaned back in his chair. "I'll manage my own affairs, MacGuinness," he said. "You'll be off Derleth by tomorrow night."

The big man hesitated, fingers clawing into fists until he realized that he was crumpling the precious piece of paper. Then he squared his shoulders. "You're cursed," he said. "You bear the name of Haggard. You're cursed, Captain. Bad luck on you."

He looked for a moment at Alice, waiting just outside the door, then went down the stairs.

"Roger." Alice hurried into the room, leaned across the desk to hold his hands. "You *will* give up the army?"

"No."

She released him and straightened, pink spots in her cheeks, while Meg gave a wail and jumped to her feet.

"I'll give up the army when the war is over," Roger said. "It must end sometime."

"You'll go away," Meg wailed. "You'll be killed. After all, you'll be killed."

Roger got up to take her in his arms. "Now, Meg, of course I won't be killed. I've never been killed before, have I?"

"It'll never end," Alice said. Slowly she sank onto the chair before the desk. "How can it end? Bonaparte is in Moscow. All Russia belongs to him. But he can't invade England. Why should it ever end?"

"It will end," Roger said, feeling Meg squirming against him once again, her fingers tight on his shoulders. "Someday. Someday soon. I'm sure of it. But I cannot desert my men now, Alice. Not until . . ." He squeezed Meg close. "Look, I promise you, when we have freed Spain of the French, if there is no sign of peace then, I will come home. I promise you."

"Oh, Roger . . ." She leaned across the desk again, her eyes glistening. "If only I could believe you."

"I have promised you," he said.

"But who will manage the estate until then?"

"You will," Roger said.

Alice turned on the seat, face twisted. "Me?"

"You reminded me at the tomb, you've been the one who stayed with Father, all of your life. You must know more about Derleth than anyone else."

"But . . . what of the magistracy?"

"It'll stand vacant. You may rely on your neighbor Burton of Plowding to sit for you. He's a good man."

"It cannot be," she protested. "Who'll take orders from a woman?"

"They'll take orders from whoever I tell them to, Alice. And when you get married, there'll be a place here for your husband, as well."

"Married?" She flushed, suitably distracted, as he had intended. "I'll not marry."

Roger returned round the desk, sat down, still holding Meg's hand; she stood beside him. "Why not?"

"Well . . . how can I? I'm thirty-one. I'm . . ."

"As lovely as ever you were. Of course you'll marry. There'll be no Father to stand in your way now. But first of all, the estate. Listen carefully. You'll rebuild the mill, as Father wished, but you'll make it more healthy. You'll put in windows, and proper toilets. And you'll pay the wages while it is being built. Father promised them that. And it's right. *They* didn't burn it down."

Alice chewed her lip.

"You'll dismiss whichever of the servants from here you see fit, and replace them with others."

Alice frowned at him. "Why should I do that?"

"I don't know them. I don't know which of them will serve us, now Father is dead. Mary Prince . . ."

"Mary hasn't slept with Father in ten years. She's a good housekeeper."

"Didn't she have a son?"

"What difference does that make? He was sent off to Canada, oh, ten years ago. Father did that."

"I said, the decision is yours. We'll have another chat before I go."

"When?"

"I must be off, tomorrow, I think. As soon as—"

"Tomorrow?" Meg cried, throwing her arms around his neck.

"I must, sweetheart. I was recalled a week ago. I must. But listen to me." He held her hands. "You'll stay here. You and Emma. You'll live here, with Alice, until I come back."

"Live here?" Meg looked around her, left and right, as if expecting the oak paneling to rot away before her eyes, the draperies to collapse on the floor.

"Wouldn't you like that?"

"Live *here*?" she asked again, her voice sinking to a whisper.

"Oh, it'll be marvelous," Alice said. "You, and Mama . . . here with me. It'll be marvelous. I'm so glad."

"And when I come back," Roger said, "we . . . we'll marry." There, he'd said it. Why? It wasn't necessary. He had lain on her belly once in his life, and been ashamed. Her maidenhead had already been lost. He had watched her laugh, and thought then how lovely she was, how like his memory of her mother. But was having loved the mother, who had acted as his mother too, a reason for marrying the daughter? The child of a tinker and a Gypsy, brought up to scrape what living she could by any means she could, to steal and cheat and poach, if need be. Even to prostitute herself, if need be? How could she ever be the mistress of Derleth?

But Alice was a lady, simply because of her upbringing. Surely she could teach her own half-sister a similar style?

Alice was gazing at him, her face a picture of consternation. Did she know what that proposal had cost him? Or did she know, far more than himself, the dangers involved?

"Marry?" It had taken some seconds for the words to penetrate Meg's consciousness. "Marry? You'll marry *me*, Captain Haggard?"

He kissed her on the nose. "Only if you'll call me Roger."

She stared at him as if he were a stranger. Then she pushed him away and ran onto the landing. "Ma," she shouted. "Ma," she screamed. "Captain Haggard's going to marry me. Ma."

Alice got up. "You can't carry all the guilt of this family on your shoulders, Roger," she said softly. "Not even you."

He forced a smile. "Guilt? What nonsense. I love the girl. I loved her the moment I set eyes on her."

Alice gazed at him for some seconds; then she shrugged. "And Johnnie?"

"She no longer cares for him. Nor he for her."

"I was wondering how he would take to her as a sister-in-law. Supposing you can save his life."

"I have already done so, by being Haggard."

"And legally? He was condemned in a court of law."

"An irregular court of law, in my opinion." He came round the desk, squeezed her shoulders. "He'll not hang, Alice.

You've my word on that. But legally, why, we'll wait on Lord Byron. He rode to the duke. We'll wait on him."

George Gordon, sixth Lord Byron of Newstead Abbey in Nottinghamshire, sat a horse well. Mounted, his somewhat heavy body and his club foot were equally well concealed, and one was aware only of the arrogant beauty of the face, waving dark auburn hair, the infectious glamour of his personality. When excited, as now, he dominated the landscape, galloping his exhausted horse up the drive to Derleth Manor, kicking and whipping at the same time as he gave a tremendous shout. "Haggard," he bellowed. "Haggard."

Grooms hurried forward to secure his bridle and bring the horse to a halt. Roger was already waiting in the doorway, Alice hurrying down the stairs behind him. "What news?"

"News?" Byron cried. "News?" He limped toward them, thrust a sheet of paper into Roger's hands. "I'd appreciate a glass."

"Champagne for his lordship," Roger said, leading them into the downstairs parlor as he read the letter. "Champagne for us all. His grace considers that the proceedings *were* irregular, in that no father should be permitted to sit in legal judgment on his own son. He pronounces them quashed, and . . ." He raised his head to stare at Byron. "Requires a new trial?"

Byron seized a glass from Nugent's tray, drained it, took another. "Well, man, what would you? Johnnie was out breaking frames."

"And that is a hanging crime, no matter who the judge."

"Oh, my God." Alice sat down.

"Is that fellow going to stand there the day?" Byron demanded.

"Put the tray down, Nugent," Roger commanded. "And close the doors."

Nugent bowed and obeyed. Byron took his third glass.

"Well?" Roger demanded.

"A very private message, from the duke," Byron said. "Having regard to all the circumstances, as I outlined them, he is of the opinion that were Mr. John Haggard Junior to take himself from England in great haste, never to return, proceedings would be dropped."

"From England?" Roger repeated.

"Never to return?" Alice was on her feet again. "But where?"

"Well . . . what of Canada? The Americas . . ."

"Barbados," Roger said, snapping his fingers.

"Barbados?" Alice and Byron asked together.

"Why not? He'll manage Haggard's Penn."

"Johnnie?"

"Well . . . he can hardly make a worse job of it than Ferguson has been doing these past twelve years." Roger ran to the door, threw it open. "Nugent, Nugent. You'll go to the inn and fetch Master John here. Wait, I'll give you the authority." He went to the table in the corner, pulled a sheet of notepaper from the drawer, wrote the necessary instructions. "Now, hurry."

Nugent touched his forehead, left the room.

"Barbados," Alice said. "Four thousand miles."

"It may be the making of him," Byron suggested.

"And you, better than anyone, my lord, should know how much needs to be done."

Byron met her gaze without a blush. "Indeed, Alice," he said. "I would agree that I have been more a brother to Johnnie than you have ever been a sister."

Alice did flush, while Roger hurried forward to take both their hands. "Whatever the outcome, my lord," he said, "we are both eternally grateful to your efforts. As will Johnnie be."

"Friendship demanded nothing less," Byron said.

Roger felt Alice gently tugging her hand free. "There are things to which I must attend." In the doorway she paused. "Believe me, my lord," she said, "as Roger says, I am in your debt, forever."

"A strange girl," Byron said. "But a most handsome and elegant one. I wonder she never married. Do you know, Haggard, were she not seven years my elder, I would beseech her hand of you?"

He was smiling, that utterly charming smile which melted every female heart, and even, so it was said, a goodly number of male ones as well. Friendship. In the name of friendship this man, the current literary toast of England, with all of London anxious to throw itself at his feet, had not only stayed on Derleth to support Johnnie during the trial, but during the last forty-eight hours had ridden close to a hundred miles at breakneck speed. All on behalf of someone he must consider his social inferior. They had been at Cambridge together, but Johnnie had been a freshman in Byron's fourth year. Then Byron had gone abroad for very nearly three years. Yet on his return, the friendship had resumed, as close as ever.

Friendship. But did Lord Byron *have* any friends? Were there not only lovers?

Roger realized he was himself flushing, and squeezed Byron's hands once again. "I would give her to you, my lord, were you but to ask," he said.

"Partners in crime, by God," Byron said, and released him to find another glass of champagne. "And she has everything I require, I do assure you, from beauty to expectations. But I'd not inflict myself upon you as a relative, Haggard. That were to make us enemies." He raised his glass. "I'll give you a toast. Master John Haggard." Once again the smile, but this time accompanied by a singularly meaningful look. "At the least, he can come to no harm in Barbados."

"Barbados." Johnnie Haggard had inherited his mother's beauty; the pale, delicate features sat oddly on top of the tall, lanky Haggard frame. Now he raised his glass, looked through it at the light before drinking. "Can hanging be that much worse?"

"Johnnie!" Alice admonished. "After all Lord Byron has done for you."

Johnnie made a mock bow to the poet. "And I am grateful, my lord, believe me. Perhaps it is that I never expected to find myself standing here again. And in such strange company."

The huge drawing room was quiet. And incongruous. For if the three men had dressed for dinner, as had Alice, Emma and Meg's best gowns were hardly better than rags; Alice was too tall to be of any assistance to them in the immediate matter of clothes. Now Meg flushed, as she caught Johnnie's gaze, although why *she* should flush, Roger thought, when he was the one who had run away and left her to fight as best she could, and suffer as best she could . . . He supposed he would never like his half-brother, would always indeed be close to hating him. Not only for what he had allowed to happen to Meg, but because he was Alison's son.

Yet tonight was not an occasion for hate. It was Roger's hope that hate might have fled Derleth forever, as its principal instigators both lay securely locked in the family vault. "You'll like Barbados," he said. "Like it. You'll love it. I did. And so did Alice."

"It was a happy place," Alice agreed.

"The happiest I have ever know," Emma said.

Meg looked from one to the other; poor child, Roger thought, she does not even know where Barbados is. So much to be done, for her and to her and with her. But was not that a main part of the pleasure to come?

"And hot," Byron said. "A heat which will warm your bones, Johnnie, boy. No more rheumatics. Why, I've almost a mind to come with you."

"My lord?" Johnnie's petulance disappeared as his face lit up.

"Almost," Byron said. "There is too much to be done here. But I do like the heat. The Mediterranean. There is the place to be. The fount of all our knowledge, all our history, all our glory. There is where I shall end my days." He smiled. "Who knows, perhaps you may be able to join me, one day."

"One day," Johnnie said.

"It may be possible," Roger agreed. "But a spell in Barbados first. You must be away tomorrow."

"Tomorrow?"

"Well, we are engaged in perverting the course of justice, are we not? I do not suppose his grace would like you to remain around for too long. Besides, I am returning to London tomorrow as well, to find a ship for Lisbon. So I will be able to see to your affairs personally."

"Tomorrow?" Meg cried, tears starting to her eyes.

"Now, my darling girl, I have explained it to you."

"There were arrangements," Emma said in a low voice.

"Alice will see to everything."

"Everything?" Emma asked.

"Well . . ." Roger put down his glass, held her hands. "I am trying to do what is best, for us all. A public announcement would be unwise, at this moment, as I am going to be away for the next few months. But here and now, before us all, and before Lord Byron, who may be my witness"—he released one of Emma's hands to take Meg's—"I declare my love for Meg, declare my intention of marrying her and of making her mistress of Derleth House." He raised his head to meet Johnnie's gaze, watch the sudden quickening of breathing which dilated his nostrils, so like Alison.

"By Gad," Byron said, and raised his glass. "A toast to the happy couple. And a kiss from the blushing fiancée." He put his arm round Meg's waist to give her a squeeze and a kiss, and her threatening tears dissolved into a giggle.

"Then I must congratulate you too," Johnnie said. "Forgive me, Roger, for not stepping forward immediately, but you took me by surprise." He held out his hand, and Roger shook it. "I sometimes suppose," Johnnie said very quietly, "that Father is not dead at all, only somehow miraculously made younger. Save of course that Father would never have married the girl."

Roger stared at him, fingers tight on his. Were you not my brother, he thought, I would sight you down the end of a pistol. Or leave you to choke on the end of a rope. He smiled. "As you say, Johnnie, Father would not have married the girl."

"And you would give her all of this?"

"To your exclusion, dear brother? I will give her what she deserves. As I will give you what you deserve."

Johnnie pulled his hand free, lifted his glass. "Then here's a toast to us all," he said, his eyes simmering pools of light blue anger.

"To us all," Alice said, and kissed Roger on the cheek. "To us all. I think dinner is ready."

Roger Haggard stood at the window of his bedchamber, looked out at the night, still not entirely gathered, to leave the trees in the deer park billowing shadows in the evening breeze. His trees now, as the stags which wandered beneath them were his stags. His cotton mill and his coal mine. He had not been over there since his father's death. This was cowardly of him, even if he could tell himself there had not been time. But he hated them both. He hated the thought of human beings shut up for hours on end to work at an endless, repetitive labor, even as he hated the thought of the men, and the boys and girls, dispatched a hundred feet and more under the earth, to struggle on their hands and knees, naked in the grime, inhaling the coal dust which would send them to early graves.

But there was nothing he could do about them. They were part of his wealth, and were he to close the mine and the mill, they would starve, while he would dwindle. It was a cruel world. As a career soldier he could have no doubt about that. He could only hope to alleviate their misery to the best of his ability.

By running off to the war? Because he knew that was what he was doing. The army was the only life he truly knew. Life on Derleth, life as an English gentleman, and as a Member of Parliament—because Derleth returned its own M.P., and he was traditionally the squire—would all have to be learned, and it could not be learned while his emotions were in so chaotic a state, his ambitions so distorted by memory. There was no escaping Father, for the moment. Every time he looked at Emma, there lay the memory of Father. Even in Mary Prince, one of those Father had seized from the coal face in his lust for experience, for young female flesh; the servants whispered that he had taken her to his bed without washing, so that in the morning the sheets had been stained black. Father had to be escaped. The many complexities and problems that went with being squire of Derleth had to be escaped, for a season, in the clear-cut business of fighting and killing, of knowing your enemies and your friends, of surviving.

Of being heroic while knowing that one had run away, leaving the truly difficult task to one's sister. But he would run away to return. And when he returned, he would be ready to be Haggard. He would *be* Haggard, in mind as well as body.

"You'll take a glass, sir?" Corcoran asked, anxious to please as ever.

Roger shook his head. "I'm for an early night. We've a long day ahead of us tomorrow."

"Oh, aye, sir. And sorry I'll be to be leave this lovely place."

Roger got into bed, and Corcoran carefully adjusted the nightcap.

"You'll be coming back, Corcoran. I promise you that. Good night to you."

"And to you, sir." Corcoran blew out the candle, tiptoed to the door. A happy man, Corcoran. He had been a fresh recruit when he had first seen action, at Talavera, under the watchful eyes of his strange, silent sergeant major. And following the metamorphosis, he had attached his star to that of the new officer's, never dreaming it would take him so high, to a squirearchy, and the wealthiest inheritance in all England. No wonder he could see little sense in returning to risk his life all over again.

No one could see any sense in it.

Haggard sighed, closed his eyes, and opened them again at the soft scrape of fingers on his door.

He sat up, pulled the nightcap from his head. Again the coward. After dinner he had sent them all to bed, left only Johnnie and Byron sitting up over a glass of port, as they liked doing. And what else did they like doing? Sodomy was another capital offense. But what they did, what road to ruin they took, was their business. He had saved Johnnie from execution for frame-breaking and murder, as he had sworn to do. Next time the boy could look out for himself.

Something to be anticipated? But he had fled them as well, while Meg had stared after him with those wide brown eyes. She had been sending him messages, and he had refused to accept them. Knowing all the while that she would come?

The door opened, closed again. Now he could smell her. No perfume for a tinker's daughter, but a glorious freshness such as he had never known before.

"Captain Haggard?" she whispered.

"The name's Roger."

"Roger." She stood by the bed, a tiny wisp in a white cotton nightdress. "You're leaving tomorrow."

Roger swung his legs out of bed. "For a brief while."

She sat beside him, rested her head on his shoulder. "Too long. I've nothing but you, Captain Haggard."

"You've Emma, and Alice. And you've Derleth. You'll be so busy you'll not notice I'm gone."

"During the day. Now . . ." She took his hand, placed it on her breast. The thin material might not have been there at all; the swelling flesh, the pointed nipple, seemed to suck into his hand, and her mouth was turned up for his kiss, while when his tongue touched hers she gave a little wriggle and her own hand slid down his shirtfront as she searched his breeches.

He took his mouth away. "No," he said. "You're to be a lady."

"And ladies do not fuck?"

"They do not use that word, for a start." He kissed her again, quickly and lightly, moving his hand to hold her shoulders. "You are going to be a very great lady, Meg. Margaret Haggard, mistress of Derleth, and of Haggard's Penn as well."

"But you will . . . lie with me, Captain Haggard? Say you'll lie with me?"

"As your husband, Meg. As your husband. I'm sorry about what happened in the wood."

"Sorry?" she cried.

"I mean, it was wonderful. I knew then that I loved you. That I would always love you. But now we're betrothed, why, I must wait. We must wait. Nothing must spoil what we are going to have. Can you understand that?"

Her body seemed to subside; her flesh slid through his fingers. "I understand that it is what you want, Captain Haggard." She got up, hands hanging at her side. "You'll say good-bye to me in the morning?"

"Of course I will. Early, mind."

She nodded, went to the door, hesitated. "You do *want* to marry me, Captain? It's not just . . . well . . ."

"I want to marry you, Meg. I love you. I have never loved anyone before you, as you. I want to marry you. I am going to marry you."

He heard the rush of her breath in the darkness as she smiled. The door opened. Then her head turned again. "You do·*like* to fuck, Captain Haggard? Don't you?"

"You'll do well, Nugent old fellow. I expect to see Derleth blooming when I get back." Roger shook both the butler's hands, smiled at him. "And don't forget. Miss Alice will see to everything. She has complete powers of attorney. You may rely on her, utterly, as I am relying on her, as I am relying on you."

Nugent sighed, and nodded. "Of course, Master Roger. When you come home . . ."

I will no longer be "Master Roger," Roger thought. Not even to you, Nugent. I'll be Squire Haggard. "When I come home," he said, and walked quickly down the line of footmen and housemaids, to smile at them all, and take each one's hand, cook and the grooms and yardboys, and at the end, Mary Prince. Mary Prince was two years younger than himself, and knew so much more. They all did, but Mary was unique. At least so far as was known.

"You'll help Mistress Alice, Mary," he said.

"Of course I will, sir."

"Of course you will."

Alice stood alone, part of the establishment, while Emma

and Meg, together a few feet farther on, were strangers. He kissed his sister on each cheek, then the mouth. "I feel a rat."

"But you are going."

"Yes."

Her chin came up. "Then be sure, brother, that Derleth will be waiting for you when you return."

"Had I not been sure of that, Alice, I would stay, at whatever cost to my honor." He hesitated, bit his lip. "Alice, there is something . . ."

"Something you lack the courage to say?"

"Am I that conspicuous a coward?"

She smiled at him. "No. Never a coward, Roger. You are that conspicuously confused. And now you fear that Harry Bold may come back."

He frowned. "How did you know that?"

She shrugged. "What else can you *have* to fear?"

"And if he does?"

"You must leave him to me, Roger."

How strong was her face, how determined. Did he have that strength, after all? "He will have rights, I suppose."

"None which will stand up to what you intend." Her fingers closed on his, squeezing. "You do intend, Roger. You *do* intend?"

"Yes," he said. "I do intend, Alice."

"Then Godspeed, dearest brother. Only, be sure you come back to Derleth."

He kissed her again; then it was time to embrace Emma, before turning to Meg. Another embrace, a kiss, a deep and lasting kiss, a squirm against him. But he was in a hurry to escape, a hurry to avoid the possibility of her tears. Because he had none of his own?

"Free," Johnnie Haggard yelled, kicking his horse to send it galloping down the turnpike. "Free. Free of Derleth." He drew rein, looked over his shoulder. "How I have always hated that place. Will I be free in Barbados?"

"As free as air," Roger promised, smiling despite himself.

"Free," Johnnie shouted again, and resumed his gallop.

Roger and Byron rode stirrup-to-stirrup, more slowly, Corcoran and Byron's man Fletcher a respectable distance behind. "You cannot blame him for being happy," Byron said.

"I do not blame him for being at least relieved," Haggard agreed.

"But you will be pleased to see the back of him."

Roger gave him a glance. "I won't deny that. He is even more confused than I."

"Confused," Byron mused, perhaps to himself. "You'll forgive me for thinking that you are a considerable fool, Roger Haggard."

"I'm not sure I should forgive you for saying it."

Byron smiled. "I speak my mind. To my friends, I speak it more often than perhaps I should."

"And I am your friend?"

"I should not like to have you an enemy, Captain Haggard. Believe me, I understand your problems, the thoughts that must be hurling themselves against each other in your brain. And yet, to give up all this, for a bullet in Spain . . ."

"I shall be back."

"That is surely in the hands of the gods. And then, to limit your future to such an extent . . ."

"You tread on dangerous ground, my lord."

"Yet must I say it. You mean to marry that . . . that Gypsy?"

"I do."

"But why? You've bedded her, I have no doubt. And she will be happy to come to you whenever you wish, for the rest of your life."

Roger drew rein. "Byron—"

"Listen to me. *Then* challenge me, if you wish. Just remember that you may be a soldier, but pistols are my hobby. And listen to me. A man should marry for posterity. Position, family, wealth . . ." A peculiar expression crossed his face. "That, at least, is not your problem. But sex, never. Where is the point of it? Whoever you marry, my dear Haggard, will bore you within the year. Without the ties of mutual advantage, it will be a disaster. And to *marry* a disaster . . . Hear me. I meant a social disaster. Do you suppose a single door will be open to you, with Margaret Bold at your side?"

"My father sought all his life to open doors, my lord," Roger said, speaking quietly and evenly. "He married, to open doors, as you would suggest. Thank God, in my years as a common soldier, a fate which overtook me thanks entirely to his desire to open those doors, I learned that there are more important things in life than position or the ability to pick up the right fork at dinner."

"Spoken like a man," Byron said. "And a Haggard. Man, were all England composed of people like you, we'd have no fear of the future. But the future . . ." He touched his horse with his heels, sent it walking along the road toward the next rise, where Johnnie Haggard waited for them. "It is desperate. Desperate, Haggard. This Tory government is so hellbent on bringing down Bonaparte, supposing such a thing is possible, that it pays no attention to what is happening under its very nose. You'd not see a guillotine set up in Whitehall, now, would you?"

"I do not expect to."

"It can happen. There is not that much difference between England in 1812 and France in 1792. Last week, before all this happened, you were kind enough to listen to me."

"So I did."

"And I gained the impression you were not altogether a hidebound Tory."

"Like my father, you mean? I hope I am not a hidebound anything, as yet."

"There'll be a few days in London before you take ship. May I introduce you?"

"I'd be flattered."

"Whigs, mind."

"I have no politics, Lord Byron."

Byron laughed, and kicked his horse into a trot. "Then we must see that when you do accumulate that curse, Captain Haggard, you fly the true colors."

"May I present your hostess?" Byron said. "Wilhelmina Favering, Countess of Alderney."

They had climbed the great staircase, and up to this moment a footman had barred their view into the ballroom. A small soiree, Byron had said; there were at least twelve carriages outside. And he had not attended a London occasion for eighteen years. But he was Haggard, no longer a terrified youth. He simply had to get used to the idea. He squared his shoulders—he wore dress scarlet—and then felt them sag again as he took in the woman before him. He had not supposed anyone quite so beautiful could possibly exist outside a dream. Lady Alderney was very small, just over five feet tall, he estimated; she was also, he had been told by Byron, approaching her fiftieth birthday, although this would have been impossible to estimate. And yet so perfectly was she proportioned, so dazzling was the raven perfection of her midnight hair, so exquisite the cast of features, each one small and perfectly fitted to the other, as if carved by some immortal sculptor, so glowing the deep amber of her eyes and so welcoming the sudden widening of her mouth, he felt for a moment like a man who has raised a glass to his lips and tossed it off at a gulp, supposing it water, only to discover too late that it is rum. She wore an absolutely plain white gown, slashed in a breathtaking décolletage, which but accentuated her coloring.

"My dear Captain Haggard," she said, her voice low and yet possessing a lilt which accompanied the rest of her like a cloak. "I have heard so much about you. Why, you are one of the toasts of London."

"You flatter me, my lady," he said.

She made a little moue, gave him her hand to kiss. "I intend to, to be sure, Haggard. But I have not yet begun. I was told you had a brother?"

"Who this morning took ship for Barbados, my lady. Business, you'll understand."

"Which is far beyond the ken of a mere woman."

She withdrew her hand, smiled at Byron in turn. "Byron, you rogue, where have you been these past few weeks? Bedding some helpless girl, I'll swear. But no matter. As you have brought Captain Haggard to me, your every sin is forgiven. For the moment."

But her smile, and her repartee, were immediately directed at the guests following behind, and it was time to accompany Byron inside. And to blink at the glowing chandeliers, the enormous area of highly polished wooden floor, for the furniture had been pushed against the walls and the carpets removed for dancing. And to feel himself flushing as the dozen or so men and women already inside turned to stare at the new arrivals.

"You said a small soiree," he muttered at Byron.

"And so it is, by darling Mina's standards. Do you waltz?"

"Waltz?" But he could take the conversation no further, as Byron had urged him into the room at the same time as he was himself apparently recognized by the ladies present, for with a combined squeal they descended upon him, and by necessity upon Haggard as well, chattering their introductions, squeezing his hand, and kissing him on the cheek. The forwardness, the abandon, with which they pursued their ob-

jectives took Roger by surprise, and he was glad to escape the
throng and find himself on the edge of the room, sipping
champagne from a glass hastily provided by one of the many
footmen who hovered at every doorway, and standing beside
a small, slight young woman with upswept golden hair and a
remarkably youthful face, not at all pretty, although intensely
animated as she frowned at the huddle in the center of the
room.

"Wretched man," she remarked. "He conceives of himself
as the sun, and the rest of us as mere asteroids. You must be
the famous Captain Haggard."

"Famous?" Haggard inquired, wondering if he should have
added a "my lady" to be safe.

"But of course. Did you not give up all—home and family
and commission and prospect—to run away and fight as a
common soldier? Tell me it was an affair of the heart."

"Well . . ."

"Of course it was. And now you are returned, to your position and your fortune, and find yourself the son of a suicide.
Why, Captain Haggard, you are the stuff of which great romances are made."

"It has not seemed very romantic to me, madam."

She laughed, and became suddenly attractive. "You have
not had the time to think about it, my dear Mr. Haggard.
Now all you need is a famous marriage, and you will go
down in history. Alas, there is no use in looking at me. I already have a husband. That lout over there."

Haggard followed the direction of her flicked fan. "But
that is . . ."

"Willie Lamb."

"Then I do apologize, my lady Caroline."

"Why should you? We have not been introduced. Ah."

For Lady Alderney had apparently greeted the last of her
guests, and had now entered the ballroom, flanked by two
footmen as Cleopatra might have been attended by her eu-
nuchs. She clapped her hands. "Ladies and gentlemen," she
said, and laughed, the most delicious sound Haggard had ever
heard, a low ripple of utter delight, accompanied by a dissolving of the flawless features into something even more
compelling. "Let us begin."

Instantly the orchestra, situated in the minstrel gallery high
on the opposite wall, began to play a waltz, and equally quickly the group broke up into couples, the men holding the

women about the waist, to Roger's amazement, while with their free hands clasped in those of their partners they whirled about the room.

Caroline Lamb glanced at Roger, and then at Byron, limping toward them, and then at Lady Alderney, who was accompanying him.

"Captain Haggard," Lady Alderney said. "Will you honor your hostess?"

"I . . ." He could feel his face burning. "I'm afraid I do not know the dance, my lady. It was not in fashion when last I attended Almack's."

A momentary stare, which quite chilled him, and then once again that unforgettable laugh. "And of course, Byron does not indulge either. Well, my lord, I will leave you to talk with Mrs. Lamb. While Captain Haggard and I discuss . . . what shall we discuss, Haggard?"

"Why . . . I have no idea." What a fool he was cutting, he thought, quite unable to get a word in edgeways. He should never have come. But at the least he would soon be away again, he reflected, with tonight nothing but a nightmare.

"Then I shall have to think of something," she said, and tucked his arm beneath hers.

"Actually, I would have you meet my husband," Lady Alderney explained as she escorted Roger through one of the inner doorways.

"Your husband?" It was impossible to think of this remarkable creature being tied to any man.

"I do have one. Tell me, what do you think of Caro?"

"Mrs. Lamb? She seemed very pleasant."

"She is as mad as a March hare. When she throws a tantrum, all London trembles. And I happen to know she has set her cap at poor George Byron. We shall have an interesting winter, I am sure. Harry, my darling, I would have you meet Captain Roger Haggard, of Derleth in Derbyshire."

They had entered a small room in which half a dozen men were playing cards around a green-baize-topped table. That they were all nobly born was quite simple to decide; which one was the Earl of Alderney was impossible to tell, as they all looked up together.

"My pleasure." A large, stout man, probably, Haggard thought, no older than his wife but looking *his* age, got up and held out his hand. "I've been hearing about you. Mina says you're no Tory."

Haggard glanced at the woman on his arm, who smiled. "An educated guess, Haggard."

"We must have a chat. Yes, a chat," Lord Alderney said, and himself glanced at his wife, at the same time sinking back into his chair. "You play?"

Haggard supposed this might be the most important question of his life. Now, why had he thought that? The champagne? Or the heady perfume drifting up his arm.

"Occasionally, my lord," he said. "But tonight I am not in the mood."

"Ha," said Lord Alderney. "Ha ha. Well, we must talk. Bring him to me at some more suitable moment, Mina. You'll excuse me, Haggard."

The other gentlemen had already turned back to their cards, and Haggard was aware of a gentle pressure on his fingers. He allowed himself to be walked across the room to a yet more inner door, resisted the temptation to look over his shoulder in case someone was watching him.

"I like your style, Haggard," Lady Alderney said softly, inclining her head to the footman who was opening the way for them. "I consider it a tragedy that I should be meeting you for the first time as you are about to leave England. But you are not *about* to leave England, are you?"

"I am on Tuesday's packet for Lisbon, my lady."

"My friends call me Mina." The door had closed behind them, and they were in an even smaller chamber, furnished with only two chairs and a settee, and an incidental table laden with gold ornaments. A window at the far end looked out onto a vast expanse of lawn surrounded by weeping willows. "You *are* going to be my friend, Haggard?"

His hand had been released, and she was walking away from him, to the table in the far corner, where there was an open bottle of champagne, and straight from the ice, as he could tell at a glance. Her footmen, he thought, must be trained like any guardsmen. But *did* he want to be her friend, with all that that entailed? Or was he entirely misjudging her?

"I should be flattered, Mina."

"As shall I." She poured two glasses, came back toward him, and their fingers brushed as he took his. "Tuesday," she said. "And today is Thursday. I go down to Midlook on Fridays, for the weekends. There is time for you to accompany me."

"To Midlook?"

"Alderney's country seat." She gave another of her little moues. "He will not be accompanying us."

"My lady . . . Mina . . ." How he hated his flush, his stammer. He felt like a schoolboy. But of course, where this woman was concerned, he *was* a schoolboy.

"I wish to talk politics, Captain Haggard," she said. "I wish you, and men like you, in support of my husband in the tumultuous times that lie ahead. Because there are tumultuous times ahead, do not doubt that." She tilted her head back to look at him. "Will you accompany me to Midlook, and be my friend?"

The face was smiling, the eyes challenging, and the champagne was cloying his senses as heavily as her perfume. He wanted no part of her, the woman. There was Meg, waiting for him at Derleth. And besides, he had experienced these society predators before, knew them for what they were.

And yet, he was inclining forward, his lips approaching hers, slowly but surely.

Lady Alderney laughed, and tapped him on the shoulder with her fan. "My carriage will call for you at eight," she said. "We must make an early start for Midlook." She stepped round him and went to the door. "Shall we rejoin the dancers?"

"Midlook," announced Lady Alderney. She had leaned forward to point, and Haggard had to look past the feathers which festooned her hat, as well as the hat itself. For the moment he was seeing only the soft black curls of her hair, and had the strangest desire to part them with his lips and reach her neck.

But her maid continued to sit opposite them, regarding him with a smile. And besides, what utter madness, even to be considered. Yet he was here, sitting beside her as he had sat beside her for the past five hours as the carriage had bumped and rumbled over the roads. He had been bathed in the beauty of her smile, the glow of her scent, the dazzle of her conversation. Was he that much of a fool? This had happened to him before, and turned out disastrously.

But would he not be equally that much of a fool, to spend the rest of his life looking over his shoulder? This woman was no relative; she could do him no harm. And probably she intended nothing more than she claimed, to spend the next two days discussing politics.

Besides, he reflected, how could he ever teach Meg to be a great lady if he did not know what great ladies were like? But would he ever wish Meg to be quite like Mina Favering?

The carriage came to a halt before the huge Corinthian pillars which supported the portico. Above them there was a forest of windows, no doubt supplying the major part of Pitt's infamous tax entirely on their own, he thought, while above even the windows the chimney pots clustered thickly against the sunlit September sky.

There were grooms and yardboys and ladies' maids and footmen and a butler, all greeting their mistress as if they had not seen her in a year, all smiling at Haggard—condescendingly? He could not be sure. But he was not the first gentleman to accompany the Countess of Alderney to Midlook for a weekend. There could be no doubt about that.

And there was a girl, a younger, much younger edition of her magnificent mother, embracing Mina and smiling over her shoulder at Haggard.

"Jane," Mina announced. "My younger daughter. My others are all married, would you believe it? I am a grandmother, Haggard."

There was no safe answer to that, so he concentrated on kissing Jane Favering's hand; she even smelled like her mother.

"I hope it will not bore you," Mina said, leading the way into the house. "With just the pair of us to entertain you for two whole days."

Luncheon was waiting, and they sat down immediately to an enormous meal of fresh trout and smoked salmon, pork chops and a side of beef, apple tarts and gooseberry pie, the whole washed down with several bottles of claret, in which Jane Favering indulged as freely as her mother.

"Do you not approve?" Mina inquired, watching him as he watched the girl. "Jane is sixteen, Haggard. And life is there to be lived. It is a rule I have practiced ever since I can remember. And it has done me well. You must join me, sir."

He hastily obeyed, and covered his confusion in some more wine. Then it was time for the port, but here Jane was dismissed. "Music, and then history, on Friday afternoons," Mina said, and herself filled Haggard's glass while her butler anxiously hovered. "Oh, to be sixteen again. Now I . . . I am forced to rest in the afternoons. Would you not like to do the same, Haggard?"

She offered him the glass as she spoke, and he was once again impaled upon her gaze. Say something, anything, to put her off.

"I *am* feeling rather tired," he said. "After that splendid meal."

"Then you shall have a siesta." She got up. "Hargreaves will show you to your room."

She left immediately, sweeping past the bowing footmen and out of the door, leaving Haggard standing rather stupidly before his place. He was once again defeated by the unexpected.

"If you will accompany me, sir," the butler said. "Your man has already gone up."

Haggard followed him up the stairs, along a gallery hung with paintings of past Faverings, and of each of Mina's daughters, every one as lovely as the next, then up another flight of stairs, and into another gallery, this one draped in crimson brocade as it was carpeted in crimson Persian to deaden all sound, and eventually into his bedchamber, where Corcoran was busy hanging up his uniforms.

"What a place, Mr. Haggard. Do you suppose Derleth will ever be like this?"

"Would you have me ape the aristocracy, Corcoran?" He sat down with a sigh, had his boots drawn off. So, after all, his fears—and his hopes—had been pointless. She wished to discuss politics. Nothing more. And he *was* tired. He stretched out on his bed, naked, allowing the gentle afternoon breeze to drift over him. For a moment there he had almost been mad. No, no, he had been bewitched, as they said Father had been bewitched by Emma Dearborn. Hard to believe, looking at Emma now. But Emma was only a few years younger than this magnificent creature.

He heard the door close as Corcoran left, closed his eyes. Well, then, would he succumb to her charms, her real charms, and join her husband's party? His father had been a Tory, even after his quarrel with Pitt. He had stood for property and power in the right hands, for the continuance of the system which had made Britain the greatest country in the world. Could his son possibly stand for anything less, no matter what his personal feelings?

But could his son resist whatever blandishments Lady Alderney was going . . . ? Another door closed, and he sat up in utter consternation. He had not known it to exist, for it seemed part of the wainscoting. But it had opened, and closed again, and Mina Favering stood there, wearing a crimson undressing robe which shrouded her from her neck to the floor.

Hastily Roger reached for the coverlet on which he had been lying, but it was securely tucked in, and he was helpless.

"Are you ashamed of your body, Haggard?" She came farther into the room. "I think it is a very nice body." She smiled at him, only two feet away now. "And eager."

"Mina . . ." He drew up his knees, and she laughed, and sat beside him.

"Did you not expect me?"

"Mina . . ."

"I hate subterfuge," she said. "Polite conversation, pointless flirting, when most men and most women know exactly what they want. Do *you* know what you want, Haggard?"

He abandoned any attempt at concealing himself, sat back, legs stretched in front of him across the bed. Mina gave another gentle laugh, got up, and released her robe. It slid from her shoulders, hung for a moment on her breasts, clouded her thighs as she inhaled, and then slipped down her legs to the floor.

"Tell me," she said. "What do you think of Jane?"

Haggard opened his mouth and closed it again. For if the face and the hair and the voice were perfection, what was he to make of the body, which was that of a girl? He realized with a start of dismay that he had never before seen a naked woman in her entirety. Alison had been in the dark, and Meg had been only half-undressed. Therefore he had nothing with which to compare. But how could any woman in the world stand a comparison with this?

"She looks very like me," Mina said, coming forward to sit beside him. "Her breasts are not so large, as yet. And she has no ugly stretch marks on her belly, as yet. That apart, we are very similar." She turned toward him, her hand closing gently on his penis as she pushed him back and lay on his chest, black hair flopping onto his face. "Were you to wish to marry her, Haggard, I think I can persuade Favering that it would be a good match."

She kissed him on the lips, drove her tongue between,

sought out his, and took possession of it. There was no other apt description. While her hand moved and was replaced by her groin as she slipped onto his stomach.

"Mina," he gasped. But his hands were closing on her shoulders, and despite himself, sliding down her back to hold her bottom, as small and compact and hard-muscled as the rest of her. "Oh, my darling Mina."

He was inside her, without realizing how it had happened. But she was very wet, and he was slipping, in and in and in, while she moved herself up and down, reaching for his mouth with her lips. "I think you are beautiful, Haggard," she said. "I think you are the most delightful creature I have seen in years. I want you, Haggard. I want you near me. Always."

He came in a vast explosion of damp heat, surged against her, and went on surging for several seconds afterward, unable to control his movements, while his hands clawed her buttocks apart and found their way between, and her lips sucked at his and then moved over his face, his eyes, and his nose, nibbled at his chin.

Then she laughed again, and shook her hair in his face again, and lay on his chest, her mouth against his neck.

"Now," she said. "Let us talk politics."

Chapter 2

The Island

"Well, Mr. Haggard, what do you think of it?" Captain Grainger was at last able to spare time from conning his ship through the maze of shipping in Carlisle Bay, and join his passenger at the rail, to gaze at Barbados.

The vessel was almost still. After four thousand miles and thirty days, her sails were furled, and she moved only very gently through the calm water, towed by the boats which would berth her alongside in the careenage. Four thousand miles of exile, John Haggard realized. But he had been realizing that with increasing force day after day after day. It had begun with a violent bout of seasickness, which had made him so miserable his earlier misery had seemed irrelevant. Besides, in many ways he was glad to be escaping England. There had been too much misery, too much hatred, too much confusion for his spirit.

Johnnie Haggard could not remember his mother; he had been but one week old when she had died of puerperal fever. The only mother he had ever had was his half-sister Alice. She had, as he recalled, been kindness itself. But he doubted she had ever loved him. For that matter, he did not suppose he had ever loved her. He was too conscious of the difference in their respective stations, for he had been the Haggard heir, then, and she was a bastard, the daughter of an indentured servant whom John Haggard had taken to his bed. The old man, for all his grimness, had been more affectionate, in the beginning. Because he had loved all of his possessions, so long as they did not ever argue with him, and his only remaining son was the most prized possession of all.

But never had it been possible for a moment, once he had

36

been sent away to Harrow School, to forget that he was the
son of the most hated man in England. Perhaps in the world.
A man who had quarreled with the Prince of Wales. A man
who, it was said, had loved his own wife—and Johnnie's
mother—to her grave. A man who had once turned out some
servants into the snow to die because he could not enslave
them. And a man who had driven his own eldest son to
suicide, it was suggested. The natural love which any son
feels for his father, and which is compounded of fear and respect as much as affection, was unable to stand up to that
constant bombardment of his senses, especially as he had
then begun to realize that Alice also hated the old man, even
if she remained at his side.

And yet he had never considered rebellion. Rebellion
against John Haggard was not a conceivable step. The rebellion, he now realized, was entirely unplanned. It had just happened, out of hatred, out of fear, out of self-doubt . . . and
out of his upbringing as well, he supposed. He had invited his
school friends, and later his university acquaintances, to visit
Derleth, and been rebuffed. Until Byron so surprisingly had
invited *him* to a weekend at Newstead Abbey. It had been a
farewell party before that strange young man had departed
for his tour, and there had been perhaps half a dozen of
them. All men, of twenty and twenty-one, save for the one
freshman of seventeen. He had not known the risks he had
been taking. But had they been risks? He had been a virgin.
They could not allow that state of affairs to continue. So he
had been placed upon the belly of a laughing serving girl,
and directed what to do. He had been ashamed, of himself
and of them, and he had not enjoyed it. What then was he
to make of it afterward, when Byron had himself wiped him
clean?

Because he had enjoyed that.

Thus guilt. All-pervading, all-consuming guilt. Friendship
of that kind, between two men, love of that kind, between
two men, was the most dastardly act any man could consider.
For Byron it was a huge joke. But that was his nature. He
loved as he lived, wildly and extravagantly, be it man or
woman, just as he challenged the law and the establishment
with the same devil-may-care gaiety. He had even invited
Johnnie to accompany him to watch the execution of two
guardsmen sentenced to death for sodomy. And then he had

departed, to the East, where, as he had laughingly said, they *prefer* you to make love to their little boys.

And for Johnnie Haggard life had been able to return to normal. Almost. For in his secret midnight hours he could still remember that soft caress, still wonder if it could ever be his again, at least, without fear of the gallows. But even memories of that nature do fade. If he had consorted with the devil, he had almost considered himself clean again, until this year, this single, tumultuous, terrible, tangled year of 1812. This year Byron had returned, to fame and fortune, certainly, but also to a resumption of his pleasures, so heightened by his sojourn in Greece. And while Johnnie had been attempting to cope with the sudden renaissance of lust and desire, there had been yet another unfaceable upheaval in his affiars: he had discovered he was no longer the Haggard heir.

That long-lost brother, who had disappeared before *he* had been born, presumed to have abandoned his commission through cowardice as his regiment had been ordered to Flanders, had reappeared. No coward, but a hero. A man who, for some social crime—no one save Father, and Roger himself, of course, had ever known the truth of that matter—had given up his birthright, not to sneak away into a corner and die, but who instead had continued his career, only this time starting at the very bottom and yet regaining his predestined rank. A Haggard with the world at his feet, tall and dark and handsome, as was his father, confident and grim, yet still with the ability to smile and even on occasion to laugh. A true Haggard, whereas Johnnie, at least in his own mind, had been nothing more than a sham.

He supposed he had always been confused. But the confusion of this spring had been unbearable, had led him to run, at least mentally, tossing from pillar to post, until he found himself in the arms of Meg Bold. What strange quirk of fate had decided that? Or was everything similarly predestined?

He did not think he had ever loved Meg. But she was a woman, and she had reminded him of the serving girl. With her he had thought he might be able to regain his manhood, whereas women of his own class, his father's class, merely left him terrified. The tragic thing was that he had never had the opportunity. At least, if he had had the opportunity, he had never used it. Meg Bold was a medicine, to be taken with care, a sip at a time. The end of the bottle had loomed a long way in the future; it had not occurred to him that that future might be clouded, that nothing could happen on Derleth, or off it, without Father's knowing, that the simple act of visiting Meg Bold, of taking her walking in the woods, could have set in motion such a train of tragedy, from Father's determination to punish the girl he supposed was taking advantage of his son, to his own anger, and the Bolds' anger, to the dreadful night when they had burned the mill and Peter Wring had tried to stop them, to the exploding fowling piece—he had never been sure whose it was—to his own arrest and trial. And condemnation, by his own father.

So at last the rebellion had been real. Like knights of old, he supposed, he and Father had met upon an open field and tilted. And he had been unhorsed. But not the loser. For having done his duty as magistrate, as squire of Derleth, and as Haggard, John Haggard's spirit had snapped.

Was he glad, or sorry, that the old man had blown out his own brains? Did he have any feelings in the matter at all? Certainly he had not believed it when he had been told. He had composed himself for his own death, had been unable to consider any other matter as important. So, what were his feelings on being reprieved? Did he need to pretend? He did not know why he was living. He only knew that his entire life seemed to have been one continual disaster. And he had known that if he was going to live, he must escape Derleth. Not only for the place, for the memories it invoked, not only for the people who stared at him, and hated him, for killing one of their own, but because even Meg Bold had reappeared to haunt him.

It was unthinkable, but it was happening. Roger had spent fifteen years of his life as a common soldier, after having had an experience—some experience with a lady of fashion—that had left him as distressed as Johnnie himself. He sought love where he could be sure of finding it, where there could be no risk of betrayal.

But Derleth, slipping into the grasp of a tinker's daughter? Had he stayed, no doubt he would soon have emulated Father, but only after putting a bullet through that silky red hair, the fount of all his misfortunes.

But exile? Thirty days of pitching and rolling, of vomiting and hating, with no past, and with nothing to look forward to. Save Barbados. A heat which had been growing day after day after day, which had the tar melting in the seams, had his shirt sticking to his back as if painted on, a sunshine so bright it hurt his eyes, and a lifetime of drudgery in a canefield, so far as he could make out.

But it would be his canefield. At this distance from England, Roger's ownership counted for little. He was the Haggard here. His spirits began to rise. No one in Barbados knew anything about him. He had actually been given the opportunity to start his life all over again. And be like his father?

Barbados. "It looks very fine, Mr. Grainger," he said.

At least the island had appeared green enough from the sea. He had come on deck at dawn, and been pleasantly surprised. At closer quarters it was less impressive. The careenage into which the *Dream of Araby* was now being towed was a long, narrow dock situated between streets out of which there rose a cluster of buildings, some wood and some stone, none higher than two stories, every one with a sloping roof to throw off the tropical rainstorms of the hurricane season, and not one with the slightest indication that it had been designed by an architect, or even put together with anything more than a hurried accumulation of ideas and materials.

The heat seemed to increase as they left the sea breeze behind, and the morning became filled with a variety of odors, almost all strange to Johnnie's nostrils, just as the air was crowded with a gabble of conversation, presumably most of it in English, but delivered in such a mélange of accents that it was hard to decide he was not entering some latter-day Babel. Everywhere he looked, there were black people. He supposed that to this moment he had seen only half a dozen men and women with skins other than white in his entire life; if his father had returned to England with several black servants, he had very rapidly got rid of them upon discovering that he could not treat them as slaves outside of Barbados. But here there were black men rowing the boats taking them alongside, and black men waiting to handle the mooring warps, and black men standing on the quayside to gaze at them, and black men and women sauntering up and down the streets, all dressed in cotton gowns or shirts and pants of varying degrees of whiteness, and not one with a pair of shoes on his feet.

"Would all of those people be slaves?" he asked Grainger.

"Most of them, to be sure, Mr. Haggard. But there are free blacks about. Oh, indeed. You'll be met?"

"I doubt that, Mr. Grainger."

"But, Mr. Haggard . . . ?"

"For the very good reason that no one knows I am coming," Johnnie pointed out. "I am the bearer of my own bad news."

"Ah. Then my agent will see to it," Grainger said. The freight for Haggard's Penn was one of his most lucrative contracts. The ship was already alongside, and the warps were being made fast, while immediately a gangway was run ashore, and up the steps there came a white man, presumably, for he was better dressed than any of the slaves about him, although like them he wore white cotton and shaded his head beneath an enormous brimmed straw hat, while his complexion was burned a mahogany brown by the sun.

"Grainger," he shouted. "I'd not expected to see you."

"A fast passage," the captain said. "You've had no storms?"

"Not one. But you saw no sail?"

"I did not, Mr. Meechem."

"You can thank God for that. You'll not have heard the news, then?"

"What news?" Johnnie asked.

The shipping agent gave him a glance, then continued to address the captain. "There's a war."

"That's news, Mr. Meechem?" Grainger asked with a smile.

"Oh, not with France, man. With America. You mark my words, if it's anything like thirty years ago, these waters will be crawling with Yankee privateers in another week. Oh, you're fortunate, man. Fortunate."

"And I'll agree with you, if what you say is true. I'd have you meet Mr. John Haggard."

The agent's brows slowly drew together in a deep frown. "Haggard, did you say? Haggard?"

Johnnie shook hands. "That is my name, Mr. Meechem."

"He seeks transport to the Penn," Grainger explained.

"Haggard?" Meechem said again. "Of Haggard's Penn? By God . . ." He seized Johnnie's hand again and shook it violently. "I knew your father, sir. Oh, aye, I did. He *was* your father, sir?"

"Yes," Johnnie said. "I'm in haste to be out there, Mr. Grainger. Can you see to my baggage?"

"Of course, Mr. Haggard, of course. But . . ."

"You'll not want to go out there now, Mr. Haggard," Meechem said. " 'Tis past ten of the morning. Now, sir, I suggest you come home with me, and meet the wife, who'll fix us some breakfast and a drink, and then you can have a siesta, and this afternoon, when the sun starts to go down, why, sir, then we'll have you out to Haggard's."

"This afternoon?" Johnnie inquired. "Why should I not go now, sir?"

Meechem looked at Grainger.

"Well, sir, Mr. Haggard," Grainger explained, "it is the sun, you see. Why, sir, you think this is hot, you'll not know it in another hour. Midday is no time for a gentleman to go riding around Barbados."

"Do you, then, work only at dawn and dusk?" Johnnie inquired.

"Well, sir," Meechem said, "in a manner of speaking. 'Tis a shortcut to an early grave for a white man to work at noon, to be sure. But we manage, sir, we manage. Now, if you'd like to come ashore . . ."

"I intend to go out to Haggard's Penn immediately, Mr. Meechem," Johnnie said. "If you won't assist me, then I'll have to find someone who will."

Meechem looked at Grainger, who shrugged.

"Well, of couse, Mr. Haggard," Meechem decided. "If that's what you want, why, sir, you have but to say so. If you'll come with me, sir, I'll see to it. Oh, indeed, sir. I'll see to it."

Johnnie shook hands with Grainger. "My thanks, Captain. If you'll see to my things . . ."

"You can leave them with me, Mr. Haggard. And I hope, sir, that I'll have the pleasure of your company again, when you decide to return to England."

"Aye," Johnnie said. "When, Mr. Grainger." He went down the gangway, nearly fell over as he found himself on dry land after so long at sea.

Meechem had to catch his arm. "Easy, sir," he said. "You'll soon find your legs. This is Mr. Haggard, Jeffries. Mr. John Haggard, come to visit the Penn."

He had spoken at large, in the general direction of two white men who were just emerging from the swinging doors of a shop. Now they stopped and stared.

"Haggard?"

"My name is John Haggard, yes," Johnnie said.

The two men peered at him as if he might be a ghost.

Then one stepped forward to shake his hand. "Jeffries is the name, Mr. Haggard. Best tailor in Bridgetown. The only tailor in Bridgetown, come to think of it. I've a card here, sir."

Haggard took the card, looked after the second man, who had raised his hat before hurrying down the street.

"Ah, Mr. Corby is an overseer, sir. On Bolton's." Jeffries paused and glanced at Johnnie.

"Bolton's?"

"It's the penn next to yours, Mr. Haggard," Meechem explained, also watching him intently. "You've not heard the name?"

"I know very little about Barbados, Mr. Meechem," Johnnie said. "I am here to learn. Now, sir, you mentioned transport to the Penn."

"Of course, sir, of course. You shall have my own kittareen. Brutus. Brutus, you black devil, fetch out my team."

"Yes, sir, Mr. Meechem, sir." A Negro lounging by the dockside hurried away, while Meechem and Jeffries escorted Johnnie into the shade of the veranda overhang, and thence into the shop itself, a large room principally occupied by sacks of what smelled like sugar, but with a counter and also a table and chairs to which Johnnie was shown.

"You're sure you won't change your mind, Mr. Haggard?"

"No, sir, I will not," Johnnie said. He smiled at them. "I am anxious to reach the Penn before news of my arrival in Barbados gets there."

"Oh, indeed, sir." Meechem laid his finger on his nose. "But you'll take a drink, sir. Oh, aye. Pontius, swizzles. And haste, you black scoundrel."

"I'se coming, Mr. Meechem." Another black man hastily set a tray on the table before them, on which there were three glasses and a huge jug filled with a foaming pinkish-colored liquid, and a great deal of ice, into which he now inserted a wooden stick with four spokes radiating from its end. This stick he held between the palm of each hand while moving the hands vigorously against each other, causing the spokes to rotate violently and increase the seething foam in the jug. He then removed the stick, and carefully filled each of the tumblers.

"Here we are, Mr. Haggard, sir," Meechem said. "Drink that, and you'll feel a new man."

Cautiously Johnnie raised the glass, and sipped, and then drank deeply. It was like nothing he had ever tasted before, very faintly bitter, but so cold that it slipped down his throat without an effort, where the cold faded and his stomach filled with a delicious heat which seemed to explode in his brain.

"What in the name of God is it?"

"Hollands gin, Mr. Haggard. With some water, and ice, and bitters."

"Bitters?"

"A local delicacy, Mr. Haggard. Made from rum, to be sure. Now, does that not feel better?"

"I am ready for my ride, if that's what you mean." Johnnie got up. Certainly he could not ever recall being filled with such a glow of well-being, even if the ground was once again a little unsteady beneath his feet. "Oh, indeed I am. Now, then, sir . . ." He paused as the doors to the shop were thrown open with quite remarkable violence and he found himself facing a woman.

Johnnie estimated she was at least old enough to be his mother, although it was difficult to be precise; her hair was white and her complexion seemed to have assumed a quality of leather, but she stood erect, and she was a tall, slim woman, and there was nothing aged about her eyes.

"Haggard," she said. "You are John Haggard's son?"

Johnnie hastily raised his hat, and discovered that there was another woman behind the first. Woman? This was a girl, and someone to make anyone stop and stare. As tall and slender as her companion, dressed in a similar pale blue muslin gown, and wearing a similar straw hat with a blue band, she possessed a quite lovely face, the features large but well-formed, and blessed with obvious traces of humor at her mouth and in her pale blue eyes—but the whole was overlaid with a remarkable smothering of light brown freckles, while her pale yellow hair was quite undressed, secured by nothing more than a bow on the nape of her neck as it cascaded down her back.

"Well?" demanded the first woman.

"Mama," said the girl, grasping her mother's sleeve. "Please, Mama."

"Oh, be quiet, Lindy. I asked the man a question."

Johnnie replaced his hat. "I am John Haggard, madam."

The woman stared at him for some seconds. Then she asked, "What brings you back to Barbados?"

"Mama," the girl whispered. "You've no right."

"I have not come *back*, madam," Johnnie said. "I have arrived for the first time. My purpose . . . why, it is to manage my brother's plantation."

"Brother? You have a brother? Of course. Roger. Does the scoundrel still live?"

"Mama," Lindy begged. And gave Johnnie a hasty smile. "I do apologize for my mother, Mr. Haggard, she—"

"Will you be quiet?" her mother snapped.

"Roger Haggard is my brother, madam, certainly," Johnnie said. "Now, if you would be good enough to introduce yourself . . ."

"And it is his plantation," the woman said, half to herself. "Do you say that John Haggard is dead?"

The room was momentarily quiet; Meechem and Jeffries, and the slaves, had all retreated against the far wall, as if for mutual support.

"He is that, madam," Johnnie said.

"Well, well," remarked the lady. "Well, well. There's an act of God for you." She pointed. "Beware, Haggard. There is no room for your sort on Barbados. Not nowadays." She turned and left the room. Her daughter hesitated for a moment, gave Johnnie another embarrassed smile, and then hurried behind her mother.

Johnnie removed his hat to wipe his brow. "What in the name of God was that all about? Who was she?"

"Ah . . . Mistress Campkin, Mr. Haggard." Meechem hurried forward. "Adelaide Campkin. Her husband owns Bolton's. Well, I suppose *she* does, but he manages it."

"You'll have to explain it to me."

Meechem exchanged a glance with Jeffries. "Well, sir, Mistress Campkin was Adelaide Bolton, you see. Only two Bolton children there were, and when Mr. Malcolm was killed, why, Miss Adelaide was the heiress."

"I see. And she married someone called Campkin. And the girl is her daughter."

"Oh, indeed, sir. Rosalind is the youngest of them. A lovely girl, would you not say?"

"She could be," Johnnie agreed. "If she'd take a little more care of her complexion. But what made Mrs. Campkin set into me?"

"Why, sir . . ." Once again Meechem glanced at Jeffries. "Have you *never* heard of the name Bolton, sir?"

Johnnie shook his head. "Father did not often discuss Barbados. At least with me."

"Yes, sir. Well . . ." Meechem sighed. "Master Malcolm Bolton, the man I mentioned just now, he was killed in a duel, sir. By your father."

"Good God," Johnnie said. "But that must have been a long time ago."

"Thirty-two years, sir, to be exact."

"And his sister still hates to that extent?"

"Ah, well, sir, it was the cause of the duel."

"Well?"

Meechem looked at Jeffries for support, and found none. He licked his lips. "Well, sir, they do say the duel was fought because Mr. Haggard, your father, sir, refused to honor a contract of marriage with Miss Adelaide."

"You'll stop here," Meechem commanded, and Brutus, the driver, instantly obeyed, straining on the reins to bring the kittareen to a halt. It was a small two-wheeled vehicle, driven by a single horse, and with room for just two passengers, who sat side by side facing forward. There was no roof, and after two hours' driving, Johnnie was beginning to understand something of Meechem's earlier protests; his clothes were soaked with sweat and his hair seemed plastered to his head, while he could feel the skin on his face and hands beginning to burn; it was turning red before his eyes.

In addition, his head ached beneath his English beaver and his eyes were watering; he could not be sure whether this was a result of the sun or the swizzle he had drunk immediately before his departure. And apart from his physical discomfort, he was decidedly upset by the reception he had received. He had walked right into the middle of a family skeleton, it appeared, still busily rattling away. Had Roger known anything of it? He had to; he had been fourteen when he had been brought to England. Just as Emma must have known as well, and therefore Alice. But they had said nothing. Had they not considered it important?

Meechem, for all his strictures about going out in the heat of the day, was in much better shape, and now that the vehicle had come to a halt, he was pointing with his cane. "Haggard's Penn."

Johnnie made himself sit up, to look down the hill, past the seemingly unending fields of waving green cane stalks—these had accompanied them, to either side of the road, since leaving Bridgetown—at what was very nearly a town. In the foreground there was row after row of neat little cottages, somewhat longer than the English variety, and lower, with troolie-palm-thatched roofs, each with its little patch of vegetable garden at the back.

"Those are the barracoons, where the Negroes live," Meechem explained.

Farther off, and commencing to climb up the next shallow hillside, was another cluster of houses, two-storied dwellings with proper tiled roofs and much larger gardens, and overlooked by a steepled church.

"That's the white township," Meechem said.

To the right of the two villages, and about half a mile from each, was yet another cluster of buildings, low huts these, lacking walls and providing nothing more than shelter from the sun and the rain, surrounding an enormous shed from which a huge stone chimney poked its way some forty feet into the still afternoon air.

"The factory," Meechem said. "Where the sugar is ground, and where your rum and molasses are also made, Mr. Haggard. You'll see the house."

In the very far distance, and at the top of the hill, there stood a large square house; the upper stories were made of wood, so far as Johnnie could decide, but the whole was set upon a stone base, itself founded firmly into the ground, so that the cellar windows were only a foot or two out of the earth. The roof of this house was of the dormer variety, and in each side there was a huge recessed window, beckoning the breeze from whichever direction it might arrive. The ground surrounding the building was divided into green lawns and many-colored flowerbeds, and indeed, the whole—the villages and the factory and the great house itself—presented a remarkably peaceful and attractive picture in its neatness and general air of prosperity, at the same time as it occurred to Johnnie that there was not a single human being to be seen, in fact, there was no life at all, save for the chickens strutting their runs behind the black village and an occasional dog stretching and moving from one piece of shade to the next.

"It is quite beautiful," Johnnie said. "I had expected nothing like it."

"There *is* nothing like it, Mr. Haggard," Meechem said. "A well-run sugar plantation . . . and when it's the biggest in the world . . . Why, do you know we've been riding over your property for the past hour? And you could keep going for another couple of hours beyond the house."

Johnnie scratched his head, hastily replaced his hat. "And everyone is in the fields?"

"Everyone is asleep, Mr. Haggard."

"Asleep? At one o'clock in the afternoon?"

"Siesta, Mr. Haggard. Drive on, Brutus."

The kittareen rolled down the hill and through the open gates into the compound. A dog barked once and then settled back to slumber. But one or two black children emerged from the shelter of their barracoons to look at the arrivals.

"Anyone could just walk in here and do whatever he liked," Johnnie remarked.

"What, for instance, sir?" Meechem inquired.

"Well, steal. Or kill."

"Steal? What are they to steal, save food? And there is enough of that. These poor devils have no use for art or literature or bric-a-brac. As for murder, why, Mr. Haggard, consider this: you have with you on this plantation approximately thirty white men, who have with *them* possibly thirty white women and a few children. You also have better than two thousand slaves. You will appreciate, sir, that should your slaves *wish* to murder you, they could do so, and everyone else on the plantation with a white skin, long before the military could arrive from Bridgetown."

"And they have no wish to do so? You mean they are content to be slaves?"

"Well, sir, I doubt they ever really think about contentment, or lack of it. But you have to remember that since the trade was ended, five years ago, there have been no new blacks arriving in Barbados. That means that all the people here have been here for some years, and most of them, sir, are second and third generation in the West Indies. But no matter. Whether from the day they landed or the day they were born, they'll have had it drummed into them by their fellows that to lift a hand against a white man, or a white woman, means death, and a pretty unpleasant death, too. They used to burn a recalcitrant slave alive, down to a few years ago. Nowadays, why, they hang him, or her, real slow, hoisting them from the ground bit by bit. Niggers don't like having their necks stretched, Mr. Haggard."

"A society existing entirely on fear," Johnnie mused. "Does it not strike you as somewhat barbaric, Mr. Meechem?"

"Ah, come, now, sir. What society is not based entirely on fear? Would not every poor workingman in England be after your money, and your hide, if he didn't know he'd suffer for it? In Barbados we've just reduced the facts of life to their simplest form. Here we are, sir."

The kittareen rolled to a halt, having labored its way up the hill. The great house loomed above them, and Johnnie noticed, as he stepped down, that although the huge front door and every enormous window stood wide to allow the entry of the warm afternoon breeze, each aperture was also guarded by a thick wooden shutter, able to be secured by steel bolts if the need arose. Because of the hurricane winds? Or because the slaves had not always been as quiescent as Meechem claimed?

His feet sounded dully on the wooden steps as he climbed onto the veranda that completely surrounded the lower floor, and looked inside at the hall, while gratefully removing his hat as he escaped the sun, and wiping sweat from his neck and forehead. Here everything was on a similar immense scale, the hall wide and deep as it stretched into the interior of the house, the withdrawing room to his right even larger, and filled with upholstered chairs and low tables laden with brass ornaments, the dining room to his left dominated by a huge mahogany table, to which there were matching sideboards clustered with crystal and silver. But the whole sadly needed dusting, the silver was tarnished, and as he stood in the hall, a large white cock came hopping down the stairs, not in the least disturbed by the visitors, pausing to gaze at them for a moment through beady eyes before continuing on his way out of the house.

Johnnie glanced at Meechem, who was also drying sweat. "Does anyone live here?"

"The servants will be downstairs, I'd say. And Ferguson . . ."

"Our manager?"

"That's right, sir. I imagine he has been using the house."

Johnnie saw the gong waiting at the entrance to the dining room. He stepped inside, seized the striker, and sent the notes reverberating through the afternoon. For a moment nothing happened; then there was a sudden babble of noise, and

black people began emerging from everywhere, men hastily
pulling on red-and-gold liveried coats, absurd because below
them they wore only white cotton drawers and had bare feet,
women hastily cramming their tightly curled hair into enormous turbans and smoothing their gowns, all inquiring among
each other, in the picturesquely broken English he had first
heard in Bridgetown, what could be the matter, whether there
was a fire or what, all clustering into the hall from various
recesses at the back of the house, to stare at the two white
men.

"But what is this?" inquired the oldest and tallest of the
men, advancing toward them. "Is war, Mr. Meechem?"

"More important than war, Montague," Meechem said.
"This is Mr. Haggard."

"Mr. Haggard?" Montague looked from left to right, and
the slowly advancing wall of slaves came to a stop, and began to retreat.

"Haggard? Haggard, you say?"

The voice came from the upper gallery, and Johnnie
looked up, to see a short, stout gray-haired white man peering
over the balustrade. He wore only a shirt, obviously hastily
put on, while at his shoulder there stood a sallow-skinned
woman with flowing jet-black hair, who had also obviously
just pulled on a robe.

"Haggard," Meechem announced, clearly enjoying himself.
"Mr. John Haggard, come from England to see to the man-
agement of his plantation. Mr. Haggard, allow me to present
Mr. William Ferguson, your attorney in Barbados."

"Dead? Mr. Haggard is dead?" Willie Ferguson sat in an
armchair in the center of the withdrawing room and
scratched his scanty hair. "I can't believe it, if you'll excuse
my saying so, sir."

"You had better believe it, Mr. Ferguson." Johnnie had remained standing, while Meechem also remained on his feet.
The woman stood in the doorway. She had not been introduced, not did she seem to find this insulting. And she was a
remarkably fine creature, tall and strong, with skin the color
of pale mahogany and bold, handsome features, the whole
submerged in the long, straight black hair, so thick and apparently heavy it only moved in its entirety; not even the
breeze drifting through the open windows could wisp it.

"But how, sir? Why, he could have been no more than

. . ." Ferguson obviously performed a quick mental calculation. "Sixty at the outside."

"He was fifty-nine, Mr. Ferguson," Johnnie said. "And he blew out his own brains." He could see no reason to be kind to Father's memory, while he was determined that there would be no whispering behind his back. Whatever had to be said would be said by him.

Ferguson's head jerked, and Meechem dropped his hat. The woman in the doorway continued to watch them, only moving to allow Montague, the butler, to enter, bearing a tray on which there were three tall glasses, very like those from which Johnnie had earlier drunk his swizzle, but these filled with a glowing red liquid in which there floated pieces of ice and sliced fruit.

"Suicide," Ferguson muttered. "My God. Suicide." He noticed Montague. "You'll take a glass of sangaree."

"Sangaree?"

"Red wine, sir, fortified with a dash of brandy and some fruit. It's refreshing."

"I have not yet had my luncheon," Johnnie pointed out.

"Faith, sir, you can't eat in this heat. 'Tis liquid you need. Drink up, sir, drink up. Suicide. My God. And Master Roger . . . ?"

"Has sent me out here to learn planting, Mr. Ferguson." Johnnie drank. It was the most delicious thing he had ever tasted. "All this ice . . . where the devil does it come from?"

"We ship it out, Mr. Haggard," Meechem explained. "Direct from the Labrador coast, great blocks packed in canvas and sawdust."

"At what cost, man?"

"Ah, well, sir, what does the cost matter where a gentleman's comfort is involved?"

Johnnie drank some more, found himself staring at the woman. She smiled at him.

"Suicide," Ferguson said yet again, and heaved himself to his feet. His glass was already empty. "You'll forgive me, Mr. Haggard, sir, but what you've told me is a considerable shock. Well, well. And Master Roger . . . is he still in the army?"

"He'll be back in Spain by now, Mr. Ferguson. He's that dedicated. But if you don't mind, I'd rather talk about the plantation."

"Of course, sir. Of course, your baggage . . ."

"Is on its way from Bridgetown," Meechem said. "All taken care of, Willie. By my firm."

"Of course," Ferguson agreed. "Well, Mr. Haggard, sir, you'll be moving in?"

"I will, Mr. Ferguson."

"Yes, well . . ." It was the attorney's turn to glance at the woman in the doorway. "You've not met Claudette. Come here, Claudette, and meet the master."

"Pleased I am, Mr. Haggard," she said, advancing and giving a little curtsy. Her voice was like liquid gold.

"Mrs. Ferguson?" Johnnie asked.

Meechem suppressed a titter, and Ferguson frowned. "Why, no, sir, she's housekeeper, you might say."

"I beg your pardon?" Johnnie hated his flush.

"Your housekeeper, Mr. Haggard. She was just acting, for me. In your absence, sir."

Once again Claudette smiled. Johnnie could just imagine what she would be like. She would envelop him, suck him into her, laughing and caressing. . . . Would she be laughing at him, or with him?

"Aye, well," he said. "You'll show me to my room, Miss Claudette."

"Is my pleasure, Mr. Haggard," she said.

"Yes." Johnnie took a step or two toward the door, and checked himself. "My thanks, Mr. Meechem. No doubt you'll render your account."

"Bless you, sir, that's all taken care of."

Johnnie nodded, glanced at Ferguson. "What is the first thing I should do, Mr. Ferguson?"

"Do? Do?" Ferguson looked at Claudette in a scandalized fashion, scratched his head some more. "Yes. Well, sir, I reckon the best thing you can do is have a rest. Then we'll make an inspection of the plantation."

Johnnie awoke to a crashing headache. Each breath seemed to lift the top from his head and then allow it to fall again; it was as if someone were banging his skull against a wall.

He opened his eyes, blinked at the still-bright sunlight that cascaded through the open windows of the enormous bed-chamber, hastily closed them again. And then opened them again. He lay in the center of a huge four-poster, looking up, not at an ordinary tester, but at a cloud of thin gauze netting, presently suspended just beneath the canopy, but ready to be dropped, or drop itself, he feared. To smother him?

He raised his head. He was naked. Someone had undressed him and put him to bed. He could remember nothing of it. He had accepted another glass of sangaree . . . and must have passed out. For the very first time in his life, and he had not lacked drinking companions at Cambridge. The heat, undoubtedly. For all his lack of clothes, he still sweated, and his skin had developed red blotches at his groin and in his armpits. Sentenced to this, for the rest of his life, he thought bitterly. Father had at least intended to put an end to his misery.

A sound had him sitting up again, and drawing up his legs in alarm. Claudette stood by the other window, her back to the light, watching him. Now she came across the room. "You needed the sleep, master," she said.

He stared at her, tugging at the coverlet with his left hand and being unable to free it, and slowly becoming aware that he need feel no embarrassment; clearly it was she who had undressed him.

"Master?" he asked. "Why do you call me master?"

"Because I'm your slave, master," she said.

"You?" He must have made a gesture of surprise which she interpreted as a beckon, because she came closer.

"Don't you like me, master?"

"I like you very much. I . . ."

"I likes you too," she said, and with a single gesture shrugged her robe from her shoulders to the floor. He supposed he had never seen such a perfectly proportioned woman, from the high, firm breasts, past the flat belly to the wide hips, and then the long, powerful legs, all coated in that delicious golden-brown skin, on which the thick black patch covering her pubes seemed almost an obscenity.

Because it was an obscenity. He rolled away from her, but she was already kneeling on the bed, her nipples scouring his back, her hands slipping in front to hold his penis. "I likes you very much, master," she said. "You ain't going to need nobody but Claudette."

Only three hours before, she had been doing the same thing to Ferguson. But how superb was her touch, the sensation of her against him. For a moment he lay back against her, enjoying the feel of her; then suddenly he saw Byron's face in front of him, smiling at him, and he remembered By-

ron's touch, the touch he would never know again, the feeling
of utter intimacy, utter rapport, he would never know again,
could never know with any woman, much less a creature like
this.

In a wave of self-disgust he thrust his elbows backward as
hard as he could, encountered soft flesh, heard her gasp and
then give a cry, before striking the ground with a thump.

Instantly he turned, on his hands and knees, brain shrieking apology and mouth about to follow suit, when he realized
that she had taken no offense. She looked hurt, and obviously
was hurt, and somewhat winded, but he was the master, and
she was the slave. There could be no question of an apology.

"I have things to do," he said, and got up to find his
clothes.

"Mr. Beddoes, the field manager," Ferguson said.

Johnnie shook hands.

"Mr. Champion, the second field manager. Mr. Pelham,
the chemist. Mr. Evans, the factory manager. Mr. Cartwright,
the assistant factory manager. Mr. Lewis, the chief book-
keeper. Mr. Robinson, the accountant."

Their names melded into a blur, much as did their faces.
There were more than twenty of them, as Meechem had
prophesied, every one anxious to be presented to the new
master. How would he ever remember who was who? Even
worse, how would he ever measure up to these keen-eyed,
suntanned men, used to living, again as Meechem had described, one in forty to their blacks, and yet to ruling, by the
power of their personalities?

"We can start on the fields tomorrow," Ferguson said, and
Johnnie realized that he had reached the end of the line. "It'll
take several weeks to inspect them all. But that's to the good;
in six weeks' time we'll be grinding. But for this afternoon,
why, you'll wish to take a look at the slaves. I've kept them
in to see you."

Mules were waiting for them, held by attentive Negro
boys. Johnnie swung into the saddle, and felt more at home.
"I thank you all for attending me," he said. "I'll hope to meet
your wives, in due course."

"Three cheers for Mr. Haggard," Beddoes shouted, and
they threw their hats in the air.

"Oh, they're a good bunch, Mr. Haggard. You'll like it

here," Ferguson declared. He looked at the house. "It's a comfortable place."

Johnnie followed the direction of his gaze, saw Claudette standing on the veranda, watching them. "How long has she been housekeeper?" he asked.

"Just one year, Mr. Haggard." Ferguson touched his mount with his knee, turned it down the slope toward the black village. "I believe in changing them, every so often. Doesn't do to get them set in their ways." He winked. "And a bit of variety is a good thing, wouldn't you say?"

"I wouldn't know, Mr. Ferguson. I'll change her again, if you please, for a man."

"Eh?"

"She's familiar, Mr. Ferguson." And her lip curled when I left the room without hauling her back into bed, he thought. But surely the biggest mistake I could make would be to become like these people. That is what is wrong with Haggard's, wrong with every plantation, the reason for the sugar profits falling so drastically. Not just the limitation of European markets, but the progressive nativization of the white staff. That is where I must start to make my reforms.

"As you wish, Mr. Haggard," Ferguson agreed. They rode slowly, approaching a vast sea of black faces, for all the slaves had assembled outside their barracoons to see the new master. "But if you've any English church-type doubts about her, sir, I'd forget them. These people don't have morals. They're animals, standing up on two feet. They expect to be bedded, the women. It's an honor."

"No doubt, Mr. Ferguson," Johnnie agreed coldly. "I'll have some information, if you please."

"Of course, sir."

"I met a lady this morning. At least, I suppose she was a lady. Name of Adelaide Campkin."

Ferguson drew rein. "You've met Adelaide Campkin?"

"I've just said that. She was uncommonly rude."

"Aye, well . . ."

"Mr. Meechem gave me to understand it is connected with a duel. Do you know of it?"

"I was your father's second."

"And it was fought over Mrs. Campkin?"

"There was a quarrel at a ball thrown at Bolton's. Old Bolton was alive then, you'll understand, sir, and Mrs. Campkin was his only daughter."

"And my father refused to honor a contract of marriage."

"Well, so it was said. Mind you, Mr. Haggard, I never knew of any contract."

"Yes," Johnnie said. "Well, perhaps Father would not have told you. But I would like to know why so much bitterness still exists, after thirty years. Mrs. Campkin is married. And surely a duel is an honorable thing."

"Aye, well, 'tis long ago, to be sure."

"I'd like to know, Mr. Ferguson."

Ferguson sighed. "Your father was the best pistol shot in the West Indies. Why, he practiced every day, for over an hour. His range is still downstairs, in the cellars."

"And Mr. Bolton was not so good a shot?"

"No, sir, and he knew it."

"Yet did he make the challenge, as I understand it?"

"Yes, sir, he did. But he was drunk when he did it. And next morning, when they met, why, he was terrified. His face was white as chalk, sir. But it was his sister involved, and he couldn't drop the matter. It was put to Mr. Haggard, Mr. Haggard. After all, there was no man in all the world going to call Mr. Haggard a coward. It was put to him that he might like to make an approach. And he refused."

"So what happened, exactly?"

"Well, sir, they faced each other, and Mr. Haggard, cool as he always was, leveled and fired, and shot Mr. Bolton straight through the heart, before the other weapon was even leveled. There were those said it was cold-blooded murder. But it was a duel, sir, legal and aboveboard. There were witnesses. Peter Campkin and me, and the doctor. We were all there. It was legal, sir."

"Cold-blooded murder," Johnnie mused. That was Father, to be sure, when he conceived himself to be in the right. But had he been in the right?

They had reached the foot of the hill, and he gazed at the black people. If the overseers and bookkeepers had confused him, what was he to make of this sea of faces, every shade from ebony to pale mahogany, men and women and children, the adults reasonably modestly clad, but the children, and well into their teens, he estimated, naked and unashamed, shuffling their feet and whispering to each other.

Ferguson held up his hands. "This here is Mr. John Haggard," he shouted. "There'll be some of you remember Mr. Haggard, who owns this plantation. Well, this is his son, come out here to see to you. You'll work hard for the master, eh?"

A low chorus arose from the throng, but Johnnie could not decide whether it was approbation or misery. And he was already distracted by a sudden shift of breeze that brought a dreadful smell to his nostrils.

"What in the name of God is that?" he demanded. "You've a dead animal, Ferguson."

"Ah, 'tis but the punishments," Ferguson said. "We'd best take a look."

He wheeled his mule and walked it round the front of the crowd, toward the rear of the black village, and for the first time Johnnie saw the five triangles set up on a row, four of them occupied. Three of the hanging figures were men, and the fourth was a woman. All were naked, and every one had been cruelly flogged, or worse, so far as he could see, for their brown skins were flecked with red where the flesh had been torn. And they had been suspended there for some time, he could tell at a glance; the smell came mainly from a pile of excreta beneath each one, while the wrists hanging from the cords securing them were cut to the bone.

"That is barbaric," he said, his stomach rolling. He reined his mule, tried to look away, and could not. "What can they have done?"

"Stealing or fighting," Ferguson said. "As I said, Mr. Haggard, they're animals. You'll want a closer look."

"Me? Why . . ." But the mule was already walking closer. Johnnie gave an alarmed glance over his shoulder at the vast concourse behind him. They were all watching him. Two white men, in the midst of two thousand blacks, about to inspect their dreadful handiwork. He became aware of a violent outbreak of sweat, while his mouth filled with saliva. "How long have they hung there?" he gasped.

Ferguson dismounted. "A week."

"A *week*? For stealing? After being flogged? My God, man . . ."

"Well, you see, Mr. Haggard, they were given fifty lashes each—"

"Fifty? Who gave that order?"

"I did, Mr. Haggard. Only the attorney, or the master, of course, has the right to order a flogging. But I reckon it's inhumane to give them more than twenty-five lashes at one time. And the jumper only comes once a week, you see, sir."

"The jumper?"

"The professional whipping man. Why, sir, I'd not trust any of my people to flog a slave. They don't have any idea how to go about it. Very likely to do them an injury, they might."

"An injury," Haggard said.

"Indeed, sir. None of the plantations permit their own people to flog. No, sir. So the jumper has a lot of work, and he can only make it to Haggard's once a week. He's due tomorrow."

"To give these people another twenty-five lashes?"

"That's it, sir."

"And meanwhile they have hung there for the entire week?"

"They'll not come down until their punishment is completed, Mr. Haggard. That would be a mistake. Never let a black man think you're soft. No, sir. *They* aren't soft." He walked up to the first black man, struck him twice smartly across the face. "You're awake, you black devil. You know what I'm saying."

The black man stared at him. "I'se awake, master," he said.

"Damned right you are. You see, Mr. Haggard, even the jumper makes mistakes. Look at this." Using his forefinger, he dug into one of the gaping, insect-infested wounds on the man's shoulder, extracted a thin sliver of steel. "Left from the cart whip, that is. Pure negligence. Shows he's not maintaining his thong properly. Oh, I'll have a word with him when he comes tomorrow. Or maybe you'd like to have a word, Mr. Haggard."

Johnnie Haggard vomited onto his horse's neck.

"A suicide." Adelaide Campkin looked down the sweep of her dining table at her husband. "Can you believe it? John Haggard a suicide."

"Idle gossip," Campkin grumbled. He was a short, thickset man with bushy gray hair.

"My dear Peter, Meechem heard the boy say it himself, to that scoundrel Ferguson. There can be no doubt. I have no doubt. I always knew that John Haggard would come to a bad end."

"I imagine, if it *is* true," Campkin remarked, "that his family probably drove him to it. One son running off to enlist as a common soldier, and now this fellow. . . . Have you heard how he puked when he saw a slave being flogged?"

"You'll excuse me, Mama, Father." Rosalind Campkin pushed back her chair and got up; she was the only other person at table, as her two married sisters lived with their husbands, one in Jamaica and the other on a neighboring plantation.

"Whatever is the matter with you?" Adelaide demanded.

"Nothing, Mama. I . . . I'm just a little tired." Rosalind left the room, past the line of bowing footmen.

"Was it something I said?" her father inquired.

"Probably," Adelaide agreed, but she was staring down the table again, her chin propped on her forefinger. "She needs a husband."

"I'm sure she does. And where are we to find that commodity at the moment? There's not an eligible bachelor in the island."

"Do you not suppose so?" Adelaide asked.

Campkin, tucking into his avocado pear, raised his head with the soft green flesh still smearing his chin. "Are you out of your mind?"

Adelaide leaned back. "Bolton's, and Haggard's. Was that not always Papa's dream? He dreamed it, for me and John Haggard. It would be the biggest plantation in the world, and the richest. He dreamed that, Peter. So did I."

"And John Haggard stood you up," Campkin said, resuming his meal. "Don't let's start that all over again."

"And now he's dead," Adelaide said happily. "And I'm still alive. And this boy is utterly unlike his father. He's a weakling. You've just said so yourself. Well, I saw it the moment I met him. But he's the Haggard heir."

"What of the other brother?"

"Roger? As you say, he went off to fight as a common soldier. He's still soldiering, I understand. And he must be well into his thirties. He'll never marry, not even if he doesn't manage to get his head blown off. You mark my words, Peter. This boy will inherit. Lindy could inherit. Haggard's Penn."

"You'd sell her off like a slave?"

"Oh, come, now, don't be absurd. You just agreed it was time she was married. She's just wasting her life. And she has character. She has strength. She'll make Master John Haggard dance, she will. If I tell her to."

"I think you *are* out of your mind," Campkin said. "Anyway, I heard another piece of gossip today. How your would-be bridegroom turned his housekeeper out the day he arrived. He sleeps alone."

"Never mind that," Adelaide said. "I have no desire to discuss male debauchery. He'll make Lindy an excellent husband." She smiled. "And I will make him an execllent mother-in-law. Haggard's Penn. After all these years, it's going to be mine at last. I know it is."

"Aye. All you have to do is make the young fellow propose. After the greeting you gave him, he's more likely to spit in your eye."

Adelaide raised her head, and the butler hurried forward to take away her chair as she rose.

"There's time, Peter. We shall hurry slowly to catch our monkey. But I think we should invite young Mr. Haggard to supper with us. After all, it would be the neighborly thing to do. And then I can apologize."

Her husband stared at her with his mouth open.

Chapter 3

The Planter's Wife

The tolling of the bell awakened Johnnie Haggard. He had been dozing for some time, for he slept badly. Partly this was caused by the heat, which left him continually bathed in a sea of sweat. Equally was it caused by misery.

He had been sentenced to a living death. For him. Because in his heart he knew that Roger had not intended it like that. Roger *had* been happy here, as had Alice, no doubt. They were planting people, just as they were Tory squires, born and bred. They knew nothing of aesthetics, had read not a line of poetry in their entire lives. They were, in reality, animals, who existed and prospered by virtue of that very animality. They understood their own desires and their own needs, and they sought them with unflinching determination. That other people might have desires and needs in opposition to their own was unthinkable; where discovered, such opposition was immediately trampled underfoot.

They were Father's children.

The door opened, and William entered, carrying a tray. "Is morning, Mr. Haggard," he said. "I'se got your coconut water."

Johnnie sat up, and William advanced more cautiously. Even after several months of valeting his master, he was confused by his position. White men in the tropics were as a rule attended by their females. He could not understand his elevation to this intimate position at all, was inclined to wonder, indeed, whether it might not have been a *demotion*. The other domestics, cruel in their wit at the master's expense, were equally devastating in their comments about his servant.

"Thank you, William," Johnnie said, and sipped the clear

white liquid. Coconut water. "It'll put semen in your prick," Ferguson had said, watching him with that sly smile.

Now, what reply would Father have made to a remark like that? Or Roger? But such a remark would never have been made to either Father or Roger. There was the point.

"I'se got your clothes here, Mr. Haggard," William said, carefully laying out shirt and pants and placing stockings and boots beneath them; nothing more was necessary on a Barbadian morning.

"Thank you, William." He finished his coconut water, swung his legs out of bed, and William beat a hasty retreat. Did *he* understand? Anything, much less the tormented thoughts that roamed his master's mind? A black penis, huge and rearing. He had seen them often enough, since his arrival. What would they feel like? What would they . . . ? He shook his head violently, as if he could dislodge the consideration, went to the window to look out at the plantation.

It was just dawn, but time for the day's work to commence. The slaves were already streaming out of their village, to be mustered by their drivers, the heads of each of the laboring gangs. And although he could not see them, the bookkeepers and overseers would be assembling around the trestle table erected every morning at the foot of the front stairs. Where he would have to join them. To give them their instructions for the day. What a farce. He sat at the head of the table while Ferguson gave the orders, only pausing every few minutes to look down at him and say, "That's what you want, ain't it, Mr. Haggard?"

What I want, Johnnie thought bitterly, as he shaved himself. At home he had always been shaved by a servant; in the West Indies men shaved themselves, and he was a man. What I want. To escape this place? But that thought was even more terrifying than the thought of remaining here for the rest of his days. Because so far as he could see, the entire world was filled only with Willie Fergusons and John Haggards and Roger Haggards and Harry Bolds. Male animals, the most vicious creatures ever placed on God's earth. To be an aesthete and a poet, one also had to be a Byron, the possessor of a flowing courage and a devastating wit. But Byron, and England, were banned to him. Here at least he was the master.

He dressed himself and went downstairs. Footmen bowed and housemaids curtsied. He passed the door leading to the pantries and thence to the kitchens, which were built away from the main building to lessen the risk of fire, and watched several of the yardboys wrestling a whole pig's carcass through the back door, while Montague, the butler, stood by beaming with anticipation. This would be his supper. Four slices of roast pork, after which the entire pig would disappear by morning. The first time it had happened he had gone to the kitchen to protest, and found himself isolated in the center of twenty bewildered stares. So he had complained to Ferguson. "I will not have my domestic people stealing," he had said.

Ferguson had been equally bewildered. "Stealing, Mr. Haggard? Why, they don't regard it as stealing. I don't think the word is in their vocabulary."

"Then shouldn't we teach them it exists? We've a cold room, in the cellar, stuffed full of ice. Why can't the carcasses be hung there to provide food for a week or more?"

"Ah, well, sir, I don't think Montague would like that. He fancies a bit of pork himself. So do his wives and daughters."

"Montague? For God's sake, Ferguson, who owns this plantation, Montague or me?"

"Why, you do, Mr. Haggard. But a man must get on with his domestics, or life can be hell. Now, as I see it, you have two choices. You either let them do as they see fit, or you scare the living daylights out of them. Your father went for the second. So if you give me the word, I'll have old Montague down to the triangles and lay his ribs bare. Mind you, sir, with a domestic being punished, the master must be there. It'd look bad if you weren't."

He had walked away, as he walked away now. But there was nowhere to walk to. For if he left Montague and the carcass behind, he was on the front veranda to meet the overseers and Ferguson. There was no escape from Haggard's Penn.

Grinding was the worst time of all. Where normally he could at least pretend to be the master, during that frenetic month he was at once clearly a supernumerary and a nuisance.

Grinding involved the entire plantation, down to the smallest slave capable of walking. The field gangs labored from dawn until dusk, cutting the ripe cane, which was then loaded into bullock carts to be transported to the factory. Here was the master's place, together with his chief overseers. And here too was a scene straight from Dante. The clanking rollers, driven by a treadmill on which platoon after platoon of naked slaves toiled, endlessly mounting, tormented by the whips of their drivers; the shattered canestalks discarded by the machinery after they had been ground three times, to be collected by other slaves for use as fuel; the seething fires, situated beneath each of the great vats; the vats themselves, slowly filling with the thick, cloying cane juice, and equally slowly being evaporated away to leave the crystalline sugar; the molasses, that part of the mingled juice and fiber that could not be crystallized, and was instead poured off, thick and black and treacly, to be used as the basis for the plantation's rum industry; the heat and the noise, the nudity, for few of the blacks wore any clothes, and the overseers were stripped to their breeches; all were suggestive of a world in which he could never participate. Because it terrified him. And it was a terrifying world, for with everyone working to the limits of their endurance and beyond, people made mistakes; machetes slipped and cut deeply into feet, hands got too close to the endless rollers and fingers were caught; men and women screamed and instant amputations were performed, while the dispensary, the plantation hospital, filled with wailing victims.

But nothing must be allowed to interfere with the rush to complete the grinding and have the hogsheads safely shipped to England. For Roger's profit.

If the factory during grinding was hell, the dispensary was a specially deep pit beyond even the tortured furnaces. Here were not only the injured from the factory. Here too were all the sick, every loathsome disease that could be imagined—or inflicted—upon people badly fed and overworked, seldom washed, and never considered. Here was elephantiasis with limbs and genitals swelling to hideous sizes, and the scab, a skin cancer which Johnnie at first sight thought was leprosy; here were women having babies and women dying of fever; here were children coughing and spitting blood and doubled up with diarrhea. Here was a stench and intimate humanity Johnnie had never really considered before and did not want to consider now. It had been the Reverend Morton's wish that the master accompany him to the dispensary every day; Morton was the plantation chaplain and took his duties seriously. But once had been enough for Johnnie; he felt ill every time he even thought of the place.

Grinding over, the plantation became almost bearable. He had to keep up the pretense of being the master, had to attend the daily briefings and had to make a daily inspection of the fields. But when he returned to the house at eleven o'clock for his breakfast and his glass of sangaree or swizzle, he could turn his back on the horrors and the humiliations for the rest of the day. After breakfast there was the siesta, and while the rest of the white men and the field gangs returned to their labors at three o'clock, he could remain at home, in what cool the great house provided, reading the books in Father's old library—untouched since the Haggards had immigrated to England, so far as he could see, and ready to fall apart unless handled with great care—and consume more sangaree and swizzles, delightful drinks which helped him to exist at all, and sit on his veranda and remember, and think, and even hope a little, for the future. If he was most certainly in prison, it could be made bearable by the alcohol and his long hours of comparative solitude—there was always at least one servant within earshot—he even managed to write a little poetry, but that was a secret to be kept even from the domestics, in case it reached the overseers and gave them something else to laugh about.

For he saw *them* as little as possible. He had invited them all, with their wives, to the great house within a week of arriving. But by then the news of his repudiation of Claudette—which seemed to have been as grave a crime as frame-breaking was in England—and of his vomiting when confronted with the tortured slaves had become common knowledge, and he was aware only of the ladies' sneering smiles. So, they could live down there, and he would live up here. They could whisper whatever they wished, and he could think whatever he wished. They could not harm him with their words.

He saw them in church for a brief hour on a Sunday morning; but as his pew was the very front, they did not even impinge on his worship to any great extent, and Morton, after one sermon on the duties and responsibilites of being a master, had let him be.

The rest of Barbados seemed to have decided to ignore his existence, with one very strange exception. Adelaide Campkin, the woman who had been so rude to him on his arrival, and who apparently hated his family with a perfectly feminine consistency, had now invited him to supper on no less than four occasions. It could only be with the intention of humiliating him, so far as he could determine. Obviously word of his inadequacies would have spread far beyond the boundaries of Haggard's Penn; in any event, Haggard's and Bolton's adjoined each other. He had pleaded his preoccupation with learning the business of planting to avoid the first three; the fourth he had not troubled to answer at all. She clearly was a woman who needed a man-sized hint.

But oh, he thought, as he sat and watched the sun begin its droop toward the western horizon, to have a single friend, a single human being to whom he could stretch out his hand, reveal his thoughts. His loneliness was leading him into some strange mental paths, to considering the possibility of the companionship of a dog—the plantation had many dogs, but they were either mongrels or mastiffs, and neither appealed so much as a lap dog, but that could only add to Ferguson's contempt—or, more attractive, someone like William.

Terrible thought. William had nothing to which he could appeal, no spark to which he could respond, save that of his manhood. And that was behind him forever. Forever and ever and ever. He broke out in a cold sweat at the thought of someone like Ferguson ever learning an iota of what went on inside his brain.

But still, a friend, if such a thing were possible . . . He sat up as he watched a phaeton rumbling up the drive to the house, and realized that he had watched it enter the compound gate, more than a mile away, without acknowledging the implications. Someone was visiting Haggard's Penn. A caller. On him? He stood up in a panic.

"Montague," he shouted. "Montague."

"I see them, Mr. Haggard," the butler said. "I got sangaree here for them. But what a thing, eh? It ain't ever happened before."

"You know who they are?"

"Oh, yes, sir, Mr. Haggard. That is Mistress Campkin's buggy. She coming here. Well, glory be. That ain't never happened before."

Johnnie sat up, spilling his drink. "Mrs. Campkin? Oh, my God. What are we to do?"

"I got sangaree ready mix, sir."

"Sangaree. Yes . . ." Johnnie advanced to the veranda rail, but the phacton was already almost upon them, and now he saw that there were two women in the body of the coach; the young one, Rosalind, was accompanying her mother. He swallowed, endeavored to straighten his cravat, realized to his dismay that he wasn't wearing a cravat; his shirt was open at the neck. How could he possibly appear before ladies while so undressed? But there was nothing he could do about it; the equipage was already at the foot of the stairs, and the yard-boys were running forward to seize the bridles.

Adelaide Campkin descended first, as stiff and as angular as he remembered her. Rosalind was much more supple, but by then he was already reaching for her mother's hands.

"Mistress Campkin, an unexpected honor."

Adelaide Campkin gave him a devastating stare. "Why have you not accepted my invitations, you silly boy?"

"Why, I . . ." He bent over Rosalind's hand. "I have been so busy." He tried a quick smile. "I'm afraid I know absolutely nothing of planting. *Knew* absolutely nothing. I am learning."

"Ah, Montague," remarked Mrs. Campkin, taking a glass from the offered tray. "This place never seems to change. You've met my youngest daughter, Rosalind, Mr. Haggard?"

"Indeed I have. On the day I arrived." What a pretty girl she was. Freckles apart—and they were not altogether ugly—her height and her composure, despite her obvious embarrassment at her mother's manners, were most attractive, and she possessed a quality of almost masculine friendliness, as opposed to feminine coquettishness, which he found delightful.

Adelaide sat down. "Well," she said. "I can tell you, Mr. Haggard, she is very upset that you have chosen to ignore us."

"Upset? Oh, I . . ." Johnnie found himself blushing as he offered Rosalind a glass of sangaree. "I did not mean to be rude, believe me. It is just that there has been so much to do . . ."

"Stuff and nonsense," Adelaide declared. "You finished grinding a month ago. I would interfere with no plantation while it is grinding, Mr. Haggard. But now you *are* finished, why, I confess that I don't know whether to take you for a monk or a criminal."

He felt his cheeks burning even more intensely, and glanced at Rosalind, who gave him a nervous smile.

"I assure you, madam," he said, "that it would give me the greatest pleasure to accept your invitations, were—"

"Well, then," Adelaide said. "We shall expect you to dinner tomorrow night, Mr. Haggard. And now I really must be on my way. I am to see the Reverend Oldham. Have you met the gentleman?"

"I'm afraid not," Johnnie confessed.

Adelaide gave him a roguish smile. "You have missed nothing, I do assure you. He is an absolute scoundrel. A Methodist, my dear Mr. Haggard, who wishes to discuss the emancipation of the slaves. Can you imagine it? What would they do, without us to see to their affairs, but starve? Supper tomorrow night, Mr. Haggard. Oh, by the way, you won't mind driving Rosalind home, in due course? I'm sure *she* has no desire to waste her afternoon talking to a Methodist."

"Why, I . . ."

"Mama," Rosalind said. "You cannot so impose upon Mr. Haggard."

"Nonsense, girl," Adelaide said, finishing her drink and going down the stairs. "I'm sure Mr. Haggard will be delighted."

Johnnie watched the phaeton dwindling down the drive, hastily offered Rosalind another glass of sangaree.

"I must apologize for my mother, Mr. Haggard," Rosalind said. "She is . . . well, Adelaide Bolton. It's a stupid thing to say, but she's been Adelaide Bolton all of her life. If you see what I mean."

"I do," he said. "My father was John Haggard all of his life."

"Yes," she agreed, and sat down.

He sat down as well, took a fresh glass from Montague's tray, wished the black devil would take himself away. Because *what* an attractive girl she was. He would not have supposed it possible, with so destroyed a complexion. Probably it was the friendliness, breaking through the embarrassment. A friendliness inspired by confidence. She was Adelaide Bolton's daughter, in the same sense that he was John Haggard's son. No, he thought, not in the *same* sense. I have never been John Haggard's son; I have just borne his name. But this girl has been a Bolton, more than a Campkin, from the day she was born.

She was also growing prettier by the moment, as he looked at her. She had none of the hills and valleys he normally associated with women, and loathed; her hips were as slender as his own, and her chest seemed even less robust. Save for her hair and her clothes, she might have been a boy.

And now she was smiling at him as she sipped her sangaree. "You *will* come to supper, Mr. Haggard," she said. "Mama is not half so bad as she appears."

Amazingly, she found herself beginning to be amused by the young man; having been brought up to loathe the very sound of the name Haggard, she had felt her initial dislike reinforced by Mama's sudden volte-face. And yet she found herself thinking as they returned to Bolton's in the cool of the evening, sitting beside him in the Haggard kittareen, driven by a black man—why hadn't Johnnie taken the reins himself—didn't he knew how to drive?—he is obviously as different from his father as it is possible to be. Contemptuously so, in the eyes of Barbadian society. In her eyes, up to this afternoon. But as he talked—and she had the feeling that he was *talking*, as opposed to communicating with his mouth, for the first time in a long while—she began to understand something of his spirit, of his love of beauty, of the attraction he found in a sunset or in a lonely bird swooping low over a copse of trees. He was a poet.

She did not suppose there had ever been such an animal in Barbados before, in all its history. Certainly she had never read any poetry, and she had regarded herself always as at once well-educated and sensitive. She could understand his revulsion at life on a sugar plantation. She had been born on Bolton's, and had grown up there. She had not left Barbados in her life. The sight of slaves, the sound of them and the smell of them, their humor and their tears, their births and their deaths, their agonies and their scant pleasures, had always been as much a part of her life as the sun and the rain, the hurricane winds and the roar of the surf at the seaside. But as she avoided the sun at noon, or saw that her windows were securely battened when the wind began to blow, so she would never dream of attending a slave punishment, or worse, a slave execution, and if her duty as Adelaide Campkin's daughter demanded that on special occasions, such as Easter or Christmas, she visit the slave village and even enter the dispensary, it was always with her face guarded by a nosegay of flowers and her spirit fortified by a gin swizzle.

None of her sisters or her friends were any different. Nor were they expected to be, as women. Those females, like her own mother, who took an active part in the management of a plantation were regarded as the salt of the earth by their menfolk; the majority, who preferred to spend their time in idle gossip and with their dressmakers or at the horse races, were at least not condemned. It was Johnnie Haggard's misfortune, she realized, as she watched him at dinner attempting to hold his own with the other male guests and having to be rescued time and again by Adelaide, that inside his male exterior there lurked a possibly female brain. And was quite shocked, at once at the profundity of the thought and then at its possible implications. He was the man her mother had decided she should marry.

It was a matter she considered very seriously. She was the youngest of three girls, and had taken her attitude to life strictly from Virginia and then Penelope. From them she had learned to sew and to cook and to play the piano; with them she had suffered the boredom of Mr. Digges, their tutor, only last year dispatched back to England after having completed his task, as Miss Rosalind had attained the age of fifteen.

The requirements of marriage, of having to be married in the first place, of having to go to bed with a man, and then of having to bear children, had also filtered down to her through her sisters. She had only been eleven when Ginny had been married, to a planter from Jamaica. The excitement of a Campkin leaving Barbados had quite overlaid any other consideration, and the fact that she had only met Mr. Marsden twice in her life had not seemed to upset Ginny. "It's a huge plantation," she had said. "Nearly as big as Bolton's. I'm going to be very happy. Mama says so."

There had been no possible argument with that, and Ginny's early letters to Penny had been full of interesting and not altogether distasteful pieces of information. She had been seasick on the voyage, but Mr. Marsden had still insisted on sleeping with her. Here the letter had descended into a sort of shorthand, for Ginny and Penny had been very close, whereas Lindy had always been an outsider. "He's so big," Ginny had written. "The pain was terrible, at first. But afterward, why, he seemed to fill me right up." And when Lindy had asked for an interpretation, Penny had merely gone into shrieks of laughter. "Goose," she said. "Don't you know, when you get married, your husband will have the right to push his tool right into you?"

Her first sex lesson, and a frightening one. Having spent her life on a sugar plantation, Lindy was under no misapprehensions as to what men looked like; black men, at least. She had never really considered the idea of white men without their breeches. When she did, following the letter and Penny's explanation, she had wanted to be sick. But had it been fear or excitement?

And soon it had been Penny's turn. She hadn't done half as well as Mr. Marsden, had had in fact to be content with the field manager of another Barbadian plantation; rich planters were becoming thin on the ground. Eligible bachelors were on the whole hard to find. By then Ginny had become a mother and had almost stopped writing, and when she did, it was mainly to moan about the trials and tribulations of running a great house and being a mother, and about Marsden's—she no longer used the "mister"—drinking. Nor had Penny given a better impression of married life. Harrison also drank, and when he drank, he beat her, so much so that after a few months she had come home again. Mama had been furious, and she and Papa had driven over to have a word with Harrison, and with his employer. After that Penny had returned to her husband, and since then she had not visited Bolton's very often. Penny had taken on a faraway look, which Mama said was because she couldn't have any children. Which annoyed Mama no end; her only three grandchildren were over a thousand miles away, in Montego Bay.

So Lindy's marriage had become a matter of some importance. And for her as well, because *having* considered the matter, she was determined that he should neither be a drunkard and beat her, nor be enormous, nor so insensitive as to manhandle her while she was suffering from seasickness. It would also help, she had decided, were he to be around her own age instead of old enough to be her father, and to this end had managed to fall in love, the previous year, with Lieutenant Brady from the garrison. He was young, he was handsome, he cut a dashing figure in his uniform, and he was quite hopelessly infatuated with her. He was also transferred to British Guiana within a week of the state of affairs becoming evident. "Marry a soldier?" Mama had demanded. "With-

out any better prospect than having his head shot off? My
dear child, I despair."

They had held hands twice, and on the second occasion, in
a spirit of true military valor, he had managed to kiss her on
the cheek before they had been interrupted. My romance, she
had thought bitterly. Because it was all very well for Mama
to have the governor send him packing; with Brady gone,
there was *no* one who could even be considered as a husband
for a Campkin on the entire island. Until the arrival of
Johnnie Haggard.

Johnnie Haggard. He had now come to dinner with them
on five occasions, and had attended several other soirees
around the island, as the rest of Barbadian society was always
willing to take their lead from Adelaide Campkin. And he
cut a more attractive figure on every occasion. He was only
six years older than she. He dressed beautifully, and he
danced divinely. He could dominate any conversation, once it
could be steered away from sugar or war or illness or disease
or the falling profits from planting. He was undeniably handsome. He had the background of tragedy that made every
woman want to mother him. And if all the men, including
Lindy's own father, still affected to hold him in contempt,
and eagerly listened to every bit of gossip from Haggard's to
show how utterly incompetent he was to manage a sugar estate, mustn't that necessarily mean that he was as unlike
Messrs. Marsden and Harrison as could be imagined? Certainly he drank sparingly when in company. And if he was
also quite unlike Lieutenant Brady in that he seemed to ab-
hor the very thought of war and killing, that was surely only
an aspect of his poetic nature. Living with Johnnie Haggard
might just be a true pleasure, and if he never attempted, on
the many occasions they were rather deviously left alone together, even to kiss her on the cheek, preferring to talk, well,
that was just English politeness. Things would be different
when they were married.

"Well, Mr. Haggard, the great day, eh? Nervous?" asked
Cartwright, the assistant factory manager, who, because he
was the senior bachelor on the plantation, had been desig-
nated as Johnnie's best man.

What a farce, Johnnie thought. A best man is surely meant
to be a close friend. But now he was descending the stairs,
and the carriages were waiting, with all the white staff ready

to accompany him, their wives in their shabby best gowns, the men discovering long-forgotten tricornes to look absolute fools in this day and age. While down the hill the slaves, given a holiday and a measure of rum to celebrate their master's felicity, stamped and danced and cheered as they saw the procession rolling away from the great house.

Johnnie sat bolt upright. It was nearly four in the afternoon, and the heat was beginning to fade, but he could feel sweat pouring out of his body.

"And she's a lovely girl," Cartwright said from beside him. "Oh, aye, a lovely girl. Slim, but she'll grow. And tall. I like them tall. I like to feel them from tit to toe, all the way down."

"Will you be quiet, Mr. Cartwright?" Johnnie requested. "You are discussing the future Mrs. Haggard."

My God, he thought. The future Mrs. Haggard. How had it *happened*? Dinner party after dinner party, dance after dance, and Lindy had always been there. It had got to the stage that had he ever attended a soiree and she *not* have been present, he would have supposed her ill. And always, at his entry, whoever was talking with her immediately made his or her excuses and melted away. Adelaide Campkin had spoken, and no obstacles were to be placed in the way of the Haggard.

And he, being several kinds of a fool, had not considered the matter in its proper light. Because, amazingly, he actually liked the girl. He liked being with her, talking with her. She was always ready to listen, she had a delightfully gentle sense of humor, and she was not at all feminine in her exchanges with him. It simply had not occurred to him that as they *did* belong to different sexes, at the end of it all there had to be something more than conversation. He did not see the necessity of it. There had been no conversation at all with the serving maid at Newstead, and his conversation with Meg Bold had been decidedly limited. Conversation was something one shared with men, and if it could happen, as with Byron, that there was an end there too, it was not very common and it was not something to be thought about.

But apparently it *was* something to be thought about with a girl, even a girl like Lindy, because girls had parents, who apparently thought of nothing else. So it had been that when he had been in Barbados just a year, one night after dinner there had been no Lindy, but suddenly Mr. Campkin instead.

A serious chat was indicated. "Of course," Peter Campkin had said, "I can see that you're head-over-heels in love with the girl. And I happen to know that she is head-over-heels in love with you. Now, I suppose that you feel that you are a bit young. Twenty-two is it? Why, man, that is an excellent age for marriage, provided a man is established. And you are established, what? At least you're older than Lindy. That's important, mind. A woman must know her place. But now you've raised the subject, I can tell you, Johnnie, that Adelaide and I are absolutely delighted. I'll confess to you, lad, tongues were beginning to wag, and in Barbados that can be a bad thing. But you leave it all to me, boy, and I'll leave it all to Adelaide, and we'll have the wedding of the century between us."

Next morning, in a cold sweat, he had written a desperate letter to Alice. He was only twenty-two and an absconded felon. He had no legal right to marry without permission of his guardian. Having written the letter, he could visit the Campkins with an easy conscience and a ready smile, to explain his situation. Much as he would adore to marry Lindy, to do so without Roger's permission would be unthinkable; he did not of course tell them the truth of the matter, merely reminded them that without Roger's support he was destitute; and Adelaide, her face taking on a peculiarly grim expression, had quite agreed. Again the fool, he had acted too promptly. Adelaide's letter had apparently traveled on the same ship. And Alice's reply had been the death knell of all his hopes.

She could think of no happier event than a uniting, after all these years, of the Haggards and the Boltons. She had received a letter from Mrs. Campkin praising him to the skies, and from all accounts—whose accounts, save Adelaide's, could it possibly have been?—Miss Rosalind was a beautiful and charming girl, entirely worthy of the name of Haggard. What a relief it was, Alice wrote, to learn that all those criticisms mentioned by Ferguson in his last year's report were entirely groundless. When Roger returned, she would seriously broach the matter of getting rid of Ferguson altogether. After all, with Johnnie soon to be a married man, a general manager was surely an unnecessary luxury. As for Roger, Johnnie need have no fears there. Roger would be delighted. It was quite impossible to contact him at the moment, as Wellington's armies were on the point of bursting into France and there was almost no communication with the line regiments, but she *knew* he would be pleased. And in any event, as he had given her complete power of attorney, including that of acting for him as regards Johnnie, her permission was all that was necessary. And she was utterly delighted as well.

She had written to Adelaide Bolton to the same effect. Adelaide Bolton, who had regarded John Haggard's bastard daughter as the scum of the earth and had said so often enough, was now amazingly exchanging letters with her. After that there had been no defense. And here he was, having made his way up the narrow aisle of the Bolton family church, his back slapped and his hand wrung a thousand times, standing next to his bride. The marriage of the century, Peter Campkin had called it, and Johnnie could well believe it as he thought of the hundreds of guests, almost every white person in Barbados save for the redlegs—the descendants of the prisoners Cromwell had dispatched here as his first colonists—of the equipages and the gaily dressed slaves, of the cases of champagne and the acres of cake waiting to be consumed, of the excitement which had even engendered a leader in the newspaper on the merits of Barbados' two leading families being at last united.

United. What a terrible thought. But as he looked down at the smiling face beside him, it occurred to him that perhaps he was unnecessarily alarmed by the situation. When all was said and done, their principal pleasure, indeed their only pleasure up to now, was in talking with each other. There was no reason for that to change because she wore his ring on her finger.

"Congratulations. Congratulations. Congratulations." The words flowed around Johnnie's head as hand after hand squeezed his own fingers, and cheek after cheek, with occasionally even a mouth, was presented to his lips. The huge withdrawing room seethed and hummed; plates and glasses rattled, champagne exploded and gurgled, teeth and jaws masticated, woman giggled and men guffawed, black servants circulated, and the air steamed. When would it be over? He had not seen his bride since he had kissed her on the cheek after they had cut the cake. She had been equally in demand, but now she had disappeared altogether, as had her mother. She was changing for her honeymoon drive to the Campkins' beach hut over on Bathsheba.

"Mr. Haggard. My congratulations."

Johnnie peered at the short, thin man with the intense features.

"Thank you, sir."

"My name is Oldham. The Reverend Oldham."

"Ah," Johnnie said.

"You have heard of me, sir? Well, sir, I am trusting that now you are married into this illustrious family, you will permit me to visit you on Haggard's."

"I'm sure you are welcome, whenever you choose, Mr. Oldham."

"Am I, sir? I have been to Haggard's four times in this past year, and been refused admittance on every occasion."

"Indeed? Not by my orders, certainly. I was quite unaware of your intention. Believe me, sir, next time you call, you shall be welcome. I shall see to it personally."

"Spoken like a man, sir," Oldham said. "And you embolden me to suggest that you may even be willing to listen to what I have to say."

"I will listen to any man, sir."

"Then, sir, I will tell you that I wish to discuss your slaves. Their condition and their future, sir. I know you for a humanitarian. I can see it in your eyes, sir. But perhaps you have not thought the matter through. Slavery cannot endure, Mr. Haggard. It is opposed to every principle of religion or indeed ethics. It must crumble, and it will crumble. The time is all but upon us. All it requires, here in the West Indies, here in Barbados, is someone to give the lead. Now, sir, Mr. Haggard, have you the courage to be that someone?"

Johnnie could only goggle at him, quite taken aback by the vehemence of the assault. He was rescued by the Very Reverend Bledy, the Dean of Barbados, who had performed the ceremony.

"Really, Oldham, a marriage is no place for a sermon. You do your cause more harm than good by these unseemly outbursts. Mr. Haggard has more important things to think about tonight than the state of his slaves. His bride is coming down."

Johnnie turned, heart beginning to pound. He was to escape, in the company of a woman he genuinely liked. Perhaps one he could even love, in time. And there she was, on the stairs, escorted by her bridesmaids and her sister and her mother, a picture in her dark green silk spencer, worn over a pale green muslin gown so sheer that despite the two petticoats beneath, it was almost possible to see her legs when she moved in front of the windows. Her bonnet was a straw poke, decorated with pale green ribbons, which all but concealed the glory of her yellow hair, and her reticule, in dark green silk, hung from the fingers of her left hand. It was a simple but tremendously effective showpiece for her height and her beauty. Because she *was* beautiful, he realized. Tonight even her freckles were beautiful.

She threw her bouquet, expertly, into the arms of some waiting maiden, then she was in the throng, and he was making his way toward her, once again running the gamut of the slapping-grasping-tugging hands and the shouting voices. Then her hand was locked in his, and she was turning up her face for a kiss, just a quick touch of the lips, before they were being half-carried down the front stairs and thrust into the waiting carriage. The door was slammed shut, and the coachman took his place, while several of the younger overseers mounted, carrying flaring torches, as it was by now quite dark, and made ready to accompany them for at least a part of their journey.

The noise was tremendous, for there was a collection of buckets and spades and old boots and horseshoes secured to the rear of the carriage, and the road to the west was by no means well-surfaced, so that they bounced and rattled in time to the clattering and banging and hallooing from outside.

"They'll soon weary of it," Lindy gasped, jolting against him as she closed the blinds.

"I was thinking what fun it all is," he said.

"I suppose it is. I remember behaving very like this at Penny's wedding," she agreed. "But I really am quite tired." Hastily she corrected herself. "I mean, of all this celebration. I'm not really tired."

"It's a great occasion," Johnnie pointed out. "For your family even more than for us, I should think."

She gave a little sigh, of relief, he thought, at his mood, and rested her head on his shoulder. "Have you ever considered what a tremendous step it is, for a woman to . . . to place herself in the hands of a man she does not know very well?"

"Stuff and nonsense, my dear," he said. "You have known me longer than a year."

"Which means nothing. For how may you *know* someone until you have actually lived with him? Or her."

"I suppose that's true. But I do assure you that what you know of me, is me, my dearest Lindy. I have no great hidden depths. Have you?"

She sat up to kiss him on the cheek. "That you will have to find out, my darling. Listen."

The halloos were fading into the distance. She leaned forward and banged on the trap. "Let's have all that rubbish off the back, Henry."

"Yes'm, Miss Lindy." The coach stopped, and the driver got down. Lindy pulled down the blind again and looked out. They were already in the low hills which spined the island, and the breeze was freshening. As with all West Indian communities, Barbadians preferred to live on the leeward, or western, side, where some shelter was to be obtained from the unceasing trade winds, which arrived strengthened by having blown across three thousand miles of open ocean, all the way from Africa, while taking their pleasures on the windward coast. And already they could hear the roar of the surf, breaking itself on the rocks that littered Bathsheba Bay, where on the leeward side all was sandy beaches and gentle ripples.

"Isn't it marvelous?" She nestled against him again as the equipage began its descent to the shore. "I love our visits to Bathsheba. I love going to sleep to the sound of the surf." Once again she seemed to realize that she might have said the wrong thing. "I love lying awake to it, too. As for . . ." But then she might be going too far the other way. "It makes me excited," she confessed in little more than a whisper.

He put his arm round her to squeeze her against him. "Me too. It makes me want to write, something dramatic, stirring . . . I sometimes suppose Byron must have the sound of surf rumbling in his ears all the time."

"Boo. I'm sure you could write as well as Lord Byron if you wished. Why don't you, as soon as we arrive?"

"I haven't brought any paper with me."

She hugged him in turn. "There'll be paper at Bathsheba."

A few minutes later they were turning into the drive of the house, a one-storied cottage this, called a bungalow in a word borrowed from similar dwellings in India. Here there was the usual retinue of slaves waiting to assist them down, and to escort them into the house, torches flaring in the fresh wind, and candles too. On Bathsheba there were no mosquitoes and no sand flies, and therefore no need for nets around the beds; the interior of the house looked almost English.

"I got supper for you, Miss Lindy," the butler said. "And champagne."

"No more champagne, Lucas. I couldn't stomach a drop. As for supper . . ." She glanced at her husband.

"I've had more than enough," he said. "And it's quite late."

"I think we shall just retire, Lucas," Lindy said. "But I would like you to provide Mr. Haggard with a pen and some paper." She squeezed Johnnie's hand. "Don't be *too* long."

She was in every way an absolute darling. Her temper, her humor, her demeanor, even such physical things as her scent or the texture of her skin, might have been created especially for him. He supposed he was really the luckiest fellow in the world. After everything that had happened, the utter disaster which had seemed about to overtake him two years ago, to be able to look forward to spending the rest of his life in the company of so delightful a creature was quite unbelievable. All that was required was to make her legally his wife. It was not something to which he was looking forward, but then, he did not suppose she was particularly looking forward to it either, hence her sudden bouts of nervousness. But it had to be done, and they both knew it had to be done, and presumably the sooner it was done, the better. Certainly he was in no mood for poetry.

He put down the pen, went along the corridor to the bedroom. Instantly Lucas, the butler, appeared behind him. "You want me to help you, Mr. Haggard?"

Johnnie glanced at him, realized he was being offered the services of a valet, not a stud. "I'll undress myself, thank you, Lucas," he said, and knocked.

There was an outbreak of giggling from inside, clearly not from Lindy, he reflected thankfully, and then the door was opened by a smiling maid. Lindy still sat before the mirror, wearing a white linen nightgown, with her golden hair completely loosed—for the first time that he had ever seen—and trailing in a straight cascade down her back almost to her thighs. She smiled at him in the glass, but she was definitely nervous; there were pink spots in her cheeks.

"No poetry tonight, Mr. Haggard?" she asked.

"Perhaps tomorrow," he said. "May I dismiss your maid?"

"Of course. Good night, Maggie."

"Good night, Miss Lindy. Good night, Mr. Haggard." The door was closed.

Lindy turned round, still sitting, and it was his turn to flush.

"Will it embarrass you if I undress?"

"Not at all, sir," she said.

He took off his cravat and his coat. "Because you do understand, Lindy, that there is a duty I must perform, we must perform."

She got up, went to the bed. "You will find that I am anxious to be your wife, Johnnie. In every way."

"I never doubted it. It is just that . . ." He turned his back on her to remove his breeches, reach for his nightshirt. "I should hate to cause you any pain."

"I doubt you could ever do that, my darling."

Damnation, he thought. He was not hard. Of all the absurdities. He had been hard enough when he had been placed on the belly of Byron's maid. But that had been because there had been male hands holding him there, male hands squeezing his buttocks, male hands . . . He stood by the bed. She sat up, the sheet folded across her lap, the pillow bunched behind her back. And she did, after all, have breasts; he could see their shape beneath the linen; the material was so thin he could even make out the darkness of her nipples. Oh, damn, damn, damn.

He sat beside her, held her hands. "I do love you, Lindy. I have never met a woman I have so instantly liked so very much."

"As I love you, Johnnie. Love you, love you, love you." She half-pulled him forward while rising herself, and their lips met. But instantly hers parted and he was aware of saliva, and her tongue brushing his. He felt quite revolted, jerked away. She released his hands, and frowned at him. "Did I hurt you?"

"Hurt me? Of course not." He got up, went round the bed, sat on it. To get beneath the coverlet would be to risk touching her legs with his own. But he had to. He had to want to. "Do you think I could blow out the candles?"

"Of course you can. I would prefer it."

He left the bed, snuffed the candles, made his way back through the sudden darkness, crawled onto the mattress, and had his hands seized to bring him once again against her.

"I do love you, Johnnie," she said. "But I'm so afraid. Johnnie, now, now, please . . ."

He attempted to push her away, and found that he was pressing his hands against her breasts. He released her and fell back, and she lay beside him.

"Johnnie . . . ?" There was a note of anxiety in her voice.

"I . . . I am not hard, Lindy. I could not penetrate you, at this moment."

Her breath rushed against his cheek. "Then you are afraid too. I'm so glad. I'm so glad we're both young, and we know nothing. There's so much to be learned, just you and me. But Mama has explained it to me. Hold me in your arms, Johnnie dear. Would you like me to take off my nightdress?"

"No," he said. "No." For God's sake, no.

Her head was on his shoulder, her breasts pressed against his arm. "But I must help you," she said. "Mama did explain to me. I must help you, Johnnie dear." Her hand slid over his thighs, across the nightshirt, and just as gently touched his penis, hesitated, and then her fingers reached down to raise the nightshirt. In a moment she was going to be holding him. And then no doubt he would come hard, and she would wish him to push into her . . . His stomach seemed to roll, and he thrust down with his hands to push himself up and reach his feet, standing beside the bed.

She lay half on her side, sprawled where he had left her. "Johnnie? Please, Johnnie."

"You mustn't touch me," he snapped. "I hate being touched, by . . . by anyone."

"You were going to say by me," she accused, raising herself on her elbow.

"Of course I wasn't. I hate being touched, by anyone. Just leave me alone. I will enter you, Lindy. I promise you. I will enter you. But . . . but not tonight. As you said, I'm nervous. And we are both tired. But I will enter you. I give you my word."

Chapter 4

The Prodigal

Alice Haggard stood on the steps of the inn, used her handkerchief to wipe the last of the ale from her lips. The inn was not a place she habitually visited on her daily inspection of the valley, nor did she normally drink beer, but today was special. "You'll post a notice, Mr. Hatchard," she said to the publican. "And remember, free drinks for all."

"That I will, Miss Alice," Hatchard agreed. "That I will. Oh, they'll be some celebrating tonight."

"I look forward to it." She gave him a smile, went down to be assisted onto the seat of the gig by Doughty. She preferred to drive herself, allowing the coachman to sit beside her, a post he greatly honored. It was an honor for anyone in Derleth to be associated, in however minor a way, with Miss Alice. Her handsome looks, her splendid deep auburn hair, the readiness of her smile alone would have accounted for her popularity, even had she not been the squire's sister, and had she not demonstrated, time and again during the past bitter two years, that they were *her* people, that as far as she could permit it, their bad times were her bad times.

And in the end, all had come right. She almost wanted to cheer herself. Certainly she was near to tears as she wrapped her dark blue redingote closer around herself—although it was nearly the end of April, the weather remained chill—adjusted her bonnet, and clasped the reins in her strong gloved fingers.

The gig's next stop was the manse, but Mr. Shotter, who had replaced the Reverend Malling, had seen her coming, and was waiting with his wife and daughters on the step.

"Miss Alice," he shouted. "You've heard the news? Bonaparte has abdicated."

"Of course I have, Mr. Shotter," she said, "You'll ring the bells, if you please."

"I've sent for the lads now, Miss Alice. Oh, what a great day. Mr. Haggard will be coming home."

"I hope so, Mr. Shotter. I do hope so. And now we're no longer fighting the French, we'll soon settle with the Americans, and then we'll have some cotton again."

"Glory be," Shotter agreed, seeming about to fall to his knees. "What a great day it is, to be sure."

"A great day, Mr. Shotter. Good day to you, Mrs. Shotter. Children."

Alice drove on, down the main street of the village itself. Now every doorway was filled, with men as well as women, as well as children, while their dogs barked and even their cats seemed to sit up and take notice. They looked happy, at last. And they should not be here at all. They should be over in the mill, spinning cotton into cloth, English cloth, to dominate the haberdasheries of the world. Supposing they could find the cotton.

"Is it true, Miss Alice?" a man asked. "Boney's done a bunk?"

"Better than that, Mr. Martin." Alice laughed. "He's been arrested."

"Will there be cotton, Miss Alice?" asked another man.

She kept her smile fixed with an effort. "There'll be cotton, Mr. Carson. If we can beat the French, we've naught to fear from the Americans. Now, get you down to the inn and have a drink. Ale is on the squire today."

They gave a cheer, and came flooding out of their homes, while Alice flicked the whip and Rosebud resumed her leisurely trot through the village. "Poor devils," Alice muttered, half to herself. "Am I not shamefully deluding them?"

"There'll be cotton again, Miss Alice," Doughty said. "Things always come again."

"And men and women starve when the essentials are absent."

"Not on Derleth, Miss Alice. Never on Derleth. Not with your relief. Why, miss, I've heard that over on Plowden a fellow really did starve to death this last winter. Squire Burton don't believe in poor relief, except where the law says he must. But on Derleth, why, miss, I'd wager there ain't no happier village in all Derbyshire, cotton or no cotton."

"Which doesn't mean to say they're happy, Doughty," Alice argued. "The happiness you are talking about is a degree. I suppose a drowning man is happy to come to shore, even if it is a desert island on which he will surely die in lonely misery."

"Ah, but then, miss, what *is* happiness? The happiness you're talking about. I don't suppose it exists. Even for a king."

Least of all for that poor old madman, Alice thought. But philosophy, from her coachman? On the other hand, was he not right? Had she ever been truly, irreproachably, unarguably happy? Had Roger? Had even Father, for all his wealth and his power?

She guided the gig through the cut into the hills, to emerge in the next valley, where the river bubbled, and from where the canal stretched, a long straight liquid road, all the way into the next county. Here stood the rebuilt mill. It was something she was proud of, because in its sanitation and its windows, its space and its air, it was the finest cotton mill in the country, perhaps in the north of England. But today it stood empty. She could obtain enough cotton only to provide work for two days out of five. There was no man in Derleth could support his wife and family on what he was currently earning.

Save he worked down the pit. For farther on, closer to the canal which floated the barges, the huge black scar, made to seem greater by the slag heap which towered beside it like some obscene pyramid, was as usual throbbing with activity. Alice hated the pit. She hated the very thought of it, but to have to visit it every day, to have to watch the men, and more especially the children, come crawling up, faces and bodies blackened, coughing out their lungs as they reached the open air . . . Yet it provided employment, and money. However revolting it might be to think of a twelve-year-old girl crawling naked along a low filthy passage a hundred feet below the surface, in famine times like these it was her meager wage kept her family from depending entirely on the squire's charity.

"Good day to you, Miss Alice." Truff was the pit manager, a short, thickset man who presumably had once worked a coal face, although it was impossible to imagine when, regarding his overfilled belly. "There's a rumor—"

"No rumor, Mr. Truff. Bonaparte has abdicated."

"Well, hallelujah," Truff said. "Shall I tell the lads?"

"You tell them, Mr. Truff. Tell them today is a holiday, and there's free beer at the inn. Tell them to celebrate."

"I'll do that, miss. I'll do that. Ah, there's this gentleman wishing to have a word with you."

Alice glanced at the other man. She had assumed him a buyer from Manchester; they sometimes came down to inspect the quality of the coal at the face. He was taller than Truff, but equally broad, and equally prosperous in appearance.

"Brent is the name, Miss Haggard," he said, coming forward with outstretched hand. "James Brent. I've heard a deal about you."

"Then you have a considerable advantage over me, Mr. Brent," she said. She closed her eyes as Truff started beating the gong which would reverberate down the passageways and summon the miners to the surface. "What can I do for you?"

"Ask instead what I can do for you, Miss Haggard," Brent said. "I'm selling."

"What?"

Brent opened his bag, took out a roll of stiff paper. "A machine, Miss Haggard. If you'd care to look . . ."

Alice gave the reins to Doughty, climbed down, Brent's hand on her elbow. "What sort of machine?"

"We call it Puffing Billy. You'll see those fellows over there?"

He pointed at the dozen men whose duty it was to work the air pumps that did something to alleviate conditions under the ground, now relaxing their labors as the word spread that the rest of the day was going to be a holiday.

"I do, Mr. Brent. They're my own people."

"Of course they are, Miss Haggard. But could they not be better employed? Our machine will provide ten times as much air, driven harder and more consistently, so that your passages will be twice as clean and healthy as they are now."

"How?"

"Steam, Miss Haggard. Steam. You understand the principles of steam?"

"Not very clearly."

"Well, miss, to put it in a nutshell, when you heat water

sufficiently, it creates a vapor, and it has been proved, time and again, that that vapor has a force, has energy, Miss Haggard. It can lift things and it can drive things. Why, do you know that the *Times* newspaper . . . do you read the *Times*, Miss Haggard?"

"I do, Mr. Brent."

"Well, Miss Haggard, I can tell you that its presses are now being driven by steam."

"And steam will drive your machine?"

"Yes, indeed, Miss Haggard."

"This has been proved?"

"One of them is already in use, Miss Haggard. At Wylam Colliery."

"Of course," Alice said. "I'd heard they were trying some newfangled piece of machinery." She gazed at the drawings. "What sort of a price?"

"Ah, well, miss, it's not cheap. But think of the labor-saving, and the improvement in conditions for your people."

"It's the second interests me, Mr. Brent." She straightened. "You'd best come back to the house with me, and we'll talk about it."

A machine, for pumping air. The answer to a miner's dream. But the cost of it. On the other hand, it was progress, and with every year it was becoming necessary to drive the mine shaft deeper into the earth. Even Father had been grumbling that they would soon run out, not of coal, but of the man-energy to get air down there. Roger would certainly agree. Or should she wait until he returned? It could not really be long now.

She smiled down the luncheon table at Emma. "What do you think?"

"I hate machines," Emma said.

"My dear Mrs. Bold," Brent protested. He was in a happy glow, at the claret wine which had been provided, at the thought of sitting down to table in Derleth Manor at all, and with three such attractive ladies. Even if he obviously could not understand the situation at all. But Meg could pass for a lady now, after eighteen months of concentrated schooling.

And today, if Brent was in a happy glow, what was Alice to make of Meg? She had hardly touched her wine or her food. Roger was coming home. It seemed as if all the happiness in the world was suddenly being aimed at Derleth

Manor. Johnnie married—she had not received a letter from him since the great day, but no doubt he had enough to occupy his time—and Roger coming home. The fighting and the killing were done. After more than twenty years. It was an almost incredible thought. She had been eleven years old when the French had cut off the head of their king and the war had started. Twenty-one years.

She signaled Nugent, and her chair was pulled back. "Well, Mr. Brent, it has been a great pleasure. Bring me the contract for the machine when next you're in Derleth, and I'll sign it." She held out her hand.

"The pleasure has been mine, Miss Haggard. Oh, indeed." He bowed to the room at large. "Ladies."

"Is it really called a Puffing Billy?" Emma asked.

"I'm afraid so. But as long as it works . . ." She nodded to Nugent, who had returned from seeing Brent to the front door. "I shall retire for an hour, Nugent."

"Of course, Miss Alice. But Fred was asking if he could have a word. He's waiting now."

Happiness, as she had remarked to the coachman, was too transient a frame of mind to be appreciated. Alice sighed. "I'll come now. You'll excuse me, Mama. Meg." In the doorway she hesitated. "Will you be going out, Meg?"

"I thought I'd take my block," Meg said. "Into the park."

Because Alice had been determined that, if she was going to be a lady, Meg should be able to display some talent. It had been far too late to consider teaching her the piano, and her embroidery was clumsy, mainly because it very obviously bored her. But she had revealed an unexpected gift for drawing, and this Alice had encouraged, buying her crayons and writing blocks by the coachload.

Who would have supposed that so innocent a pastime could possibly endanger her?

"The park," Alice said. "I suspect it may well rain this afternoon. Wouldn't you prefer to stay indoors?"

"Oh, it's such a lovely day, Alice," Meg protested. "Couldn't I go, Ma?"

"I'm sure Alice is just worrying about your health," said Emma, who didn't understand the situation at all. "Especially with Roger coming home. Just stay in sight of the house, in case it *does* come down to rain."

"Oh, I shall. I'm off."

She ran from the room, and Emma raised her shoulders helplessly. "You'll never change her completely."

"I don't want to change her completely," Alice said, and went outside. If she were going to stay close to the house, there should be no problem. But she would have to make sure. "Well, Fred?" She closed the pantry door behind her.

Fred Loon had succeeded Wring as head gamekeeper. Now he twisted his hat between his hands. "There again today, Miss Alice."

"How many?"

"Two, maybe three. Now, if you'd let me set those traps . . ."

Alice turned away, chewed her lip as she gazed out of the window. Father had always maintained mantraps in the woods beyond the park. He had no intention of permitting poachers to take his birds and his deer and his trout. And for more than three years there had *been* no poachers on Derleth land, save for Harry Bold and his son. Since they had fled, nearly two years ago, Loon's task had been virtually a sinecure. Until last month, when he had found human footprints by the stream. Poachers, driven to the woods because their families were starving? Or something even more sinister, Roger's nightmare coming true?

She had seen a man taken in a trap once. It had closed on his ankle, by bad luck missing the boot, and the steel claws had driven right through his flesh, so that when he had been released it had been possible to see his bones. She had sworn to herself that if ever she had the power there would never again be a mantrap on Derleth. Not even to trap Henry Bold? Her mother's husband, but a man she loathed and feared, as a villain and a murderer. And a man whose return could bring nothing but disaster.

Thus it was not a problem to be discussed with Emma. She had no idea how Emma would react. Surely this was what she had always wanted, to live at Derleth in the style to which John Haggard had made her accustomed before he had so cruelly thrown her out. But Harry Bold was her husband, had been her husband for twenty years. There had to be some love there, some affection at least. And some mutual interest. But what interest could Harry Bold have in Derleth that would not be disadvantageous to the name of Haggard?

And Meg. She claimed to hate her father as much as anyone, and to hate what he had done. But she was his flesh and blood, and Tim was her brother, only a year older.

Never had she felt so lonely. But surely her loneliness was as transient as anything else. Roger was coming home. Perhaps in days. Certainly in weeks. It was only a matter of holding the fort until then.

She turned back to Loon, still twisting away in his anxiety. "There'll be no traps, Fred. All we have to do is keep an eye on things until Mr. Roger gets home. I'm relying on you. And I'm relying on you to keep an eye on Miss Margaret as well. She's out in the park now, so far as I know. You watch her, Fred."

"And if I sees a poacher?"

"Fire at him. But not to kill. I'll not be responsible for anyone's death, Fred. Just until Captain Haggard comes home."

"Aye," Fred agreed. "Until Captain Haggard comes home."

"Paris, in the spring," declared Major Trumley Sparrow. "Can there be a more beautiful place, Roger?"

The two officers were returning from having billeted their men. Now they walked their horses up the Champs Elysées, stared at the half-completed Arc de Triomphe, the monument with which Bonaparte had been going to make his conquests immortal. Would it ever be completed now?

"A defeated city, in a defeated country," Roger pointed out.

There was sufficient evidence of that. Fierce mustachios, gathered on street corners to stare at the red jackets in turn, too many of them now reduced by an arm or a leg, but nonetheless obviously dreaming of past glories more than recent defeats; scampering girls, skirts swirling and heads bobbing as they smiled at the Englishmen, uncertain whether to regard them as enemies or possible keepers, sure only that they were preferable to the Prussians or the Austrians and the Russians—they paid for what they took; members of the *ancien régime*, once again thronging the boulevards with their powdered wigs and their sword canes, their sneers and their pomades, apparently unaware of how out-of-date and out-of-fashion they now were, openly hostile to the occupying troops, for were not these men, their saviors, the enemies of France? And distraught officials, suddenly having to cope with the collapse of an empire, the resurrection of a kingdom.

And, of course, the conquerors. For if his grace the Duke of Wellington had insisted that discipline in the British army remain as severe in the days of triumph as ever it had done during the long March across Spain, such an attitude clearly did not prevail among the other nations. There were cossacks sprawling at the café tables, drinking wine by the bottle where they had only ever known vodka, intent upon forgetting the miseries of their existence as rapidly as possible; there were Austrians, white-coated and stiff-necked, flirting with the ladies and quarreling with each other; and there were black-coated Prussians, with a century of Louis XIV's marauding adventures across the Rhine to avenge, glowering in doorways and, to judge from the occasional shriek which emanated from an upstairs window, doing more than that once they got inside.

Yet above and beyond them all, there was Paris. No longer the Paris of history, Roger supposed. Bonaparte had gone a long way toward cleansing the stench and the narrow, verminous alleyways which had provided such a haven for thieves and murderers, but nonetheless the capital of the French, living by and on and round the Seine, accompanied always by the nostril-tingling fragrances of fresh baking bread and unfading garlic. To have come here at all was a great adventure. But to be here at all was to remind him of how good it would be to get home.

Supposing he wanted to go. Supposing he wanted to return to Derleth, to the problems of a nation which, if Alice's letters were to be believed, had in its determination to throw over Bonapartism throughout the world reduced itself to a poverty which this conquered city certainly did not share.

Supposing he wished to return to Meg.

But of course he wished to return to Meg. He loved her. He could not possibly love anyone else. No matter what had happened during that glorious, unforgettable weekend before he had left England, it could never be anything more than an episode. Had he been guilty? At the time. But guilt had very rapidly faded. Mina Favering was a unique woman, a memory to be treasured. Presumably she had thought very little of him, whatever she had pretended. He did not doubt that she was Byron's mistress, in reality, and was but taking a private revenge for Byron's dalliance with Caro Lamb. If he had permitted himself to dream of her occasionally, during the nights before Vittoria and Toulouse, such diversions must now be behind him forever. The war was won. It was time to return to Derleth, time for Major Haggard to cease his existence and Squire Haggard to begin his. And time for Meg. The discharge papers were in his pocket, and Trumley would accompany him. The very best of friends. Introducing Trumley Sparrow to Derleth was going to be a pleasure.

They drew their horses to a halt to watch a retinue of carriages rolling down the street.

"From England, by gad," Sparrow commented. "The aristocracy wishes to gawp."

The aristocracy. Roger saluted as the women leaned out of their windows to wave at the redcoats, and then felt every muscle in his body stiffen and begin to tingle as he found himself smiling at the Countess of Alderney.

"Good day to you, vicar. A splendid sermon." Alice shook hands with Mr. Shotter as she led the procession out of church.

"Thank you, Miss Haggard. Thank you. What news of the major?"

Alice could not stop her smile from fading. But she regained it immediately. "He will be back, Mr. Shotter. Soon. But of course the army of occupation must be organized, at least until the new French government can be established. He will be back. By autumn."

And it was already July. Perhaps she had been too optimistic. Obviously the mere fact of Bonaparte's surrender could not mean the immediate disbandment of the entire British army. But what bad luck that Roger should have been one of those required to remain in Paris. Why, had he even been so unfortunate as immediately to be dispatched to America, as had so many regular regiments, he would at least have had a week's leave in England first. Now, after so long, every day's delay seemed interminable.

She worried most about Meg, whose disappointment must be even greater than her own. Or was it? They sat together in the carriage for the drive back to the manor house, Emma in the middle. Like her mother, Meg was given to smiling and bowing at the villagers, who always lined the road to wave at them. Meg already thought of herself as the mistress of Derleth. Well, there was no reason why she shouldn't, Alice supposed; it was her appointed station in life. But was she enjoying it the more because there was no squire to steal her thunder? And dominate her bed? But there was a subject of which Alice knew absolutely nothing. She had never even been kissed lovingly by a man. Having observed many of the miseries which seemed to follow such a mishap, for either sex, she was inclined to consider herself one of the few really fortunate people on earth. But Meg, whether she felt that way or not, could only attain the position to which she aspired by accepting Roger as her husband. It was a cruel world. But it was what Meg wanted more than anything else. She would have to accept the rough with the smooth.

As if Roger could ever be rough, with anyone. If *only* he would come home.

"I shall write some letters," she announced when they regained the house. "You'll excuse me, Mama."

"Of course. Will you write Johnnie?"

"I suppose so. I think he owes us some sort of a progress report. I was hoping to obtain a portrait of his bride, but apparently there are no such people as portrait painters in Barbados. We shall have to make do with his description." She frowned at Meg, picking up her sketching block.

"It's a gorgeous day," Meg said defensively.

"Yes," Alice agreed. "But, Meg . . . what about that man?"

"Oh, for heaven's sake, Alice. Fred Loon chased him away. Not that I think he needed chasing. He looked a very personable young fellow."

Alice looked at her mother, who came to her rescue.

"Personable young men do not prowl around other people's woods, Meg. The country is filling up with itinerants nowadays. It's all the fault of the war. You do want to be careful."

"There's always Fred Loon," Meg pointed out, pulling on her coat. "Even on Sundays, there's Fred Loon."

She hurried down the corridor to the side door before they could say anything else. Silly women. As if she could ever be afraid of any man after what John Haggard—Alice's own father—had done to her. She had been laid on the ground and raped by five men. There was nothing, absolutely *nothing*, that could ever happen to her again which could possibly be as bad as that. She could remember every second of it as if it had happened yesterday. She had begged and she had shouted and she had wept, and they had taken their turns, silently, hurting her as they pleased themselves, driving their fingers where not even she had explored before. For a year she had lain awake every night, shivering with fear and with distaste.

And then it had passed. It had happened, and she was alive, and she could feel. She had realized this by herself, but her recovery had been completed by Roger. Dear Roger. He was quite unbelievably innocent. When he had first come to her father's cottage, intent only upon seeing Emma again after twenty years, and she had watched him striding through the door, she had thought to herself, now, should I ever lie with a man again, that's who it should be, someone tall, and distinguished, and rich, and wearing a red jacket. That he had been wounded had only added to his attraction. And amazingly, it had happened, only a week later. That she had followed *him* into the wood, and sought him out, had not seemed to occur to him. He had been terrified of her, and of what he was doing to her; he had not imagined that she might be the one doing. It had been a triumph. Her triumph, not only over the Haggards, but over all mankind.

That it would have had such an effect upon him that he would propose marriage still seemed a dream. Mistress Haggard, of Derleth Manor. The richest man in all England, they said, thanks to his West Indian sugar. Her husband.

But did that mean she must turn up her nose at every other man who crossed her path? And the poacher, for presumably he had been one, had been a good-looking young fellow, far, far younger than Roger, although strangely he had somewhat resembled him, and as cool as a cucumber. When he realized she had seen him, he had raised his hat. Almost she thought he might be about to speak, when they had heard Fred Loon's shout. Then he had taken to his heels, but he had stopped, at the trout stream, to wave his hat again.

No doubt he was now in Nottinghamshire. But it had been sufficient of an adventure to make her blood tingle, and it was a long time since that had happened.

She reached the door, pulled it open, and heard Mary Prince.

"Miss Margaret?"

Her voice was hardly louder than a whisper, and when Meg turned, the housekeeper seemed to have seen a ghost. Her cheeks were pale, and Meg was sure she was shaking.

"Mary?" she asked. "Whatever can the matter be?"

"There . . . there's someone wishes to speak with you, Miss Margaret," Mary said, and made a gesture with her hand. Round the corner of the corridor, from the direction of the pantry, there stepped the young man from the wood.

"You?" Meg cried. "But you can't come here."

"Ssssh," he said, smiling at her. He *was* a handsome fellow, tall and well-built, only a year or so older than herself, she estimated, with strong, almost Haggardian features, as she had noticed at their first meeting, and a deliciously crooked smile. His hair was black and curly, and his brown eyes sparkled. His clothes were poor and his boots worn, but Meg was no connoisseur of fashionable male clothing.

"That's what I keep telling him, Miss Margaret," Mary Prince said, regarding the young man with a most peculiar expression. "But he won't listen."

" 'Tis a duty I perform, Mistress Prince," the young man said, and removed his hat. "Jeremy Woodsmith, at your service, Miss Bold."

"Jeremy Woodsmith?" She thought she had never heard so delightful a name. "A duty?"

"A message I bring. From someone very dear to you."

"Someone dear? Not from France?"

"France?" He obviously did not understand.

"You'll not listen to him, Miss Margaret," Mary Prince begged. "Send him packing before Nugent discovers him. It'll be prison if he does."

"Prison?" Meg felt utterly bewildered.

"Mistress Prince would keep a man from his daughter," Jeremy Woodsmith said. "And a daughter from her father. Now, would you really do that, Mary Prince?"

Mary bit her lip, and flushed scarlet.

"Father?" Meg cried, and hastily lowered her voice. "You've a message from Pa?"

"I have it here." He pulled the piece of paper from his pocket.

Meg took it, hesitated. "Pa can't write."

"True enough, Miss Meg. I wrote it for him."

She raised her head. "You?"

"At his dictation."

Slowly Meg unfolded the paper. Reading had been the first task to which Alice had made her address herself, but she was still slow.

"Trust Master Woodsmith," the letter said. "He will bring

you to me. Tim is with me. Not a word to a soul, now. Not even your mother. Dad."

Meg frowned at the young man. "Pa never dictated that."

"He told me what to say, Miss Meg. What he wanted said. I tried to put it in good English."

"And you'll take me to him?"

"That why I'm here. Risking Fred Loon and his fowling piece."

Meg glanced at Mary, who flushed again. "You can trust Mr. Woodsmith, Miss Meg."

"Is he a friend of yours?" Meg asked.

"I've known the good lady for years," Jeremy Woodsmith said. "Why, she must have dandled me on her knee when I was a babe. But I've been abroad. Now I'm back, and trying to help. You'd not turn your back on your dad, now, would you, Miss Meg?"

She was so excited she thought she might choke. Ma had been full of the direst suggestions, that Pa and Timmy were hung by now, at the best transported to Australia.

"When?" she asked.

"Tonight."

"Tonight?" she gasped.

"You're not afraid of the dark, Meg, now, are you? After you've had supper, when the ladies have gone to bed, you come out to the park. I'll find you."

"Loon walks the park at night."

"Loon will be elsewhere. I promise you. Will you come?"

Once again she glanced at Mary Prince. You can trust him, Mary had said. But now she was looking terrified. Yet if she could trust him, then he must be telling the truth about Pa. And Timmy. How she wanted to see them again.

"I'll come," she said. "Wait for me about eleven."

She could hardly eat a bite of dinner, which attracted comment from both Alice and Emma.

"You're sure you're not sickening for something?" Alice asked. "It really would be too unfortunate, with Roger due home any day."

Meg seized her opportunity. "I really *don't* feel very well," she confessed. "Perhaps I've a flu coming on. I'll go to bed early."

"The best thing for you, my dear," Emma agreed.

Then it was merely a matter of dismissing her maid as

quickly as possible—she just could not get used to being dressed and undressed by another woman, as if she were a babe—and climbing into her bed, and forcing herself to lie still as she listened to the clock chiming the hours. But at ten o'clock both Alice and Emma went to bed, looking in on her first, as she had expected. She closed her eyes and breathed slowly and evenly, and they went off together, muttering to each other. She heard the name Roger several times. Roger was coming home. So was what she was about to do awful?

But how could he expect her not to wish to see her father again? Anyway, he'd never know. Jeremy Woodsmith would take her there and then bring her back. Jeremy Woodsmith. What an attractive young man. But was it wrong to be thinking that of any man, when Roger was on his way home to marry her? Jeremy was coming to take her to her father. She *had* to think about him.

The clock struck half-past ten, and she sat up, heart commencing to pound. She got out of bed, changed her nightgown for a walking dress—it was a warm July night and she had never been able to understand Alice's concern with underclothing—brushed her hair, and tiptoed to the door. She left her feet bare; it was too long since she had walked across the grass, barefoot, at night. So she was not being at all the lady they expected of her; tonight she was going back to being Meg Bold. Just for an hour.

The house was dark and quiet; the servants knew Miss Alice's early habits and were pleased to take advantage of them. She went down the second staircase to the ground floor, made her way along the corridor by the pantries, found the outside door unlocked, as Mary Prince had promised it would be. And paused, frowning. It had not really occurred to her before, but she had taken Mary into her confidence. Mary Prince. Of all the Derleth domestics, Mary Prince had been the most loyal to John Haggard, and to his memory, so it was said. And therefore she would be a natural enemy to the Bolds. Yet here she was helping her to see her father.

No doubt, Meg thought, she is also hoping that Pa will insist Ma and I go away with him, and then she'll be rid of us. When she was mistress of Derleth, the first thing she would do would be to sack Mary Prince.

She went outside, closed the door behind her, waited for a moment to allow her eyes to become accustomed to the lighter gloom outdoors. Fred Loon was her problem. Fred or one of his assistant gamekeepers was on duty every night. Then she heard a distant explosion, and her heart seemed to leap into her throat. But it came from way over to the left, at the foot of the hills. Someone had fired a fowling piece. And Jeremy Woodsmith had promised that the gamekeepers would be distracted.

She scooped her skirt to her knees, and ran, through the garden and across the lawn beyond, into the first of the trees, paused there for breath, then ran on again for the stream, stopped when she could hear the rustle of the water, looked over her shoulder, but the house was now lost to sight, turned again, and stifled a scream as a hand closed on her arm.

"Ssssh," said Jeremy Woodsmith.

"You gave me a start," she complained.

"As you gave me," he said, still holding her arm, and now pulling her against him. "I've never seen a prettier picture than you running through the wood."

She freed herself, turned to face him, pushing hair from her forehead. "You'd say that to any girl."

"I wouldn't. Not unless they all had bums as round as yours."

"You've never seen my bum." But she laughed as she spoke. She hadn't had a flirtation like this since the last time she'd been to the fair, with Pa selling his pots and pans.

"I can feel it, though," he said, snatching her against him again and holding her there while his hands went behind her to hold a buttock each and give them a gentle squeeze, pulling them apart before pushing them back together again. Roger had never touched her there. Roger had never really touched her anywhere with his hands. She gave a little shiver of delight, moved her body against his, and jumped away as she felt him stir.

"I'm betrothed."

"To the squire," he said contemptuously.

"You're jealous," she said. "Where's Pa?"

"You'll have to cross the stream. Shall I carry you?"

"Bah. I'll wade." She lifted her skirt to her thighs, stepped into the water, gave another little shiver, and gained the other side. Jeremy splashed behind her.

"You don't love the squire," he said. "You couldn't. Not a great stuck-up oaf of a gentleman. And old enough to be your dad himself. You couldn't, Meg."

"Where's Pa?" she asked again.

"Through the trees. It's dark in there. You'd best hold my hand."

She allowed him to take her hand, and they walked together through the bracken. How lovely it was, she thought, to be holding hands with a handsome young man, walking through the woods. It was what she had always dreamed of. She had supposed that she and Roger would spend their time doing that at Derleth. But he had not once taken her walking through the woods. And this Jeremy so obviously knew everything she liked, everything she wanted; she could be entirely natural with him, where she was always having to be careful what she said and what she did and how she looked, with Roger.

"Hist."

"Pa," she cried, and ran forward to throw herself into Harry Bold's arms. His beard tickled her; the black was speckled with gray. But it was Pa, short and heavy and sweating as ever, his teeth gleaming at her.

"Meg, you little marvel," he said. "Christ, but it's good to see you."

"Where's Tim?"

"Distracting them gamekeepers. He sends you his love." He held her away from him, to look at her. "Still as pretty as a picture. And you've fallen on your feet, I hear."

"Well, Pa . . ." She glanced at Jeremy, waiting patiently beside her.

"How's your ma?"

"She's well, Pa. She's well."

"Does she ever speak of me?"

"Sometimes, Pa. She thinks of you a whole lot. Pa . . . you don't want us to leave Derleth?"

"Now, why should I want you to do that, child? You're going to marry the squire, I hear."

"Yes, Pa. Soon as he comes back from the war. I'm going to be Mistress Haggard."

"Bully for you. But you'd not have your poor old father starve, or hang, now, would you, Mistress Haggard?"

"Of course I won't let you starve, Pa. Or hang."

"Aye, well, there's those that would. Now, you listen to me, miss. Tim and me, we're back to tinkering, calling ourselves Smith, eh? Jeremy here has thrown in his lot with us for the time. You want to be nice to Jeremy. He's an educated gentleman, he is, fallen on hard times. He's traveled, he has. Been to Canada and back. Ain't that the truth, Jeremy?"

"That's the truth, Harry."

Meg looked at him again. To Canada. The other side of the world. As far away as the moon. He'd been there. And come back.

"Now, it seems to me, Meg, girl," Harry Bold said, "from what Jeremy has told me, that there's the place for Tim and me. A new country. Where people like Squire Haggard can't get their hands on us."

"Canada?" she cried. "You're going to Canada?"

"In time. But sea voyages cost money. You follow me?"

She bit her lip. "I don't have any money, Pa."

"You will have, soon as you're married. You'll have the entire running of Derleth Manor. And your husband will want to buy you fine things, jewels, furs . . . you'll have money. I'm not asking for much. Just enough to get Tim and me safely on our way."

"And Jeremy?" She looked at the young man.

"That's up to him. He don't have the law on him yet. Now, girl, will you help your pa?"

"Well . . . of course I will, Pa."

"Good girl. Now, listen, Jeremy here will be our messenger, because he ain't known on Derleth, see? Tim and me, we're keeping over in Nottinghamshire, tinkering. Nobody over there knows us, and the warrant against us is a Derbyshire one. So we won't be coming over here too often. Jerry can be trusted."

"Yes, Pa." Another glance. She could think of no finer arrangement. "Can I tell Ma?"

"That's up to you. Only if you reckon she's on our side."

"Oh, she will be. I'm sure. I'd like to tell Ma. And she has money already."

"Then you tell her. Careful, now. I'd like to see her again. Jerry here will arrange it. Now you'd best be going back. Tim won't keep that gamekeeper running all night. Come here and give your pa a kiss."

Meg obeyed, and he rumpled her hair. "You're a good girl. The best of my children, I always said. You'll see me right, little Meg. Now, off you go. With Jerry."

She kissed him on the cheek, ran into the wood, stopped to look over her shoulder and wave again. Jerry caught her up, held her hand again.

"He's a fine man, your pa."

"He is that," she agreed.

"Which is why he has so fine a daughter." His arm went round her waist. "You and I are going to be great friends, Meg. I've your pa's blessing on that." His fingers were under her arm, and stroking the side of her breast. "You're going to show me your little bum, aren't you, Meg, girl? Seeing as how I admire it so much?"

"Haggard, Haggard. Oh, Haggard." Mina Favering arched her back, up and up, until she was taking her weight, and his, on her shoulders, her legs round his neck, her buttocks thrust against his groin. "Oh, push," she shouted. "Push." Her arms came up as well, her nails clawing at his to bring him down, while his body surged against hers. Even after he had come, he went on moving, because to lie against Mina Favering and not move was an impossibility.

But at last even she was satisfied. Her legs slipped away and struck the bed with a thump, and he lay on her, having to hold himself slightly free with his elbows to avoid crushing her, his lips against her ear to suck the gentle sweat which rolled out of her midnight hair.

Mina Favering. Even after six months, every night more tumultuous than before, she excited him as no woman had ever done. As no woman could ever do.

"I love you," she said. "I have never loved anyone the way I love you, Roger Haggard. Christ, that so much of my life should have passed before I could meet you."

"There's enough left," he said, and bit her ear.

She gave a little wriggle of pleasure, tossed her legs, one after the other, into the air. She moved, as she thought, as she lived, like a girl.

"Is there?" She rolled over to face him, nose touching nose, breaths mingling. "Did I not notice your man packing this morning?"

"Aye, well . . . I must get back to Derleth. I have remained here too long as it is. But a new year—"

"Wretched man," she said. "Wretched, wretched man." Her hands found his penis, squeezed it. "I should tear it off and feed it to the pigs."

"Sometimes I think you are quite capable of that."

"Oh, I am. And it would stop you from committing this act of madness you are contemplating."

He moved his head back to look at her.

She smiled at him, enjoying the feeling of his hardening yet again. "Byron tells me everything. He is no more sensible than you. You'll know he is also considering marriage?"

"I did not know."

"Well, he is, the poor fool. But he at least has some reasons. He is destitute."

"Byron?"

She made a moue. "Well, he owns Newstead Manor, but cannot find a purchaser. For the rest, he is in debt to his eyeballs. His creature is a simple little thing, as plain as a sheet of paper, and she *does* have prospects. You do not need prospects, Haggard. You have them all yourself. And to marry a serving girl . . ."

"Not a serving girl."

"What's the difference?"

He moved her hand, and straddled her once again, allowing their bodies just to touch while he kissed her on the mouth. "Whom would *you* have me marry?"

"Ah. Now . . ."

"You."

Her eyes opened wide, and she frowned. "Me? Are you mad?"

"I am desperately in love."

"With me? Of course you are, you darling, darling boy. Oh, push it in, Haggard. Push it in."

She seethed against him, holding him down on top of her. And then sighed, and relaxed. "But marriage? That would be a disaster. For one thing, I am married already. To obtain a divorce I would have to be even more flagrant than I am now, and Alderney would never forgive me. I'd be ostracized. I was born in England, and I intend to die there, not in some Italian village."

"Mina . . ."

"And then, there is no surer cure for love than marriage, my darling. As you will find out."

He lay on his side, raised on his elbow so that he could look down the sweep of slender white flesh, the love forest in which he had buried himself so completely for six months, the well-muscled legs, the exquisite toes.

"But if you had any sense at all, my darling, you would marry Jane."

His head jerked. "That would be impossible."

"Because you have held me in your arms? My dear Haggard, a man is not a man until he has allowed his mind to roam wide and free. To reject a thought merely because some country parson might consider it immoral is absurd. The world would never have progressed had every man been so hidebound. Now, what have you against Jane? Is she not beautiful?"

"Well, of course she is. She's your daughter."

"Exactly. And very like me, too, I can promise you that. She would make you a superb wife."

"Even if, as you say, we should immediately stop loving each other?"

"She would continue to be a superb wife, as I have always been a superb wife to Favering. I can promise you that, too. And think of it, Haggard. Whenever your mother-in-law came to visit, as she would often, especially when your wife was pregnant and therefore incapable of fulfilling her conjugal rights, well . . . would you not be the most contented man in all the world?"

He rolled away from her and sat up. "You are utterly amoral."

"I am an utterly happy woman, Haggard. And as I am foolish enough to have fallen in love with you, I am offering you a share in my happiness. Don't be silly, and come back to bed."

"I must go," he said, reaching for his clothes. "I am on the stage at dawn."

"Really and truly?"

"Really and truly, Mina."

"To hurry back to your Gypsy?"

"Mina . . ." He looked down on her. The most beautiful sight he would ever see, he supposed. Oh, to stay! "Mina, I love you. I adore you. If you snapped your fingers, I would kill for you. But I will not run behind you like a dog. Divorce Alderney, marry me. That would be to betray Meg, but I would do it. As you will not, then I have the opportunity to regain some of my honor at least."

"Some of your honor," she said contemptuously. "Oh, men, men. What fools they are. And now you expect me to fly up in a rage and throw a chamber pot at you. Because I am a woman. But I am not *a* woman, Haggard. I am Mina Favering." She sat up in turn, caught his hand, released his breeches. "So catch your stage at dawn. Go back to your Gypsy charmer and get the clap, for all I care. But come back to bed now, my darling. I love you."

Chapter 5

The Question

Where the turnpike topped the hill before descending again into the valley, beneath the shadow of the empty gallows, timbers now starting to rot from neglect, Roger drew rein and pointed. "Derleth."

Trumley Sparrow squinted in the afternoon sunlight, at the straight street and the neat little cottages, the pruned rosebushes and the dormant potato patches, the ducks proceeding in stately order across the pond, the children just bursting out of the schoolhouse; it was three o'clock in the afternoon.

And beyond was the manor house, thrusting its tower above the trees which surrounded it; there was still snow in the park.

"I don't see how you have managed to stay away so long," he remarked.

"'Tis a neglect I mean to remedy," Roger agreed. He kicked his horse and sent it cantering down the slope, Sparrow beside him, Corcoran and Smellie, their servants, hurrying behind. The drumming of hooves caused windows to open, old Hatchard to emerge onto the steps of the inn, to watch the approach of the four redcoats with a puzzled frown, until they came within range of his dwindling eyesight.

"Hatchard," Roger shouted, slowing his horse to a trot. "It's good to be home."

"Major Haggard," Hatchard shouted in turn, and bellowed over his shoulder at his wife. "Squire's home."

The children took up the cry, running into the street so that the horsemen had to draw rein to avoid them. "Squire's home," they shouted.

Roger and Sparrow rode side by side, between the houses

now, waving and smiling at the people who filled the doors and windows. Women, in the main; they were here instead of at the mill, on a working afternoon. Roger sighed. Alice's letters had been too descriptive. And then he frowned as he saw a group of children, aged in their early teens, playing in the meadow behind the church. But surely nothing could have gone wrong at the mine. He drew rein beside four men standing in a communal vegetable garden and watching his approach. They were not smiling. And he recognized at least one of them.

"Hulloa, Peter Larkin," he called. "Is it a mining holiday, then?"

Larkin grudgingly removed his cap. "No holiday, Mr. Haggard," he said. "No holiday."

Roger rode on. There was a mystery. But Alice would explain it. He urged his horse faster, now that he was clear of the village, waved to Mrs. Shotter, standing outside the church, cantered up the drive to the manor house, giving a great halloo as he approached. But the word had already spread, and people were pouring out of the stables and the gardens and the house itself, grooms and yardboys, footmen and maids. "The squire's home," they shouted at each other. "The squire's home."

Roger swung from the saddle, clapped Nugent on the shoulders. "It's good to see you again. And I've a guest. Major Sparrow will be staying for a season. Corky, you'll see to Smellie."

"That I will, Major." Corcoran also dismounted, shook Nugent's hand. "I'm that glad to see you again, Mr. Nugent."

"And are you home for good now, Mr. Corcoran?" asked the prettiest of the housemaids.

Corcoran pinched her bottom. "You can say that again, miss. I'm done with soldiering and wandering. Ain't that right, Mr. Haggard?"

"That's right, Corky. We're home. Home for good." He slapped Sparrow on the shoulder. "Come along, Trum. I want you to meet Alice."

Because there she was, standing in the doorway, auburn hair fluttering in the summer breeze, wearing a simple house gown, looking as lovely as ever. . . . He frowned. Her always pale complexion had even less color than he remembered, and there were shadows beneath her eyes. "Alice?"

"Oh, Roger. Thank God you're back. Oh, thank God

you're back." She was in his arms, holding him tight, and then stiffening as she looked past him and realized that Sparrow was also an officer. She pushed him away, attempted to smooth her gown and her hair at the same time, and accomplished neither very successfully.

"Trumley Sparrow, Miss Alice Haggard, my sister."

Sparrow kissed her hand. "I have heard so much about you, Miss Haggard."

"I . . ." She glanced at Roger, color at last flaming into her cheeks.

"Trum is going to stay with us for a while," Roger explained. "He has a mind to become a farmer, when his soldiering days are done."

"Oh," she said. "Aren't they?"

"Mine are. All but. Trum has elected to wear the red for another year or two. Deadly stuff, soldiering in peacetime. Now, come along." He put his arm round her shoulders. "Where's Emma? And Meg?"

"They . . . they went for a walk. In the park."

"Then let's go and find them. We'll sneak up on them and surprise them."

"No." Alice spoke so sharply he checked at the foot of the stairs. Once again she flushed and glanced at Sparrow. "I have no idea which direction they took," Alice explained. "They'll soon be back. They'll always be home for tea. I must show Major Sparrow to a room."

" 'Trumley,' please, Miss Alice," Sparrow protested. "If I may be so bold."

The worry lines on her face dissolved into a smile. " 'Trumley' it shall be. I'm so glad you've brought home a friend, Roger. So glad." Her gaze searched his—looking for what? he wondered. "I'll be down in a moment. We've so much to talk about."

So much to talk about. Roger stood at the great windows of the drawing room and looked out at the park. Emma and Meg were not in sight. It was splendid to think of them walking together. Remembering? Or dreaming?

But he wished they had been here to meet him. He had come up the road from London at a rare speed, driving himself along with a whipped-up false enthusiasm for regaining everything that was his. Including his bride. To see Meg, to hold her once again in his arms, to know that they could plan again, for a future which was now very close, might just be to drive the memory of Mina from his mind.

Mina, Mina, Mina. His body ached for her as his mind ached for her. He had fallen in love, stupidly, senselessly, impossibly, with a woman fourteen years his elder. Then why not be honest about it, throw over Meg, and, as Mina herself was unobtainable, marry Jane? And never look in a mirror again. Admit that he had sold his mind and his body, utterly, to a woman for whom he was most certainly only a passing fancy. And admit that he was the second Haggard to desert Meg Bold, to turn her dreams into so much trash.

And admit too that he was setting his feet firmly in his father's footsteps. The one thing he was determined never to do.

He turned, smiled at his sister. "You're not well."

"Nonsense," she said. "I'm as well as ever in my life. But it is so good to have you home."

"Because you have found managing Derleth too much for you?"

"I . . . I do not suppose a woman is really fitted for such a responsibility," she said. "I have made too many mistakes."

"I can think of none. I can hardly wait to see this new machine of yours."

"The machine," she said, and sat down, her hands on her lap, her shoulders bowed.

"Isn't it working?" He sat beside her.

"It is working very well. Far too well."

"I don't understand," he said. And remembered Larkin. "There's been no trouble at the mine?"

"No trouble," she said. "But I am no longer welcome there."

"You? Why ever not?"

"Don't you see?" she cried. "I bought a Puffing Billy. I installed it. And the men who pumped before its arrival had no work to do. There is a dwindling market for coal in any event. Oh, people want it just as badly, but they don't have the money to pay for it. It makes no sense to cut more, when we can't sell it."

"So you had to let the pumping gang go," Roger said.

Her shoulders rose and fell. "What was I to *do*?"

"Exactly what you did do. And the others resent it also? Surely their conditions are improved."

"Very much improved, I'm told. But they feel we are going to introduce even more machinery. There's talk about machines to cut the coal itself, which will make manpower obsolete."

"Those are dreams, my dearest girl," he said. "I am so sorry you have had some unpleasantness. I'll go down to the mine tomorrow and talk some sense into them. I don't want you to give it another thought. Except . . ." He frowned, remembering. "There *has* been trouble, hasn't there? I saw some children as I came down. Shouldn't they be working?"

Alice drew a long breath. "I . . . I have changed their hours."

"I'm not sure I understand."

"Well . . ." She held his hand. "They're only ten and eleven, Roger, down in that pit from five in the morning to seven at night. I've told Truff no one under the age of twelve is to work more than ten hours a day."

Roger scratched his head. "But . . . how does the work get done?"

"They're enough children. It's just that the parents of those who always worked there feel they're being robbed of four hours' wages a day."

"I suppose they are. You'd better leave that one with me as well. Come on, now, what else have you been doing?"

"I'm so glad you're back," she said for the fourth time. "And then . . ." She hesitated.

"Go on."

She got up. "Nothing. Now you're back, everything will be fine again. I know it. Meg has been terribly lonely."

"I should hope she has," Roger agreed. "You haven't been worrying about her, too?"

Alice turned. "She's my sister. My half-sister, anyway. And she's to be my sister-in-law."

"That bothers you?"

"I'm not sure it's right."

"Do you know, I've never thought of that? I'll have to have a word with Shotter. But it will *be* all right."

"Because you will make it so? Regardless of any consequences?"

He crossed the room, held her shoulders. "Consequences? What consequences? I love her. She loves me. What other consequences can there possibly be?"

Alice gazed at him for a moment, then turned away again. "Here she comes now," she said.

● ● ●

He looked down from the window at the two small figures, each wrapped in a hooded pelisse and wearing boots, making their way across the park toward the house. As they approached, they looked up, and he waved. To his surprise, they stopped as if they had seen a ghost, seemed to huddle together for a moment. Perhaps they did not recognize him; Emma was certainly a trifle shortsighted, and it was possible Meg had inherited the defect. He waved again, both hands, and this time they apparently did know him, because Emma gave a tentative wave back, and then Meg did too, before they hurried for the side door.

"*They* look well enough," he remarked.

Alice was standing beside him. "I am sure they are," she agreed.

It was an odd way to speak of one's mother and half-sister. But then, perhaps he had never realized just how strange a girl Alice was. He kissed her cheek and hurried to the entrance to the hall, got there as Emma emerged up the lower stairs.

"Emma," he said, and held out his arms.

She came forward, uncertainly, he thought, allowed herself to be embraced and kissed.

"You are frozen," he said. "Even walking must be approached carefully, in January."

"The exercise does us good," she said, speaking as if she were still short of breath and looking, not at him, but past him at Alice. Exchanging messages with their eyes? What secret could they possibly share that they were afraid to divulge to him?

But then he saw Meg, who had climbed the stairs more slowly than her mother. He released Emma and went forward again, arms outstretched. "My darling."

She stopped before he could get to her, and curtsied. "Mr. Haggard."

He stared at her, and then smiled. She was showing off her skills. "You *are* a fine lady, Meg. But I am 'Roger,' remember? Come and give me a kiss."

She came forward even more slowly, stood on tiptoe, kissed him on the cheek. As if she were his daughter. When he remembered how she had clung to him two years ago, squirmed against him, come to his bedroom two years ago. Then the fool was himself, for having stayed away so long.

The poor child could not really believe it was still going to happen.

"Oh, Meg," he said, and caught her again to bring her close and give her a hug and a kiss, but when he searched for her lips, he found them only in passing. "It's so good to be home."

Because it was good to be home. Good to be back, and able to take command of a situation which was obviously proving too much for Alice. Good to be back holding Meg in his arms. She was not Mina Favering, and she would never be Mina Favering. She would not even ever be Jane Favering. But she was his Meg. She was the girl on whom he had stumbled so strangely when she was so in need of help, and she was the girl in whom his entire honor was bound for the rest of his life.

As for this sudden feeling of strangeness between them, it would be overcome in a day or two. He had no doubt about that. With his arm around their shoulders he faced Alice. "United again, and for always. Was I worth waiting for?"

"You are always worth waiting for, Roger," Alice said, but although she smiled, her eyes were tortured as she said it. Alice, too, regarded him as a stranger all over again, where when he had returned from his twenty-year absence, in 1812, there had been no barrier at all between them. Even Alice.

He was glad to hear Trum clearing his throat behind them. "Trum," he cried, turning again, and again carrying Emma and Meg with him. "I'd have you meet my fiancée, Miss Meg Bold, and her mother, Emma."

"Ladies. This is a very great pleasure." Trum kissed their hands in turn. And once again they exchanged those secret and frightened glances. But at least Sparrow's appearance had brightened Alice. This time her smile was genuine, as it had been at their introduction. "The pleasure is ours, Trum," she said. "Come and sit down, and tell us about Paris. What are the women wearing this year? Meg, would you be so good as to ring for Nugent? We'll have some mulled wine and biscuits, together with a pot of tea. Roger, come and sit down. We are all too overcome by your sudden return."

Sudden? he thought. After six months? But as he looked at Meg and Emma, he realized that Alice spoke nothing more than the truth. They *were* overcome. By his return.

"A splendid machine, Mr. Truff." Roger walked round the

air pump. "It certainly lives up to its name." For it did puff, as it exhaled steam, and drew its power from the roaring coal-fed furnace beneath the boiler as it clanked remorselessly on. It reminded him of the factory in Barbados, a self-perpetuating process, fed by crushed canestalks in order to crush more canestalks. Here the fuel and the product was coal, but the principle was the same.

"Oh, aye, Mr. Haggard," Truff agreed. "A splendid machine."

"But the men don't care for it."

"Well, sir, it's not the machine, you understand. Those passages, why, sir, they're cleaner than they have ever been. It's the consideration, sir, that where there's one machine, there'll soon be others."

"Machines will never replace men, Mr. Truff," Roger said. "Least of all on the coal face. You tell them that. In a hundred years' time we'll be taking coal from that seam, and it'll be their grandsons working it. You tell them that, Mr. Truff."

As if, he thought, as he remounted and allowed his horse to pick its way through the snow toward the cut in the hills which led to the village, the faithful Corcoran ever at his heels, anyone could possibly desire his grandson to work down a coal mine. Yet these people wanted their sons and daughters down the mine for every waking moment. Would he reverse Alice's decision? He thought not. If one or two grumbled, the wage distribution would be more evenly divided over the entire village.

His grandson. He would have to get a move on, or Johnnie would beat him to it. There was an amazing sequence of events. After all his suspicions about Johnnie and Byron . . . He had not felt so relieved in a long time. Indeed, he thought, when Derleth is again running smoothly and prosperously, I might just take Meg on a honeymoon to Barbados.

At least there was no need to reassure the people at the mill. The American war was over, after nearly three utterly pointless years, and the cotton would soon be arriving again. There would be work for them to do, and he would be able to pay them a full wage again. Whether it would be a living wage, whether any workingman in England would ever have a living wage again, was another matter entirely. He had never known prices to rise so steeply and so quickly; he supposed one would have to go back to the days of Elizabeth for a comparable inflation. And there was no end immediately in sight. There would be an end. He had no doubt about that. The mistake was to suppose that the abdication of Bonaparte would immediately restore England to the prosperity it had known in 1792. Just as there had been those that had supposed the collapse of France would immediately reopen the European markets to West Indian sugar. He doubted that *would* ever happen. By virtue of Napoleonic decree, the people of Europe had become used to beet sugar, and to growing it, too.

He reckoned there were grim times coming. The world was in one of its periodic stages of change, and it was his bad luck to be taking control of Derleth just as that was happening. But it was a challenge, too. He squared his shoulders, sat straight in the saddle. He had never refused a challenge.

If only there were not quite so many looming challenges on the domestic front. And there he could admit, at least to himself, that he could see no clear way ahead. Last night at supper the conversation had been carried entirely by an embarrassed Trum and a frightened Alice. The fact that the pair of them seemed to be finding each other mutual refuges in the storm everyone appeared convinced was about to break was the only truly happy thing about his homecoming. Because something had happened during his absence. And apparently no one was prepared to tell him what it was. Well, he could be as patient as any man. Certainly he had no desire to provoke a crisis.

"We'll ride through the park," he told Corky, and turned off before the drive. Here the snow lay thicker, and Hannibal picked his way more carefully. But soon he felt grass beneath his feet, and Roger could stop stooping in the saddle or twisting to avoid too-low-slung branches that flicked at his shako. Another prospect of change. Presumably he should abandon this uniform, which he had worn for twenty-one years, now that he was on dischargement leave. How odd life would seem without a sword at his side.

"Holloa there, Fred Loon," he shouted, drawing rein.

The gamekeeper looked up. He had been lugubriously breaking the thin layer of ice on the trout stream, using a long pole. Now he laid it down and came toward his master.

" 'Tis good to see you home again, Mr. Haggard," he said, and reached up to shake hands.

"It's good to *be* home, Fred," Roger lied. But Loon at the

least could have nothing but good to tell him. The park, and the wood beyond, looked in perfect winter condition. "How are the deer?"

"Well, sir, they're as well as can be expected."

Roger frowned at him. "They've survived colder winters than this, Fred."

"Oh, aye, sir. 'Tis not the cold I was thinking about."

"Then what are you thinking about?"

"Miss Alice hasn't talked with you, sir?"

"We haven't really had time. You've poachers?"

Loon sighed, and nodded. "Started last summer. Not many. But two or three persistent."

"After deer?"

"Well, sir, there's the funny thing. They *have* taken a deer, and one or two brace, and even a trout or two. Nothing serious, from our point of view. Save that they're there. Almost like as if they was looking the place over."

"And you've caught no sight of them?"

"Oh, aye, sir, I have. I've seen them several times, at a distance. Fired me piece at them, too, and hit one, once. I'm sure of that. There was blood on the ground when I got to the spot."

"Bully for you, Fred," Roger said. "That must have discouraged them."

"Well, sir, it didn't. It upset Miss Alice, you see. She said she wasn't going to have nobody killed on Derleth if she could help it. 'Those poor men are starving, Fred,' is what she said to me, sir. 'Starving. If you see them, you can chase them off, but no more shooting.' "

"Good God," Roger said.

"Yes, sir," Fred agreed.

"I'll speak with her, you may be sure," Roger said. "I'm surprised we haven't attracted every layabout in the north of England, if word's got out we won't protect our land."

"Yes, sir," Fred agreed, suggesting by the tone of his voice that that might just have happened.

"Well, I want it stopped, and right away," Roger said. "Recruit a couple more fellows from the village and make sure they've plenty of shot. You drive those fellows off, Fred."

"Yes, *sir*," Loon agreed. "Mind you, Mr. Haggard, it's a lot of ground to cover. Now, sir, if I could lay a trap or two—that'd discourage them quicker than any pellet. Once they knows there's traps about, why, they'll soon move on again."

Roger hesitated, pulled his nose; Father had believed in mantraps, whereas he always had considered them a hideous form of barbarism. But if things had really been allowed to get out of hand . . .

"All right, Fred," he said. "Put out one or two. Just for this winter, mind. And for God's sake tell Mistress Bold where you've put them; she seems to have taken up walking in the wood."

"Yes, sir," Loon said enigmatically. "Miss Alice isn't going to like it, sir."

"Miss Alice no longer manages Derleth, Fred."

But discussing poaching with Alice would wait. The last thing he wished to do at this moment was upset her, after she had managed so well for two years. Besides, she seemed sufficiently upset by his mere presence, accompanied him into the office, and stood by the window as he opened the huge green account book.

"Won't you sit down?"

Alice sat in the chair before the desk.

"And don't look so haunted." He smiled. "I don't expect any profits. I just want to find out the size of the losses." He opened the book, ran his thumb down the page, moved on to the next. The room was silent, save for the sound of Alice's breathing.

"What do you think of Trum?" he asked without raising his head.

"I think he is charming," she said.

"The best fellow in all the world. I've a mind to offer him a position, when he gets out."

"Has he nothing of his own?"

Roger shook his head. "His father was a country vicar. A wealthy uncle paid for his commission, but they have since quarreled. Derleth needs a sound business manager, and I would like to have a friend about the place." At last he raised his head. "Would you object to that?"

"Of course I wouldn't." But she was flushing.

"Good," he said. "Now, let me see . . . you've been uncommonly generous with the poor relief."

"Well . . ." Another sharp intake of breath. "You'd not have them starve, Roger. They're your people."

"I'm aware of that. But we mustn't ever be so charitable as to take away a man's will to work. We can't go on supporting all of Derleth all of our lives. And I am thinking of even when the mill is again in full production. Some of them will have to move on."

"You couldn't," she objected. "They're Derleth people."

"A village, a valley, like this one, can only support so many, Alice. Sometimes it is kinder to be hard. Man is essentially a lazy animal, you know. We make it too easy for them here, and they'll never do an honest day's work in their lives." He had been continuing to examine the entries while he spoke. "Meg must have quite a wardrobe. And Emma too."

"You wanted them fitted out." Her tone was defiant.

"Indeed I did. And I think they look splendid. You've done a magnificent job. I suppose I'm afraid I shall never understand the economics of a woman's clothes. Meg seems to be buying a shawl a week, just about. What does she do with them all?"

"I have no idea," Alice said. "She asks me for the money whenever she and Emma go up to town. And they like to do that at least once a week." She leaned forward across the desk. "You can't begrudge them that, Roger. They've been poor all their lives. Meg has, anyway. And Emma . . . well, she always knew she was nothing but an indenture. This is the first opportunity they've had to *live*."

Roger closed the book. "I don't begrudge them a thing, my dear. I'm concerned with her character, that's all; spending money just because you are bored, as I suspect is happening, is not sound." He got up, held out his hand for her. "Now, come along. Let's join them for a glass of sherry wine. I'm not displeased with you, Alice. I've nothing to be displeased about. You've done magnificently." He squeezed her fingers as they climbed the stairs. "But I suspect Derleth is ready for a touch of a man's grip on the reins, wouldn't you say? This poaching business, for instance."

They had climbed the stairs and arrived at the entrance to the withdrawing room; Emma and Meg were already inside, passing the time of day with Trumley Sparrow. Now Alice checked.

"What poaching business?"

"Now, sweetheart, I've been talking with Fred Loon. You have been posing him quite a problem."

Alice looked into the room; the others were watching her, and they must have heard what was being said.

"No damage has been done," Alice said.

"Not as yet. But they will grow bolder, you may be sure of that. And think of the possible dangers." He walked into the room beside her. "Have you seen any poachers in the woods, Emma? Meg?"

"No," Emma said. "Of course we haven't."

"Yet Loon assures me they are there. And two defenseless women . . . You can let softheartedness go a little too far, Alice. Anyway, it's time to put a stop to it. I've told Loon to recruit some extra help, and to make sure they are well armed. And I've told him to put out some traps, so I'd be obliged if you'd—"

"Traps?" Alice cried.

"Traps?" Meg screamed.

"Oh, my God." Emma sat down.

Roger looked from one to the other in surprise. "Just for the next couple of months, until these chaps have learned their lesson."

"But you'll hurt them," Meg cried.

"Well, I mean to."

"You can't use traps," Alice begged. "Father used traps. You said . . ."

"I hate the things," Roger agreed. "But I'll not have poachers or worse prowling Derleth. This is a law-abiding community. I mean to keep it so."

"It is best, Miss Alice," Trumley said. "Once let this sort of thing go unchecked, and it's nearly impossible to stop."

Alice stared at him.

"I hate you," Meg suddenly shouted. "I think traps are horrible. Ugh. I hate you." She ran from the room.

"Who'd be a landowner?" Trumley Sparrow remarked. He and Alice sat in the winter parlor before a roaring fire, sipping their port. Dinner had once again been a disaster. Meg had refused to come down at all, and Emma had sat stiffly silent throughout the meal. Afterward Roger had retired to the library, and Emma had soon gone to bed. Only Alice had preserved the manners necessary to a guest.

"But you agree with him," she said.

"I'm afraid I do."

"Have you ever seen a man taken in a trap?"

"I have, as a matter of fact. It's horrible. But . . ."

"The law is the law," she said bitterly. And then smiled. "I don't blame you, Trum. I think men and women will always see things like that differently."

"Not all women."

"And not all men."

"An impasse." He raised her fingers and kissed them. "I don't imagine you have many secrets from your brother."

She gave a start, and her head swung; her hand remained in his. "What makes you say that?"

"I formed the impression you are very close."

"I've seen very little of Roger, since we were children," Alice said. "As you are his friend, you will know something of his history."

"I do. And as you are his sister, you will know something of mine, and my prospects."

"Well . . ." She took refuge in her port, at last withdrawing her hand. "I know he very much wishes you to stay in Derleth."

"Charity, do you suppose?"

"Good Lord no. Roger is a very lonely man. I would say you are the only friend he has in the world. Only true friend, I mean. I should rather say he is being selfish, in never wishing to let you go."

"And if I said that I could think of nothing finer than to stay here . . . with you . . ." He hesitated. "With you all?"

"Then we would like you to." It was her turn to take his hand. "*I* would like you to, Trum. Roger needs you."

Spring, in Derleth. The most beautiful time of the year. A time to be happy. And with reason. Cotton was arriving again; the mill was working six days a week. Why, Roger supposed, even the squire was making a profit at last.

And now, he could get married. He picked up Mr. Shotter's letter again: ". . . and having regard to the quite unusual circumstances, sir, although the bishop feels that it is certainly necessary to apply for a dispensation, he can see no reason why such a dispensation should be withheld."

Shotter was a good man. And Meg would be happy. *Should* be happy. But she had not seemed particularly unhappy when he had told her that it would be necessary to take advice on the matter before he could proceed with the marriage. She had merely shrugged and walked away. The fact was, they were complete strangers again. The girl who had lain with him on the grass in Plowding Forest, and the girl who had come to his bedroom the night before he had left Derleth, had disappeared as if she had never been more than a dream. This was a young lady he now encountered; at least, although there were still many slips, she was trying consciously and very hard to *be* a young lady.

The terrible problem was, he was not sure he liked this Gypsy-become-lady as much as her previous self. And it was his business to *love* her. He did not like her sudden taste for extravagance, or her manners, which she no doubt thought aped those of the aristocracy, but which led her to abruptness and cold attempts at wit, nor her sudden propriety, which caused her to avoid wherever possible being left alone with him. All of which added up to a wall which had mysteriously and invisibly appeared between them. A wall on the far side of which Emma, always dear, reliable, friendly, wise Emma, had also taken her stance. Because she had found out that they had slept together? That seemed incredible, from Emma.

And a wall on which Alice, most uncomfortably, sat astride, apparently unable to make up her mind to come down. He would not beg her. He would not beg any of them, as they so determinedly opposed his plans for ridding Derleth of poachers and for putting it back on a viable economic footing. But could he marry Meg while in such a frame of mind?

The fault was his, he knew. His entire attitude to her, to any woman, to life itself, was colored by those six months in Paris. Six months which, after all, were not going to fade into oblivion quite as easily as he had hoped. Because Shotter's was not the only letter on his desk.

"Brussels is the place to be, my darling, darling, darling Haggard," Mina had written. "I have never had the pleasure of living in an army headquarters before. It is all gay uniforms and dashing young men, and balls and cards and rides in the country. Now that summer is coming, I am even contemplating a visit to the seaside. Because Jane is with me. Or did I mention that before? My dearest man, as I study the *Gazette* every day, and have not yet discovered your marriage, I must suppose that you remain England's most eligible bachelor, if only for the nonce. So why not undertake a last fling, and come here for a week? I promise to make you comfortable. Comfortable, my sweet Haggard."

Oh, to be in her arms again, for just a moment. But were not thoughts like those entirely responsible for his present dilemma? No doubt Meg, with her womanly instincts, could tell that his love was at least partly elsewhere. My God, he thought, clapping himself on the brow, is it not entirely likely that someone had written either her or Alice, telling them of my affair with the countess? Of course. And he could imagine who it was: George Gordon Byron, the scoundrel, always against the match with Meg in any event, and determined to tie Derleth to the Whip party by hook or by crook.

The more he thought of it, the more convinced he became. It would explain everything—Meg's aloofness, Emma's obvious concern, Alice's fear. All their hopes must rest on this marriage. George Byron, he thought, when I get hold of you . . .

But for the moment, everything could be put right. For if the final part of their dismay had been caused by his announcement that the marriage must be postponed, then at last he could set their minds definitely at rest. He got up, folded the letter from Shotter in his pocket, went outside, and was arrested by a tremendous noise welling up the road from the village. He went down the stairs instead of up, joined Nugent and Corky and Trum Sparrow and the grooms on the front lawn, to watch a red-coated horseman flogging his mount toward them, while behind him there trailed the village housewives and those of the men still on relief.

"Major Haggard," the dragoon shouted. "Major Sparrow."

"We are here," Roger said, himself catching the man's bridle. "He's done in, Nugent, fetch some port. Get down, sir, and rest yourself. Where are you from?"

"From Derby, your Honor," the soldier said. "With urgent dispatches. 'Tis a matter of life and death."

"There's a revolution," Trum ventured.

"Worse than that, sir. Far worse. Boney's back in France."

"In France?" Roger shouted. "How?"

"When?" Trum wanted to know.

The man drank his port, seemed to collect himself. "In the south, sir. Fréjus. He landed there three weeks ago."

"And the news has only just reached us?"

"Well, sir, the roads are bad, and the matter was discounted in the beginning. But now, sir . . . the King has fled Paris, and it is war again. And orders have come from headquarters in Brussels that all leave is canceled and officers must rejoin their regiments by the earliest available means."

"Bonaparte," Roger said.

"Back to it," Trum said. They looked at each other, trying to appear to reflect the gravity of the event, unable to prevent their eyes from dancing.

"Back to it," Roger said. Back to Brussels. My God, back to Brussels, if only for a single night. The call of duty.

"You'll not go," Alice said from the doorway. "Roger. You'll not go. You have retired from soldiering."

"I *am* retiring from soldiering, to be sure, my pet. But I am most definitely still on leave."

She stared at him for a moment, then at Trum. "For God's sake, Trum, talk some sense into . . ." She frowned. "You want to go. Both of you. You *want* to go."

Roger caught her hands. "I must go, my sweet. Believe me, this *will* be a short campaign. It has to be, because were Bonaparte to be allowed to reestablish himself . . . why, it would mean another twenty years of war. But that is why every man is needed. He must be crushed before he can gain strength. You do understand that?"

She withdrew her hands. "I understand that fighting is the only life you know," she said. "Or wish to know. When will you leave?"

"Now, immediately. As soon as Corky can pack my bag and saddle a horse."

She glanced at Trum. "And you as well?"

"As Roger says, Miss Alice, we must go."

She sighed, and nodded. "And what of Meg? Do you not suppose she has waited long enough?" ·

"She has suffered most grievously, and I am sorry for it," Roger said. "But it will be for only a very short time more. Where is she?"

"Walking, with Emma."

"As usual," he remarked. And smiled. "Send someone to fetch her in, to wish me good-bye. And do not look so worried, my dear. A letter from Shotter. We will have the dispensation. We will be married as soon as I am back from the war. I promise it. Now I must dash. Come along, Trum."

He went inside and ran up the stairs. Alice turned to look after them, holding Shotter's letter in both hands. "As soon as you are back from the war," she said. "Pray God you are not too late, dearest brother."

Chapter 6

The Riot

"Stand to," someone called, a voice breaking through all the other sounds, the groans and the shrieks, the moans and the sighs, which had accompanied the night. "Stand to."

Consciousness returned. A private sat up, screaming, "The French, the French," and was comforted by his fellows. And with consciousness came awareness, memory of what the previous day had spewed forth, awareness of what the spreading daylight would reveal.

"Stand to."

Roger got to his feet, stood at attention. Behind him the remnants of his company fell in, forty-seven men where ninety-one had marched gaily out of Brussels in yesterday's dawn.

The Duke of Wellington pulled his horse to a stop, his staff a bedraggled group behind him. It had rained during the night, if not as heavily as the night before. And these men had not slept.

"Well done," the duke said. "Well done, my fine fellows." He leaned from the saddle, shook Roger's hand. "Well done, Major Haggard. Well done."

"And today, sir?"

Wellington straightened, drew the back of his hand across his forehead. "March your men back to Brussels, Major. The Prussians will continue the pursuit. Rest your men, Major Haggard."

"Three cheers for the duke," Roger said, and raised his hat.

"Hip hip . . . horray," they shouted. "Hooray. Hooray."

The staff walked on; Roger faced his men. "You heard the

orders, lads," he said. "Back to Brussels. And bed. Sergeant Major, form them up."

Did he have any subalterns left? Young Hutchings had fallen early on, he remembered. Baines had disappeared when they had been ridden over and momentarily scattered. His body would be lying in some ditch. But it would have to be sought later; his first duty was to those of his people still living.

The entire British army was on the march, back from Mont St. Jean, back from Hougoumont and La Belle Alliance, back from the most terrible day any of them could remember, away from the heaped corpses, of redcoats and bluecoats, away from the shattered horses and the discarded rifles, the bloodstained grass. The last battle. It had to be the last battle. He would never kill a man again. On that Roger was resolved.

"Roger." Trum held out his hand. "By God, but I didn't think to see you. When that square broke . . ."

"We survived," Roger said. "Some of us. . . . But you . . ." His friend had lost his hat, and one epaulet was also gone, while his trousers were split and his jacket was covered in mud.

"I was dismounted, would you believe it? Poor Betsy was shot." He patted the farm animal he rode. "Hence this sorry state of affairs."

"But you . . ."

"Sound as a drum. And you?"

Roger nodded. The two companies marched side by side, feet tramping, the hooves of their officers' horses clip-clopping on the cobbled road. Now they were through the trees of the forest, and in front of them the rooftops of Brussels sparkled in the morning sunlight. And now, too, spirits began to rise. The battle was over. The last battle. Those who had lived would be able to tell their grandchildren of the day they had faced Bonaparte, and for the first time in his career forced the greatest soldier of all time to admit total defeat. Suddenly it was a day to be alive. A day to cheer and to shout, a day for officers to allow discipline to relax, just a little. A day to remember.

And a day for others to remember, too. Out of Brussels came those who had waited, listening to the rumble of the guns, terrified when the Hanoverian cavalry had ridden from the field and through the streets of the city, screaming that all was lost, that the French would soon be among them, and thus the more hysterically happy as they watched the victorious redcoats coming toward them. Women squealed their joy, broke the ranks to hug and kiss the soldiers; great ladies, still wearing their ball gowns in some cases, although that famous occasion was now twenty-four hours in the past, leaned from their carriages as they blocked the road, shouting and cheering, threw ribbons and hats and far more intimate pieces of apparel to the happy troops. It was going to be a long time before he got these men back to their cantonment, Roger realized.

"Haggard. Oh, Haggard."

He had known she would be here. They would both be here. He pulled his rein, looked from left to right.

"There," Trum said, pointing to several carriages grouped on a hard shoulder just off the road, and separated from them by a mass of milling excited women and soldiers. "You go," he said. "I'll herd your people."

Roger slapped him on the shoulder, pushed his horse into the crowd, moving slowly but surely toward the faces leaning from the window. Mina wore black, only the whiteness of her face breaking the breathtaking somberness of her attire. But Jane wore white, and was equally lovely; men kept reaching up to touch their fingers.

"Oh, Haggard." He was there at last, leaning from the saddle to kiss her on the mouth. "Oh, Haggard."

Jane's fingers closed on his, long and strong, cool and purposeful. What did she know of her mother's secret ambitions? The night before last, they had waltzed and waltzed, while Mina had sat and smiled at the skill of her pupil. In the heat of the evening they had strolled on the patio, still holding hands, and she had rested her head on his shoulder. He was comfortably old enough to be her father, but she made no bones about her adoration. Because he was her mother's lover?

And he had been inflamed enough, with wine as well as the certainty that soon battle would be joined, to have kissed those splendid lips. He had touched her tongue, or her tongue had touched his; he could not be sure. And that touch had reawakened his manners and his awareness. When they had returned to the ballroom, he had had every intention of taking her mother to bed, as usual. Instead he had been sent off to fight and kill. And, amazingly, not be killed.

"Haggard," Mina said, at last releasing his mouth. "Oh, Haggard. I thought you dead."

He smiled at her. "And wore your mourning just in case."

She made a moue. "I am mourning all those who *did* fall. You have not kissed Jane."

He bent his head again, and once again the tongue slipped shyly through her lips. "I was worried too," she said.

"With two such guardian angels watching over me," he said, "how could I fall?"

"And now we shall go home," Mina said, "and you shall have a hot bath, and then—"

"I must billet my men," Roger said.

She raised her eyebrows. And shrugged. "Oh, very well, Haggard. But come to us afterward. Soon. Hurry."

"And then I must return to England, as soon as I am relieved of my command. I am nothing more than a volunteer, you know."

"Haggard, you are the most infuriating of men. I had supposed—"

"I came to fight Bonaparte," he said. "And to see you again, my dearest Mina. There, I can be honest too, you know. But—"

"But you are betrothed," she said, "to a Gypsy." It was the first time he had ever seen her angry, because, he suddenly realized, she *was* angry. He glanced at Jane, but she had leaned back into the carriage and it was impossible to see her face clearly. Besides, she took her lead only from her mother.

"Yes," he said. "I am betrothed. And I have an estate to be managed." He looked into her eyes, but it was not possible to see to the bottom of Mina Favering's eyes. "And I must see to my men," he said. "I shall try to be with you for tea."

"No," she said. "Don't come for tea, Haggard. "Don't come again." She smiled. "If you are so determined to leave me, then leave me. Don't come again."

"They kept coming." Trumley Sparrow stood in the center of the drawing room of Derleth Manor, arms spread wide as he attempted to illustrate the scene. "More than five thousand of them. The finest horsemen in Europe, they say. Well, I'd argue about that, thinking of our own Grays. But they made a splendid sight. The sun had come out, you see, and reflected from their cuirasses and their helmets. Oh, it was a splendid sight."

He paused, to take a fresh glass from Nugent's tray. Nugent wasn't going very far, and indeed most of the servants were clustered in the open doorway, listening to the tale. Alice leaned forward, mouth open. Emma twisted and untwisted her fingers. While Roger sat next to Meg on one of the settees. Her hand lay in his, but nothing Trum could say had made *her* fingers tighten.

"And then they charged," Trum said. "Oh, it was splendid."

"But how did you survive?" Alice asked.

"We formed a square," Trum explained. "They could not break the square. Except one."

"We were slow," Roger admitted. "We were ridden over."

"Oh, *Roger*," Alice cried. "It must have been terrible."

"It was touch and go for a while, and we lost too many good fellows. But we reformed in the end."

"And now you're here," she said. "Both of you." Her eyes shone.

"Never to roam again, I promise you that. We're here to be married." He squeezed Meg's hand. "Both of us."

"Both?" Alice flushed scarlet.

"A double wedding." Roger put his arm round Meg's shoulder, gave her another squeeze. Her head moved, almost so that it wouldn't have to touch his. "Trum and Alice, Meg and I. Come, Nugent, a toast."

Alice gazed at Trum, eyes wide; his face was a matching scarlet to his tunic.

"I . . . we talked of it, Alice," he said. "It is something I have dreamed of."

"Oh, Trum," Alice said, and extended her hand.

Roger got up, carrying Meg with him. Nugent had the champagne ready. "Come on, Emma. A toast. To us all. To all the happiness that we are going to know, here on Derleth."

He raised his glass, and Trum and Alice and Emma raised theirs. Meg gave a choking cry, freed herself, and ran from the room.

Slowly Roger lowered his glass.

"She's overcome," Emma said, face pale. "I'll go after her."

"No," Roger said. "I wish to know the truth of the matter."

"The truth?" Emma gave Alice a startled, terrified glance.

"Meg acts as if she hates me," Roger said. "Where once she showed me nothing but love. Can she be that angry at my desertion? She knew I was coming back. Does she suppose I still love Mina Favering? That business is over and done with."

"Mina Favering?" Emma and Alice spoke together, their bewilderment too utter to be pretended.

Roger looked at Trum, but Trum was too embarrassed to say anything.

"Will you permit me to speak with my sister alone for a few moments?" Roger asked.

"Of course," Trum said.

"With me? Roger . . ."

"With you," Roger said, and went to the door, the servants fleeing before him, scrambling downstairs and upstairs to be out of his way.

"I know nothing of Mina Favering, Roger," Alice said. "Save that she is Countess of Alderney, and reputed to be the most beautiful woman in England."

He nodded. "I understand that. Therefore you must know a great deal about something else, of which *I* know nothing. Will you come?"

Alice hesitated, gave a despairing glance in Emma's direction, then went toward her brother.

"Alice," Emma said. It was half a warning and half a plea, Roger thought.

Alice checked again. "I shall not be long, Mama," she said.

Roger waited for her, escorted her down the stairs and into the office.

"I imagine we make fine sport for the servants," she said with a nervous smile.

"And no doubt we shall go on doing so." He closed the door, indicated a chair. "God knows I do not wish to persecute you or anyone, or even to interfere where it is not my business. But Meg is to be my wife. I would hardly expect her to share my bed while she is in such a mood of continuous resentment, directed entirely against me, so far as I can see. I will have to know the cause."

"This Mina Favering . . ." Alice ventured.

"Has been my mistress. It is well known in London and in Belgium. She does not conceal her conquests. And she is against my marriage—to Meg, at least. But I have broken with her. Definitely and irrevocably. I had assumed Meg had heard of it and taken offense."

"Is that not a possibility?"

"Without you or Emma learning her feelings?"

"Well," Alice said. "Now I come to think of it, I do remember . . ."

Roger sat behind the desk. "Alice, my sweet, if *you* start lying to me, I shall be unable to trust anyone in the world."

She raised her head, her eyes full of tears. "Oh, Roger, I am so miserable. And I should be so happy. But if you *knew* . . ."

"Tell me."

She hesitated, seemed to be gathering her strength. "I must have a promise, first."

He shook his head. "No promises, Alice."

"But . . ."

"Save one that I shall do what I think is right."

"Like Father?"

"Do you really suppose so?"

She sighed, and her shoulders sagged. "No. No, I did not mean that. Well, you foretold the future yourself."

"Bold?"

She nodded slowly. "And Tim."

"The poachers?"

Another nod.

"I see. And understand. But they have been here for over a year, and not come to see Emma?"

"They meet in the wood. They mean no harm, Roger. They wish to immigrate. To Canada. All they require is funds."

"And Emma and Meg have been providing out of their pin money?"

Alice sighed, and nodded.

"For a year," Roger said. "In the name of God, why didn't you tell me before? Why the secrecy? Did you not suppose I would finance them?"

"They are absconded felons," Alice said.

"And you and Emma presumed I would hang my own prospective father-in-law? God Almighty. Tell me how to find them. I'll settle this once and for all. When I think . . . Over a year, and all you had to do was tell me."

Alice said nothing.

Roger got up, went round his desk, rested his hand on her

hair. "Don't take it so. I'm not angry, really. I'm just distressed that you have been so miserable when it has never been necessary. I'll see to it, believe me."

She raised her head, and he frowned at the misery in her eyes.

"There's something else."

"Of course there isn't," she said. "I'm just so happy, so suddenly. I don't know what to say."

"Something else," Roger repeated. "Loon hit someone last year. Was it Tim? Or Bold himself?"

"It was Tim," she said. "But it was not serious. Only some pellets in the leg. Not serious, Roger."

He continued to frown at her for some moments. Then he smiled. "I believe you. Now, tell me where they can be found, and I'll get over there as soon as I can."

"They are just across the border, in Nottinghamshire. The village of Lowden. Harry's gone back to tinkering, under the name of Smith."

"A tinker called Smith, in Lowden. Why, that's just beyond Plowding. I'll go over there this afternoon." His smile widened. "I'll bring them back with me, to say good-bye. I'll leave you to tell Emma and Meg what I'm about. And for God's sake, ask them to smile when I come home."

She caught his hand. "Roger . . ."

"They cannot stay in England, Alice."

"I know that. I . . ." She sighed. "Be careful."

"Of what?"

"They'll not know of your intentions. You are magistrate of Derleth, and it was a Derleth magistrate issued the warrants against them."

"I'll not go alone. Trum and Corky can accompany me." He squeezed her fingers. "It is going to be all right. Everything is going to be all right. I only wish you'd told me sooner. But everything is going to be all right."

And he had imagined so many different reasons for Meg's strange behavior. While all the time it had been fear for her father and brother. An explanation which covered everything, surely. He rode his horse through Plowding Forest and on to the turnpike that formed a border between the two counties, drew rein to allow Trum and Corcoran to catch up with him. They had made good time and it was just after four of the afternoon. They would not get back before dark, but what a splendid evening it would be. Why, he thought, I might even entertain Harry and Tim to supper at Derleth House before sending them on their way. There would be a historic occasion.

The village of Lowden lay about three miles farther on. They cantered across the empty meadow, walked their horses down a shallow slope, entered the main street. And drew rein in dismay. Here was the true face of an England which had spent twenty years and more at war, dilapidated cottages, a total absence of paint on any wall, roofs with gaping holes, a group of half-starved children in threadbare clothes, staring at the horsemen with ravenous eyes, huge potholes in the road they must follow . . . "My God," Trum said. "You'd think it had been fought over."

Roger did not reply, urged his horse toward the inn, dismounted. "Will you come in?"

Trum shook his head. "We'll wait for you here."

Roger nodded, lowered his head, stepped inside the gloomy taproom. Conditions were very little better inside than out, save that it seemed half the male population of the village were in here, sitting or standing, drinking beer, and talking. But the conversation slowed and then stopped, and heads turned, as the soldier stood in the doorway.

"Good evening, landlord," Roger said.

The man behind the bar nodded. "What's good about it, sir?"

"It is not raining," Roger pointed out.

" 'Tis beer you're seeking?" the landlord inquired. "There's naught else."

Roger placed a silver coin on the counter, and heard a sigh go round the room behind him. "Not for myself, landlord," he said. "But for these good fellows, in exchange for some information."

The landlord stared at the coin for a moment, then picked it up. "You hear that, lads? Gentleman's buying."

They surged against the bar, almost curshing Roger in their anxiety.

"And what information would you be seeking, sir?"

"I'm looking for a man calling himself Smith. A tinker. Short and heavy, with a black beard. Has a son called Timothy."

"Oh, aye, we know Harry the tinker. Parks his caravan on the other side of village, when he's not on the road."

"Is he here now?"

"Oh, aye, was yesterday, anyways."

"Thank you. Then I shall be going over there." He endeavored to extricate himself from the crush.

"You've business with a tinker, sir?" the landlord asked.

"Business." Roger nodded.

The landlord scratched his head. "May I be after inquiring your name, sir?"

"Why, it's Haggard," Roger said. "Major Roger Haggard, of Derleth in Derbyshire. Good day to you, landlord."

He got outside, remounted.

"Thought we'd lost you," Trum remarked.

"It's the other side of the village," Roger said, and smiled at the women and girls who had collected around the horses. They looked as poor and as desperate as their menfolk, and there was no beer for them. "Mind the hooves, ladies," he said, and walked through them.

Trum drew level with him. "What happens to these people, Roger?" he asked. "They are starving. And this is high summer."

Roger nodded, and sighed. "Things *must* improve, Trum, now the war is finally over."

"Aye. But how soon, d'you think?"

"I have no idea. I shall play my part, so far as I can. I intend to represent Derleth in the Commons, for a start."

"One voice," Trum said.

"There'll be others. There have to be others." He pointed to where a wisp of smoke emerged from a copse of trees. "There's our man."

"Let me go first, Mr. Roger," Corcoran offered. He remembered the Bolds too well.

"We'll go together, Corky." Roger loosened the pistol in his saddle holster. "But no shooting unless I say so. We've not come to fight with them."

"Aye," Corcoran muttered, without conviction.

They walked their horses through the trees, and now could see the tinker's wagon, and the horse grazing a few feet away. There was a fire before the step, but no sign of humanity.

"Holloa, there," Roger called. "Holloa, Harry Bold."

A shot rang out, and Trum gave a gasp, half-turned, and fell over his horse's neck, hanging there for a moment before plunging to the ground.

"Christ almighty," Corcoran shouted, dragging his fowling piece from its sling behind his saddle even as he dismounted.

"For God's sake, Harry," Roger shouted. "It's me, Roger Haggard. You've no quarrel with me."

His horse continued to move restlessly, and it was to this he owed his life, for now two shots were fired, and he could almost feel their wind. He dismounted himself, knelt beside Trum, who was writhing on the ground and clutching his shoulder, blood welling from between his fingers. "Take cover," he muttered. "They'll bring you down as well."

"Not until they've reloaded," Roger pointed out. "Up you get."

Between them they lifted Trum to his feet and back into the saddle, mounted themselves.

"We'd best retire a way," Corcoran suggested, and Roger led Trum's horse back up the track. There he paused and faced the now distant wagon.

"You hear me, Harry Bold?" he shouted. "You're a fool, man, a fool. I came to help you. Now, throw down your weapons and come out, or by God I'll hang you myself."

There was another explosion, and they heard the bullet crunching into a tree trunk only feet away. Trum gave a groan, and swayed.

"Begging your pardon, Mr. Roger," Corcoran said. "But Major Sparrow is losing blood."

"Aye," Roger said, and wheeled his horse. "We'll back to the village. You'll be stopped up, Trum."

Trum did not reply, his teeth gritted together against the pain. They rode up the track and came to the village street, and the entire village, it seemed, men and women and children and even dogs, gathered to bar their way.

"There they are," shouted the landlord. "That's Major Haggard, the Derleth magistrate. He's over here to arrest Harry Smith, I'll be bound. You've no jurisdiction here, squire."

"You mistake the situation entirely, my good fellow," Roger explained, riding closer. "I but wished to see Harry Bold . . . Harry Smith, on a business matter. He opened fire on us, and my friend is hurt. Now I require your assistance, bandages and a bed for Major Sparrow, and a posse to surround that camp and obtain Smith's surrender."

A stone whistled through the air and almost removed Roger's shako. This was followed by another, while the crowd surged forward.

"Go back to Derbyshire," they shouted.

"You've no place here, Haggard."

"Harry Smith'll not hang."

"Hit the bastard."

Trum almost fell again as a stone struck him on the chest. Corcoran seized his bridle while Roger stared at the mob in impotent anger, fingers closing on the hilt of his sword.

"You can't fight more'n a hundred people, Mr. Roger," Corcoran begged. "And Major Sparrow is hurt bad."

Roger pulled his bridle round, was struck on the shoulder by a stone, and kicked his horse into a canter. The crowd booed and cheered, and some more missiles were thrown, but these fell short.

"Where to, Mr. Roger?" Corcoran gasped. "Derbyshire's thataway."

"Aye, well, we need help sooner than that. And a Nottinghamshire warrant. We'll to Squire Hutchinson, in Benligh."

James Hutchinson was a large, stout man who revealed his emotions in every movement of his body. When he laughed, he trembled from head to foot. When he was angry, he bristled in a similar comprehensive fashion. Tonight he was very angry indeed.

"Lowden," he roared, seeming almost about to thump himself on the chest. "Lowden, by God. A set of scoundrels. Oh, aye, I know them well."

"They are starving, Hutchinson," Roger pointed out, sipping his port as he watched Mrs. Hutchinson, as small as her husband was large, and her rather plain daughter tenderly removing Trum's bloodstained shirt in order to strap his shoulder; the bullet had passed right through, fortunately, and the wound was clean if jagged.

"Starving, by God. They'll be hanging soon enough. Mobbing a serving officer of the King? And a squire? By God, sir, they shall pay for it. I've sent for the yeomanry. Oh, aye, I've sent for the yeomanry."

"We merely wish to talk with Harry Bold," Trum protested faintly. "Not start a war."

"Major Sparrow, in view of the fact that these people brought you low, your forbearance does you credit. But per-

sonal feelings do not enter into it, sir. This country is in a
parlous state. No doubt about it. It needs time to regain its
feet, and that time, sir, must not be used by mobs or rabble-
rousers to commence a revolution. Our instructions are plain,
sir, from the Secretary of State himself. You'll have studied
the matter, Haggard?"

"I have had very little time to study anything since my return," Roger pointed out.

"Ha ha. But it is there, for your perusal. Orders from London, sir. Civil disturbances must be stamped out. Stamped
out, sir, at the very source, before they can swell, and grow,
and burst to poison the entire country. Oh, aye, sir, stamped
out. You'll ride with us, Haggard? As a veteran of Waterloo
you'd be more than welcome."

Roger stared at Trum, who shrugged with his eyebrows.
But there was no going back now. The business had been
started; he had no alternative but to see it through. "I'll ride
with you, Hutchinson."

"Good man. Good man. Now, sir, have some more port.
And you, Major Sparrow."

"I do think, Mr. Hutchinson, that Major Sparrow should
be put to bed," Mrs. Hutchinson ventured.

"Bed?" Hutchinson roared.

"Bed?" Trum inquired more quietly.

"Bed," Mrs. Hutchinson said firmly. "You have received a
nasty blow, sir, and with exhaustion, a fever may well set in.
Is Dr. Rowland coming with the dragoons?"

"Well, I sent for the fellow," Hutchinson said.

"Then he will wish to examine you, Major Sparrow, I am
sure of that. Raison, you'll assist the major."

The butler hurried forward, and Trum was helped to his
feet.

"I do apologize for all this inconvenience," he said. "And,
Roger, to leave your side now . . ."

"I'm sure Mrs. Hutchinson is right, old fellow," Roger said.
"I am only happy to see you in such good hands. I shall send
my carriage for you as soon as this business is over. Now,
rest."

"Brave fellow," Hutchinson said, shedding a tear into his
port. "Oh, brave fellow. How I wish I had been at Waterloo
myself. Oh, indeed. Hark."

The night was filled with the jingle of harnesses. Roger accompanied his host onto the patio, watched the troop of yeo-

manry, some seventy strong, he estimated, a glitter of
bearskins and bright yellow jackets, ordering themselves in
the yard below.

"Is that you, Richardson?" Hutchinson called.

"I am here, Hutchinson," the colonel, squire of a neighboring village, replied. "We have come with all haste, as you required. Frame-burning, is it?"

"Worse, far worse," Hutchinson declared. "Lowden. The
entire village set upon Major Haggard here, and gravely
wounded a friend of his with solid shot. You'll go upstairs,
Rowland, if you please."

The doctor dismounted, nodded to Haggard, entered the
house. The colonel also dismounted, came up to shake hands
and have a glass of port. Footmen circulated among his men
with trays of ale. "Haggard, of Derleth," he said. "I had an
acquaintance with your father."

"Pleasant, I hope," Roger said.

"I found nothing ill with the fellow, whatever his manners," Richardson agreed. "At least his politics were in the
right place. You'll ride with us to teach these fellows a
lesson?"

"Indeed I will," Roger agreed. "But I suspect the entire situation is a misunderstanding."

"Misunderstanding?" Hutchinson was being inserted into a
yellow jacket himself, while a footman stood by with his
bearskin cap, and another waited with his sword. "They fired
on you."

"They did not," Roger said. "A man called Bold fired on
me, suspecting I was about to arrest him. The villagers
merely sided with their own."

"That is rebellion, sir, against a magistrate and therefore
against the crown itself," Colonel Richardson declared. "It
must be crushed."

"How, exactly?" Roger asked, finishing his port and mounting; Corcoran was already in the saddle, and their red jackets made a vivid splash against the yellow behind them.
"There is an entire community there, women and children as
well."

"We'll not trouble their families, saving they do not trouble
us," Richardson said, taking his place at the head of his
troops and regarding Hutchinson with some impatience as the
squire slowly got himself mounted, assisted by three grooms.
"But we'll arrest the ringleaders. Oh, aye, we'll not have

rebellion in these parts. Are your men ready, Sergeant Major?"

"Ready they are, Colonel Richardson," the sergeant major agreed, and Roger winced. But these men were but part-time soldiers. And therefore, he realized with a start of concern, the more difficult to control when loosed. But he could do nothing more than ride along with them, heels clip-clopping on the turnpike, until they came in sight of the houses of the village.

"The buggars have flown," Hutchinson exclaimed in disgust, examining the empty street through his glass.

"They'll not have done that," Richardson said. "They'll not leave their houses. Look." He pointed at the lights in the window of the inn. "They're celebrating, I'll be bound. Rats in a trap." He drew his sword, raised it above his head. "Men of Notts, are you ready to do your duty?"

"We are," the troopers answered with one voice.

"Then follow me," Colonel Richardson said, and walked his horse down the street.

"Oh, my God," Alice said. "Oh, my God. Trum . . ."

"Will be well," Roger assured her. "A clean wound. He may have some difficulty with his arm, but it will enable him to bring forward his retirement from the army. There is naught to worry about."

Alice gazed at her mother with stark eyes.

"Fired on you," Emma said. "Oh, God. You should've taken me, Roger. You should've taken me."

"How was I to know he'd . . . ?" Roger sighed, interrupted by a fresh howl of anguish from Meg, weeping her heart out on the sofa. "For God's sake, Meg, no one was hurt, save Trum. They were all in the inn. Your father and Tim as well. There was no resistance."

"And now they'll be hanged," Meg wailed. "They'll all be hanged."

"They will not be hanged," Roger said. "I have withdrawn frame-breaking charges against them."

"Yet will they be punished," Emma said.

"Well, civil disturbance is a serious matter. This country is still under martial law. They will be sentenced to transportation."

"Transportation?" Alice whispered.

"Transportation?" Emma cried.

"Transportation?" Meg screamed.

"I'm afraid so. They will be sent to Australia, possibly for ten years. For heaven's sake, Emma, Meg, they are fortunate at that. They wished to immigrate, anyway. There is not that much difference between Australia and Canada."

"There is a difference between going as a free man or as a convict," Alice pointed out.

"Aye, it's cheaper as a convict," Roger said with an attempt at humor. "Listen to me. They'll have to work for the government there. But if they behave themselves, the life will be easy, and at the completion of their sentence, why, if they do not wish to return to England, they may obtain land for themselves, to farm, to live on with prosperity, perhaps."

"Australia," Emma muttered. "The end of the world."

"A huge and promising country, I've been told," Roger argued.

"Begging your pardon, Mr. Roger," said Mary Prince.

Roger turned. He had not realized the housekeeper had entered the room. "Yes, Mary."

"The men who were arrested, Mr. Roger. Can you tell me their names?"

"I have no idea of their names, Mary. Save for Harry Bold and Tim."

"But . . ." Meg had stopped crying for the moment. Now she bit her lip.

Roger frowned at her, then at Mary, and then looked at Alice, who turned scarlet and got up. "I must get over to Benligh, to see Trum," she said. "You'll allow me the use of the carriage, Roger?"

"Of course. But . . ."

"I'll come with you," Emma decided.

"And me," Meg cried.

"Miss Alice . . ." Mary begged.

"Wait a moment," Roger said. "I'll have an explanation, if you please."

"An explanation?" Emma cried. "I wish to see my husband and my son. Meg wishes to see her father and her brother. We may never see them again."

"And you, Mary?" Roger asked. "Whom do you wish to see?"

Mary Prince gazed at him for a moment, and then burst into tears.

The eight men arrested in Lowden had been removed to Benligh, where Squire Hutchinson had erected a jail. Here they were guarded by his own gamekeepers turned into constables, while curious villagers paraded outside in an attempt to catch a glimpse of the desperadoes who had attempted to raise the Jacobin flag in peaceful Nottinghamshire—or so the rumor went.

"I'll not come down with you," Alice said. "I couldn't. I . . ." She stared at her mother. "Besides, I must stay with Trum."

"And welcome you are, my dear," Mrs. Hutchinson said. "The news of your arrival has cheered the poor man most pleasantly."

"I wish I could understand all this," Hutchinson said, glancing from Meg to Emma to Mary Prince, all red eyes and evident handkerchiefs, and then to Roger. "I wish you'd explain it to me."

"It is very simply this, Hutchinson," Roger explained. "This young lady, as I have told you, is my financée, and Mrs. Bold is her mother."

"Mrs. *Bold?*"

"That is what I am trying to explain to you. Harry Bold is Emma's husband and Meg's father."

"By gad," Hutchinson declared. "By gad." He looked around himself in a scandalized fashion, and Raison, the butler, hurried forward with a glass of port. "You propose to marry a tinker's daughter?"

"I'll not take offense, Hutchinson," Roger said. "In the circumstances. But you are right. That is what I propose to do. And I'd be obliged if in the future you take care with your words."

"By gad," Hutchinson said again. "By gad. But the fellow shot at you."

"Indeed he did," Roger said. "And will suffer for it, no doubt. Meg is not responsible for her father's deeds."

"By gad," Hutchinson decided. "And this woman? Or is she . . . ?"

"Miss Prince is my housekeeper," Roger said.

"And she also has a relative in my jail?"

Roger looked at Mary. "I have no idea."

"Oh, God," Meg moaned, as she had moaned throughout the journey from Derleth. "Oh, God. Where are they, Mr. Hutchinson? Where are they?"

Hutchinson stared at her for some seconds from under arched eyebrows, apparently unable to make up his mind how to address her.

Raison came to his rescue, clearing his throat. "If you'll permit me, Mr. Hutchinson, the . . . ah . . . men are downstairs now."

"Ha," Hutchinson said. "I must have a closer look at these scoundrels." He hesitated, flushed, glanced at Roger. "I beg your pardon, Haggard, and yours, er . . . ma'am, but to my mind they *are* scoundrels."

"Just take us down to them, Hutchinson," Roger said.

"Yes, well . . . you'd better show the way, Raison," the squire decided.

Roger reached for Meg's hand, but she pulled it away. Her hatred seemed to have grown overnight. And he could not blame her. He had meant well, and he had landed her father and brother in the deepest trouble of their lives. Senseless to argue the fault was theirs, for having fired at him in the first place. It had been equally senseless of him, blindly confident, to ride over to make his peace. Out of it had come a total disaster, a village ruined, with five of its leading men sentenced to exile, and the country a seething mass of discontent. Perhaps it would have happened anyway. Perhaps where people are starving, an explosion is inevitable. But it had been he who had sparked it.

And what lay ahead? Only time, for the scars to heal, for the memories to fade. Only time.

They reached the foot of the stairs, faced the three men. Three men? He had only requested that the Bolds be brought out. He glanced at Mary Prince. Her face was white, and there were tears dribbling down her cheeks.

"You've done me at last, Haggard," Harry Bold said. "'Tis my only regret the ball took your friend, and not you."

Roger gazed into the hate-filled black eyes. "You're a fool, Harry Bold," he said. "I came to give you the money you wanted."

Harry glanced at his wife, who gave a sob. "That's what he intended, Harry. I swear that's what he intended."

"And you believed him," Tim Bold said contemptuously. He was a conscious copy of his father, even down to the beard, in his case still scanty.

"She believed me because it was the truth," Roger said. "I'm sorry for what happened. But you bring your misfortunes on yourselves." He looked at the third man. Not a great deal older than Tim, he thought, and much taller and better built, with fine features. Vaguely familiar features, although he was certain he had never seen the fellow before. "Who may you be?"

"His name's Jeremy Woodsmith," Harry Bold said. "And he's our friend."

"It was his shot hit the major," Tim said.

Jeremy gave the boy a glance which boded no safety for when they were next alone, and Tim flushed.

"Then you're to be congratulated, Mr. Woodsmith," Roger said. "On your markmanship. But it was an unlucky hit, for you."

Woodsmith stared at him, and then glanced at Meg, his mouth twisted.

"Could . . . could I speak with Mr. Woodsmith alone for a moment, Mr. Roger?" Mary asked.

"You, Mary? Is this your interest? But he's young enough . . ." He bit his lip. It was no part of his plan to hurt his housekeeper.

"I think we should both have a word, Major Haggard," Woodsmith said. "With you. Alone."

"I've nothing to say to you," Roger said. "You'll receive a fair trial. But your crime has just been admitted."

"I want none of your justice," Woodsmith said. "I want your aid."

"My aid?" Roger demanded. "Now, why should I aid you, you scoundrel?"

"Because I'm your brother," Woodsmith said.

Mary Prince gave a stifled scream, but Meg did cry out, while both the Bolds, and Emma, turned to stare at the young man. Hutchinson retired against the wall, to be revived by his butler and a fresh glass of port.

Roger gazed at him, and knew he had just heard the truth. The face, so familiar, was almost pure Haggard. Yet he was already denying the likeness. "You?" he asked. "You're a dreamer."

"I'm as much your brother as Alice is your sister," Jeremy said. "Or as that ratbag in Barbados is another brother. Mary Prince is my mother. Your father, Roger Haggard, took her from the coal face to his bed, and sucked me out of her. But I wasn't to be left around the place, so when I was old enough, he packed me off to Canada. Your father, Roger. My father too."

"By gad," Hutchinson remarked. "By gad."

"Is this true, Mary?" Roger asked.

"It's true, Mr. Roger. As God is my witness, it's true."

"You can't transport your own brother," Emma said.

And for the first time since his return from the army, Meg seized his arm of her own accord.

My brother, he thought. My God, what a legion of illegitimate or half-legitimate monsters my father raised to haunt me. But there is only one Haggard, and I am he. This man, whatever his name, is a felon, convicted out of his own mouth. And I have another felon as a brother, too.

"You'll have a pardon for me, Roger," Jeremy said. "Just as you had a pardon for Johnnie."

"Johnnie had no pardon," Roger said. "I would not have sought one. He's transported for life. You may be luckier. But you'll go, Jeremy. You'll go."

Jeremy stared at him with his mouth open.

"No, Mr. Roger," Mary Prince cried. "Please, Mr. Roger . . ."

Roger felt Meg's fingers drop away.

"I'll intercede for none of them, Mary," Roger said. "A man lives, and suffers, and dies, on account of the life he has lived, his deeds. And when he commits a crime, he must pay for it."

"What crime?" Emma screamed. "What crime has any of them committed? They defended their home. They thought you were coming to arrest them. Can that be a crime?"

"By gad," Hutchinson said, having regained his breath. "They fired on a magistrate."

"You're afraid," Meg shouted. "You're afraid, Roger Haggard, that Jeremy will prove more of a Haggard than you. You're afraid."

"Now, Meg," Roger said, "I know you're upset . . ."

"If . . . if you send him away," Meg said, backing slowly across the room to stand beside Jeremy, "I'll go with him."

Roger could only stare at her in total amazement.

"Oh, God," Mary Prince whispered. "Oh, God."

"Meg . . ." Emma said.

"I will," Meg shouted. "What do you think I am, some whore, to be dressed up in fine clothes and told to crook my little finger when I drink tea? Mistress Haggard of Derleth.

Fuck that. Do you think I want to be married to that long streak of lard? Oh, *you* wanted that, Mama, and Pa wanted that, so you could skim off the cream. You never thought about my feelings."

"But . . . you know this chap?" Roger asked, feeling a perfect fool.

"Know him?" Meg laughed, and tossed her head as she held Jeremy's arm. "Oh, aye, Squire Haggard, I *know* him. And he knows me."

"Now, Meggie," Jeremy said. "Be careful."

"I don't want to be careful," she said furiously. "I love him," she shouted at Roger. "I love him because he's a man. He don't mind what I say. He likes to feel my bum. And when he comes . . . Oh, God, how he comes!"

"By gad," Hutchinson said.

"Oh, Meg," Emma said.

Mary Prince wept softly.

"So you save him, Roger Haggard," Meg said. "Or you lose me."

Roger stared at her. He had not supposed she possessed so much character. But then, he had never supposed she had any character at all. She was Meg Bold. She had been ridden over by life, and he had happened along and lifted her up. And he had looked no further than gratitude. He was the wealthiest man in England. How could any girl not want to live with him, marry him—any girl, from the highest in the land?

But not, apparently, Meg Bold. She wanted only a hard stick between her legs. And suddenly he was angry, with an anger he had not known since the night Alison Haggard had laughed in his face. He had been betrayed and fooled by women all his life. Every one. To avoid their laughter and their contempt, he had turned to Meg Bold. And she was no different from any of the rest. He could feel his hands closing into fists, his heart slowing with pure hate, for every living creature in a skirt—and more than one dead one, too.

"That's your choice, Meg," he said. "He's shot my friend, and he shall pay for it. What you do is your choice." He turned and went up the stairs.

Chapter 7

The Catastrophe

Rosalind Haggard sat on the front veranda of Bolton's great house and sipped tea as she watched the work gangs filing out of the slave village toward their afternoon's work in the field. She had rested, and she had bathed, and she felt reasonably clean and relaxed, save for the nagging worry that this afternoon she must return to Haggard's Penn. Whenever she visited her mother, and she did this as often as could reasonably be arranged, it was with every intention of staying forever. But Adelaide would not hear of it.

"My dear Lindy," she had said in those patiently condescending tones of hers on the occasion of the first flight, immediately after the honeymoon, "you are making far too much of it. I can tell you, there is many a girl would far rather have a husband with a certain inadequacy than one who commits virtual rape every night of the week."

"Certain inadequacy?" Rosalind had cried. "For heaven's sake, Mama—"

"I am the one who should be saying 'for heaven's sake,'" Adelaide had said severely. "How old are you, seventeen? And you expect a man like John Haggard to go wild with passion every time he looks at you?"

"*You* expected that of *John* Haggard, Mama," Rosalind had pointed out. "All *I* am asking of *Johnnie* Haggard is that he at least indicate that he does not find me absolutely repulsive."

"What nonsense," Adelaide had said. "The marriage has been consummated. Hasn't it?"

Rosalind had sighed, and nodded.

"Well, then . . ."

"It took him near an hour," Rosalind had shouted. "And my God, he was doing me a duty."

"Hoity-toity," her mother had retorted. "Who's the great lover, then? The day will come, my dear girl, when you will pray for a man to spend an hour inside you. And find no one to oblige. As for Johnnie Haggard, if you are not to each other's tastes, that is entirely irrelevant. You are his wife. Nothing can be done about that now, thank God. In the course of time you will bear him a child, and that child will be the fulfillment of everything I . . . of everything you want from life. I promise you that, my dearest Lindy. And I promise you further, that once you are pregnant, if you wish to sleep apart from your husband for the rest of your life, then I shall see that you attain that desire."

Once I am pregnant, Rosalind thought bitterly. Two years. But once I am pregnant, I can set up a separate establishment. Mama has promised.

Adelaide stood at the rail, also watching the blacks. "You'd think they would be happy," she said. "Bonaparte finally crushed, Europe at peace, trade routes opening up; I see us entering a period of enormous prosperity. And they glower. Now, why? Not one has been flogged in a fortnight. *I* am happy. *You* are happy. But they are not. Do you know what I think? I think it is all the fault of that damnable man Oldham. He has been filling their heads with nonsense, that the English government really intends to make them free, but has been waiting for the defeat of Napoleon to do it. Can you believe it? Can you imagine *any* English government actually wishing to free the slaves? Why, it would mean their ruination as much as ours."

"I am *not* happy," Rosalind remarked.

Adelaide gave her a contemptuous glance, then set down herself. "You are not going to moan again, Lindy. I do hope not."

Rosalind set down her teacup, leaned forward. "Mama, Johnnie and I have been married for two years. And I have hated and been humiliated every second of those two years."

"Exaggeration is a fault to be deplored," Adelaide pointed out. "Now, tell me. Does he beat you?"

"Of course not."

"Does he limit your expenditure? Stop your dressmaker visiting you?"

"Oh, Mama . . ."

"Does he drink to excess? Does he maintain a black mistress in the house? Does he swear at you?"

"Mama, if you are not going to be sensible . . ."

"As I understand it," Adelaide continued, "he sits with you every evening, he reads to you from some carefully selected book, he enjoys listening to you play the piano and sing for him . . . why, do you know—and considering his parentage, it is an utter miracle—I think Johnnie Haggard is the most admirable and blameless of men."

"He does not fuck me," Rosalind shouted.

Adelaide threw up her hands, forgetting that in one of them she held a teacup. Servants hurried forward with mops and pails. "Rosalind," said her mother. "Where *did* you hear that word?"

"Ginny uses it, and Penny," Rosalind pointed out.

"They are old married women."

"And I am not? Two years, Mama, and he has shared my bed four times. Once on our honeymoon, once when he was drunk, and on each Christmas day. It is my present."

"Oh, go away," Adelaide snapped at the girls who were still polishing and listening. "If you wish to know the truth, miss, the fault is entirely yours."

"Mine?" Rosalind cried.

"Yours. I have never heard of a wife who would permit such a state of affairs to exist. I have no wish to be indelicate, but really and truly, you are a lovely young woman, and he is a handsome young man. And you cannot attract him to your bed? Really and truly."

"What am I supposed to do?" Rosalind demanded. "Strip off before him and waggle my ass?"

Adelaide gave her a cold stare. "I simply do not know where you learn your language. But since you ask, yes. If that is what is necessary, do it."

"And when even that does not work?"

"Have you tried?"

"I wouldn't dream of it. I'm Lindy Haggard, not the town whore. But it wouldn't work. He just doesn't find me attractive." She leaned forward, held her mother's hand. "Mama . . ."

"No," Adelaide said. "No, no, no, no, no. I will not hear of it. What grounds would you propose? That he will not honor your bed? You would be the laughingstock of Barbados. Of the entire Caribbean. Just be patient. It is impossible for two healthy, attractive young people to live together and not become . . . well, suited. I'll hear no more of it. Strolo is waiting."

The kittareen had been brought to a halt before the steps, and Rosalind's valise already placed in the back. Strolo, the coachman, smiled at her. He was an old friend, not very much her elder; they had played together as children. Rosalind sighed and got up; if only she had been able to play with Johnnie Haggard as a child.

"And do tell your father to come home," Adelaide said. "I'm sure he's finished that business by now."

"What business?" Rosalind asked. "Papa is on Haggard's Penn?"

"Oh, didn't you know? They've decided that the time has come to make an example of Mr. Oldham."

"They? Who? What sort of an example?"

"Silly girl. Your father, and your husband, and one or two others. They're going to arrest him."

"Arrest Mr. Oldham? You can't arrest a parson."

"He's not a parson. He's a Methodist. That's not the same thing at all. And even a parson can be arrested, if he's caught preaching sedition. And he is, you know. That's why your father won't have him on Bolton's. But Johnnie, now, has been allowing him to preach to the Haggard blacks, simply because, having once given permission, he doesn't know how to withdraw it. So Johnnie came to your father for advice, and your father said to give him enough rope to hang himself. They're going to surround one of his meetings today, and catch him in the very act." She squinted at the sun. "I suppose it's all over by now, and they're sitting down to gin swizzles. You send him home."

"But, my God," Rosalind said. "What will the blacks say?"

"The blacks?" Adelaide raised her eyebrows. "What have the blacks got to do with it?"

Rosalind ran down the stairs, ignored Strolo's waiting hand, and climbed into the kittareen. "Take me home," she said. "Quickly. Take the track through the fields."

"Right away, Miss Lindy." He got onto the perch, flicked the whip. Rosalind gave her mother a perfunctory wave, threw herself back against the cushions. Of course Oldham preached sedition. He kept telling the slaves that they ought to be free, suggesting that the British government actually wanted them to be free, but was prevented from implementing that desire by the planters and the West India lobby in the House of Commons. But what the newspapers would say, what the government would say, to the news that the planters had actually arrested a parson . . . And what *would* the blacks' reactions be?

And did it matter?

She took off her hat to fan herself, in time to the bouncing jog of the wheels. Dust flew, and already they were beyond the canefields of Bolton's and slowing on the slope to the wooded hill that separated the two plantations. Imagine Johnnie Haggard taking a leading role in such a decisive step. Johnnie Haggard. She lowered her hat, chewing her lip. Mama simply did not understand. And it was not something she could put into words. Johnnie was not only totally uninterested in her. He was not visibly interested in anything female. He had made it plain enough that he did not like her breasts or the width of her hips; he did not like to see her legs, and he thought her pubes obscene. So what weapons did she have left?

The kittareen pulled to a halt on the top of the hill. "Eh-eh," Strolo remarked. "But what is that?"

Roselind sat up. Below her began the Haggard canefields, stretching five miles into the distance. In that distance there was the next low hill, crowned by the great house. And the great house was on fire. She blinked, quite unable to believe her eyes. But smoke was issuing from the roof, and when she blinked again, she saw that smoke was also issuing from some of the houses in the white township farther down the slope.

"Oh, my God," she said.

"What we must do, Miss Lindy?" Strolo asked. "I am thinking—"

"Get down there," Rosalind shouted. "Something has happened. Get down there."

"Miss Lindy, I am thinking we should go back to your mummy."

"Oh, for God's sake," she cried. "My home is on fire and you want me to go home to Mama? Drive on. Hurry."

"If you saying so, Miss Lindy." The whip cracked, and the kittareen jumped forward, charging down the slope, following the track which led between the towering green stalks. Now the hill was lost to sight, and the breeze disappeared; but always there was the pall of black smoke staining the sky.

"Can't you go any faster?" Lindy demanded, hanging on to the strap.

"Miss Lindy," Strolo gasped, "if I drives any faster, we going be thrown out."

Her hat came off, fell to the seat beside her, and she only just grabbed it before it floated away. Presumably he was right. They were going far too fast as it was. But what on earth could have happened? A slave revolt? That was impossible. Nothing like that had happened in Barbados for fifty years. It had to be just a fire. But a fire, in Haggard's great house?

She looked up again, hoping that the smoke would have disappeared, but it was still there. And then the kittareen stopped.

Strolo had thrown his entire weight onto the brake; wood screamed against wood and began to smolder. The horse, feeling the drag suddenly doubled, whinnied and rose on its hind legs. The seat tilted and the traces broke, and Rosalind hit the ground with a thump which knocked all the breath from her body, still sitting, but on her back, with her legs pointed at the sky, while dust eddied onto her face.

It was several moments before she could move. Then she cautiously pushed with her hand, thrusting herself backward so that her legs came down and she could straighten her skirts, at the same time prodding herself to make sure nothing was broken.

"For God's sake," she said. "Strolo? Strolo, where are you?"

Cautiously she pulled herself to her feet, holding on to the upturned kittareen, and gazed at three men. It had been their presence that caused the accident, for they had been standing in the middle of the path. Now they had advanced to stand beside the broken equipage. They were most certainly slaves—indeed, she recognized one of them; but they carried not only their normal machetes, but muskets and cartridge belts. Her mouth opened, and then closed again.

"Is the mistress," said the man she knew.

"Yes," Rosalind said. "And I'm very angry with you, Derwent, for frightening the horse. You might have killed us all."

"Oh, yes, mistress," Derwent said. "We going to kill you all."

Rosalind's heart gave a little pitter-patter, and she involuntarily stepped backward, tripped over the seat, and sat down again with a fresh jolt which left her once again winded.

"But not this one," said one of the other men.

"Not until them boys have her," said the third.

"But we got her first," Derwent said, advancing again so that he stood immediately above her. Now her heart seemed to be climbing up through her chest into her throat, and she was aware of a tremendous sweat breaking out on her shoulders. She had to think. But more than that, she had to get up. Whatever had happened, she was the mistress, as they had just reminded her. They would not touch the mistress, standing up and looking at them.

"But what is this?" Strolo reappeared, having climbed out of the irrigation ditch into which he had been hurled. "You boys mad or what?"

"You from Bolton's?" Derwent demanded.

"Yes, man, and this is Mistress Haggard. You knowing that?"

"You run back to Bolton's," Derwent said. "You tell them boys the white people done take Mr. Oldham. You tell them boys that we ain't standing for that. Mr. Oldham, he say these people wrong, and the King in England going make us right. We ain't standing for that."

Strolo gaped at them. Rosalind realized her own mouth was open, and closed it. Cautiously she began to ease herself backward out of the seat.

"So you hustle back to Bolton's and tell them boys to join with we. Because you know what we done?" Derwent asked. "We drive all them white people out of Haggard's. Man, they run so quick when they see us coming. We got Haggard's men, and we going have Bolton's, and then we going have the whole island. Man, we going have Bridgetown and all."

"They got soldiers in Bridgetown," Strolo pointed out. "You knowing that?"

"We caring? They got maybe two hundred soldier in Bridgetown. Man, we got two thousand people on Haggard's, and you got two thousand more. We caring about two hundred? Man, you should have seen them white people run."

"So you go tell the Bolton's people we's coming," said one of the other men. "And they'd best be ready for us."

The third man grinned. "Unless you wanting a piece of this one first."

Strolo gazed at Rosalind, and attracted the other three.

And she had just freed herself entirely from the seat. But there was no point in delaying any further. They meant to kill her, after . . . She couldn't imagine what would come first. She turned on her knees, pushed down with her feet, and was kicked in the bottom. She lost her balance and sprawled on the earth, and had her arms seized by a man kneeling to either side.

"This one got hair," Derwent said, digging his fingers into her chignon and pulling the pins free. "I ain't never seen hair like this one."

Her scalp seemed to be lifting from her head and her eyes to be popping out of her skull. "Please," she gasped. "Please." And hated herself.

The pressure left her scalp, and her head flopped forward again. She took a mouthful of dust, and tried to move, but they were still holding her arms, and she dared not kick, in case her skirt rode up. . . . But hands were on her thighs, and her skirt was ripping. With it went the petticoats, and she had always refused to contemplate the new fashion of wearing drawers.

She jerked her head, and attempted to kick after all, and suddenly felt the heat of the sun on her legs and bottom. The knowledge that she was naked from the waist down struck her like a blow, and she flopped forward again, into the dust.

"You taking she from that side?" inquired one of the men.

"Not this time," Derwent said. "Turn her over."

Rosalind closed her eyes, and then found them open again. She stared at faces. But they were strangers. Even Derwent was a stranger. The face she found herself looking at was that of Strolo, standing behind Derwent, staring at her. He was afraid, and he was concerned, but he was fascinated as well.

She kicked again, involuntarily, and Derwent caught her thighs, and knelt between. He had already taken off his drawers, his only garment. Rosalind gasped, sucked air into her lungs. "Help me," she shouted. "Help me," she screamed. "Strolo . . ."

He was inside her in a tremendous burst of pain. Oh, God, she thought, he's going to kill me. He's going to tear me apart. Oh, God. She rolled her head from side to side, worked her hair in the dust, felt him on her body and sucking at her chin, and then he was gone again. Her eyes opened, and she blinked at the sun, and at Strolo, being seized by the shoulder and thrust forward. "You," Derwent said. "You next."

"Me?" Strolo asked. "Man . . ."

"You ain't never want to put your hand on she?" Derwent inquired.

"Man . . ." Strolo gazed at her. "Them boys . . ."

"They going have they turn after," Derwent assured him. "But you. You must be wanting this one a long time."

"Well, man . . ." Strolo continued to gaze at her. No, Strolo, she thought. Oh, no. Not you, Strolo. "I did want to feel she bubbies."

"She got bubbies?" one of the men holding her arms asked.

"She must be got bubbies," Strolo argued.

"Well, look, huh?"

Strolo knelt beside her.

"Strolo," she whispered. "Please, Strolo . . ."

"Man, mistress, these boys going kill me if I ain't running with them," he said, and tore down her bodice. Heat all over now. Heat and hands, all over. She thought she would never forget the hands. If she lived to be a thousand and one, she would never forget the hands, exploring her breasts and her buttocks and between her thighs, her mouth and her ears and her eyes and her nose, and her hair. Hands, and dust. And flies. Beside all of those, the swelling flesh that filled her time and again seemed almost irrelevant. She was utterly surprised to find herself suddenly on her feet, dragged there by the hands holding her wrists, just as she was utterly surprised to find that she still wore her boots, her stockings collapsed around her calves.

"Now we kill she?" asked one of the men eagerly. "I always wanted to kill a white woman."

"Just now," Derwent said, and slapped her on the backside. "Walk, huh? We going to take she back to show them boys."

"Holloa," shouted Peter Campkin. "Holloa."

He led the group of horsemen up the drive to Bolton's Penn, waving his arms and shouting. Slaves on their way back from the fields paused to gaze at their master, and beyond at the cloud of smoke which darkened the western sky.

"Watch those black devils," Peter called to the cluster of men behind him, and swords were loosened in scabbards, pistols in their holsters.

Adelaide Campkin stood on the veranda to watch her husband gallop to a halt, take off his hat, and fan himself.

"Are you all right?" he shouted.

"Don't I look all right?" she demanded. "Where have you been?"

"Been?" he cried, dismounting and running up the stairs, seizing a gin swizzle from his butler's tray and downing it at a gulp. "Been? I've been to hell and back." He waved his arm. "We've all been to hell and back."

Adelaide gave him a contemptuous look. "You certainly look as if you've been frightened by the devil." She surveyed the rest of the men, some twenty of them, Bolton's overseers as well as Haggard's, with Johnnie Haggard in their midst, every man enjoying a drink from the trays being circulated by the busy footmen. "Will somebody tell me what has happened?" she asked. "Where is Oldham?"

"On his way to Bridgetown, with the others, Mrs. Campkin," Willie Ferguson said. "And our women and kids."

Adelaide put up her hand, almost as if she would scratch her head, but remembered in time who and where she was. "Your women? To Bridgetown?"

"They're up," Peter Campkin said, busy with his second drink. "The black devils are up."

Adelaide looked at the smoke. "That is from Haggard's Penn?"

"Where else?"

"But . . . why aren't you over there?"

"Over there, Mrs. Campkin?" asked one of the men. "We've been over there. My God, we've been over there. But when they came at us . . ."

"Thousands of the black devils . . ."

"Waving their knives . . ."

"It was terrible."

"We didn't stand a chance."

"Shut up," Adelaide shouted. "Shut up, all of you. Do you mean to say you've abandoned Haggard's to the blacks?"

"Well, Mrs. Campkin, it was them or us," Ferguson explained. "Two thousand of the devils, armed with knives, and only forty of us . . ."

"Armed with swords and pistols," Adelaide pointed out.

"Not much use against all of those numbers. So we decided to fall back on the house, and they kept coming. So we decided to get out. We sent half the men and the women and kids, and Oldham, to town, to call out the military, and the rest of us came here. We've time, Mrs. Campkin. Just bring what you can carry, while we alert the women, and we'll move out before these niggers know what's happening."

"You *abandoned* Haggard's to a bunch of slaves?" Adelaide asked, her voice dropping to little more than a whisper.

"Now, Adelaide," Campkin said. "You weren't there. You—"

"You abandoned *Haggard's?*" his wife demanded again. "And now you want to abandon Bolton's? Christ in heaven, what did I marry?" She turned back to the rail. "You, Johnnie Haggard, you abandoned your birthright?"

"Well, Mrs. Campkin," Johnnie said, "like Mr. Campkin says, you weren't there. And Mr. Campkin—"

"Do you suppose your father would have left? Do you suppose your brother would have left?" Adelaide shouted, every word searing the evening sky.

"Well . . ." Johnnie bit his lip.

"Oh, my God," Adelaide said. "Oh, my God." She sat down.

"Adelaide?" Peter Campkin bent over her chair.

"Lindy," she said. "Lindy left here two hours ago to go home."

"Lindy?" Johnnie's voice was high. "But . . . we never saw her on the road."

"You came by road?" Adelaide said. "Why in the name of God did you come all the way round by road?"

"Well . . . we thought the blacks might be in the fields, waiting to ambush us."

"You thought . . ." Adelaide said, and got up again. "You sniveling little rat. You bet your life the blacks are in the canefields waiting to ambush you. But they got Lindy first. She took the track through the fields. She and Strolo. Nobody else." Her hand flung out, the finger pointing. "Your wife, John Haggard, and my daughter, has been in the hands of those people for nearly two hours. Your wife!" she screamed. "My daughter! In the hands of those devils."

"Oh, Christ," Johnnie said. "Oh, Christ." A tear rolled down his cheek.

"And you sit there and *cry!*" Adelaide shrieked. "What in the name of God are you, John Haggard?"

He raised his head, wiped his eyes. "Well, Mrs. Campkin . . . Oh, God, what can I do?"

"You can ride over there and get her," Adelaide said.

"Me?" Johnnie looked from left to right, seeking support.

"Now, Adelaide," Peter Campkin said. "The military will soon be riding out from town."

"It'll be dark before they get here. And you know Walter Lithgow better than I, Peter Campkin. You think he's going to launch any attack at night? You intend to leave your daughter in the hands of those black men for twelve hours?"

"But . . ." Campkin gazed at the overseers helplessly. "We can't leave you, Adelaide. We can't leave Bolton's. With a slave revolt on our hands."

"It isn't a revolt yet," Adelaide said. "If it can be confined to Haggard's Penn, it'll never be a revolt. And I can tell you this, there isn't going to be any revolt on Bolton's. You can leave that to me."

"There's only twenty of us now, Mrs. Campkin," Ferguson said. "They'd chop us to pieces."

"They've got at the magazine by now," said somebody else. "We'd be killed."

"Then get over there and die," Adelaide commanded. "But take some of them with you. And take Lindy with you, too, if you can't save her."

The men looked at each other.

"Do that," Adelaide commanded. "Or get down on your knees and crawl, and don't ever stand upright in my presence again. You, John Haggard. I was fortunate enough to know your father. So he blew out his brains. Now I know why. He had you for a son. But by God, if you don't ride after Lindy, I'm going to put a bullet through your brain myself."

Johnnie felt as if he were awakening from a very deep sleep. He had no idea what had happened this afternoon. It had seemed an admirable plan, to arrest Oldham, and arrest him when there could be no doubt about his guilt, so that no pension-minded governor in Bridgetown could possibly consider making his peace with Whitehall by pardoning the scoundrel. There had been forty of them, well-armed. There had not seemed any posssibility of a mistake.

Until the slaves had realized what was happening. The cry had been taken up, from field to field, and they had come streaming out from the canestalks, hundreds and then thousands of them. He had never seen anything like it, as the setting sun had sparkled from their machetes, as he had seen that sea of faces, which had so terrified him on that very first afternoon three years ago. He had looked to Campkin for leadership, and Campkin had opted to withdraw rather than face them down. Then the afternoon had dissolved into streaming terror and screaming hell. He had not supposed men and women who had lived for so long in omnipotent command of their lives could be so quickly reduced to belly-dissolving fear. It had been contagious, and he had been afraid in any event. He had tried to take comfort from the supposition that these men had faced situations like this before and coped with them. Now he knew better. They had ridden wildly, desperately, their only coherent action, apart from sending their womenfolk and their prisoner into town, being the decision to evacuate Bolton's.

But there was no revolt on Bolton's. At the moment. And Lindy . . . He felt sick. He did not love the girl. He had been wrong there. She was not a boy dressed in women's clothing. She was a woman, and considered life from a female point of view. But she was his wife. And she was the second woman he had ridden away from and left to her fate. At least up to now it had not been intentional. Up to now.

He raised his head, gazed at Adelaide Campkin. He looked from left to right, at the faces watching him. Suddenly it occurred to him that he had been made their leader. By Adelaide's tongue-lashing. It was his wife, and Peter Campkin had proved a broken reed. So they would certainly die. But dared he live any longer, with an even greater stain than before on his character?

He wheeled his horse. "Who'll come with me to Haggard's?" he asked.

There was a moment's silence, and then Willie Ferguson, of all people, the man he most loathed in all Barbados, fat Willie Ferguson, who thought only of his belly and his balls, but had served John Haggard and his son faithfully for thirty years and more, Willie Ferguson kicked his horse and rode out of the group. He looked highly embarrassed, took off his hat, and put it on again. "We'd best make haste, Mr. John," he said.

"Then let's go," Johnnie said. He gave rein and cantered out of the compound. Behind him there came a ragged cheer, and he did not have to look over his shoulder. Twenty men, challenging two thousand. Christ, he thought. What am I doing?

Ferguson pulled alongside. "What do you reckon?"

"You do the reckoning, Willie. There must have been slave revolts before."

"Oh, aye, fifty years ago."

"And what happened?"

"Well . . . a couple of plantations were overrun, but then the devils broke into the liquor store and began to drink, and the military didn't have too much trouble with them."

"And have they changed that much in fifty years?"

"Well . . . I suppose not." They had topped the rise, could see the red glow where Haggard's Penn still burned in the dusk. "What about the men in the fields?"

"Will there be any men in the fields, Willie? When all their friends are busy getting drunk?"

"By God, you're right. But shouldn't we slow to a walk? They'll hear us coming."

"I want them to hear us coming," Johnnie said. "I want them to think the whole goddamned British army is coming. Ride, men, ride."

They rode down the slope, and through the cane. It was nearly dark now, and the sand flies and glowworms seethed in the fields to either side, disturbed by the drumming of the hooves. That drumming, Johnnie reckoned, must be carrying two or three miles, drifting on the gentle breeze toward Haggard's Penn, encountering another noise now, a wailing, chanting song, rising and falling as the slaves, free for this one precious moment in their lives, sought to celebrate. But they would hear the noise, were already hearing it. Soon the cadence broke, to resume again as someone decided it was but heat thunder. Then it dropped again, and the night became filled with a gigantic whisper, sparked only by the occasional clash of steel.

"They know now, by God," someone called from behind him.

"They'll be waiting," said someone else.

They debouched from the last of the fields, at the foot of the hill, looked up at the immense concourse, milling about the factory, where the rum was to be found, running through the white township, setting fire to houses, and looting where they could, or dancing round and round the great house, watching it burn, enjoying the end of two centuries of tyranny, like the children they were.

Johnnie drew rein and held up his hand. The party behind

him panted to a halt. At the foot of the hill, and facing them, there were several hundred people, also milling about, chattering among themselves, clearly debating the best course to follow. By God, Johnnie thought, what would I give to have Roger at my elbow. Roger at one elbow and Byron at the other. What would I *give*.

"There's a hell of a lot of them," Willie muttered.

"They've no formation," Johnnie said. "Now, listen to me. We charge together."

"Charge *that?*" Peter Campkin demanded.

Johnnie looked at him in surprise; he had not suspected his father-in-law had followed them.

"It's our only hope," he said. "We'll charge them, and up the hill. Then we'll regroup, and we'll charge them again from the other side. We'll charge them until they break and run."

"Or until they kill us all," someone said.

Johnnie gave him a cold stare. "That's right, Mr. Hutchings," he said. "It's them or us. Gentlemen, will you draw your swords?"

The steel rasped behind him, and he heard someone cock a pistol.

"Steel, gentlemen," he said. "Steel."

His entire being seemed possessed by a tremendous surge of careless courage. He was about to die. He had no doubts about that. He would be chapped from the saddle by a swinging machete, and that would be the end of John Haggard Junior. But the world would remember his death. In that one moment of flying steel and flying blood and unending pain, he would atone for all the disasters of his life.

He kicked his horse in the ribs, sent it cantering up the gentle slope, rose in his stirrups, and pointed his sword at the dark mass before him. "Charge them," he shrieked. "Charge them."

Hooves drummed, and the overseers joined him in their paean, their cry for blood against the people who had so badly frightened them. With a roar and a rush they reached the slaves. But the blacks were already wavering. They had no experience of charging horsemen, even so desperately small a band: they had not even the literature of heroic military deeds to spur their memories. They were the children and the grandchildren of slaves, and a white man with a whip was an irresistible monster. A white man on a charging horse and armed with a sword was Lucifer himself. Only one or two of the younger and bolder spirits stood their ground. A man leveled a musket at Johnnie Haggard and pulled the trigger. The barrel went up in the air as it exploded, and the boy staggered backward. Johnnie's sword took him in the neck with a jar that nearly tore the weapon from his grasp, but then he was riding on, sticky blood coating his wrist. He had killed a man, and now he was about to kill another, for someone was running away from him, immediately in front of his horse. The sword point sank deeply into the man's back, and he tumbled forward with a scream.

Then all the horsemen were through, galloping up the slope, firing their pistols now and still screaming their halloos. They rode nearly to the great house, scattering the dancers and sending them running into the fields. The horses halted, thoroughly blown.

"Wheel," Johnnie shouted. "Regroup. Stand together now, reload."

They jostled each other, gasping and panting, blurting their experiences in exhilarated phrases.

"See the buck . . . ?"

"Sliced his head right off. . . ."

"Hear that scream . . . ?"

"Two men . . . *two*."

"Where are they now, d'ye reckon?"

Johnnie got his breathing under control. "Number!" he shouted. "One."

The call was taken up. Not a man had fallen.

"At the trot," Johnnie commanded. Downhill was going to be easier, but the horses had had an exhausting afternoon. The small group moved down the hill, but there was nobody left to oppose them. Only the triangles, over to the left of the slave village, from which there hung the naked body of a woman.

Lights flared in Bolton's great house as the horsemen returned. Their shouts and their halloos had been heard for miles, and Adelaide Campkin had made sure her footmen were turned out with their trays of sangaree for the victorious warriors.

She stood at the top of the stairs, flanked by the maids she knew were going to be necessary, watched the group approach.

"Whipped them, Mrs. C.," someone shouted.

"Scattered them."

"Lord, it was glorious," called someone else.

"Johnnie Haggard," shouted Willie Ferguson. "Three cheers for Johnnie Haggard."

They cheered with uproarious happiness, while Johnnie brought his mount to a halt before the steps, and Adelaide stared at the girl in his arms, her yellow hair drifting down his arm.

"Is she . . . ?"

"She's alive." Johnnie handed Rosalind down to the waiting slaves, and she suddenly came to life.

"Don't touch me," she screamed. "Don't touch me." They stepped back in surprise, and she landed on her feet, the blanket in which she had been wrapped slipping from her shoulders.

"Help her," Adelaide snapped, and Johnnie leaped from the saddle to pick his wife from the ground. She gave a sigh, and subsided against his shoulder.

"What did they do to her?" Adelaide asked.

"I don't know." Johnnie carried her up the stairs, while the men behind him fell silent.

Adelaide stared at her daughter. "Lindy . . . ?" she asked. "Lindy . . . ?"

Rosalind raised her head, attempted a smile. "Mama," she whispered. "I should've stayed."

"Oh, my darling," Adelaide said. "My darling, darling girl." She embraced her, held her close. "Meely," she commanded. "Is the bath ready?"

"Yes'm, Mistress Campkin."

"Then you'll assist Miss Lindy."

"No," Lindy said. "No."

They stared at her, and she gradually freed herself from Johnnie's grasp. She held the blanket close about her chest and shoulders, but it stretched no farther than her thighs. There were red weals on her legs, together with dirt and the dust, but no blood.

"Lindy . . ." Johnnie said.

"I am quite capable of bathing myself," Lindy said, and went through the door.

"What did they *do* to her?" Adelaide asked again.

"She wouldn't say," Johnnie said.

"And you are going to accept that? Go to her, Johnnie,

stay with her. Only you can save her mind. For God's sake, you've proved you're a hero. I'm sure these people can crush the rebellion without you, tonight."

Johnnie glanced at the overseers.

"You stay here, Johnnie," Campkin said. "We'll join the military and make sure it's over and done with. You stay here."

He hesitated, and a servant gave him a glass of sangaree. He gulped it, slowly mounted the stairs. He was a hero. All the world would know he was a hero. Roger, already a hero, would know it. Alice would know it. Would Father, from that very deep pit in hell he must be occupying, also know it?

And Meg Bold would know it.

He reached the landing. He felt sick, his belly filled with air. But filled with other things besides. What *had* happened to her? And why did he feel so excited that it should have happened to his wife?

He knocked on the door.

"Leave me alone," Rosalind said.

"It's Johnnie."

A moment's silence. Then she said, "It's open."

He turned the handle, stepped inside. The tin tub had been placed in the center of the bedroom, and she was soaking up to her shoulders, slowly massaging her arms and legs. She had wet her hair, and it lay in a dark yellow stain on her back.

"Lindy . . . ?"

She turned her head, gazed at him, and then looked away again; a rosy flush began at her neck and seemed to spread upward and downward at the same time.

"If you talk to Papa," she said, "I'm sure it can be arranged."

"What?"

She shrugged. "A divorce. An annulment."

He sank to his knees beside the tub. "Why should I want an annulment?"

She soaped, slowly and rhythmically. "For God's sake, Johnnie, no one is going to *expect* you to stay married to me."

"You're my wife."

Her head turned again; he leaned forward and kissed her on the lips, very gently. There was no response, but she stayed looking at him.

"Tell me what happened," he said.

The soap slipped from her fingers, fell to the floor with a dull plop. He held her hands and lifted her from the tub, wrapped her in her towel.

"Tell me," he said.

She sighed, and shrugged. "What do you think happened?"

He sat her on the bed; water ran out of her hair and down her legs. "Tell me."

"They held me down and pushed it in. Pushed *them* in."

Black penises, pushing into his wife. The sexual urge seemed to fill his entire body. "How many?"

"Just four."

"Four?"

She turned her head again, to look at him. "There were going to be others. But when they took me back to the Penn, they gave me to the women and children first."

"Tell me."

"They chased me, and they rolled me in the dust, and then they put me on the triangle and they beat me." Another shrug. "They only had sticks, not cart whips." This time her shrug was a shiver. "And they told me what they were going to do to me. They were going to cut off my hair, and then my breasts, and they were going to put ants . . ." She shuddered.

"What did you do?"

"I screamed. For God's sake . . ."

"I can't help you if I don't know."

"Well, now you know," she said. "And then you came. You came and rescued me, Johnnie." Her tone filled with surprise. That had not occurred to her before.

"I would rescue you again, now," he said. He had never been so hard in his life. Hard, with lust for a woman. With lust for his wife. He could not believe it. Gently he slipped the towel to her waist, held her breasts.

She stared at him. "You . . . no." Her hands closed on his. "Please, no. No. Johnnie . . ."

He pulled the towel from her fingers, dropped it on the floor. "But I must, Lindy. Don't you see?"

"No," she begged. "For God's sake, no. I couldn't bear it. Johnnie . . ." Desperately she caught his hands. "I must have time. Johnnie, I hurt. Johnnie . . ."

He pushed her back, straddled her thighs. "I must. Oh, I must."

"Johnnie . . ." she said. "No. Oh, please God, no. Johnnie . . . no."

Her wailing scream drifted through the house, and Adelaide Campkin, waiting on the front veranda, smiled.

"Dr. Waley is delighted," Adelaide Campkin said.

Lindy lay on the bed, a pillow hugged in her arms, and faced the window, looking west. Over there, out of sight beyond the canefields, Haggard's great house was being rebuilt. No time wasted about that. And over there, too, were the slaves who had seen her marched through their midst, naked, and crushed. When the Penn was rebuilt, she would have to return there and face them. She would have to be their mistress.

No matter that the three men who had raped her, and Strolo, had all been hanged. So had some sixty others. But everyone would know. Everyone in Barbados would know. And now . . .

"I would have supposed you'd be delighted," Adelaide said.

Lindy rolled over and sat up, the pillow still clutched against her breasts. "I want an abortion."

"Are you out of your mind?"

"I sometimes think I'm the only sane person around," Lindy said. "Mama, for God's sake, I've had black men inside me. I can't have this baby. I can't."

"You've had Johnnie inside you," Adelaide said, crossing the room to stand by the bed. "He realized at last how much he loved you. Oh, I know you have had the most horrible experience possible. But it's over and done with. And you've benefited. Your husband loves you. Everything is going to be all right. And now you are bearing his son."

"How do you *know?*" Lindy screamed. "How can anyone *know?*" She seized her mother's hands. "Mama . . ."

"You listen to me," Adelaide said, squeezing her fingers. "Everything has turned out for the best. Johnnie is a hero. After being the laughingstock of Barbados for three years, he has become a real-life, genuine hero. People raise their hats to him in the street. You can only benefit from that. So you were raped by black men. That's not important, set beside the fact of being John Haggard's wife. He loves you. He'll be at your side always. And you'll be the mother of his child.

Don't let me ever hear you mention the word 'abortion' again. This is everything we have ever hoped for."

Everything we have ever hoped for, Lindy thought bitterly. She sat on the veranda and looked across the canefields, hands clasped on her belly. Haggard's great house was complete, waiting only for its mistress to return. But she had obtained one concession, at the least, that she would remain on Bolton's until her baby was born. She could feel it now, moving inside her. It would be any day now, according to Dr. Waley. At least there had been no difficulty in working out the time, exactly; he had known where to start.

"Sangaree, Miss Lindy?"

The servants were solicitous. Adelaide, full of her own ideas on medicine, had forbidden gin. But Miss Lindy was to be given all the sangaree she wanted, to keep her good-humored and relaxed. Miss Lindy was to be pampered in every possible way. But what did they say about Miss Lindy in the kitchens? What did they say in the barracoons? And this was Bolton's.

She had not left the plantation since the day of the revolt. She had not wished to visit Haggard's, and the thought of Bridgetown was approximated by hell. People had come to see her. Ginny had come all the way from Jamaica, Penny from the north of the island. They had sat and held her hands, their minds and their eyes filled with questions they dared not ask. But Johnnie had asked. Again and again he had asked. "I cannot help you," he had said, "unless I know."

And her answers had made him hard. In that sense she had thanked God for her pregnancy, because Adelaide had forbidden intercourse from the first break in her menstrual pattern. But her husband wanted her, because she had been raped by black men. And soon, very soon, he would be in a position to have her again.

She drank deeply, watched the horsemen walking up the drive. Johnnie and Papa were great friends now. If everyone in Barbados knew that Papa had played the coward, he had ridden back with Johnnie at the end, and heroism can brush off. Besides, to have a hero for a son-in-law was kudos enough for any man.

A hero. A man who did not like women; she was not prepared to take the thought any further, because she did not know how far it was possible to take it. Save when the woman was his wife and had been raped. And she was married to him, married and married and married, for the rest of her life. Adelaide had said, once you have a child, you need never sleep with him again. Adelaide would see to that. But Adelaide also intended that the child should inherit, and therefore that it should continue to be Haggard, which meant that its mother had to continue being Haggard as well. So, would she ever have sexual intercourse again, without being raped?

And could she ever have sexual intercourse again, without screaming in pain and terror and self-horror?

And would she ever *want* sexual intercourse again?

The horsemen dismounted at the foot of the steps. "My sweet Lindy," Johnnie said. "It really is complete now. The last stick of furniture is in place. It looks superb. Better than it can ever have looked before. I can hardly wait to show it to you."

"And I can hardly wait to see it," she lied.

"And there are letters," Johnnie said. "Letters from England. From Roger." He took a glass of sangaree, sat beside her. "I'll read it to you. He says, 'I really am quite overwhelmed that everything should have turned out so well. Of course I'm sorry that you have had so much trouble and that the house has been burned. But I can't help reflecting that from your point of view that has been a fortunate event. The house was always Father's house, and in view of everything that has happened, I think it is to the good that you and Lindy should have a new one, something you can call entirely your own. It will cost us all of this year's profit, but it is worth every penny. Johnnie, I am proud of you, of the way you handled the revolt. I know Alice is proud of you too. We are both longing to hear of Lindy's successful confinement, and we both long to meet Lindy as well. If you are not careful, we may well pay you a visit in the not-too-distant future!' " He smiled at her. "Roger is an absolute brick. He's been a soldier all his life, you know. He understands what soldiering is all about. He got an award for bravery at Talavera. And he fought at Waterloo, virtually as a volunteer. You'll like Roger. And Alice. I wonder . . ." He frowned.

"What?" she asked. Because she was interested, despite herself. Here was an entire family of which she knew nothing, save through her mother's hate.

"Well . . . Roger was betrothed, when last I heard. To a

girl called Margaret Bold. But he does not mention her in the letter."

"You will have to write him and ask," she suggested.

"Hardly my place." His head raised as she caught her breath. "Lindy . . . ?"

"Yes," she said. "Oh, my God, yes."

"Mrs. C.," he bawled, springing to his feet. "Mrs. C." He bent over her. "Shall I help you, my sweet? Let me help you."

"I can manage," she said. "Just . . . just hold my arm."

But by now the entire veranda was filled with anxious servants, marshaled by Adelaide, taking her upstairs, putting her to bed.

"Off you go," Adelaide commanded to Johnnie. "There's nothing for you to do here. We shall call you after the child is born. Go and have a drink with Peter."

Lindy's forehead was swabbed, and she was put into her nightdress, while the midwife arrived and began her gentle but insistent ministrations. Adelaide sat by her bed and stroked her hair. The spasms came more quickly, and she was aware of pain, but never half as bad as she had anticipated.

"You're doing splendidly," Adelaide said. "All my girls have always done splendidly," quite forgetting poor Penny. "Childbearing has always been easy for Boltons. Oh, you're going fine. Come on, now, just a last push. Here he comes. Here he comes."

A tremendous relief, and a feeling of utter exhaustion. And the sudden wail of a baby inhaling for the first time. It was done. What Mama and what Papa and what Johnnie had wanted for so long was done.

And herself? Now it was done, she wanted it too.

But the room was strangely silent. And they had not given her the baby. She raised her head, stared at Adelaide, who stared back, stared at the maids, who stared back, stared at the midwife, holding the woolly-haired little boy in the crook of her arm.

"Oh, my God," Adelaide said. "Oh, Christ, that such a thing should have happened."

Lindy's muscles gave way, and she fell back on the pillows.

"Haste, haste," Adelaide said. "The child was born dead, of course. There is no necessity for Mr. Haggard to see it at all. Bury it, Johnston." She glared around the room. "And so help me God, if a single one of you ever so much as breathes a word of this, I shall skin you alive."

The girls shifted their feet anxiously.

Lindy pushed herself up again. "Give me my baby," she said.

"Now, Lindy . . ." Adelaide hurried to her side, smoothed hair from her forehead. "There is nothing for you to concern yourself with. There will be other children. Of course there will. You'll have so many children you won't know what to do with them."

"Give me my baby," Lindy said.

"Lindy . . ."

"Give me my baby," Lindy screamed, and got out of bed, falling to her knees beside it. "He's mine. You made me have it. He's mine. Give me my baby."

Chapter 8

The Fugitive

"Holloa," Roger Haggard shouted. "Holloa."

He walked his horse down the long, curving drive of Mid-look House, swaying occasionally to escape the low-hanging branch of a tree, swaying more often for no other reason than that he found it difficult to sit straight in the saddle.

"Holloa," he bawled.

Lights flared as the front doors were opened, as grooms hurried from the stables.

"Who's there?" someone shouted.

"Major Roger Haggard, damn your eyes," Roger shouted. The horse stopped because it had come to the foot of the steps, and the suddenness of the movement finally dislodged its rider; Roger's toes came out of the stirrups and he slid sideways over the animal's neck.

"Help the major, there," commanded the butler, having arrived on the scene to take control, and hands grasped Roger in time to prevent his falling to the ground. "You have lost your hat, sir."

"Hat?" Roger put up his hand, ran his fingers into his hair. "By God, sir, but you are right. I had it when I left London."

The butler peered at him. "You have ridden from town, sir? This evening?"

"Of course I have, you great oaf," Roger said. "Har-greaves, is it? I remember. Hargreaves. Well, Hargreaves, I am in need of a drink."

Hargreaves, having been inhaling his breath, sighed. "And perhaps a bite to eat, Major Haggard."

"Drink," Roger said firmly, starting up the shallow steps

165

and retreating down them again. "Damnation. Can't you keep your people still?"

Hargreaves caught his elbow, while signaling a footman to assist on the other side. "It is a turbulent night, sir," he agreed deprecatingly. And cleared his throat. "Her ladyship is not in residence, sir."

"Eh?" Roger stopped at the top of the steps, turned his head from side to side.

"The countess is away for the weekend, sir," Hargreaves explained.

"By God," Roger said. "By God."

Hargreaves assisted him through the front door. "Perhaps she was unaware of your intentions to call, sir."

"Unaware," Roger said. "Unaware. By God, she was unaware, Hargreaves. I never told her. Ha ha. What d'ye think of that?"

"Well, sir . . ."

"Thus it seems I must make you welcome, Major Haggard," Jane Favering said.

Roger's head tilted as he peered at the stairs. Jane was on the first landing, wearing a pale blue undressing robe over her nightdress. Her midnight hair was loose, and like her mother's, reached to her thighs. Her face was quite lacking in makeup and looked paler than he remembered in the flickering candlelight, but was the more beautiful for that.

"Jane?" he asked owlishly, and attempted to raise his nonexistent hat.

Jane Favering continued on her way down the stairs. "You are drunk, sir," she said. "And this is an unusual hour to call on a lady uninvited."

How old was she? Roger tried to remember. Somewhere in the neighborhood of twenty, he supposed. A perfect copy of her mother, lacking only the additional thirty-four years' experience. Or did she lack experience?

"You are right, my lady," he agreed. "I am drunk. Drunk with despair, at having been separated from you for so long."

Jane almost smiled. "I am sure Mama will be flattered, whatever her present feelings for you. Will you not come inside?" She walked before him into the withdrawing room. "Hargreaves," she said, "you had best provide the major with a glass of port, to fortify him before he begins his journey back."

Roger found himself standing above a settee, and sat

down; his legs would support him no longer. "Journey back?" he inquired.

Jane stood before the smoldering fire. "I am alone in this house, sir," she pointed out, her face severely composed.

Hargreaves gave a gentle cough and withdrew to the company of his maids and footmen.

"Ah," Roger said. "And suppose, my lady, that I claim to have come all this way just to see you?"

"Then would you be telling a lie, sir," she said. "For which I should forgive you," she added, her face softening, "as it is also a compliment. But which would do nothing to raise you in my esteem. Ah, Hargreaves, you may serve the port."

Hargreaves held the tray to Roger, who took a glass.

"Will you not join me, Jane?"

She hesitated, then took a glass herself. "I suppose it would be discourteous not to. You may close the door, Hargreaves." She sat opposite Roger, on a straight chair, sipped her drink. Some color appeared in her cheeks. "My mother is going to be very angry with you, Major Haggard. I suppose she would call herself a romantic, but the romance has to be entirely on her own terms. She no longer counts you among her favorite gentlemen, and I'm afraid it is your duty to wait until, if ever it happens, she once again invites you to attend her. A boorish act such as to call on her unannounced, when the worse for drink, is likely to make that day very remote in the future."

Haggard drank some more port, sat up straight, endeavored to tidy his cravat, and only succeeded in pulling it loose altogether. "I apologize, Jane, both for my appearance and for my behavior. I am drunk, as you have observed, but my reasons are sound enough, believe me. I was summoning my courage, at best a difficult creature, merely to enable me to ride down here. I have not come to see your mother. At least, I did wish to *see* her, but entirely to discuss a project in which we were both at one time interested. As she is not here, may I be bold enough to discuss it with you instead?"

"You may discuss whatever you wish, sir," she said. But her breathing had quickened.

"I have come to ask for your hand in marriage," Roger explained.

She gazed at him for some seconds. "A *project*, sir," she said at last. "In which you and Mama were interested? I feel like a cow in a ring, being examined for my better points."

"Oh, my darling girl," Roger said, leaning forward to take her hand, and, unable to reach, sliding off the settee to kneel before her. "How I would adore to examine you for your better . . . My God, I do beg your pardon."

Jane Favering smiled. "Mama always said that one of your more endearing traits was a West Indian uncouthness, which she found refreshing. Major Haggard, I should tell you that Mama and I have no secrets from each other."

"My dear Jane . . ."

"And therefore I am aware that you have refused the notion of me as a wife on several occasions." She gave a little sigh, and then a moue exactly like her mother's. "I had supposed myself doomed for a life of spinsterhood."

"You mean there is no one else?" He had advanced across the floor on his knees, and now did take her hands.

"For the moment, sir. Which is not to say I accept you. What, marry one of Mama's cast-off lovers? And especially one who is only here because his intended has reverted to type?"

Haggard frowned at her. "You know of that?"

"Mama makes it her business to know everything about those in whom she is interested," Jane pointed out. "Has the girl really departed to Australia with a transported felon?"

Roger sighed, and nodded.

"Who also claims to be your half-brother?"

"I'm afraid he *is* my half-brother. My late father . . ."

"Sewed a crooked pattern, Major Haggard. Now, tell me, sir, has anything I have just seen or heard been of the quality to convince me that I should place my maidenhead in your keeping?"

Roger discovered that she had not pulled her hands free; indeed, the fingers were quite tight on his. "Indeed not. I am the most wretched fellow in England. I loved Meg Bold, but more than that, I felt I owed her a duty, because of her circumstances and mine. To that end I rejected your mother's proposal that I should marry you, no matter what my personal feelings. And now I find that I have been pretending to love a chimera, which never truly existed. I was too old for her, and there's the truth."

Jane gave a gentle laugh. "So far as I am aware, the young woman is older than I."

"My God," Roger said. "I am being a perfect fool. But you, Jane, you—"

"Are precocious. Oh, indeed, Mama has seen to it. Yet do I still *have* a maidenhead, and therefore scant experience in that direction. It is a matter of some concern to me, sir, to whom I entrust it. Especially as I now know that Mama would disapprove."

"Would she?"

"A Favering spurned?" She smiled, and stood up, freeing one hand but leaving the other in his. "But in all the circumstances, I do not think I will expel you once again into the night, after all. Hargreaves will find you a bed for the night, Major Haggard. And possibly we may be able to pursue this discussion in the morning, when our heads are less fuddled."

There was no Corky. My God, he thought, sitting on the bed and scratching his head. Where the devil is Corky? But he had left Corky in his London lodgings before undertaking that fruitless hunt for Mina. The poor fellow would be out of his mind with worry by morning. Or would he have the sense to know that his master would have gone down to Midlook?

Anyway, morning was a long time off. For the moment there were more pressing problems—no nightshirt, for instance.

"Ahem," remarked Hargreaves. "His lordship is a trifle shorter than you, sir, but this will at least, ah, protect you from the draft."

Roger allowed the linen shirt to be dropped over his head. "I feel I should apologize, Hargreaves, for arriving like this."

"It is my pleasure, sir," Hargreaves said skeptically. "I will provide one of the lads and a razor in the morning, if that is suitable."

"Suitable. Oh, indeed, it will be suitable. And no doubt you will be able to have my trousers pressed and my boots blacked, as well?"

"That shall be done, sir, and your linen washed and dried, before you awaken."

"Hargreaves, you are a splendid fellow," Roger said, and lay down, drawing long breaths. But deep breathing was not going to solve his problem this night. No sooner had Hargreaves left than he was out of bed, exploring the wainscoting. But this was a different room from that he had occupied four years before, and he could find no trace of any secret doorways. And anyway, he thought, once again sitting on the bed, are you out of your mind? The girl is but twenty, and as she has repeatedly explained, a virgin. On the other hand, he argued, I do mean to marry her, even if it requires eloping to Gretna. Now, why? Is she not right, and you are reacting entirely to Meg's betrayal?

Was it a betrayal? His thoughts were leading him down some strange paths tonight. But when the matter was considered, had Meg ever had any chance to reveal her own thoughts on the matter, from the very beginning? He had used her body, and told her he would marry her. Not proposed to her. *Told* her. Was he not being entirely unfair to her in condemning her for falling in love with someone else? A condemned felon, on his way to Australia? But also a Haggard, which he supposed was by way of being a compliment to the family. My God, he thought, there will soon be Haggards scattered all over the globe, from Barbados to Australia. Haggards and Bolds. Poor Emma. But she too had revealed her sense of honor in electing to accompany her husband and family into exile.

And none left in England? Not if he could help it. But did he love Jane? Did that matter? She was beautiful, she was well-connected, she was not obviously unsympathetic to him—in fact, he rather felt . . . And he wanted her so very badly. She would make the most perfect Mrs. Haggard of Derleth Manor, a fact readily observed by her mother. It would be a splendid match, physically as well as financially. And it was the financial aspect that would interest Mina and Alderney. He could think of nothing finer than to spend the rest of his life with Jane Favering at his side. And if she was exactly half his age, well, Father had married a girl half his age.

Disastrous thought, because that had been a disastrous marriage. But it was almost blasphemy to approximate Jane Favering in any way with that beautiful green-eyed snake.

And how he wanted her body. If he could not hold her in his arms this night, he must attend to himself, and it was a long time since he had had to resort to that. Besides, if she *was* interested, she was not yet convinced. Now was the time to play the lover, and be accepted, utterly. Or rejected, utterly. Certainly he could not wait.

He tiptoed down the hall, wondering where to begin. But there was no other way than by trying them all. The first door was clearly a dressing room, then two empty bedrooms in turn, then one that smelled of Mina's perfume but was clearly not hers, then a rather masculine room, and then another gentle scent . . .

"Major Haggard?"

He blinked into the darkness.

"I see I have made a mistake," Jane said. "And should indeed have sent you back to London."

He stepped inside, closed the door behind him. "I am here to plight my troth."

"And do you not suppose we may well wind up plighting a great deal more than that, sir?"

Cautiously he advanced across the room. "That is my fervent desire, certainly."

"Major *Haggard*!"

Her voice was very close, and now he could see the draperies immediately in front of him.

"Will you, then, scream for help?"

He heard her smile. "I have never screamed, for anything, in my life. But that does not mean I shall submit to rape."

He opened the draperies, could see her, a white wisp sitting up in bed. "I had always supposed the very word presupposed submission."

Another smile. "I very much doubt whether any single man, Major Haggard, would succeed in raping me, however big and strong and experienced. Save you were to beat me insensible first. And I should not like that. Indeed, sir, my first action on recovering would be to blow out your brains."

He sat on the bed. "Do you not find this conversation absurd?"

"That depends, sir, on what you propose. It may turn out to have been deadly serious."

He touched her arm; she did not move it. His fingers slid up the velvet of her flesh to her shoulder, stroked her hair. "I am here to make love to you, Jane," he said. "I propose to do so until you slap my face. Then I shall withdraw, and you shall not see me again, I swear it." He leaned forward, and her lips touched his, and once again her tongue, shyly questing, came between her teeth to caress his, before withdrawing again.

"Do you not suppose, sir," she whispered, her lips moving on his, "that such an ultimatum will but harden my resolve?"

"By God, but it hardens mine," he said.

She gave a little shriek of laughter, and hugged him close,

then allowed her left hand to drop onto the skirt of his night-shirt. A quick touch, and she was gone again.

"You will do me an injury, Major Haggard."

"Oh, Jane. My darling, darling Jane." She fell back across the bed, and he was lying beside her, half across her, his hand going down to scoop her nightdress to her waist, to slide his hand up her thigh, to quest into the silky dark hairs he had dreamed of for so long.

"Wait," she said, her breath rushing against his face.

He hesitated, and she sat up, moved his hand, and got out of bed. He watched her shadow cross the room to the still-smoldering fire, and dip in a candle. A moment later, to his amazement, the room flared with light.

"I like to see what I am doing," Jane said, setting the candle in its holder. "What I am enjoying." She turned to face him. "You must take me as I am, Major Haggard. I am Mina Favering's daughter." She lifted the nightdress over her head, allowed it to fall to the floor.

Haggard reached for her, brought her against him, kissed mouth and eyes and nose and chin, slipped lower to kiss her nipples and her breasts, lower yet to lose himself in the soft dampness of her groin, hands tight on her buttocks. He felt her fingers closing on his hair. Then she was on the bed and he was kneeling above her, his own nightshirt discarded, her legs spread, his heart pounding.

"Wait," she said again.

He sat on his own heels, gazing at her white-skinned perfection.

"I really do not wish to be hurt," she said. "And you are quite the biggest fellow I have ever seen."

"Ever seen?" he asked.

She smiled. "I have often watched Mama, secretly. Oh, with her permission. I have watched her and you, Major Haggard. There is a box of ointment in that drawer, if you will pass it to me."

Wondering if he was dreaming, Haggard opened the drawer, found the box. She removed the lid, took a little of the ointment on her finger, herself anointed each of them in turn. "Now," she said. "Now, Haggard, you can take me now."

Mina Favering's daughter, an unbelievable wonderland of delight, brought to perfection, it seemed, just for him. Mina Favering's daughter, into whom he could slip and slip and slip, feeling warmer and happier by the moment, with whom he could explode in passion and feel her move against him, from whom there came not the slightest murmur of pain or even discomfort, and who then stared at him through enormous dark eyes.

"Do you love me, Major Haggard?"

"I am going to love you, Jane. My God, I am going to love you."

She smiled. "Then I shall love you. But, Major Haggard, however like my mother I may seem, I am not my mother. I shall love only once. I swear it. It shall be you. But you shall be mine. So help me God, if you betray me, I will destroy you."

"A rogue," Mina Favering said. "The very devil of a rogue." But her smile was brilliant. "And you, miss, yielding your all. My God, I'd be entitled to have you flogged. Locked up, certainly."

"I did what I supposed you would have done, Mama," Jane explained. She looked ravishing in dark blue. Haggard supposed it was utterly, masculinely unfair of him, but he did not at this moment see how he had ever fallen in love with Mina, lovely as she still was.

"Wretched girl," Mina said. "But to have you as a son-in-law, Haggard, why, I am prepared to forgive a great deal. And now, there is so much for us to talk about."

"We must tell Daddy," Jane said.

Mina gave her an old-fashioned look. "Whatever for?"

"Well . . . he is my father."

"Ah," Mina said. "Now, there is something we must discuss."

"*Mama!*"

"Well," Mina said, "there comes a time in every life when a mother must be honest with her daughter. And her prospective husband. Would it greatly distress you to think of marrying a bastard, Haggard?"

"I'm marrying Jane," he said. "It might be interesting to know the name of her father, but not important."

"Autumn of ninety-five," Mina said. "My God, I was thirty-two. Oh, Haggard, if you'd known me when I was thirty-two."

"Saving the point . . ."

"That you would have been nineteen. But I think I saw

you, at a ball at Almack's, just before your strange disappearance from the social scene."

"Yes," Roger said. Alison's night.

"You must tell me about that, sometime."

"No," he said. "You tell me about the autumn of ninety-five. When you saw me was two years before."

"Oh? How memory does play tricks. Well, there was . . . I shall have to look up my diaries."

"But not Daddy," Jane said regretfully.

"My dear girl, you are far too quick-witted to be Favering's. No, I think we may say not Daddy. Although I should hate this to be bruited abroad."

Haggard nodded.

"But yet you are a trifle pensive," Mina observed. "I suspect your liberal intents do not quite match your Tory upbringing."

"I have received a letter from Barbados," Roger explained. "This very morning."

"Don't tell me the price of sugar has fallen again?"

"Nothing so serious as that. There has been a revolt."

"A revolt?" Jane cried.

"A slave uprising."

"My God," Mina said. "But . . ."

"There is nothing to worry about. These things do happen from time to time. Never during my sojourn there, to be sure, but then, I have always been fortunate. Yet the whole thing is rather gratifying. My brother—"

"Whom I have not yet met," Mina pointed out.

"Well, up to this morning I would have counted you fortunate. But it seems that he has played rather the hero, leading a cavalry charge, at odds of fifty to one, which scattered the insurgents. I find it difficult to believe, but it is supported by a testimonial from his mother-in-law, so believe it I must."

"And has there been a great deal of damage?"

"Oh, Haggard's Penn? Yes. Nothing that cannot be restored, at a price. It was the loss of life I was considering. Still, we must be grateful. It could have been far worse." He squeezed Jane's hand. "You are marrying into the business rather than the social community, my dearest one. I hope that does not alarm you."

"I find it fascinating," she said. "And now, Mama, I should like Roger to take me for a walk in the park."

"And I should like him to remain here, with me," Mina said. "To discuss certain points of view."

"Mama . . ."

"My dear girl, I shall not even cast an eye in the direction of his breeches. But there are matters I, as your mother, must discuss with your future husband."

Jane hesitated, then squeezed Roger's hand and got up. "Then I shall leave you to discuss your points of view."

Mina waited until the door was closed; then she sighed. "I am, of course, overjoyed that you should have come to your senses at last, my darling. Although I could wish you had done so in less dramatic a fashion. All London is abuzz with the tale of how you stormed my daughter in her bedchamber."

"I don't see how anyone can know of that," Roger protested.

"The actual facts of the case? Why, no one does. Sufficient that you arrived here in the middle of the night, when she was alone in residence, and remained here for two days. Busy imaginations require very little else upon which to grow. But as I say, I am delighted. I see before you a long and prosperous and happy life. But there are certain responsibilities you must contemplate."

"My solicitors are drawing up a contract which will please even you, Mina," Roger said. "Jane will never want for a penny, nor any of her children. Their only problem will be how to spend all I mean to bestow upon them."

"I am sure I did not come down here to discuss money," Mina pointed out. "That truly is a matter for solicitors. No, no. I am concerned with more important matters. There is shortly to be an election."

Roger shook his head in wonderment. "Does politics run in your veins, instead of blood?"

She made one of her moues. "You should know the answer to that as well as any man, Haggard. But politics is exciting. Almost as exciting as sex. It is the future of a nation we toy with here. You will take the seat for Derleth?"

"I thought your friend Russell did not approve of pocket boroughs."

"He doesn't. Neither do I. But as they are there, for the moment, we at least intend to use them. You'll adhere to our cause?"

"Ah," Roger said. "It's a matter I have been considering."

"You'll not backslide on me, Haggard."

"I had not intended to, certainly. I but wish to be sure where I am going. And where those who would accompany me are going. There is no doubt that this recent slave revolt in Barbados was inspired by too much liberal sentiment reaching the West Indies through the mouths of the missionaries."

"And you, being a slave owner, cannot contemplate possible emancipation?"

"Being a businessman, I find it difficult to contemplate a sugar plantation earning a profit without slave labor, whatever Adam Smith may say. And no profit means no sugar plantation. Which means starvation for the people employed in that direction."

"And a considerable drop in Haggard wealth."

"Mina . . ." He held her hand. "You are becoming angry."

She smiled at him. "I am endeavoring not to. I will confess the West Indies is a subject I know very little about. I am sure we can all arrive at some sort of a compromise on the subject of slaves. My concern is more with the conditions of freeborn Englishmen."

"They are all human beings."

Mina threw up her hands. "For heaven's sake, what are you arguing *about*?"

"I do not think those people who rioted in Lowden, or any of those who are rioting in different parts of the country right this minute, are any different from the slaves in Barbados. In Barbados we call their riots a slave revolt, and we hang their ringleaders without trial. In England we call them riots, and we transport a select few ringleaders, after trial. The difference is in our treatment of them, not their attitude to us."

"My God," she said. "And no doubt you conceive that because people like the Bolds have been transported rather than hanged, England is the most liberal country in the world."

"You miss my point. I do not think you can allow it to filter through to the common people that those in your position, or mine, oppose the government in every way, and would change the system if we had the chance, without risking the possibility that uneducated hotheads may assume they have but to resort to force and we will support them, too. This reforming business, to my mind, must be hurried very slowly, for all of our sakes."

"You *are* nothing but a dyed-in-the-wool Tory, when you come down to it. Just like your father."

"I have no desire, and no intention, to see my house burned, Jane raped, and myself hanging from a lantern, if that is what you mean. Nor do you, I suspect, for all your fine words. Once loose the mob, Mina, and you will need a Bonaparte to confine it again."

"Bonaparte is the greatest man who ever lived."

"Oh, no doubt. But greatness does not always mean the same thing as universal happiness. Had you campaigned through one or two burned-out villages, you'd know that."

"Ha!" She got up. "You make me very angry, Haggard. Indeed you do." She smiled. "But I will forgive you, if you will but promise to listen from time to time. Will you do that?"

"I give you Major and Mrs. Trumley Sparrow."

The table burst into applause as Roger raised his glass, all heads turning to look at the couple, Alice blushing and Trum looking as proud as a peacock.

"Only the first of this summer's weddings on Derleth," Roger pointed out, to renewed applause, and smiled at Jane, seated beside her mother. It was their first visit to Derleth, both to attend Alice's wedding and to inspect Jane's future home. Alderney, predictably, had not come, but there were several of Mina's Whig friends, including John Russell and Francis Burdett, but not, to Roger's disappointment, George Byron. But then, that young poet was newly married himself, and also apparently gainfully employed, at least, in managing the Drury Lane Theater. Nor, according to his letter, did he much care for marriages, "for I will confess to you, Haggard," he had written, "my own has turned out to be a damnably rum affair." With which enigmatic remark he had changed the subject. Roger had pressed Mina, but she had merely frowned and said, "He flies too near the sun, our darling B. Like Icarus, he will one day find that his wings have melted right away and he will come tumbling from the sky."

Well, Roger thought, no doubt if he needs my help he will call for it; he can have no doubt that I will respond. And today was Alice's day. To see her so utterly happy, after the existence she had been forced to lead, kept virtually a prisoner by her father, and more recently attempting to support her mother and her half-sister, and even protect a stepfather she hated and feared, robbed throughout her life of any friends, her hopes of marriage early dashed, and then her recent misery at Emma's and Meg's decision to accompany their menfolk into exile—Mary Prince had shown more sense in electing to remain where she had always been, but then, Mary had already been separated from her son for most of their lives—and yet, apparently, this day able to put it all behind her. Because of Trum. Gallant, splendid Trum. No man could ask for a better friend, and therefore no woman could seek a better husband, surely.

"Your brother has been the best friend I have ever known," Trum confessed, his lips against Alice's brow. "Without him I should not have found you, nor even a home."

"He loves you, my dearest Trum," she said, nestling closer into his arms. Alice Haggard, she thought, naked in the arms of a man. It was not something she dared believe. She had feared embarrassment, and he had smiled as he had lifted her nightgown over her head, gently but insistently. She had feared brutality, and his touch had been like a feather's. She had feared repulsion, and his questing penis had been the most beautiful sensation she had ever experienced, resting now on her thigh, moving against her. So it had a duty, as did she, soon to be performed. Even Trum, so determined that it should be easy for her, would not wish to wait all night. So, did she still fear agony? There could be no agony with Trum.

He shrugged against her, and winced. His shoulder was all but healed, yet the inner pain remained. "I feel like a man carrying in his arms a set of the most perfect Dresden china ever made," he confessed. "And thus afraid to make the slightest stumble lest he drop his load and watch it shatter."

"Why should you stumble, dearest Trum?" she asked. "Why should you stumble?"

"Because . . ." He rose on his elbow to look down on her. "I do not want to hurt you, my darling girl."

She smiled at him. "But I want you, Trum. I want it to happen. I want to love. You. If I love you, you can never hurt me." She lay on her back, and smiled at him. "I love you, Trum. Oh, how I love you."

I love you, my dearest Jane, Haggard thought, looking down the sweep of the table, to where she sat at the other end. The dining room at Derleth glittered tonight, from the crystal chandeliers to the exposed shoulders and bosoms of the women, gleaming white, to the no less snowy perfection of the gentlemen's cravats; these men might claim to be the most liberal thinkers in the world, but they would not yet permit the new-fashioned spots and stripes introduced by Brummell to influence their dress.

And they were happy. Or was it only because *he* was so happy? But there could be no doubt about Trum and Alice, seated beside each other halfway down. And the rest were at least excited, and well fed and wined, and boisterously conversational.

"I expect a blow-by-blow description, my dear Haggard, of every moment of your honeymoon," Mina said. She was seated on his right, as Alderney, at last persuaded to leave London to welcome the happy couple back from Scotland, was beside his daughter.

"I suspect one honeymoon is very like another," Haggard pointed out. "As it rained a good deal of the time, we were not encouraged to spend our time roaming over the heather."

She made a moue, and tapped him on the shoulder with her fan. "But it is very important. Honeymoons make or mar a marriage. I do believe that poor Byron's every trouble started on *his* honeymoon?"

"He's not in trouble?"

"Trouble? Ha. Where *have* you been?"

"In the Highlands, my darling Mina, as you well know. You are the first breath of London gossip which has reached my ears in a month."

"Well," she said, "it is hardly gossip any longer. The things they are saying. Really, they are quite unimaginable."

"Tell me."

She arched her eyebrows. "Are you sure you want to know? You are by way of being a friend of his."

"All the more reason *to* know."

"Well . . ." She sipped some wine, well aware that everyone seated within earshot was also listening intently. "You've never met Mrs. Leigh, have you?"

Haggard shook his head.

"She is Byron's half-sister. Rather the same relationship as Alice is to you. Well, Haggard, you will not credit this, but the talk is that Byron has taken her to bed, and more, has even fathered a child by her."

Haggard frowned at her. "That is incredible."

Mina shrugged. "Is there anything incredible, where Byron is concerned? But that is not all."

"Can there be anything else?"

"Well . . ." Mina glanced from face to face. "It is said that on his honeymoon . . . well, he entered his wife . . . well, up her ass." She leaned back in her chair and gazed at them, little pink spots in her cheeks.

"Oh, come, now, Mina," someone said.

"It is not denied," Mina pointed out.

"Well, I say . . ." The speaker went very red in the face. "Really, I don't see how——"

There was a shout of laughter. "You've never been hard enough, Ramsay," someone cried.

"Well, I say . . ." Ramsay protested.

"Surely," Haggard said, "what a man does with his wife is his concern, and his alone, provided the lady consents."

This time it was Mina who laughed. "Annabelle Milbanke? She is the most prudish prude I have ever encountered. Would you believe, Haggard, that she did not really understand what was happening? Until much later."

"And it is she making this story public?" Burdett demanded. "I cannot credit that of any woman."

"She has demanded a separation," Mina said. "And when he resisted the demand—there is a child, you know—threats were brought to bear." She leaned forward, her face suddenly intense. "This is actually no laughing matter. He is being done up. Oh, if all is true, he has behaved abominably, but no more so than most of the gentlemen here tonight, I'd wager."

There was a chorus of embarrassed protest, led by her husband.

"Hypocrites," she said. "Why, when I publish my memoirs, I'll lay a few tales, you can rely on that."

"Memoirs?" Alderney demanded. "Are you writing your memoirs, Mina?"

She smiled at him. "I might. But that's by·the by. He was caught at it, there's the sin. And he's deep in debt, no doubt about that. But how many of you here tonight are not deep in debt? Yet Byron is being pilloried, threatened with jail and worse for unnatural practices, all his peccadilloes being dragged into the open . . . and shall I tell you why? It is because he makes no secret of his beliefs, cocks a snoop at the government whenever he can, calls Wellington a butcher, which he is. That's why George Byron is being driven into exile, my friends. So what are we going to do about it?"

The table became silent.

"If it's a matter of debt . . ." Haggard said at last.

"That is the least of his problems now," Burdett observed. "But I really do not see what we can do about it, Mina, save pursue the course we are now taking. We must be legal, and we must be seen to be legal. Now, you have yourself admitted that Byron has behaved in an outrageous manner, *and has been found out*. There's the rub. He must be prepared to accept the consequences. We shall be losing a faithful adherent, but I will confess that he is sometimes an uncomfortable bedfellow, if you'll pardon the simile. Carrying on the way he does endangers the entire Whig party."

Mina sighed. "So we do nothing, save piously pray that he goes away, and soon. There's friendship for you."

"Friendship has nothing to do with it," Burdett argued seriously. "We are in pursuit of a great and glorious cause, nothing less than the reform of the entire system of government in this country. We seek democracy instead of oligarchy or aristocracy. We wish the ordinary people to have a greater share in the election of Parliament, and we wish Parliament, once elected, to be required to account for its actions more often. To be more responsible, in fact."

"An important point," Lord Russell agreed. "Seven years is too long."

"It's an abomination," Burdett said. "Parliament should be freshly elected every year."

They stared at him.

"Every *year?*" Alderney demanded.

"Of course. How else can it be held responsible to the people in these turbulent times?"

"And who would elect these parliaments?" Roger inquired.

"Every man in England."

Heads turned to look at each other.

"*Every* man? Your two-thousand-a-year gentleman and your twopenny-a-year scoundrel?" Ramsay asked.

"A man is a man," Burdett said.

"Ha," Mina said. "And why not every woman as well?"

"Oh, come now, Mina," Burdett protested. "Governing is a male business."

"I wonder who pointed that out to Queen Elizabeth," Jane said, coming to her mother's aid.

"That is not the same thing at all," her father reminded her.

"Listen to me," Burdett shouted above the din. "Do you doubt the yeomen of England are incapable of electing a true and just government? Of course there will have to be other changes. There will have to be equal electoral districts, and there will have to be a ballot. But these are details—"

"Details?" Alderney roared.

"Anyway," Haggard said, "I'm afraid I very much doubt that the yeomen of England *are* capable of electing a true and just Parliament. At least, I'm not sure whom I'd include in the ranks of the yeomen. What of those fellows who stoned poor Trum and me last year?"

"Even gentlemen occasionally break the law," Burdett pointed out with dignity. "And they have to suffer for it."

"And do you suppose any of the people in Lowden or in Plowding, for instance, would vote for any of us, if they had the choice?"

"They must *have* that choice, inevitably," Burdett argued. "You would go against the tide of history."

"If going against the tide of history means protecting the English way of life, the very greatness of this country, which depends not on those layabouts over in Lowden, but on men like my father and his father—"

"And like yourself, in fact, Roger," Russell said with a smile.

"If you insist upon it, my lord," Roger said, also smiling. "But it is people like myself who pay the taxes which enable our armies to fight and our navies to sail, and indeed, our government to govern. I'm all for democracy, but, gentlemen, even the Greeks gave the vote to only those of their citizens considered worthy of the honor."

"Not quite right—" Russell began.

"You, sir, are a Tory," Burdett accused.

Roger smiled at Mina. "So I have been called. Can I not be a *liberal* Tory?"

"A second Canning, by God," Ramsay declared.

"Gentlemen, gentlemen," Alderney said. "Let us at least keep our tempers, and allow that our host has every right to an opinion of his own. I would propose that we abandon politics for tonight, and instead devote ourselves to the ladies, who are likely to be far more rewarding."

"Motion carried." Roger laughed, and discovered that Nugent was at his elbow, trying to attract his attention. "Yes?"

Nugent spoke in a whisper. "There is someone to see you, sir. A person."

Roger frowned at him. "I am entertaining, Nugent. Send the fellow off."

"It is a lady, sir. At least, it is a woman."

"A woman? What difference does that make? Send her away. Tell her to come back in the morning."

Nugent's face was growing longer by the second. "The fact is, Mr. Haggard, sir, she says her name is Haggard. Mrs. John Haggard, sir. From Barbados."

PART TWO

THE WHIG

Chapter 1

The Massacre

Haggard pushed back his chair, stood up. "You'll excuse me, Jane, Mina, ladies and gentlemen. There's a matter to which I must attend."

He met his wife's gaze, raised his eyebrows in an attempt to convey to her that it was something too urgent to be neglected, and left the room, Nugent hurrying in front of him to open doors.

"Where is she?"

"In the downstairs parlor, Mr. Haggard."

Thoughts whirled through his brain as he ran down the stairs. Obviously something had happened to Johnnie. But there was no point in attempting to consider what it might be. So long as the young idiot had not decided to return to England . . . The door was opening in front of him, and he gazed at the young woman. Because she was very young, he realized, certainly not much past twenty, and as she stood up on his entry, he could discover that she was tall and slender, with fine golden hair lying straight past her shoulders and quite undressed in any way, a splendid face, intelligent and well-formed rather than beautiful, a pale complexion most delightfully scattered with freckles, and clear blue eyes. Her clothes were as simple as her hairstyle, for her pelisse was open and the blue gown beneath might have been worn by one of his mill hands, quite lacking in ribbon or furbelow, while to complete the peasant picture she held a small child in her arms, wrapped in a shawl but obviously only a few months old.

Her mouth opened slightly as she saw him, and color flared into her cheeks, but she did not speak.

"Rosalind?" he asked. "You are Rosalind? Johnnie's wife?" She nodded.

"But . . ." He stepped forward, hesitated, and then kissed her on the forehead. "Welcome to Derleth, of course. But . . ."

"There is a letter," she said.

"Ah. From Johnnie?"

"Johnnie . . ." She bit her lip.

"Is he ill? Dead?"

She shook her head. "The letter is from my mother. Adelaide Campkin. Do you know her?"

"Indeed I do. Look here, let me call one of the girls to take your baby, and then you must come upstairs and meet my friends. I am entertaining."

"No," she said. "No. If it is inconvenient, I will leave. I saw an inn on my way here . . ."

"What nonsense," he said. "You stay here. I will . . ." He turned as the door opened, gazed at Jane. "Rosalind," he said. "Johnnie's wife. There is some mystery . . ."

"I have left my husband," Rosalind said, speaking very carefully. "By mutual consent. He does not know I am here. There is a letter . . ."

"Oh, my darling," Jane said, hurrying forward to put her arm round Rosalind's shoulders. "Oh, my dear girl. You shall come with me, and I shall see to you and your baby. Is it a boy?" She gently pushed back the shawl from the child's face, gazed at Roger in consternation.

Jane Haggard sat up in bed and reread the letter for the third time. "It really is quite horrible, even to think about," she said. "I mean, I just can't imagine . . . ugh." She raised her head; Haggard had just come in from his dressing room, fully dressed. "Can you imagine it?"

"I'm afraid I can," Roger said.

"And then to be pregnant . . . Why in the name of God didn't she abort?"

"That I shall have to find out."

"And then, well . . . I can understand Mrs. Campkin's being on the side of her daughter, Roger, but really when she says that your brother gave her the choice of abandoning the baby or being thrown out . . . I can sympathize with his point of view."

"You cannot," Haggard pointed out. "Until you have heard both sides of the question."

"Mmmm. I suppose you're right. And then . . . why send her here?" She found the right place on the page. " 'She is a Haggard now,' she writes. 'Taken into the bosom of your family, and not lightly to be discarded. If your brother will not recognize his duty as her husband, then I hope and pray, and earnestly believe, my dear Roger, that you will understand your duties as a brother-in-law—as your dear father would have done—and care for this poor misguided creature so cast adrift on the waters of life.' My God. She should have been a poet. And she obviously has a different opinion of your father from those *I* have heard. Did she know him very well?"

"They were betrothed, briefly."

"Oh, then she must have loved him very much."

"She hated him very much."

Jane thrust both hands into her curling black hair. "I'm in a fog. I mean to say, Rosalind is her *daughter*. God forbid, but if I ever had been raped, apart from by you of course, Mama would never have sent *me* off. She'd have kept me by her. Always."

"You're missing the point, my sweet," Haggard said, sitting beside her and holding her hands. "The fact of the rape is not important. But it was by black men, and in the West Indies that is very important indeed. And then, to bear a black child, and actually want to keep it . . . Rosalind would never be able to walk down a street in Bridgetown again. Of course Adelaide doesn't want her around."

"I see. But . . . she's a West Indian herself. Rosalind, I mean. So how can she . . . well . . . ?"

"That's something else I mean to find out. But the really important point is, do you want her to stay?"

"Of course I do. She's my sister-in-law. She's welcome to stay for as long as she chooses."

Haggard leaned forward, kissed her on the forehead. "I hoped you'd say that. Now I must go along and have a chat with her." He closed the bedroom door behind him, walked down the hall. It was still very early and none of the guests was up and about yet, so far as he knew. But they were certainly curious about what had happened last night. Some sort of explanation would be needed.

He almost smiled. They claimed to be the most liberal minds in Great Britain. But where did liberalism end and prejudice begin?

And where, indeed, did it begin and end in him? Or was he more aware of the possibility of prejudice because of his West Indian background? What would have been his reaction, for instance, to such a tragedy overtaking Jane? Save that it was impossible to imagine such a tragedy overtaking Jane. There was the point.

He knocked gently.

"Who is it?"

"Roger Haggard."

A brief hesitation. Then she said, "Come in, please, Mr. Haggard."

He stepped inside, closed the door. The draperies were open and the chamber flooded with sunlight, which made him blink.

"I'm afraid we were all so taken aback last night, we didn't respond very readily," he said. "Jane will select a maid for you this morning."

"You are being very kind."

He could see, at last. The draperies were drawn back round the bed as well, and she sat up, the baby at her breast; one shoulder of her nightgown was pulled down.

"Oh," he said. "Shall I come back later?"

"If I embarrass you, Mr. Haggard."

"Good Lord, no." He took a step farther into the room. "I was thinking that you might be embarrassed by *me*."

She smiled. "I have had to develop a very thick skin, Mr. Haggard. Very quickly."

He stood by her bed. Her breast was larger than he had expected. Because of course it was filled with milk. It was the most beautiful breast he had ever seen. But he was still virtually honeymooning. "I . . . both Jane and I are delighted to see you, Rosalind," he said. "And by the way, my name is Roger, you know? We want you to remain with us for just as long as you wish. The rest of your life, if that's the way you wish it. I do want you to understand that."

Her gaze was remarkably steady. "Mama said that was how you would be."

"Um. But you'll forgive me if . . . well . . ."

"My side of the story? I wanted my baby, Mr. Haggard. Roger. I wanted my baby. It is as simple as that."

"Even after . . . well . . . ?"

"At first I wanted it aborted," she said, still speaking perfcotly quietly and evenly. "And they wouldn't let me. They said I must have it."

"Why?" he asked. "Why on earth . . . ?"

"Because I wasn't only raped by black men, Mr. Haggard," she said. "I was raped by my husband, immediately afterward."

He stared at her.

"It . . . it excited him," she said. "I don't know how well you knew your brother, Mr. Haggard, but he is not . . . normally interested in women. Did you know that?"

Roger sighed. "I suspected it."

"Yes. Well, it was an ordeal for him to consummate our marriage, an ordeal for him to sleep with me at all. Until the day of the rape. Then he was excited. Then he wanted it."

"My God," Roger said. "Our hero."

Her head came up, pink spots in her cheeks. "He *is* a hero, Mr. Haggard. No one can take that away from him. He charged two thousand people, with only twenty at his back. His weaknesses have nothing to do with his heroism."

"I suppose you're right. But afterward . . ."

"Strolo is mine, Mr. Haggard." Her arms hugged the baby tighter. "So he was born of a rape, and I am sure at least that Johnnie wasn't the father. But would it have made any difference if he was? Strolo is mine. He is all I have got out of the entire business. I'm going to keep him."

"Strolo?"

Once again the quick flush. "It is the name I gave him."

"Strolo. Well, that is his name, to be sure. Strolo Haggard. Rather attractive. But, Rosalind . . . don't you suppose you may regret him, later on?"

"Why should I do that, Mr. Haggard?"

"Well . . . I shall of course be writing Johnnie. Does he know you're here?"

She shook her head.

"I'll have to tell him."

"I'll not go back to Barbados, Mr. Haggard. You may put me out to starve, but I'll not do that."

"I wasn't thinking of that," he said. "But it should be possible to obtain you a divorce." He peered at her. "Wouldn't you like that?"

She shrugged. "It makes no difference now, Mr. Haggard."

"Of course it does, my dear child. You are young, you are extremely handsome, you have everything to live for. You must turn your back on the past, look into the future. I shall certainly sponsor you. We shall find you a perfect husband, in the course of time. Certainly a divorce. But the boy, Strolo, may well prove a stumbling block to your future ambitions."

"I have no ambitions, Mr. Haggard, save for Strolo."

"My dear Rosalind, you future husband—"

"There will be no future husband, Mr. Haggard. I swear to you, if any man ever puts a finger on my flesh again, I shall kill him."

"Awaaaay. Awaaaaay," roared the people of Derleth. The crisp sound of the bat echoed through their shouts, and the leather ball was bouncing across the meadow in the direction of the trees, chased by four of the Benligh side, while Trumley Sparrow and the other Derleth batsmen raced up and down the rolled strip of grass, grounding their bats, panting, and running again.

"Nine for the stroke, Mr. Haggard. Nine for the stroke," Mr. Shotter exclaimed, himself cutting the series of little notches in the wooden wand. "A brilliant hit, sir. A brilliant hit."

Roger applauded with the rest, although really he understood very little about cricket. It had been played at Eton, of course, but he had spent only three terms there before his first quarrel with his father had seen him hurled into the army, and since then he had been continuously campaigning. But he had willingly supported Shotter's aspirations—the parson had played the game at Cambridge—had allowed him to prepare a pitch here in the manor park, and this game against Benligh was to be the beginning of what Shotter claimed would be a splendid summer season.

Certainly he had never seen the park looking prettier, the grass and the trees in all the bloom of early May, the playing area ringed with his tenants and their children, their dogs and their amusements, and in front of the house itself, the multi-colored marquee in which he sat with his family and his guests. His family. Already increasing, although no one but he and Jane knew it. She was leaning forward as she chatted with Mrs. Shotter, still as slight as the day he had married her, but soon to grow, and grow. Alice was next to her, eyes sparkling as she watched her husband bat. Alice's blooming happiness was almost Haggard's greatest joy, her inability to have children his only sorrow. And beside *her,* her so-strange sister-in-law, also apparently enjoying the game, Strolo in his pram by her side. He was a year old now, and the darling of the domestics. That his blood was mixed could no longer be doubted by anyone, but there was no one going to question either the squire or the squire's sister-in-law concerning what had happened. He undoubtedly was a problem for the future, her future, but if her future was to be as she saw it, then not so much of a problem at all. Haggard was determined to help her wherever he could, but she did not seem to want his help in that direction. Johnnie had written back to say that he would be content with whatever Roger wished done, but when he had reflected, the publicity and the expense attendant upon obtaining a divorce were hardly worthwhile unless Lindy had been anxious about it. As she was not . . . And she made such an attractive complement to Jane, while he could not help but admire the levelheaded way in which she had accepted her fate. She never wailed or moaned, concerned herself with assisting Jane in the management of the house and in caring for Strolo, for she nursed him herself. Her outburst on that first morning had not been repeated, and even then she had spoken in such measured tones that it could hardly be considered an outburst. It was a deeply taken, deeply determined decision. Which was a waste, he thought as he watched her, but a pleasure for everyone on Derleth.

The ball was retrieved, the batsman prepared to face the next delivery. And Squire Hutchinson sadly added up the number of notches on the various Derleth wands. "Only fourteen to win," he remarked. "And six men to go in. I suspect I must concede, Haggard. But you'll give us a return, at Benligh?"

"I'm sure we shall," Haggard agreed.

"Oh, indeed, sir, you should." He leaned across, his voice a hoarse whisper. "That brother-in-law of yours is a brilliant fellow. Brilliant, sir. Without him . . . But what would you, it is only a game. And yet, let me put this to you: cricket is the backbone of old England. Without it, sir, why, I swear we would have had trouble on our hands ere now."

"You wouldn't say we already had trouble on our hands, Hutchinson? Riots in Spa Fields, riots here in Derbyshire, somebody shooting at the Regent, habeas corpus suspended—why, sir, writing with hindsight, to be sure, are not our historians describing the French Revolution as having begun with far less sinister portents?"

"Exactly my point," Hutchinson argued, and paused to peer at the field. "There he goes again, my God. That is going to be at least another nine. Dear God, for a bowler who could pitch with accuracy. However, sir, as I was saying, *the French do not play cricket*. There is the difference, sir."

Roger waited for the applause to die, for Trum to resume resting on his bat, drawing deep breaths. "An interesting concept. But surely not everyone in England plays cricket?"

"Everyone of character, sir. Everyone of character. The rest, why let them go." Once again he leaned close. "You've lost people from here, of course."

"Two families. For the United States."

Hutchinson nodded. "Seven from Benligh. And Lowden— why, it is almost deserted. A result of that business two years ago."

"A sad occasion," Roger said. "I cannot help but feel we used a hammer to crush a nut."

"And if Louis XVI had used one or two hammers, sir, there would have been no revolution in France, cricket or no cricket. Good riddance to them, I say." He stared at the pitch as a new burst of applause rippled over the ground. "My God, you've won."

The Derleth people were running across the pitch, to surround Trum and slap him on the shoulders, and eventually to chair him, laughing and protesting, and bring him up to the marquee in triumph.

"Fifty-one runs, Mr. Haggard, and not out," Mr. Shotter said enthusiastically. "There is a remarkable score. Why, sir, I will submit his name to the Marylebone Club. He is a batsman of parts, sir."

"I am too old for this sort of thing," Trum panted as he was set in their midst. "I shall be stiff as a board in the morning."

"You are a hero, Trum," Alice said, putting her arm round his waist. "To these people you are a hero."

"And indeed he should be, Miss Alice," Shotter said. "I have never seen a finer inning."

"Congratulations, Major Sparrow," Hutchinson said grimly. "If you've a mind to move to Benligh, I'll find a position for you. Indeed I will."

"Derleth is my home, Hutchinson," Trum said, shaking Roger's hand.

"Beer for the team, Nugent," Roger said, beginning the walk back to the house. "For both teams. You'll be staying for supper, Hutchinson."

"Kind of you, Haggard. Kind of you. Why . . ." He paused as they approached the patio, and faced the Countess of Alderney.

"Mama," Jane screamed, and ran forward.

"Why, Mina." Haggard followed his wife. "What a pleasant surprise."

"I came as soon as I got your letter," Mina said, kissing them each in turn. "Is it really true?"

"We think so, Mama," Jane said. "Three months."

"Then it *must* be true. I am so happy for you." Mina linked arms with them, ignoring the rest of the party. "But I am surprised at you, Haggard. Cricket, is it? With a campaign to be fought?"

"Campaign?"

She frowned at him. "You are aware that Parliament has been dissolved?"

"Indeed I am."

"And that the country is in a ferment? Thus the dissolution, indeed. The Tories know they have tyrannized us far too long. We shall topple them, Haggard. I know it. But we shall need every man. I know you have no opposition here in Derleth, but yet I would have thought an assembly like you have here today would be ideal for an address. A man's caliber is tested by his demeanor on the hustings."

"Ah," Haggard said, walking them slowly up the stairs to the drawing room, while the others trailed behind. "I have not yet decided to stand."

Mina stopped, and as her arm was linked with his, he and Jane stopped also. "Not decided? You mean you'll not take your seat?"

"That is exactly it. I cannot see myself away at Westminster with Jane confined. My heart would not be in it."

"My dear Haggard, you astound me. Of course you must take your seat. We need you. But anyway, you will go mad, sitting up here in Derleth with no politics to distract you."

"I doubt that."

They resumed their climb. "I see, you will play cricket."

"I have no talent in that direction. I shall work, my dear

Mina. You probably have no idea what is involved in being squire of Derleth."

"Perhaps you should tell me."

"Well . . . I am about to deepen my mine. We have worked out the best surface coal, yet the seam runs deep, deep into the hills there. But to do that I must improve the conditions for my miners. You know Davy?"

"He has a detestable wife."

"I've not met her. But he is a brilliant man. I am purchasing some of his new arc lamps. They enable a man to see in the dark as no lantern can do. Then, I have my people developing a new strain of worsted thread, somewhat stronger than the material we have hitherto been producing. The clothes it will make will be less elegant, perhaps, but far stronger. And then, why, I am importing some Jersey bulls, to improve my strain here on the farm. Now, that is going to be quite fascinating—"

"Lamps," Mina cried. "Thread. Bulls, my God. Haggard, I despair of you. Jane, you should see to your guests." She squeezed Haggard's arm, led him toward the windows. "Domestic bliss is all very well, my dear boy. But there is more to life than wallowing in either a bed or a farmyard."

"I will not quarrel with you, Mina," he said. "Tell me of Byron."

"Oh, *him*. Well, when last heard, he was in Venice, or Ravenna, or some such place; now he wallows in dissipation, which is at least a pleasurable occupation. Speaking of which, my darling, you know my views on intercourse with pregnant women, so I sincerely hope you have given it up, with Jane. On the other hand, I would not have you spilling your splendid seed all over the ground, or into some serving maid. I think I shall take up residence in Derleth for the next few months. That way I shall be able to guide you. In your campaign, of course."

Haggard freed his hand, leaned forward to kiss her on the nose. "Your place is in London, dear mother-in-law. I'm afraid you would find Derleth too boring to bear. There will be absolutely nothing for you to *do*."

"Excellent," said Dr. Maltby. "Excellent. Your wife, Mr. Haggard, is one of those remarkable creatures specifically designed for the bearing of children. Well, I suppose you could say that all the delightful members of the fair sex were so designed by God, but shall we say some have more felicity in that direction than others. Mrs. Haggard, why, not only is she healthy and young and strong, but her equanimity of spirit is quite marvelous. I assure you, sir, that while I shall of course take every precaution and visit her at least twice a week from now on, neither you nor I have anything to fear. Anything at all, sir."

"You're a reassuring fellow, Maltby," Haggard said. "I suppose I worry because both my mother and my stepmother died in childbirth."

"More than twenty years ago, sir. Twenty-six years. Our science has advanced a long way in twenty years."

"Indeed it must have done. Well, have another glass of port."

"Bless you, sir, but I must be on my way back to Derby. I've other patients to attend to. I'll wish you good-bye, sir, and I'll be in again on Wednesday."

Nugent was waiting to show him out. Haggard climbed the stairs to the tower suite he had taken for Jane and himself, smiled at her. "How do you feel?"

"Ravenous. But he says I mustn't eat too much. I'd love a nice cold ice cream."

"I shall have some made up immediately."

She squeezed his hand. "You poor darling. Here am I, starting to resemble a barrel of beer, and able to do nothing but lie about the place. You must be bored out of your mind. Why don't you go down to London for a week?"

"I don't think I'm the most popular fellow there," he confessed. "With either party." Because although he had accepted his election, he had not yet taken his seat, despite urgent calls from both the Tory and the Whig whips, as the increased Whig representation—only part of Mina's hopes had been fulfilled, and the Tories still commanded a reduced majority—had begun to challenge the government's program of continued restraint and repression. "Anyway, I've more than enough to do here, with drilling my fine fellows."

For he had decided to form his own troop of yeomanry, in Derleth. Not only did the idea appeal to him, as an ex-soldier, and to Trum, but it seemed to him that this was a far more positive way of keeping his people happy than playing at cricket. He was supplying his men with horses, and with uniforms, in royal blue with red facings, and dragoon helmets, all at tremendous expense, but the miners and mill-workers were delighted to strut the main street on parade afternoons, showing off their finery to the girls and describing what they would do to any Frenchman who dared show his nose in Derleth, supposing such a thing were ever possible. Men banding together with an *esprit de corps* and a common objective, his years of soldiering reminded him, were men prepared to work together, and if need be, suffer together, for the reputation of their regiment, or, in this case, their village.

If only their parades, and the other numerous activities in which he busied himself as squire of Derleth, could keep *him* happy. Was he then damned to a lifetime of restless consideration because of a lifetime of soldiering? Was having everything any man could desire, from a lovely wife to a splendid home and a prosperous and successful life, never to be sufficient? Or was it, terribly, unthinkably, that while Jane was Mina's daughter, and like her in almost every way, she was still Jane and not Mina? For a man to realize he does not love his wife is one of the most heart-searching of all circumstances, certainly where *she* has been blameless.

But the most terrible realization of all was that he no longer dreamed of Mina, either.

He sat his horse in the park to watch his company performing their maneuvers, controlled by Trum with all the energy of a drill sergeant, leaping on and off their trotting mounts, drawing their sabers and presenting them, making mock charges, all with the complete earnestness of boys with new toys. Which is what he supposed they were.

"Well done, Trum," he said. "Well done. Dismiss them now." The best part of the day, because on drill afternoons, twice a week, they each received a free glass of ale at the inn, paid for by the squire. So, he supposed, he was shamelessly buying their affection and their respect. But in keeping his very limited body of electors happy, he was doing nothing more than was practiced by every Tory squire in the country. And he was succeeding; Derleth was an oasis of peace and tranquillity, and even comparative prosperity, in the seething caldron of discontent and riot that was the North and Midlands.

A groom was waiting to take his horse as he dismounted at the patio, strolled along to where Lindy was seated, watching Strolo crawl at her feet. And felt his heartbeat quicken, because Jane was pregnant, because he had so foolishly refused her invitation to go up to London and lose himself in the arms of a whore, or even her own mother. It had to be no more than that.

"You've done wonders with them," she said. "Considering it has only been two months. I must confess I doubted they'd ever drill after that first afternoon."

"Men will always drill." Haggard took off his helmet, sat beside her. "It is in their nature, to be herded."

"That's very cynical."

"I spent more than twenty years as a soldier."

"I keep forgetting," she admitted. "One always thinks of soldiers as hard, aggressive men." She smiled. "Not you at all. But both you and your brother seem to have it in your blood."

"God knows where we got it." He took two glasses of port from Nugent's tray, gave one to her. This had become a daily ritual; apart from her wine with dinner, she did not otherwise drink. He watched her as she sipped. They had never talked, since that first morning, about anything important. About her. There was so much he wanted to ask her, so much he wanted to discover. But would not that merely put him in the same class as Johnnie, fascinated because he was sitting beside a beautiful woman who had been raped? Was not that the quality which had first attracted him to Meg, although he would never have admitted it? Poor, poor Meg. He hoped she was happy, in her log hut on the shores of Sydney Bay, or wherever she was now situated.

"Penny," Lindy said with her quick smile. "For a moment there you looked uncommonly serious."

"I was thinking about you, as a matter of fact."

Her smile faded. "There's an unprofitable subject."

"Can any human being be an unprofitable subject?"

She glanced at him, then stooped to pick up Strolo. "Time for his supper, I think."

Haggard stood beside her. "I'll carry him."

"You?"

"Well . . ." He flushed. "Don't you suppose I should get into practice?"

"I had not considered that." She allowed him to take the little boy.

"I have also been thinking," he said as they climbed the stairs together. "About his future."

"It is not a subject I dare consider."

"Well, I think you should. Will you choose Harrow, or Eton? I went to Eton, and Johnnie to Harrow. So you can have an opinion on each product."

She glanced at him, a slow flush filling her cheeks. "He would not be accepted at either."

"What nonsense. He is a Haggard."

"He has no Haggard blood, Roger."

"Then he is a Haggard by proxy, as he will certainly be by adoption and upbringing. I propose to deal with him as I will with my own. Well, save in the matter of inheritance, of course. But I do promise you he will never want."

They had reached the top of the stairs. Now she faced him. "Why? For God's sake, why? I am nothing to you. My mother hated your father with all the venom of a cobra. She does still hate the very name of Haggard. Don't you realize that? Her sole ambition is to get her hands on Haggard's Penn. That's why I'm here. Don't you understand *that*?"

Haggard snapped his fingers, and a footman emerged from the servants' corridor. "I'm going to give Master Strolo a treat tonight, Haskin," he said. "And let him be fed by the maids. Mind you don't overdo it, now."

"But . . ." Lindy began.

Roger touched her lip with his finger. "I think you and I should talk. We haven't talked for some time."

She gazed at him, her eyes wide. They were the most splendid blue eyes he had ever seen. My God, Haggard, he thought. Be careful what you do here. Be careful. But it was not a process that could be stopped. Already he was showing her into the privacy of his office.

She stood before the desk, her back to him, while he closed the door. A tall, young woman, slender without being thin, with long golden hair and a mass of freckles. And the most beautiful breast he had ever seen. A breast which led his mind into so many dangerous channels. Would there be freckles on her body as well? Would her pubic hair be pale or dark? Would her legs be as delightful as the rest of her? Would she moan, or purr, or laugh, at the moment of orgasm?

His brother's wife. Who had suffered the ultimate fate to which any woman can be exposed. He was, then, no different at all from Johnnie. As she would know.

He closed the door, came round the desk. "I'm not going

to lecture you," he said. "Please sit down."

She remained standing, her blue eyes absolutely steady. "I think I should leave Derleth," she said.

He shook his head. "Never. You will never leave here, Lindy."

She opened her mouth, faint color creeping up from her neck to fill her cheeks, and he stretched out his hand and drew the forefinger down the line of her jaw. "You *will* have to kill me, first."

Almost she smiled. "That was fear. I don't think I would ever fear you, Roger Haggard." Her hand went up and closed on his wrist, holding it against her cheek. "But I cannot stay. Not now."

"Did you know this would happen?"

She hesitated, and then sighed, and nodded. "I knew it *was* happening. But I thought . . . It is how almost every man looks at me, and thinks of me, because when a man who knows of me thinks of me, he sees me lying in the dust of that canefield, or hanging from that triangle. I am a *thought* to men, Roger, an obscene thought. Never a woman. Never a person."

"And now you have changed your mind?"

She shook her head. "Now I no longer care. I think to myself: If only Johnnie had been the least like you."

He leaned across the desk, and she closed her eyes. He brushed her lips with his, felt her breath on his face. When he moved his head back, her eyes were open again.

"But I must go," she said. "Jane has befriended me. And she is to be a mother. I am Johnnie's wife. I must go."

"No," he said, and went round the desk to take her in his arms. "No." He held her close, kissed her mouth. After a moment her lips parted, and her tongue touched his; then her hands got between them and she pushed him away.

"It will be a crime."

"My crime." Roger Haggard, son of John. There could no longer be any doubt. John Haggard had told the world: Hate me if you will, I am Haggard, and will pursue my own destiny. Could his son really expect to be any better than that?

Her head was shaking. "I do not know if I can love. I will scream. I will hate it. And you."

He kissed her again. "You can love, Lindy. You have just proved that."

Her eyes were shut again. "They did not kiss my mouth, Roger. Nor did Johnnie. They did not kiss my mouth."

He put his arm round her waist, walked her to the door.

"The servants . . ." she said.

"Will consider nothing. Walk in front of me, up the stairs, and to your room."

He opened the door, and she stepped outside. She climbed the stairs before him, her shoes emerging from the hem of her gown and disappearing again, her hair moving slightly. My God, Roger Haggard, he thought, what are you doing? But she wants it. Lindy, magnificent, tortured Lindy, *wants* it, however she may fight it. She wants you. She loves you. She wants to be loved by you. His heart seemed to be swelling out of his chest.

But what you are doing is a crime. A crime to Jane, a crime to your unborn child. A crime in the eyes of the law and a crime in the eyes of the church.

And most of all, a crime to Lindy herself. But not if you can make her happy, even for a moment. A lover's logic.

And irrelevant. Only a bullet in the brain was going to stop him now.

They reached the upper hall, and she hesitated. They had passed two footmen on the way. But there was no cause for comment. The squire and his sister-in-law were on their way to dress for the evening. He touched her hand and she moved again, opened the bedchamber door. He glanced up and down the empty corridor, stepped inside behind her. The door closed, and she leaned back against him, her eyes once more shut. His arms went round her waist, clasped themselves on her stomach, wishing to move, afraid to move.

"Don't let me scream," she said. "Don't let me scream."

His hands came up slowly, parting, each one to hold a breast, through gown and petticoat, to feel them swell as she inhaled, to feel her head flop back against his shoulder, her mouth working.

One hand went round her shoulders, the other under her knees as he swept her from the floor, carried her across the sitting room and into the bedchamber itself. Her eyes remained shut, but her lips continued to move, and her face was twisted. He had thought, at Mina Favering's reception, that his decision whether to remain with the gentlemen or accompany her might be the most important of his life. This was the most important moment of Lindy's life, and her entire future was in his hands.

He laid her on the bed, stooped to kiss her lips. This time they opened readily, and suddenly her tongue was hungry. But she did not move. She was surrendering herself, entirely. But how to undress a woman who has once had the clothes torn from her body, and not reawake her agony?

He slipped her shoes from her feet, stooped to kiss her stockinged toes. A slow ripple of feeling trickled up her legs. Her skirts were back to her knees, and he need never have feared. Her legs were but a part of the splendid whole.

He straightened, and she rolled away from him, presenting her back, the buttons which followed the course of her spine. Slowly he undid them, stooping to kiss the nape of her neck, his lips parting the golden hair, and then the middle of her back. No freckles here, but the whitest skin he had ever known. She rolled back again, and this time her eyes were open, watching him, her mouth still twisted. Almost she seemed to be holding her breath.

He kissed her mouth, and she raised her thighs for him to slip the gown down, and lay it on a chair. Now she breathed quickly and tumultuously, as he eased the straps for her petticoat from her shoulders, removed them as well, gazed at her corset, and lower. Dark hair, like silk, splendidly luxuriant. He lowered his head, and her knees came up. He waited, his mouth only an inch from her flesh, and felt her hand take his. Then slowly her knees went down again, her legs lay straight. When he kissed her she shuddered, and then he felt her hands on his head, pressing him harder into herself.

The door to the outer room opened, and they heard Mary Prince talking to Strolo. Haggard remained still, kneeling beside the bed, afraid to move. Roger Haggard, squire of Derleth, afraid in one of his own bedchambers. But it was only for the woman.

And it was unnecessary. She slid from beneath him, got out of bed, pulled on her undressing robe, and opened the door, just wide enough to allow herself through, closing it behind her.

"Has he been a good boy?" she asked, her voice as calm as ever.

"Oh, yes," Mary said. "He ate all his dinner."

"Ma," Strolo said. "Ma."

"Bedtime," Lindy said. "I'll see to it."

"Yes, Mrs. Haggard."

Roger listened to the door closing, pushed himself to his feet. He opened the bedroom door, watched her bending over the cot, her hair clouding forward to either side of her face.

"Sleep," she said. "Go to sleep, my dearest."

Strolo gurgled, and commenced to suck his thumb. Lindy straightened, blew him a kiss, turned slowly, gazed at Haggard. But he could do nothing. He did not know if the spell had been broken, if they were to be saved from themselves.

As if two people, who want so very badly, can ever be saved from themselves. Lindy blew out the candle nearest the cot, came back across the floor, noiseless in her stocking feet. She stood beside him, and waited, and was in his arms. Now her arms went round him, her hands tight on his back and shoulders, and now he could crush her against him and know that she wanted.

And that she would not scream.

"What will you do?" Emma had once asked him. "What will you do?" And he had thought: I am Haggard. I can do anything. But not everything. Lindy knew that, and thus she did not ask. A man may not marry his brother's wife, even be she a widow, much less after a divorce.

She lay with her head on his arm, her face tucked into his chest, half-smothered by her hair. She breathed slowly and evenly; he could feel her breath on his chest. As it was a warm evening, they had not used the covers, and he could look down the long white sheen of her body. She did possess the most beautiful breasts he had ever seen, empty of milk now, and thus smaller than when he had first looked at them, but still perfectly shaped, with eager, alert nipples. Her small bottom and her long legs were the answer to a dream. But her physical delight was only a fraction of the woman. Over the past seven years, after so many years of abstinence, he had come to know four women in rapid succession, from the eager squirming of Meg Bold, through the utter passion of Mina Favering, to the cool sophistication of his wife. But now there was Lindy. One does not fall in love with a woman simply by taking her to bed. But one can become aware that the possibility of love is there. And where the woman is also aware of the possibility, love is already on its way.

But did she love? Could she love? Or did her silent ecstasy, the smile that had lit up her face, the soft murmur of contentment as her body had moved against his, merely signify the end of the mental agony she had endured for too long?

And did it matter? A man may not marry his brother's wife. A man may not *love* his brother's wife. Once that is conceded, all else is meaningless.

He raised himself on his elbow, looked down on her face. "This is your home," he said. "Now and forever."

She gazed at him, waiting, for something more, or something less.

"Now and forever," he said.

Because he was Haggard, and he could do anything. A man who can do anything can also do nothing, with equal success. So then, he thought, in a continuous spasm of guilty self-condemnation, there is the final end of Roger Haggard, the knight-errant who would set right every ill perpetrated by his father. He could condemn even his own reforms in Derleth. His mill might be the most sanitary in the country, but it still contained men and women working in endless repetition, far from the sun and the refreshing breeze. His miners might use the latest equipment, but they still inhaled coal dust as they penetrated deeper and deeper into the earth. And in Barbados his slaves still suffered under the lash, he had no doubt at all; certainly profits had picked up since the revolt, which suggested Johnnie had hardened his attitude considerably since the breakup of his marriage. His lack of political interest might be a personal matter, however irritating to those who sought his support, but whereas Liverpool and the Tories merely regarded him as lazy, Russell and the Whigs had no doubt that he was in reality Tory to the backbone, an opinion confirmed when he made one of his rare visits to Westminster to vote against Burdett's absurd ideas for the reformation of Parliament. "No doubt," he said, "the honorable member is correct in supposing that this great institution must at some time bring its composition into line with the changing face of British society, but *his* proposals would place the nation in a condition of holding a continuous election, to the detriment of business and government."

The bill would have been lost anyway, as the Tories possessed a sufficient majority, but whereas he was congratulated on his speech by the Prime Minister himself, his erstwhile Whig friends pointedly refused to shake his hand. Even

Mina abandoned any discussion of politics with him, however he remained her favorite son-in-law.

While his domestic arrangements did not bear consideration in the rational light of day. Henry Haggard posed no problem. It was, as Dr. Maltby had prophesied, an easy birth, soon after the turn of 1819. But then, Jane needed time to recover, and she also wished to feed the boy herself. "I know I am being a perfect beast, Roger," she said. "And I do assure you that I miss your embrace as much as I know you miss mine. But for the needs of the flesh, why, I am sure you can discover a pretty child among the maids to please you, for the moment. I just do not wish to know of it."

A pretty child among the maids. No doubt, he supposed, the maids did know of it. With the utmost discretion it is simple enough for a chambermaid to decide when a bed has contained two people rather than one, especially when those two people are lovers. But he was the squire, and he could do what he wished, even with his sister-in-law. The maids might shed a sigh that he had chosen her rather than one of them; they were not likely to permit their gossip to reach the ears of their mistress.

While Lindy remained, simply Lindy. Haggard deduced that she had always been a thoughtful, introspective girl, as much from her conversation as from his observation of her. The burden of being a Campkin, and therefore by derivation a Bolton, she had always found a heavy one, just as she had found the position of constant companion to her mother, following the departure of her two elder sisters, a source of continual embarrassment. The disaster of her marriage, the catastrophe of her rape, had merely turned her even more in on herself. He deduced that she had had some sort of a breakdown, and indeed it would have been surprising had she not. Out of it all she had rescued one prop to her sanity and her womanhood, her child. But as he was the principal cause of her condemnation and exile, he was not a reason for joy, but rather for possessive love, complete dedication to his health and his future, for only in his success could she envisage any reason for her to continue living.

As this was undoubtedly an unhealthy attitude, he could reason that he had almost acted the doctor, and not only in restoring her confidence in herself as a woman. Now she had two interests in life, and if she seldom smiled in conversation, and he despaired of ever hearing her laugh, the eagerness with which she reached for him, the expression of utter pleasure on her face when she held him in her arms, could leave him in no doubt that he provided the only real happiness in her life. They never discussed the rights and wrongs of the situation. He would not have dared in any event, for fear of losing her, but in fact he doubted she ever considered them. Her concern, apart from loving him, was not to become herself pregnant, and this she managed admirably, although whether by good fortune or some West Indian skill, he could not be sure. She had realized that he was the only true happiness she was ever likely to find, and she was not prepared to analyze the situation into guilt and conscience. Thus their relationship did not even affect her manner with Jane. The two women remained the best of friends, with Jane obviously delighted that her sister-in-law was settling in to contentment in Derleth.

So could a man ask for anything more? A beautiful and obviously prolific wife, an equally attractive and utterly compelling mistress. Save that he loved the mistress and not the wife. With every day this became more obvious to him. Jane was everything that the wife of the wealthiest man in England should be, a glittering jewel set in the Derbyshire countryside to attract attention from miles around. But like the diamond she resembled, there was no softness, no true affection in her character. She had enjoyed sex with him before her pregnancy, and he had no doubt at all she was looking forward to it again when she considered herself ready for it; like her mother, she could transport herself into ecstatic convulsions of pure physical pleasure, and as he was her husband, that animal delight was devoted to him—but he could not escape the feeling that it would not have troubled her a great deal had her husband been someone else, provided he also was endowed with a penis and a pair of hands and inexhaustable wealth. Similarly she managed his household with effortless efficiency, but utterly cold efficiency as well. The slightest shortfall in anything, be it a slice of meat too few on a plate or the breaking of a china cup, was deducted from the culprit's wages; untidiness among the maids was rewarded with a whipping, carried out with relentless vigor by Mary Prince under the eyes of the mistress herself. Almost as if the girls had been slaves, Haggard thought, listening to one fifteen-year-old wailing in time to the crack of the cane. As no doubt they were, slaves.

And now there could be no doubt that she would be bringing up her son in the same atmosphere of ice-cold efficiency.
No doubt correctly. Roger supposed he was in no position to
judge. *He* had been brought up by his black nurse and then
by Emma, and neither had possessed the necessary character
for the imposition of discipline, while Father, during the
years in Barbados, had been totally uninterested in his children. The first time they had clashed, indeed, had been the
beginning of their total estrangement, and if Roger had then
been pitchforked into the grim realities of life at Eton and
soon the even grimmer realities of life as a private soldier, it
had seemed to him a personal misfortune rather than a realization that he was for the first time joining the mainstream of
the country's youth. So no doubt, he supposed, he should be
grateful to his wife for supplying the domestic discipline he
would be incapable of implementing.

But none of these obvious virtues made her a lovable character. Even she had not yet risked attempting to impose her
strict pattern of life upon her husband, but he suspected that
this too was a future prospect, as she grew older and more set
in her ways. But that future, or any future, was not something that he was prepared to contemplate. If it loomed, filled
with problems and potential disasters, nationally as well as
domestically as the government continued to answer expression with repression on an increasing scale, here in Derleth the summer of 1819 was the most splendid he had ever
known, with cricket matches every week, with an improving
economy as the Bank of England at last found itself able to
resume specie payment, which meant there was actually some
cash to be obtained, and as he could move with pride between his healthy son and his beautiful wife, and his utterly
entrancing mistress. It was a summer he wished never to end.

But summers always do.

James Hutchinson of Benligh bristled, as ever. "Drilling,"
he said, walking up and down the drawing room of Derleth
Manor and waving his arms. "Bands of six and seven thousand men, drilling, sir. Well, now, if that is not incipient
revolution, I should like you to tell me what is. This fellow
Hunt is behind it, of course, a very devil, sir. A latter-day
Robespierre, to be sure."

It was a delightfully warm August afternoon, and the windows stood wide. Derleth valley hummed with contented ac-

tivity. And outside, it seemed, the world hummed with *dis*contented activity.

"I had no idea things had reached such a pass," Haggard confessed.

"Well, sir, if I may be so bold, you remain here in a fool's paradise. Oh, aye, everyone knows that Derleth people are better off than any others, thanks to your generosity. Misguided generosity, if I may say so, Haggard. A villain is a villain, and there's an end to it."

"But our people here on Derleth are hardly villains, Mr. Hutchinson," Jane protested. She sat on the window seat, her sewing on her lap, so that she could keep an eye both on Henry and Strolo, in the garden with Lindy.

"They'll sing the *ca ira* along with the rest of them, madam," Hutchinson said. "You may mark my words. The rumor is that these scoundrels, Hunt and Healey and the rest, are saying that next Sunday is their *last* drill day. Now, Haggard, does that not sound sinister to you?"

"I suppose it must do."

"Then you'll lend support? We need reliable men. And yours are that."

Jane smiled. "Five minutes ago you described them as scoundrels."

"I did not refer to those who have donned uniforms, Mrs. Haggard," Hutchinson pointed out.

"And that is almost every able-bodied man in Derleth," she replied. "We muster eighty."

"You shall not be alone, of course. I am taking my own troop, and there will be regulars as well, a regiment of hussars and one of foot. Why, I believe there will even be a muster of artillery, as well as the special constabulary."

"Does that not seem an inordinate amount of force, Mr. Hutchinson?" Alice Sparrow asked quietly. "To disperse a public meeting?"

"Public meeting, madam? Why, it is an illegal gathering. The Manchester magistrates have warned these people, publicly and repeatedly, that such a monster gathering will not be permitted. And *they* have announced their intention of proceeding, despite all. Well, madam, to my mind that is revolution. It smacks of 1789, or worse."

"I had heard their intention was to present a petition to Parliament," Trum suggested.

"Petition, sir, petition? Why, that is their declared purpose, to be sure. But consider this, sir. They are meeting in Manchester. I am told a gathering of forty thousand is anticipated. And from there they will march on London. Now consider, sir, that is an army I have just described. An army which will gain strength with every mile. Why, sir, I can see half a million men before they reach the Thames. What then, sir? What then?"

Haggard and Trum exchanged glances.

"And don't tell me it can never happen here, sir," Hutchinson insisted. "I was in town during the Gordon Riots, in 1780. Just a lad I was then. But the city was in the hands of the mob for three days. It was not something I propose to forget."

"Aye, well," Haggard said. "As you put it that way . . ."

"You'll lend support? I knew you would."

"It seems the devil of a way to ride," Trum complained. "All the way to Manchester, for an hour's meeting?"

"Your men will be looked after, sir. And yourselves. Oh, indeed. I can vouch for that."

Haggard sighed. "Well, then, my people will be there. Here's my hand on it."

Because even Jane, daughter of the most liberal countess in the realm, could see the necessity of quashing such a possibility before it could gather strength. Lindy was even more concerned. "I had supposed such things could only happen in Barbados," she said.

Haggard kissed her nose. "Believe me, they are likely to be less dangerous there than anywhere else. Save that here we command more force with which to oppose them."

She clung to him. "You'll take no risks."

It was her first-ever vocal confession of her feelings for him. "You have naught to fear, my darling. I have written you into my will."

"Do you think I am concerned about money? Or lack of it? You are the only man I . . ." She hesitated, and sighed. "I care for only two people in the world. Without either of you I should have no wish to continue living."

Another kiss. "The finest soldiers in Europe spent twenty years trying to dent my flesh, my darling. They succeeded twice, in twenty years, and neither was fatal. I'm not likely to succumb to a mob."

But he was uneasy. Not about himself. He remembered too well the furious enthusiasm with which Hutchinson and

Richardson had led their men into Lowden. That there had been no bloodshed on that occasion had been entirely because the men of Lowden had been, literally, drunk with their apparent victory and unable to raise a finger to defend themselves. But on this occasion . . .

"Colonel Lestrange," said the mustachioed regular. "Colonel Haggard, is it?" He shook hands. "It is a pleasure, sir, indeed a pleasure, to meet someone with your distinguished record. Alas, sir, I was unable to take my part in the fight against the French. I envy you, sir, upon my soul I do."

"It was an experience, to be sure," Roger agreed. "I'd have you meet my adjutant, Major Sparrow."

"My pleasure, sir, my pleasure." Lestrange beamed at the eighty troopers. "What a splendid turnout. It is well said, sir, that the men of Derleth are the equal of any in the land."

Roger glanced at the hussars, all red jackets and capes, at the infantry, in their gray trousers and tall shakos, at the blue-clad artillerymen, and wondered how many times Lestrange had used those very words this morning. Such an array of soldiers looked out-of-place amid the gables and gutters of an English town.

"You flatter us, sir. May I ask to have a word with Sir John Byng?"

"Ah," Lestrange said. "Well, sir, Sir John is not present today."

"Not present? I understand he is military commander of the area."

"Indeed he is, sir, but the magistrates thought it best not to inform him of their dispositions."

Roger put up his hand to scratch his head, remembered he was in uniform. "You'll consider me a dolt, sir," he said. "But are you not a regular soldier?"

"Indeed, Colonel Haggard. The Thirty-first. Those are my fellows over there."

"And do you not take your orders from General Byng?"

"Well, sir, it is a knotty point. General Byng does not consider civil disturbances, the possibility of civil disturbances, to be in the proper province of the military. He is confident that a suitable force of special constables should be sufficient to deal with any such situation. I do not happen to agree, and being in command of the Manchester garrison, I have placed my men under the orders of the magistrates, for this day, at least."

Roger glanced at the half-dozen very well fed gentlemen who were at this moment drinking port in front of the inn.

"And they, Colonel Haggard, have been good enough to ask me to command all the military present. So, sir, I would be grateful if you'd take your instructions from me."

Roger looked at Trum, who waggled his eyebrows.

"Well, sir," Roger decided, "as I have agreed to lend my people to the preservation of law and order, I feel obliged to accept. I have the confidence as a retired regular myself, that I shall be required to do nothing contrary to my honor."

"Indeed, sir, on that you may rely. My orders are these. The meeting is to take place in an open area called Peter's Field, not far from here. Now, sir, it would be unjust for us to occupy the field to prevent its use by anyone about his lawful business. On the other hand, should it be used for an unlawful purpose, it is our responsibility to disperse and arrest the lawbreakers. I would therefore have you position your men on the southern road leading to the field, and remain there until you receive further instructions. Instructions which I fervently hope will not be necessary."

"Amen," Roger agreed, and gave the orders for his men to walk their horses out. "But tell me, Trum, what would you do in this position?"

"I'd occupy the square," Trum said. "And the hell with justice. The surest way to keep order is utterly to prevent any risk of *dis*order."

Roger nodded, and smiled at the people who had assembled to gawp at the soldiers. There were a great many of them. And there were already a great number of people in the square itself. But hardly well-drilled revolutionaries. Here were men and women out for an afternoon stroll; ribbons and parasols were everywhere, children laughed and screamed as they ran to and fro, lovers smiled.

"These," Trum said, and pointed his gauntleted finger. Approaching them down the street opposite was a very large body of people, not fewer than five thousand, Roger estimated. But again, there were very nearly a third of them women, and while they marched in good order, and obeyed the commands of their stewards, he could perceive not a single weapon, not even a stick, among them. So much for Hutchinson's prating about revolution, he decided; we have had a journey to Manchester for nothing. On the other hand, he supposed it was a useful exercise for his company.

"That's Ramford," Trum said, using his glass.

"I thought he was rather a moderate," Roger remarked.

"I'm sure he is," Trum agreed. "Question is, whether his people are."

"There's another lot." Roger pointed at another very large body of men and women debouching into the square.

"And another," Trum said.

They watched the square fill, with perhaps twenty thousand people, jostling together, exchanging greetings, very good-humored, and still without a sign of arms, so far as Roger could see.

"No sign of Hunt, as yet," Trum remarked.

Roger was more interested in the military, which, having allowed the people through, were slowly taking up their positions around the square. Most of them were in solid bodies, but he noticed that the local yeomanry were somewhat dispersed, and indeed almost mingling with the crowd, over to the north.

His attention was distracted by the arrival of a horse and cart in which there were three gentlemen. This came to a halt before the platform, and two of the men stepped down, while the several musicians in the crowd struck up tunes such as "Rule Britannia" and "God Save the King." The crowd roared their approval, while the man who had remained in the cart, and who was obviously "Orator" Hunt, the leading figure of the radical movement, held up his hands for silence.

When at last he began to speak, removing his white hat and waving it in front of him, the crowd fell silent for a moment, although Roger could hardly hear what was being said, when suddenly there was a shout of "Soldiers!"

It was impossible to decide who had raised the alarm, nor did it make much sense, as the presence of the soldiers was obvious to everyone there. Yet the cry had the entire vast crowd heaving and swaying, and suddenly closing upon the Lancashire yeomanry, divided, as he had earlier noticed, into groups of twos and threes at the far end of the square. Voices were raised, there was a great deal of noise, over which Hunt and his fellow principals vainly called for silence.

Colonel Lestrange himself suddenly appeared beside the Derleth yeomanry.

"Cavalry," he said. "Horses. You must extricate those fellows, Colonel Haggard."

"Use the hussars," Roger suggested.

"No, no. Regulars should be used only in an emergency. I
wish you to ride your fellows across the square and disperse
that mob."

"And I, sir, am of the opinion that these people mean no
harm," Roger protested.

"You volunteered your support, sir," Lestrange shouted,
going red in the face. "And having done that, I am your
commanding officer."

"I accept that, sir," Roger retorted. "I am merely asking
you to consider the situation more carefully. This crowd is
perfectly civil, so far as I can make out. To introduce cavalry
into their midst—"

"Look, sir, look," Lestrange bawled, rising to his stirrups to
point. "Those are your fellows, sir, over there, being roughed
by the mob. You cannot stand by, Colonel Haggard. You
cannot." He drew his sword, waved it round his head. "Men
of Derbyshire," he shouted. "Charge those people."

"No," Roger called. "Stand fast."

But the yeomanry were already moving forward, swords
drawn, and those of the crowd nearest to them were shrink-
ing away, shouting their fear, sending a tremor of panic
through the entire vast gathering. Roger realized he could
bring his men under control only by placing himself at their
head, and urged his own mount forward.

" 'Tis Haggard," someone bawled. "He was at Lowden."

Roger looked left and right to discover who had spoken,
but it was too late. The cry was taken up, and the panic
spread. And now the yeomanry were crashing into people,
women and children as well as men, while to their left the
hussars were moving forward in support. The square became
a place of screaming fear, of falling bodies, of angry shouts,
of flying bonnets and tumbling legs. Desperately Roger tried
to stop his horse trampling those already on the ground, but
it was impossible to avoid them. Desperately he abandoned
the attempt in his anxiety to reach the front of his men, using
his knees and occasionally his boots to drive away those who
attempted to stop his progress, watching with a sickening
heart as the yeomanry, attempting to use the flats of their
swords, to be sure, yet sliced and cut to send the blood dribbling over the cobbles. And desperately he reached his position, rising in the stirrups to wave his arms and shout himself
hoarse, and eventually bring his men to a halt.

Peter's Field resembled a battlefield, with bodies scattered in clumps all over the cobbles, most still moving, if slowly and painfully, but too many lying in the awful stillness of unconsciousness or death. Those who had kept their feet continued to flee, jamming the approach roads as they wailed their fear and their horror and their anger. The principals remained on the platform in the center, now entirely surrounded by hussars, and clearly about to be arrested. And the soldiers stared in horror at what they had done. Trum's face was ashen, and he wiped his brow with a kerchief. Roger faced Lestrange, picking his way through the fallen. "A successful charge, Colonel Haggard," he said. "Oh, successful. They'll not try that again in a hurry."

Roger stared at him. "Try what, Colonel Lestrange?" he asked, his voice thick with outrage. Lestrange opened his mouth in surprise, and Roger pulled his horse past him. "You'll order these fellows and commence the march back to Derleth, Trum," he said. "We'll not billet here. We'll camp on the road."

"Aye," Trum agreed, and signaled the sergeant major. Roger rode in front of them, through the dead and the injured, listened to the curses surrounding his name, reached the inn where the magistrates had remained throughout the incident, surrounded by a body of special constabulary.

"There are men and women hurt over there," he said. "Have you no aid for them?"

"Radicals, Colonel Haggard," someone said. "We have no aid for Jacobins in Manchester."

Roger turned away, walked his horse down the street, encountered another horseman, gazed at Francis Burdett.

"Well, Haggard," Burdett said. "A proud day's work. You'll sleep easy in your bed this night." His face was white with suppressed rage and disgust.

But is mine any different? Roger wondered. "Who ordered this?" he asked.

Burdett shrugged. "Oh, the magistrates, to be sure. The city fathers. But they do nothing more than reflect the attitude of the government. The government you support, Haggard. The government composed of men like you, who buy their election, have never to answer to the country for their deeds and their misdeeds. Mark my words, Haggard, the people you rode over today will not forget. And one day you *will* have to answer."

Haggard stared at him. "Then answer I will," he said. "Ride with me, Francis."

"With you? I'd sooner follow a hearse."

"Ride with me," Haggard said. "For London. I wish to talk with Russell."

Burdett frowned at him. "You'll find no sympathy there, Haggard. When Russell hears of this . . ." He looked to left and right, and sighed. "His friendship, like mine, is kept for those who oppose Toryism, not those who support it, carry out its bidding."

"Aye," Roger said. "So ride with me, Frank. I'll bring Liverpool down. I swear it, if it takes me the rest of my life."

Chapter 2

The Exile

Jane Haggard and Alice stood in the doorway to watch their men return. "There has been some disaster here," Jane said.

"No disaster." Haggard swung himself from the saddle, took her in his arms. "Nothing like a disaster. Merely a massacre."

She pushed him away to stare at him, never having known such a bitter anger in her husband before. Then she looked at Burdett. "Frank?"

"The magistrates ordered a charge," he said.

"Oh, my God," Alice said. "Oh, my God."

"We need something to drink," Haggard said. "Trum, you'll dismiss the troop. Tell them no blame can attach to them; they but obeyed their orders. Tell Hatchard to see to their wants at the inn."

He turned, saluted his men. They stared at him in turn. They had indeed but obeyed their orders; there was not a man among them would not be haunted to his dying day.

"Wine," Jane said to Nugent, walking up the stairs with Roger's arm held tightly. "Were there many killed?"

He shook his head. "Six, at the last count."

"And some two hundred injured," Burdett added. "Women and children."

"It's not the injured," Haggard said. "It's not even the dead. It is the deed. It is the thought that this could have happened at any time in the past three years. It could have happened at Lowden, the way we so carelessly rode into the village with a company of half-trained troopers at our backs. It could have happened at Spa, or anywhere else. It could

217

happen again, with every day that Liverpool and his cronies sit at Westminster."

"What will you do?" Alice asked.

"A vote of censure, to begin with," Burdett said. "The very moment Parliament reassembles."

"And *you* will vote with the Whigs?" Jane inquired.

"Now, and forevermore," Haggard declared.

"Oh, Mama will be so pleased," she cried.

"You will be as unpopular in Derbyshire as ever Father was for being too hidebound a Tory," Alice pointed out.

"Well, perhaps I have courted popularity at too great a price." But his attention was wandering. He had returned, and she was not here. "Is Lindy well?"

"I think so," Jane agreed. "Like us all, she has been concerned these past few days."

"We had supposed fighting and killing were behind us," Alice said.

"So had I," Haggard said. "So had I. I'm for changing this uniform. It is not my proudest possession, at this moment. An early supper, Jane, my love. Frank and I must be off to London in the morning, to tell our friends what has happened, what we propose."

"Of course," she said. "I'll instruct Nugent. Francis, another glass."

Haggard left the room, heart beginning a slow pound. She had been as concerned as everyone else. And before he had left, she had for the first time shown that concern. That spirit, so long crushed, brought back to uneasy life by himself, was at last about to *feel* again.

He took the stairs three at a time, reached the top, and faced her.

She took a step forward, checked herself. Her mouth was slightly open, and color flared in her cheeks, causing the freckles to glow.

Haggard reached for her, held her shoulders, kissed her on the forehead. "I had thought you dead," she whispered.

"There was never any risk," he said. "Not to me." He was half-carrying her along the corridor toward her room. "Where's Strolo?"

"In the garden. Oh, Roger . . ."

The door was open, and they were inside; then it closed again, and he could kiss her eyes and her cheeks and her nose and her mouth, and feel her move against him. She moved as Meg had done, with the same instinctive abandon. But she had never moved like that before.

"If you were to die . . ." she said.

"You'll have to be patient." He laid her on her bed, as he had done that first time, and she caught his arm in alarm.

"At five in the afternoon? With Jane . . ."

"I have missed you," he said.

Always before, she had surrendered. He had never doubted her pleasure, but it had been passive, a requirement that he be gently insistent, that he accomplish his own purpose, and in doing that restore her to physical as well as mental sanity. But suddenly this changed. Suddenly she *loved*, as his knowledge of her told him she could never have loved before, but as so clearly she had always dreamed of loving, at least since her first taste of it with Johnnie. Suddenly he was the receiver, and Lindy entirely the giver. He was on his back and her lips moved from his throat to his knees, kissing and sucking, occasionally biting, softly. She moaned her pleasure, sat astride him and used her body as a weapon, drawing him up and laying him down again, lowering to kiss him and rearing upright again so that he could touch her breasts. He realized he was witnessing an emotional watershed, all the pent-up desire and fear and lust of a woman who had but scraped the surface of love, and loving, in the most vicious possible way, but who yet wanted to experience, wanted to feel, wanted to *do*.

He realized too that it was the supreme moment of his life, as a human being, to share such a moment with another.

He realized that he too was in love.

"A toast," Mina Favering said, raising her glass. "To the future."

"Where's the point in that?" her husband commented. "We failed. Your people failed, Russell."

"Well, what would you? A vote of no confidence is only effective if sufficient government supporters cross the floor. We obtained but one."

"But what an adherent," Mina said, linking her arm with Haggard's. "Worth an army in himself. Thus I toast the future. Do they not say that Canning cut you dead in the lobby yesterday morning, Roger?"

"Indeed he did. And several others besides."

"*They* know the importance of your voting with us. And we are going to have sufficient ammunition to dent their armor yet. You've heard of this ridiculous suggestion that Princess Caroline is to be divorced, and denied the title of queen? Oh, that will be a great occasion for sport, I promise you."

"At her expense," Burdett grumbled.

"At Liverpool's expense. And Canning's. And Peel's. And Huskisson's. And most of all at the butcher Wellington's expense. We'll make them crawl. And in time we'll bring them down. The country is with us."

"It's a pity you're only a woman, Mina," Russell said sadly. "I'd give a deal to have you sitting beside me on the front bench."

"Put Haggard there," Mina suggested. "We think alike. And now, supper. Roger is leaving early in the morning. He wishes to get home to Jane and Harry. And whoever is next on the agenda."

She was excited, and febrile, and delighted. As much by the change in his opinions as by the news that Jane was again pregnant. He had not intended that. But how may a man not sleep with his wife when she is beautiful and passionate and once again in the best of health? For were she ever to find out that his heart was elsewhere . . . He wondered if he feared her. More probably, he supposed, he feared her mother. Mina believed in the most open-ended of marriages, but these flights of fancy should be abovestairs affairs, worn on the sleeve, and never should cross the bounds of blood or perversion.

But Lindy, utterly magnificent Lindy. He could not truly understand it. She was not so beautiful as Jane, and if no doubt the Boltons, as among the very oldest of planting families, would consider their blood to be as blue as that of the Faverings, her birth and upbringing were not so readily apparent. Nor was she as lasciviously passionate as either Jane or her mother. But she *loved*. In every movement, every touch of her hand, every ripple of her smile, every flick of her golden hair. With Jane and Mina he had never been able to escape the feeling that their attitudes and even their movements were deliberate. They seemed to say to themselves: We are to make love, therefore we must throw abandon out of the window. Much as they might say: We are to take a ride in the country, therefore we may as well gallop. With Lindy everything was real. She needed to be awakened, to an awareness of herself, and of him. But the pleasure in watching, and feeling, that slow awakening transcended anything he had ever known, and her silent but utter convulsion at the moment of orgasm, when legs and arms would be thrown wide as her head twisted from side to side in sheer ecstasy, made all other women seem as toys.

As if it mattered. With Lindy he for the first time understood that love, however linked to physical passion, is not dependent on it. It was sufficient just to sit with her on the terrace, neither saying a word, or just to lie beside her in bed, only their hands touching, or to look at her the length of the dinner table, with smiling faces to either side, and know that she was the only woman in the world. For a forty-four-year-old man such total surrender to the goddess of love seemed absurd in the cold light of day. But it was not an emotion he envisaged ever wishing to combat, however much he had to conceal it most of the time.

Undoubtedly she was a looming disaster. She and Strolo both. The boy was three years old now and certainly resembled his father more than his mother. No problem, at three. But what of thirteen, and then twenty-three? And how much of his brain, his ambitions and his hatreds, would be inherited from his father? While Lindy held within her love for him the seeds of catastrophe to the very name of Haggard.

He squared his shoulders and his chin as he rode down the drive. Because he *was* Haggard. He could do anything he chose. Now, how long was it since he had thought that?

"What news?" They were all in the drawing room, even Lindy on this occasion, Jane seated, as her stomach was just beginning to show, while Alice and Lindy and Trum stood.

"We were defeated, naturally enough. I could persuade no other Tory to cross the floor."

"But *you* did?" Trum asked.

Haggard nodded, frowned at them. They were being no more than polite. "Now, what has happened here?"

They exchanged glances, and he looked at Lindy. Because she was in the most apprehensive state of all, her face pale and constantly biting her lip. My God, he thought, catastrophe has arrived sooner than I had supposed. But if Jane had learned of their affair, she was looking most remarkably relaxed.

"Nothing has happened here, as yet," she said. "But I'm afraid it may soon be about to." She held out a letter she had been holding on her lap. "Johnnie has fled Barbados."

The fact is, Colonel Haggard [Ferguson had written], that what happened during the slave revolt had a powerful effect on Mr. Haggard. Well, it had a powerful effect upon us all, and it would have been surprising if it hadn't upset him more than anyone else. But, sir, it is the *way* it affected him was strange. You, sir, or I, would have hated the blacks for having raped our wife, just as we would have held them in contempt for having so easily been scattered by our charge. But Mr. Haggard, sir, appeared to like them the better for what had happened, what they had done. It is not going too far to say, sir, that his whole attitude toward the slaves changed from that moment.

Well, sir, you may believe me when I say that no white man or his wife has entered the great house for two years. But the blacks are in and out of there all the time. It is a fact, sir, that I have not been permitted to flog any man, woman, or child for eighteen months. Well, sir, Mr. Haggard never did take kindly to seeing people flogged, but we had to persuade him that it was essential to the well-being of the estate. And to speak frankly, Colonel Haggard, when Mr. Haggard first arrived, we weren't disposed to take too much notice of his likes or dislikes. But it is difficult to go against a man who led a charge the way he did. Because his personality has changed too, sir. In the past three years he has fought five duels, and if I may say so, sir, not even your late father had so keen an eye with a pistol. He is so accurate, sir, that he has not yet found it necessary to kill a man, but there are three cripples walking the streets of Bridgetown.

Well, sir, I would be failing in my duty if I did not report that discipline on the plantation has suffered as a result of the abandonment of the whip. On the other hand, sir, I would be perpetrating a calumny did I suggest it has deteriorated to the extent I cannot regain control. The fact is, Colonel

Haggard, that the blacks seemed to like Mr. Haggard as well. The real cause of trouble has been the attitude of the rest of the white people here. Mr. Haggard quarreled with his parents-in-law anyway when he sent Miss Rosalind away, and he soon managed to quarrel with almost everyone else on the island. If I may be so bold, sir, it was very much like when your late father was living here, when you were a little boy, save that Mr. John never shut himself up on the plantation, but went into town whenever he felt like it, and as I have said, sir, whoever insulted or annoyed him found himself on the wrong end of a pistol muzzle in very short order.

There is another difference between Mr. John and the late master, sir, and here I must ask you to bear with me if I appear to go beyond the bounds of propriety. Your father, sir, shut himself up with Miss Dearborn, whom no doubt you remember. Mr. John, sir, does not permit any woman in the house at all, even for domestic purposes. He has dismissed old Montague, the butler, as well, and is served entirely by young black males he has selected himself. Well, sir, not to put too fine a point on it, there is talk. Talk not only among the white people but among the black. Now, sir, I was never one to report scurrilous gossip, and I have no firsthand evidence to offer, for as I have written above, I have not been allowed inside the house this last year and more, but, sir, I have to report that the domestics are a peculiarly well-satisfied lot, whom more than once I have observed to be the worse for liquor, and who in general seem to regard themselves as a cut above the rest, and even, on occasion, as equal to a white man. I can tell you, sir, that it has been a disturbing period.

Now, sir, what brought about Mr. Haggard's decision to leave Barbados, I cannot tell. I *can* tell you that he has been exchanging letters with people in Europe, in Italy and suchlike places, but I cannot say what was in those letters. I can say that he appears to have confided his purpose to no one save the captain of the ship on which he departed. It

was reported to me but three days ago, by one of
the domestics, that Mr. Haggard had left the plantation the previous night and had not returned. I
was not at that moment concerned, sir, as Mr. Haggard has amply demonstrated that he can take care
of himself. But when he had not returned after
forty-eight hours, sir, I went into Bridgetown myself, and dispatched riders to all the neighboring
plantations. And learned, sir, that Mr. Haggard had
been seen on the waterfront at about three in the
morning, boarding the ship *Dream of Araby*, cap-
tained by Thomas Grainger, the same ship, sir, on
which he first made his passage here eight years
ago. I was able to learn that Captain Grainger's
first destination was Havana, in Cuba, and thence,
so Mr. Meechem, the agent, tells me, he was bound
for Bristol.

　　Well, sir, I have immediately penned these words,
and now, sir, if I may, I shall report upon the general condition of the plantation. . . .

　　Haggard raised his head. "Poor old Ferguson. His life has
not been an easy one."

　　"Bristol," Lindy said. "He could be here tomorrow."

　　"You've read this?"

　　"We all have," Jane said.

　　"Bristol," Alice said. "He *could* be here tomorrow."

　　"I doubt he means to come here," Roger said. "He is still a
wanted criminal in England. I think he means to get to
Italy."

　　"Italy?" Trum asked. "Whatever would he wish to go there
for?"

　　"He's been corresponding with someone in Italy," Roger
pointed out. "According to Ferguson. And I know who it
probably is. Byron is in Italy."

　　"Byron," Jane said contemptuously. "A gathering of the
sodomites."

　　"Very probably," Roger agreed.

　　"But what will you do?" Alice asked.

　　"Do? Why, nothing. Unless he comes here. He was never
happy in Barbados." He looked at Lindy. "And yet, while he

was there, his presence was always to be considered. We shall wish him joy, in Italy, with Lord Byron."

"Havana, Boston, Bordeaux, Marseilles—why, what a globe-trotter you have become." Byron slapped Johnnie Haggard on the shoulder. "And what a man, too. I hardly recognized you." Now his arm went right round Johnnie's shoulders as he faced the men and women lounging on the patio, with the warm blue water of the Gulf of Genoa in their background. "Johnnie here is one of my oldest friends. Why, we were at Cambridge together. Johnnie, I want you to meet the Countess Teresa Guiccioli."

An extraordinarily attractive woman, all soft rounded curves, of face as well as figure, Johnnie estimated, small, with the most splendid auburn hair. She reminded him of Meg Bold, save that Meg had never been the possessor of such calm assurance, such contented laziness. He kissed her hands.

"Mary Shelley."

An entirely different sort, tall and slender, with almost perfect features and a wealth of golden hair, but abrupt in her movements and indeed in her speech, to suggest some continual inner conflict.

"Ned Trelawny."

A swashbuckling fellow, with a large mustache and a generally raffish air. And then a succession of others, until Byron said, "Percy Shelley, my dearest friend."

Johnnie disliked the fellow from that instant. And truly, he was as grotesque a human being as he had ever seen. Shelley was nearly seven feet tall, so far as he could judge, with a curiously gentle face sitting oddly on top of the huge but underfleshed frame. Besides, his cheeks had an unhealthy flush which suggested consumption well advanced. But he seemed friendly enough, embraced Johnnie, and demanded, "You must tell us of your adventures. I must confess that Byron has spent a lot of time talking about you. Frame-burning, was it? My God, I should have loved to be there. Tell us of Barbados."

Johnnie obliged. He had no doubt that it was very necessary to make his mark with this strange group, and immediately. How he wished they weren't there. He had dreamed of escaping to join his idol, for so long, had spent so much time accumulating the courage to take the decisive step, sure only that once it *was* taken he would be entering a heaven of perfect companionship. But all these people, and *women*, at least one of whom Byron was certainly very fond.

"Cavalry charges? Duels?" Another hug. "Where is the lad I once knew and loved? Still, no doubt I shall know and love this new fellow the better, eh?" He laughed. "He shall become my bodyguard."

Johnnie flushed, and looked from left to right, uncertain whether he was being made the butt of a joke. But he could do nothing until he could find his friend alone, which occurred after dinner that night, when, remarkably, the ladies both departed, together with the gentlemen.

"I must confess I don't understand the situation at all," he said.

Byron stretched out his legs and poured himself a drink of gin from the tumbler at his side. Johnnie observed that he seemed to consume a great deal of this liquor, without apparently having suffered any diminution of his mental brilliance.

"Well, what would you, Johnnie my lad. I love the girl."

"You?"

Byron gave a lazy chuckle. "And should I not? You have had a wife."

"Whom I got rid of as soon as possible."

Byron sighed. "Would that I could have been so fortunate. Dear Belle hangs around my neck like the proverbial millstone, poisoning the atmosphere with her strictures." He winked. "You cannot be sure yours will not be doing the same."

"She can hardly increase the burden where I am already universally condemned. Byron, I am destitute."

"Did you never ever love the girl?"

"Well, I thought I might. She really is a most pleasant creature. But then . . . No, I never loved her."

"It was cruel, to send her packing after she had been raped."

"There was more to it than that."

"There always is. Well, we shall have to find you a suitable companion for your reflective hours."

"A woman?"

"The right woman is an absolute treasure. Teresa is the mainspring of all my writing. And I am writing well, Johnnie, better than ever before. I will give you something of it to study. No stentorian bellows, mind. But a poem nonetheless. Of man, and woman, and fate, and laughter. I am calling it *Don Juan*."

"I still do not understand about Teresa," Johnnie said resentfully.

"Ah, well, she was the victim of one of those arranged spring-and-winter marriages of which the Latins are so fond. We met, and fell in love. And are still in love. But she cannot utterly abandon her husband, you see."

"You mean he is *here*?"

"Good God, no. I should have strangled him long ago. No, no. He lives in Ravenna. And Teresa has obtained a legal separation on the grounds of cruelty. But she must live with her father, and if all of Italy knows that we are lovers, there is no one capable of saying so in public."

"I had never thought to discover you so obedient to opinion."

Byron smiled. "Love, my dear Johnnie. It makes servants of us all. And besides, I am grown lazy in my old age. My concern for the well-being of my more common fellow creatures has put me in as bad an odor in Italy as ever in England. I am persona non grata in the Papal States. And here in Tuscany I am welcome only so long as I behave myself and do not take part in any anti-Austrian politics. So I sit, and drink, and love, and write. And do just a little dreaming. I have thought of immigrating to America. There's a great country, where a man is what he is and not what his neighbors think he should be. Or I have thought of going off to fight in a war. How my blood tingled when you related your deeds of derring-do. Tell me, truthfully, were you not afraid? For I will be true with you and confess that your past did not suggest you would ever be a hero."

"It is easy to be a hero," Johnnie said. "When you no longer care whether you live or die."

"There's a profound thought. But what of the duels?"

"Those too. I did not care. Up to the moment I set foot here, I did not care. I treated Lindy dreadfully. I know that. I have treated everyone dreadfully. God truly must have turned his back on the world the day I was born."

"Oh, come now."

"Yet it is true. But when I am at your side . . ." He leaned forward, seized his friend's hand. "Why do we not immigrate together? To America?"

Byron shook his head. "Teresa could never accompany us. You see, if she makes a public show of loving me, her entire family is disgraced, and forever. She has unmarried sisters."

Johnnie sighed, released the hand. And then brightened again. "Well, then, what of this war you mentioned? Is there one? A short war, where we could fight together."

Byron laughed. "The great adventure, eh? There is always a war, Johnnie. There has never been a day in the history of the world that man has not been at war, somewhere. Nor will there ever be such a day, I promise you. War is mankind's natural state. And there is even one close at hand. The Greeks are revolting against their Turkish overlords. Did you know that?"

"I had not heard of it."

"Well, it *is* happening. Slowly and clandestinely, at this moment, but gathering strength. They need aid, and leaders. They have already approached me."

"And . . . ?"

Byron shrugged. "My history of opposition to tyranny is well known, and besides, they assume any English milord is necessarily as rich as Croesus. And when I explained that I was no more than comfortably situated since I managed to sell Newstead, they said, well, then, come yourself, lend us the power of your strength and your name. Why, would you believe it, Johnnie, they even hinted at a crown?"

"Then why are we sitting here?"

Byron stretched, and drank some more gin. "Because I like sitting here and watching the sun set over the sea. Because I could not take Teresa. Because civil wars, especially civil wars of pure rebellion, are the most frightful of all forms of conflict. And because I am happy, for the first time in my life. I have my perpetual symposium. You will like them better as you grow to know them. You will love Shiloh."

"Shiloh?"

"My name for Shelley. He is the most splendid fellow imaginable. A poet too, you know. And the most confirmed free thinker in all history. Oh, he is the best of company."

Johnnie got up, walked to the edge of the patio, looked down at the sea. "I doubt I can stay here. Or should."

"Why ever not?"

He turned. "I have no such talents as your friend Shiloh. Nor do I have any contentment of spirit." He gave a twisted smile. "And I am destitute."

"What nonsense. You are my friend. I have enough for your needs as well as my own, Johnnie. Of course you shall stay here. You shall write poetry again. I will help you. You will stay here and keep my company. And I will teach you to be happy."

"You do not understand the truth of it, Mr. Haggard," Mary Shelley explained. "His daughter Allegra has just died."

Johnnie could only stare at her with his mouth open.

"A few months ago," she said, sitting beside him in the cool of the patio. "A fever . . ." She sighed. "She was at the convent recommended by Teresa. Well, the countess went there herself. But it is in the Romagna, and here they are on the other side of Italy. Teresa is heartbroken. It is not her child, of course. The mother is a stepsister of mine, Clare Clairmont. Her grief is terrible to watch. And Byron . . . Byron wonders why. Why he is here and she was there. Why she had to die at all, so young, and so full of life. He is a man quite cast adrift by fate, at this moment."

"I had no idea," Johnnie said. "He never mentioned it."

"Nor will he. Nor should you ever mention it to him. He will know that you know, and understand. And then, there are other worries. You have met Leigh Hunt?"

Johnnie nodded. "I do not quite understand his presence."

She shrugged. "It is Shiloh's doing, partly. Hunt is a journalist, you see, imprisoned a few years ago for his radical views in England. I think Byron knew him then. And Shiloh is convinced that Byron is just rotting, sitting here. He is doing nothing good with his pen, his ability, spends his time on that long, obscene poem of his. Do you know, Shiloh wanted him to write a history of religion. And Byron laughed."

"He is hardly the man for it."

"Perhaps. But he must do something. So Shiloh thought of a newspaper. An organ through which Byron could reach the world with his own views. It seemed a good idea. It *is* a good idea. But of course someone had to be found to edit the paper and do the daily grind. Thus Hunt." She sighed. "It has been a mistake. Have you been to his floor?"

Johnnie shook his head.

"Well, he has arrived in company with his wife and seven children. Would you believe it? So Byron gave him the entire downstairs floor. And they have turned it into a positive pigsty. Hunt does not believe in disciplining children, you see. It is quite terrible. And a constant source of irritation." She took his hand. "I am so glad you have come, Mr. Haggard. These last couple of days Byron has been himself again. Almost. And Shiloh and I cannot stay."

"But . . . where are you going?" Johnnie cried in sudden alarm. For if he would not be altogether sorry to see the back of Shelley, Mary was the only member of the group who had really attempted to befriend him. Besides, she was the only one who would consistently speak English.

"We have a place just north of here, at Lerici. Our children are there, and Clare as well, from time to time. It really would not do to leave her alone for too much longer. And besides, I am once again on the way to becoming a mother. But we shall return. And meanwhile . . ." She smiled. "Take care of him."

Easier said than done, he realized. For the old arrogant, contemptuous laughter, at life and propriety and law, was very seldom in evidence. He soon discovered that Mary had spoken nothing less than the truth about the Hunts; they irritated him as much as they did Byron, and Mrs. Hunt made it plain that she regarded him as just another layabout come to sponge off his lordship's limited income, without having anything to contribute to the well-being of the little community. Several of the other men also seemed to resent his presence, as much as they disgusted him, for they quite openly sat around Byron's table making notes, sure that in the years to come they would be able to offer to posterity intimate glimpses of England's greatest living poet, at ease among his friends. He spoke to Byron about it, and Byron merely shrugged. "Let them copy down whatever they wish, my dear Johnnie. 'Tis probably my only claim to immortality."

Teresa was actually his best friend, once Mary had left, and much to his surprise. But as she had only a few words of English, and he was slow to pick up Italian, it was difficult to communicate, except by smiles and glances. It could not be denied, even by himself, that she genuinely adored Byron. Indeed, as they had now lived together for three years, although the first flush of romantic love had worn off, she was as much a wife to him as he desired or required, and undoubtedly the arrangement by which, after spending all day at Byron's villa, she returned to her father's house after supper, suited the poet to the ground. For he could then pursue his peculiar habits of drinking gin until past midnight before sitting down to a bout of furious and often inspired writing which took him nearly to dawn, at which time he went to bed and remained there until noon. Johnnie, trained for more than eight years to arise at dawn and siesta in the afternoon, when Byron was just coming to life, found this new system difficult to accommodate. But far more than any personal inconvenience was the feeling of disillusion. In Barbados he had been a prisoner. In the beginning he had not supposed it possible to escape, and had given himself up to despair. Even his marriage to Lindy had been an act of despair. The strange events of that terrible day in the canefields, when he had deliberately set out to court death, to commit suicide, and instead had triumphed in a manner he had never supposed possible, had left him in a complete limbo, uncertain even of who he was. His outbursts of haughty anger had been a result of the same suicidal tendency, a desire for someone to take him at his word and bring him down. A cry for pity, perhaps, he thought, with a bullet lodged in him—he had not really considered death—even Roger would have to relent and allow him back to England.

And instead he had shot down every one of his opponents, just as Adelaide Campkin, whatever her fury at his arrogant dismissal of her daughter, had bowed to the inevitable. Without quite knowing how or why, he had become Haggard. And from understanding that to making the plans for his escape had been a short step. Only he knew this latter-day Haggard was a total sham, driven by loneliness and self-despair, by guilt at his secret desires and by fear of their discovery. Haggard the hero, the greatest coward who ever walked the earth.

He had dreamed only of regaining the company of Byron, a true hero. Let him bask in that unending sunlight, drink from the fountain of that bottomless genius. A man who no longer existed. This Byron sulked as often as he smiled, drank gin and scribbled doggerel. Even the doggerel had the mark of genius in every line, but *Childe Harold* might have been written by an ancestor. He found himself longing for Mary's return, even if it meant the presence of Shelley, and was doubly disappointed when the huge young man did appear, together with a friend of his named Williams, but without Mary, who had suffered a miscarriage.

As it happened, however, Shelley returned at an opportune moment, as Byron was in the midst of a more than usually acrimonious quarrel with the Hunts. He stayed for some days, and brought about a considerable reconciliation. "But I must go home," he explained. "I have bought myself a yacht, Byron. Oh, nothing so grand as your *Bolivar*, but I have named it *Don Juan*. I hope you do not mind?"

"I am flattered," Byron said. "Where do you keep this famous vessel?"

"Well, she is at present lying in Leghorn harbor. I shall go up there tonight to sail her back to Lerici. You will see her next time I am down."

"You'll sail her alone?"

"Good Lord no. Williams will accompany me. He served in the navy, you know. And we have an English lad with us as well. Oh, I am well crewed, my lord. But I would like to sail tonight, so I shall bid adieu."

"A grand fellow," Byron said over his gin. "The very best. You do not mind my saying so, Johnnie?"

"Why should I mind?" He was himself in a good humor this night; Byron had not been so relaxed since his arrival.

"And talented," Byron remarked. "Why, if he would but give up these grandiose schemes he has to write epic poetry and epic plays, to be another Shakespeare in fact, he would do something really worthwhile. One cannot *write* an epic, Johnnie. One can only write what is in oneself, and if your ambitions lie in that direction, hope that it may be *considered* an epic in later years. No man can write something greater than himself. Do you agree with that?"

"I do not," Johnnie said. "From all accounts, Shakespeare was no great fellow, in himself."

"Who knows?" Byron said. "Who will ever know?" He got up. "I'm for bed."

And hope to sleep, Johnnie thought. And not be awakened by fears for the future, by uncertainty, which is worse by far than fear, and by guilt, the worst of the three. But eventually awaken, to great noise and excitement, and to Trelawny, flushed and emotional, blurting out the news that Shelley had been lost at sea.

"Lost at sea?" Byron demanded. "How can they have been lost at sea?"

"They have disappeared," Trelawny insisted.

"You saw them?"

"I saw them off, certainly. They did not leave the night before last. They were going to go in the morning, but then a thunderstorm delayed them and it was noon before they put out. I watched them go, until a squall came down and blotted them out. Oh, maybe ten miles out."

"Just a squall?" Johnnie inquired. "You do not know they sank."

"They never got to Lerici," Trelawny insisted.

"But you do not know they sank," Byron repeated. "Could not *Don Juan* have ridden out the storm?"

"Of course she could, properly handled."

"And Shiloh has been sailing for years. Is it not most likely that they were driven out to sea, perhaps as far as Corsica? They were well provisioned."

"Of course it is a possibility," Trelawny said. "But nonetheless, we cannot sit here and wait for news. They must be found. Would you, my lord, agree to us using *Bolivar* for a search?"

"Of course. Take her as far as you wish."

"Then I shall leave immediately."

Johnnie stared at Byron. "Do *you* suppose he is dead?"

"Shiloh can never die," he declared. "Never. I will have a drink."

Clearly he feared the worst. And that evening Mary and Jane Williams arrived, Mary looking drawn and exhausted by her illness as much as by grief.

"To go missing at sea is nothing," Johnnie insisted. "Why, ships crossing the Atlantic are sometimes weeks overdue, but they usually turn up in the end. It is all a business of the wind."

Mary squeezed his hand, but clearly did not believe him. Nor did he believe himself. But it was tragic to see the effect even the possibility of such a mishap was having upon this tightly knit little circle of exiles. Because they all dreamed of better times to come? Of greatness and of reputation? Or because they all knew that the loss of Shiloh would be a blow greater even than the death of Allegra, that Byron would never recover, that the days of the perpetual symposium were coming to an end? Because soon enough the bodies came ashore. Williams and the boy first. And then Shelley's, farther up the coast. The Italian authorities had immediately buried each of them in the sand, for fear of infection, but Trelawny had seen them first, and had identified them.

"What, Shiloh left to rot on an unmarked beach?" Byron

shouted, his face convulsed. "He must be buried properly, in the Protestant cemetery in Rome. You must see to it, Ned."

"I doubt we shall obtain permission," Trelawny said, "but I will see what can be done."

"Forgotten in the sand," Byron moaned. "Forgotten in the sand. God in heaven, it cannot be."

His grief was quite terrible to behold, and even Hunt no longer attempted to spur him into writing. The entire group sat and waited, and watched their leader seem to consume himself, drinking vast quantities of gin, hardly speaking, even to Teresa, who sat by his side in silent sympathy.

It was nearly a month before Trelawny returned. "They will not allow burial," he said. "But I have obtained permission to burn them on the beach."

"Burn them," Byron muttered. "Burn Shiloh?" Then he raised his head. "Aye, and why not? A very Viking end, by God. We'll burn them. We'll send their ashes screaming up to heaven." He leaped to his feet. "Come along, Johnnie. Come along, Hunt. We'll give them a sendoff never to be forgotten."

Trelawny had already been busy and had constructed an iron box, resting on four legs, in which the bodies were to be consumed. This was sent up the coast on board the *Bolivar*, which was anchored off the beach where Williams and the boy had been buried. He had also prepared two leaden boxes for the bones and ashes, and these traveled with Byron and Hunt and Johnnie in the coach from Pisa. It was the most remarkable sensation Johnnie had ever known, sitting in the coach as it left the road and bounced onto the beach. It was a stiflingly hot August day, every bit as warm as it had ever been in Barbados, which but added to the almost sinister macabreness of the situation. He wondered why he had come. But they were doing Byron's wishes.

Byron himself leaned forward, looking out of the window, but not moving as Trelawny and a companion named Shenley superintended the uncovering of the first body, and then dragged the shapeless corpse across the sand with boat hooks.

"I must look at it," Byron said, and got down. Johnnie and Hunt exchanged glances, then followed.

"It could be anyone," Hunt said, holding his kerchief to his nose. "How can we know it is Williams?"

Johnnie stared at the ghastly, fleshless skull, which had

fallen back, allowing the mouth to droop open and reveal the teeth.

Byron pointed. "Those are Williams' teeth," he said. "I'd have known them anywhere." He shuddered. "Yet you are right, Hunt. It could be the body of a sheep, as much as human. Consider that we shall each resemble that, one day."

He walked away, stripped off his clothes, and waded into the sea. The *Bolivar* was anchored perhaps five hundred yards from the shore, and he swam toward it with strong, steady strokes. Johnnie recalled that swimming had always been Byron's favorite sport at Cambridge, but he was too fascinated by the horror in front of him to follow. Trelawny gave the orders, in Italian, and the gravediggers heaved the corpse into the box. The fire was then lit, and immediately the stench became so terrible that they had to throw incense onto the flames, as well as salt, sugar, and wine.

"Far better to burn," Trelawny said, "than to rot with worms in your belly."

Johnnie wiped his brow, was alerted by a shout from the water. Byron was about three-quarters of the way to his schooner, and was beating the water and splashing.

"He's been attacked by a fish," Hunt cried.

"Cramp, more likely," Trelawny said, running down the beach.

Johnnie raced beside him, taking off his clothes as he did so. The wild thought crossed his mind that Byron might have opted for suicide, because of Shelley, but the cries were genuine enough. He splashed through the shallows, reached the deep water, struck out with all his strength, Trelawny puffing behind him. Byron went down once, surfaced again, gave another shout, and Johnnie reached him.

"Easy, old friend, easy," he gasped.

"Cramp," Byron panted. "I cannot move."

"Lie on your back," Johnnie said. "Trelawny is here."

Between them they managed to get him on his back and tow him toward the shore. Gradually his breathing returned to normal, and soon he was able to swim himself, Johnnie to one side and Trelawny to the other. "My God," he said, kneeling in the shallows. "My God. You should have let me drown. I did not mean to call for help. You should have let me drown."

"You'll not drown, Byron," Johnnie said. "You'll never die, while I am at your side."

Byron turned his head, gazed at him for some seconds. "You love me, Johnnie lad," he said. "I doubt any man has ever had a truer friend." He got up, water running down his legs, dripping from his hair, stared at the fire. "Is it done?"

"It's done," Hunt said, coming toward them. "You should lie down and have a rest, my lord."

"There's Shiloh," Byron said, and went up the beach toward his clothes.

Shelley had actually come ashore considerably higher up the coast, and it was after all necessary to spend the night in Viareggio. But it was a terrible night, for Byron refused to go to bed and instead sat and drank until dawn. Then he did rest for an hour, while Trelawny went on ahead to superintend the digging-up of the corpse. But when Johnnie and Hunt and Byron finally arrived, Shelley's body had still not been found.

"For God's sake," Byron shouted. "Why the delay?"

"It is simply that we were given the wrong directions," Trelawny explained. "It must be here somewhere." Once again he thrust his spade into the disturbed sand, and immediately there was a clang. "Bones, by God."

"It'll be his skull," Byron shouted, falling to his knees. "Be careful, for God's sake, Ned. To preserve that skull, that famous home for so famous a brain . . ."

"I shall be careful," Trelawny said, and turned his attention to digging from the other end. Slowly the feet and then the body came into view, as horrible as had been Williams', a mess of nauseous putridity, flesh and clothing alike turned black by the action of the quicklime in which he had been soaked before interment.

"Oh, Shiloh," Byron moaned. "That you should have come to this."

"For for the head," Trelawny grunted. Gently he thrust his spade into the sand, turned it; there was another clang, and the skull shattered into several fragments. "My God."

Byron stared at it.

"It was too delicate," Hunt muttered. "Too delicate." He crammed his kerchief into his mouth and ran back to the carriage.

Like Byron, Johnnie could only stare at it. It had been a fine head, and according to his friend, it had housed a fine brain. All to fall into pieces at the touch of a spade.

"I am sorry, my lord," Trelawny said. "But we must fin-ish."

Byron sighed, and pushed himself to his feet. Johnnie re-mained at his elbow while the body was placed in the box.

"Will you pray, my lord?" Trelawny asked.

Byron stared at him, then shook his head. Trelawny glanced at Johnnie, who also shook his head.

"He was our friend," Trelawny said, and threw some in-cense over the corpse. "I restore to nature through fire the el-ements of which this man was composed, earth, air and water; everything is changed, but not annihilated; he is now a portion of that which he worshiped."

Byron gave a sob and ran down the beach. Johnnie made to follow, but Trelawny caught his arm. "Leave him be."

"And suppose he is again attacked by cramp?"

"Then we will rescue him again. For the moment, leave him be."

The fire was lit. Johnnie watched Byron swimming slowly but surely out to the *Bolivar*, then turned his attention back to the flames. They roared and leaped, and filled the beach with the stench of burning flesh.

"What do you think truly happened?" Johnnie asked Tre-lawny. "We heard a rumor at the inn this morning that they may have been attacked by pirates."

"I doubt that," Trelawny said. "I believe they had some money with them, but not much. And anyway, it would have gone to the bottom with the boat. No, no, a sudden squall, with perhaps too much canvas up, and she'd go over before anyone could do anything about it."

More than an hour passed, and Byron began his swim back. Now the flames were dying down, and by the time he gained the beach they had almost entirely burned themselves out.

"Will you look?" Trelawny asked.

Byron nodded, walked toward the still-glowing box, peered inside, and gave a shout. Johnnie ran to stand beside him, held his arm as he saw that while the body was entirely con-sumed, the heart remained, glowing red with heat, but none-theless still *there*.

"My God," Trelawny said. "There is a singular sight. Will you have the heart, my lord?"

"You'll give it to Mary," Byron said, and turned away, once again walking down the beach to the sea.

"You'll not go in again, Byron," Johnnie begged. "In this heat, and after so much, you'll have a seizure."

Byron remained gazing at the sea for some seconds; then he turned. "I'll not go in again, Johnnie lad," he said. "I was but thinking. A man lives, as best he can, all the time slipping into a rut, wallowing like a beast in the field, content only to see the sun rise and the sun set, to be fed and washed and mated, to *exist*, until he dies. Do we live at all, Johnnie?"

"You cannot change the life cycle. Not even you."

"Indeed I cannot. And no doubt the vast majority of mankind is content with so preordained a fate. I cannot stop myself from dying, Johnnie. But I can make my life *alive*, so long as I am breathing. You came here in search of adventure, and you found a drunken sot. Well, by God, you will have your adventure, Johnnie my love. You and I are going to challenge the gods themselves. You spoke of a war. We'll find ourselves a war." He threw his arm round Johnnie's shoulder. "You and I are for Greece, lad. A crown or a coffin, we'll find one or the other. But by God we'll know we're breathing."

Chapter 3

The Hero

"There," Byron said. "To see it, so close. Why, I swear I could throw a stone that distance."

They stood, as they had so often stood these past few months, on the beach of the island of Cephalonia, and stared across the channel at the mist-shrouded mountains of the mainland. It really was, Johnnie supposed, incredible that they should have come so far, so quickly, and then been forced to remain in these Ionian islands, under the protection of the British flag—for Great Britain had been given a mandate to govern them following the end of the war with Napoleon—for so very long.

In the beginning, all had been haste and bustle, for Byron, once he had made a decision, was never one to hesitate. Letters were written, to secure friends, and weapons, and uniforms—he was determined to cut a splendid figure when he set foot upon Greek soil—and funds, as he cashed every penny he had on deposit, and even a new ship, for the *Bolivar* was decidedly unsuited for an adventure of this nature.

Supporters had certainly arrived in great numbers, although how many of them were serious in their support of the Greek cause was to be doubted; everyone was certainly anxious to get his hands on some of Byron's money. The friends on the spot had been a more serious problem. Teresa, predictably, had been horrified at the entire concept, and was only partially persuaded to allow her lover to go by the decision of her younger brother Pietro to accompany the expedition. Mary Shelley had already sadly departed back to England, but the Hunts were scandalized, seeing their hopes of a prosperous sojourn in Italy dashed to nothing.

And what did *he* think of it all? Johnnie had wondered. He had been rather disturbed when he had learned that their first destination would be the Ionians, and British law. But surely, he reminded himself, after twelve years his name would be forgotten, if it had ever been known to Napier, the governor, one of Wellington's peninsular captains, and a man hardly resident in England for more than a few weeks in all that time. As for the war, the Great Adventure, as Byron called it, it meant very little to him, in reality. He was running, as he had spent his entire life running. That he was running toward possible danger did not seem very relevant; he had discovered that physical fear in no way compares with the terrors that lurk inside the human mind. And now he would be running with Byron. Indeed, in the sense of intimacy for which he was searching, he would have him all to himself, at last. The others—Trelawny; Byron's doctor, Bruno; the servants; even Pietro Gamba—were no more than acquaintances, leeches that had attached themselves to Byron's hurtling body as it careered through space and time. He and Byron *knew* more, about each other, about what they were seeking.

If the Byron he had known and loved any longer existed. This was a haunting consideration. That he had taken to drinking a great deal too much gin had been obvious from the start. He claimed it assisted the process of writing, freed the imagination, inspired the pen. Perhaps he was right. Certainly the great poem *Don Juan* seemed to bubble along whenever he was in the mood to write. But equally certainly, alcohol had changed his personality, or perhaps brought out some latent aspects of it, making him into a man of moods, some of them black as the pit, and a man of strange hesitancy, too, where the Byron of Johnnie's boyhood had regarded life as a perpetual challenge, to be perpetually defeated.

But far more serious were the indications of a total breakdown in health, and more especially in mental health, which too often made sudden and horrifying appearances. Mary Shelley had hinted that such things had happened before, and Johnnie had been prepared to dismiss the suggestion as womanly jealousy. But immediately following Shelley's cremation, Byron had burst into a mood of violent invective, against himself and all the world, shrieking his horrors and his fears and his hatreds to the evening sky, and collapsing into a stupor which had terrified everyone save Teresa, who had apparently encountered this before.

"The exertion," Trelawny had said, with his usual immediate decision. "Swimming out to the *Bolivar*, twice in two days, and in that heat. It is not in the least surprising that his brain is touched."

For next day Byron could remember nothing of the outburst. Grief and exertion. As Trelawny had said, quite understandable causes for a brief dementia. But there could be other causes as well. Soon after their arrival in Cephalonia, there was another outburst, again occasioned by exertion, certainly, as it happened after a visit to the neighboring isle of Ithaca during which they had done a great deal of walking in the heat, but also undoubtedly prompted by frustration as well, for since their arrival nothing had gone according to plan. The warships promised by the Greek general Mavrokordatos, the information as to where their services could be best put to use, even the money Byron had summoned from all over Europe, were all lacking, and they could do nothing more than stand on the beach, as now, and stare at the mountains of the mainland.

It had been frustrating even for Johnnie, content only to be in Byron's company, and to be free, after so many years, of convention and restriction, of criticism and of responsibility.

But Byron's outburst on this occasion had been quite horrific, as he had drawn a sword and threatened all who came near him with death, and eventually barricaded himself in his room, to emerge pale and exhausted next morning, once again quite unable to remember a moment of his outburst.

Grief and frustration, allied to exhaustion. But when is a military campaign not composed of those very three elements? It was a disturbing thought for the future.

This day, however, all fears and doubts were dissipated before the magic of his personality. They walked together back up the road to the little house in which they had established their headquarters, Byron's huge Newfoundland dog, Lyon, padding at their sides. Their band had dwindled somewhat, as Trelawny, despairing of ever leaving Cephalonia, had gone off on his own, into the Morea, where the Greek rebels were in control of the country, and where he hoped to make contact with some leader more vigorous than Mavrokordatos appeared to be.

"Pietro," Byron shouted at the young Gamba. "What news? As if I should waste the time in asking."

"No news from the mainland," Pietro said. "They continue to wrangle among themselves about what is best to be done. It is a stupid way to run a war, in my opinion. But there is some news. There are credits for you."

"Here?" Byron cried.

"In Zante." He pointed over the headland at the island farther to the south, a dim smudge on the horizon. "Several thousand, I am told."

"Why did the messenger not bring them up?"

"They are to be delivered only to you personally, by the agent there, my lord."

"Credits, in Zante." Byron walked to the edge of the patio, once again gazed at the distant mountains. "I think we have stayed in this misbegotten place long enough," he said. "I do not think they will ever decide where they want me. I think I should make that decision myself."

"You will go to the Morea?" asked Dr. Bruno.

"The Morea? Now, why should I do that? I came here to fight the Turk, not quarrel with the Greek. Do the patriots not hold anywhere north of the Isthmus of Corinth?"

"Indeed they do, my lord. They hold several fortress points on the Gulf of Patras, including one on the north shore."

"Where?"

"A town called Missolonghi, my lord. It was commanded by the great Bokkaris, and was a thorn in the Turkish side. But Bokkaris was killed in a skirmish last year, and since then the town has been in a state of siege."

"Missolonghi," Byron said. "It rolls off the tongue. A thorn in the Turkish side, by God. Aye, that's what we shall be, Johnnie, me lad. Several thorns. Perhaps, in time, several thousand thorns. We'll show these Greeks how to wage a war. Send word to Mavrokordatos, to have his warship out in the gulf, just in case we are hounded by the Turks, Pietro. How soon can you reach him?"

"A fast small boat, under the cover of night, will be in Missolonghi by dawn. But we will need larger vessels."

Byron nodded. "Find me two. A fast one, and a larger one for our gear and the rest of our people. And send a messenger off tonight. The day after tomorrow, we sail for Greece."

He threw his arm round Johnnie's shoulder. "For glory or for death."

It would, Johnnie reflected, be a damp glory and probably a damper death. He stood in the porch of the house, the rain dripping steadily past his nose, watched the walled courtyard in front of him, at best a place of muddy desolation, turn into a pond, the bronze cannon resemble more and more some primeval aquatic monster. He could thank his fortune that his dragoon helmet was also made of bronze, or he had no doubt it would be rusting on his head; certainly his sword was rusting in its scabbard.

It had rained, often and heavy, in Barbados. It had in fact rained far more heavily there than ever in Greece. But those had been storms, fierce passages of wind and water which had left him breathless but basking in the sudden hot sun which had immediately followed. It had rained, damply and consistently, over more than a day at a time in England, often enough. But he had never known rain like this, heavy without being hurled along by any wind, unceasing and unrelenting, turning everything into a damp soggy mess, even the blankets on his bed, and never ceasing even for an hour.

Presumably it also hampered the Turks, somewhere out there in the mountains. But presumably the Turks, in their mountains, did not have the mosquitoes to contend with. Missolonghi, in the best of weather, was situated in the center of a swamp. That indeed was its strength, in that the vast areas of stagnant water, through which only a long, narrow channel led to the Gulf of Patras, prevented assault by either land or water far more efficiently than any walls could have done. But the lagoons were alive with, it seemed, every insect known, and several unknown, so far as he could gather, all eager to wine and dine from human flesh.

Frustration, added to discomfort and dampness and personal jealousies. Missolonghi was a huge seethe of discontent, in which the Suliotes, the fierce mountain warriors who had followed Bokkaris into battle and wept when he had died, and who had been appropriated by Byron as his own bodyguard, two hundred strong, glowered contemptuously at the inhabitants of the town, who thought only of defending their homes; in which the various European groups, and there were a surprising number of these who had rallied to the cause once they had heard Lord Byron was taking an active part, differed nationally and also socially, far too many being entirely gentlemen adventurers with no knowledge of warfare, but prepared to look down on the professionals, like Captain Parry, who was busy attempting to create a rocket company which he was sure would spread terror among the Turks. And where did that place him? Johnnie wondered. At the least, he could recognize Parry's worth, and even like the man, however uncouth he might be.

And behind them all, the brooding, increasingly enigmatic figure of Byron himself. The fact was, Johnnie realized, as he had once so carelessly remarked to Lindy, Byron could only exist with the sound of surf rumbling continuously in his ears. Where that dwindled, so did he. All had been excited adventure on the voyage from Cephalonia, as they had actually been hailed by a Turkish man-of-war and forced to creep silently into the night. All had been excited ambition on their first arrival in the town, when Byron, recalling his own experiences among the fierce Albanians of twelve years before, had fallen for the Suliotes at first sight, and immediately commenced drilling them while sending messengers out of the town to make contact with any local Greek leaders, to inform Trelawny that he was here, and to reconnoiter the Turkish strongpoint of Lepanto just farther up the gulf, where he was determined to make his first assault.

And all had come to naught before Greek dilatoriness and the endless, pouring rain.

There had been a brief flurry of excitement once again, only a few days ago, when a Turkish patrol ship had run aground at the mouth of the channel through the lagoons. But no action. The Turks had taken to their boats, and before the vessel could be thoroughly looted, another Turkish patrol boat had appeared and driven the insurgents back into their marshes. That event had been worse than the all-prevailing boredom, for now there was endless recrimination as each commander felt the other could have done more to remove the cannon and ammunition from the stranded vessel.

Frustration and discomfort. No wonder Byron spent a good deal of his time in bed. At least he had had no more attacks, but that his health was suffering and his blood heated, there could be no doubt.

And what of himself? Johnnie wondered. What had he come here to find? Just Byron? In his heart he knew not. He had spent too much of his recent life in utter introspection not to understand himself very well. If on the one hand he had inherited from his mother an introverted disgust with all things exclusively masculine, he was also the son of John Haggard, and deep down within him there lurked a ferocious monster crying out for blood and mayhem. And for more than that.

How the thought of Lindy tormented him. He had not meant to send her away. Certainly he had never expected her merely to pack up and go. He had wanted to get rid of the boy, Strolo, but he had wanted her to remain, so that he could look at her, and remember in his imagination what had happened to her, and feel the blood surging through his arteries at the idea of her being held on the ground and raped. Perhaps he had even envisaged himself reenacting the whole event. But he would never have done that. He lacked the essential spark of violence, when in bed with a woman.

But in a war! At the head of a charging body of men. Civil war, the most terrible of all strifes. Certainly those who had taken part in this struggle from the beginning were not lacking in the most titillating of tales of the horrors perpetrated, both by the Turks and by themselves in retaliation, of men raped before castration, of women raped before having their breasts cut away, of writhing bodies suspended over smoking fires, of whole families herded into houses which were then set ablaze, of drowning and beheadings, of thoughts which made him feel sick even as they filled his system with a wild exhilaration. He did not know how he would react to the power to commit such deeds, whether he would vomit or shriek his joy to the sky. He did remember the wild exhilaration of the charge in Barbados, the feelings of almost curious detachment as he had sighted down his pistol barrel at another man. It had occurred to him, more than once, that if he could but stop himself *thinking* of anything more than his food and his bed and his daily affairs, he might be a completely normal human being.

But thought was with him constantly, and he could no longer alleviate it, like Byron, in poetry. Byron himself had killed that essential outlet. For if one could not write like a Byron—and who could?—then it was puerile to attempt it. So, thought—the strangest, most absurd, and most dangerous of considerations. Black people, for instance. In the beginning he had feared them, for their unknown enmity, and they had feared him, as the new master. Their fear had very rapidly turned to contempt. But then it had turned to something very akin to worship, after the revolt. Because they respected strength, and courage, even when it was displayed at their own expense, and they had known that it had been he, and he alone, had been responsible for their defeat. Ferguson and the others had but followed their leader, blindly and irresponsibly. That so many of their own had had to die had not distorted the essential fact. "That Mr. John," they had said, "he done what he must do."

There was manhood for you. They were the first people ever to regard him as anything more than a nuisance, a miscreation of a careless God. At first he had basked in it. Then, from basking to taking advantage of it, when filled with gin swizzles on a lonely evening, had been a simple, horrifying step. He still lay awake and sweated when he thought of it.

But it had all helped in the understanding of a people, an entire culture. They were beasts, two-legged animals, and far inferior to the plantation dogs. Thus Ferguson and every white man in Barbados, save possibly the unfortunate Oldham. But was not Oldham the more knowledgeable? They were men and women who dreamed, like any others. They were men and women who could remember stories handed down by their ancestors, of life and death along the great rivers of West Africa. They were men and women who had adopted entirely the English ideals, the concept of a distant king, a benevolent deity who would end all their ills. He wondered what any of them would say had they ever been confronted either by the madman farmer or by King Prinny. But they were men and women, in too many cases taller and stronger and bolder and *better* than himself. Yet an accident of history had him their master, with entire powers of life and death, of mistreatment and debauchery, of careless contempt.

He did not suppose God had ever intended anything like that to happen. Thus he had dreamed of perhaps setting it right. And when he had considered the dream in detail, he had run away from it. As he had run away from every single problem that had ever faced him.

But now he had reached the end of his flight, he supposed. There was no possibility of running away from Missolonghi.

"My God," Byron groaned. "I am shaking like a babe.

Hold that cup steady, Johnnie lad. 'Tis certain I could not do so myself."

"Perhaps something less heady," Johnny suggested.

"For God's sake, are you setting up to preach at me?" Byron shouted. "Gin is the only possible antidote to this fever. Where it comes from, God alone knows."

"The swamp." Johnnie held the cup to the dry, cracked lips, listened to the sigh of contentment as the alcohol slipped into his system. "You are inhaling all the poisonous miasmas which cling to it."

"And you are not? Why me, for God's sake? I tell you, Johnnie, I doubt I shall survive this winter."

"What nonsense," Johnnie said, a great clammy hand seeming to fix itself on his heart and stomach. The fever had been here too long. They all needed warmth, and fresh air, and above all, a cessation of this unending rain.

And perhaps some action.

"Nonsense? Of course it is nonsense. When summer comes, or even spring . . . For God's sake, we are past the middle of February. It can only be a few more weeks now." He smiled at his friend, and squeezed his hand. "You must forgive my tantrums. I am truly not used to being only half a man. What is that tumult?"

Because indeed there was a great deal of noise from outside. "I will go and discover," Johnnie said, getting up.

"Perhaps the Turks are assaulting. Oh, that would be a happy day." Byron raised himself on his elbow, peered at Parry, who came bursting into the room. "Is it the Turks? Say it is the Turks."

"Far worse," Parry panted, his normal phlegm quite disappeared. "It is warfare among our own people."

"How can that be?" Byron demanded, pushing himself into a sitting position.

"There has been a fight," Parry wailed. "Between Yiotes . . . You know Yiotes?"

He had been Bokkaris' right-hand man, and was an idol to the Suliotes.

"Of course I know Yiotes," Byron snapped.

"And the Swede, Lieutenant Sass. It seems Yiotes wished to show his son the arsenal, and the sentry refused, and called Sass, who was captain of the guard. I do not know who drew first, but Sass is dead, his arm just about severed from his shoulder. Yiotes is certainly wounded. And the Suliotes are out, declaring vengeance on every European in the town. We are quite lost."

The uproar was certainly coming closer.

"Help me up," Byron said.

"You cannot leave your bed, my lord," declared Dr. Bruno, hurrying into the room. "The fever . . ."

"Help me up, God damn you," Byron shouted. "Johnnie."

Johnnie held his arm, pulled him to his feet.

"My clothes," Byron snapped. "My helmet. My pistols. Johnnie, you'll stand at my shoulder."

"To the death," Johnnie promised. But what a way to die, in some internecine squabble in a Greek swamp.

"Open the door." Byron lurched outside, to find the inner room filled with terrified people, all clamoring that their last hour had come.

"Be quiet," Byron shouted. "Only determination will stop this becoming a riot. Mr. Parry, you'll have that cannon dragged over here and point it at the gate. Gentlemen, you'll prime your weapons and take your places here, behind the cannon. Now, Johnnie, when I give the word, throw open the gate."

"You'll not go out to them, Byron."

"I must. It is the only way." He walked forward, obviously making a tremendous effort to stand straight despite the fever, straightened his helmet, rested his hand on the hilt of his sword, and nodded. Johnnie drew a long breath, and pulled the bolt, throwing the gate wide to reveal a crowd of several hundred screaming Suliotes, now joined by a good number of the townspeople. They gazed at Byron for some seconds, and slowly the noise began to dwindle.

"What do you here?" he demanded.

"Vengeance," they called. "Vengeance."

"Against whom? Yiotes has not been killed. It is my man who has been killed. Suppose I demand vengeance against you?"

The noise died right away as they considered this point. Byron stepped to one side, arm outflung to point at the cannon and the waiting Europeans, armed and revealing at least a show of determination.

"You seek to assault me?" Byron shouted. "Your benefactor? The man who will lead you to victory over the Turk? By God, I will have discipline or I will have death. Make one move forward, nay, continue to stand there but a moment longer, and I will command my men to fire into you."

There was a moment of awful silence, and Johnnie heard Parry mutter, "By Christ, but we are done."

Then slowly the crowd broke up, the men retreating toward their homes and their tents, muttering among themselves. The Europeans relaxed with an audible sigh of relief.

"Close the gate, Johnnie," Byron said. He turned and walked through the congratulating crowd and up the stairs.

Johnnie closed and bolted the gate, hurried behind him, followed him into the bedroom. "That was quite splendid," he said. "I would give ten years of my life to possess so much courage."

Byron turned to look at him, and he took a step backward. Never had he seen so horrifying a countenance, suddenly mottled white and purple, the mouth a terrifying gash of fuming rage.

"Scum," Byron shrieked. "Shitbag. Bastard. Why must you follow me like a diseased dog? Get out, get out." He made to draw his sword, turned round, and fell across the bed. "Get out," he shrieked, writhing and kicking. "Leave me alone."

Bruno stood at Johnnie's shoulder. "You must help me."

"Help *that*?"

"If you lose your temper with him you will lose *him*. It is another seizure. Help me."

Johnnie held Byron's legs while Parry held his arms and the doctor his head and poured some laudanum down his throat. Byron continued to scream and shriek his rage at the world, and Parry stared at Johnnie with somber eyes.

Spring at last. April in the Gulf of Patras. Could there be any more beautiful place in the entire world in April? Johnnie wondered. The grim memories of February were gone, hopefully forever. Now the sun shone and a splendid breeze came down from the mountains. Even the mosquitoes had retired to their lairs, for the moment. Spring was a time for dreaming about meetings with the Greek chieftains from the Morea, at last arranged by Trelawny, and with them for planning the assault on Lepanto, Byron's dream, and with that, to anticipate perhaps a gathering momentum of strength and advance, which would sweep across all of mainland Greece, leave the Turks at nothing more than the Hellespont.

And this spring was the most miserable he had ever known.

They sat around a table and listened to Dr. Bruno. "The fever is no longer increasing," Bruno explained. "But neither is it diminishing. And we are at the best time of the year. Now, my friends, I must speak plainly to you. Lord Byron is not, and at no time this summer will be, in any condition to undertake a military offensive. The very best we can hope for is that the fever will run its course. But as a leader he is useless to you. And I have outlined the very best possibility. The worst is that as the weather grows hotter, as it will most certainly do, so the fever will increase. And, gentlemen, if Lord Byron is in Missolonghi next autumn, unless he be fully recovered, then he will die."

He paused, and they exchanged glances.

"Well, then," Parry said. "It does not seem to me to be a subject for discussion. Mr. Haggard?"

"I agree," Johnnie said. "But where can he go?"

"Back to Cephalonia," Bruno said. "Out there, in the sea breezes and far removed from these malarial swamps, with an absence of all the care that besets him here, why, there I think he will recover."

"Easier said than done," Hesketh objected.

"It would be a risky business at the best of times," von Hassell pointed out. "But with the Turkish ships so active . . ."

"It must be done," Johnnie insisted. "As it has to be done. Captain Parry, you'll send word to the Greek leaders in the Morea, that we must have a small ship here within the week. And we must have a diversionary attack, on somewhere close . . . Patras. If they would launch an attack on Patras itself, which would attract all the Turkish forces in the gulf, while we smuggled Lord Byron out of Missolonghi . . ."

"Leave it to me," Parry said.

"But, gentlemen," Bruno said, "no word of this must reach his lordship's ears. He would refuse to leave, and the resulting torment might prove fatal."

The resulting torment. Johnnie sat by the bed, the tortured fingers wrapped in his.

"So much to be done," Byron moaned. "So very much. Johnnie, are my Suliotes drilling?"

"I have them at it every day," Johnnie said.

Byron smiled, a quick flash of that unforgettable expression. "You will make soldiers of them yet. When we charge the Turks, Johnnie, I want you at my elbow. Say you will be at my elbow."

"I will be there, my lord. At your elbow. Always."

"I never doubted it for a moment." He sighed, and seemed to sleep, and then awoke. "Johnnie, I am dying."

"What nonsense," Johnnie said. "You, Byron? You will never die."

Byron smiled. "I said as much of Shiloh. Poor Shiloh. I wonder will I see him again, or are we doomed to spend eternity drifting around space, ships to be seen at a distance."

"Do not talk like that," Johnnie insisted. "There are plans afoot at this very moment to have you well again."

He shook his head. "No plans for me, Johnnie. No plans for me." He sighed, and closed his eyes. Johnnie's heart gave a tremendous lurch, and he leaned forward, but Byron still breathed.

And continued to do so for three more days. Johnnie remained by his bedside, despite the urging of Bruno and Pietro and Parry that he get some sleep. For were Byron to die . . . it made no sense, of anything in this life. That Byron, so full of energy, and genius, so commanding a personality, should die, while Johnnie Haggard, so wretched a human being in every way, should live, it made no sense of anything at all.

And so he waited, for the miracle to occur, for Byron suddenly to awake, the fever abated, that familiar smile on his lips, calling for a glass of gin, calling for his helmet, calling for his Suliotes. But he only called for his wife, and his sister, and Teresa, and occasionally for Shiloh. That was the hardest pill of all to swallow, that never once did the name of Johnnie Haggard cross his lips.

And then he sighed, and opened his eyes, and looked at the men standing about his bed, and said, "I want to sleep now," and closed his eyes again.

Twenty-four hours later, without again speaking, he died.

Johnnie Haggard carefully sealed the envelope, watching the wax harden in a curiously detached fashion. "You'll see that this reaches my brother," he told Parry.

"If need be, Mr. Haggard, I'll see to it. I still think this is a madcap venture."

"Surprise, Captain Parry. Surprise. Lord Byron and I often talked of it, when first we landed here. Two hundred bold and determined men, acting by stealth, could well seize Lepanto before the Turks even guessed what they were about."

"And will they not know you are coming?"

"They may well discover that we are about, Captain. But it will still not occur to them that we intend anything so bold as to seize the town."

Parry shook his head. "A madcap enterprise, Mr. Haggard. It goes against all the rules of war. And we know that Odysseus and Trelawny are on their way here, with men, Mr. Haggard. Come summer, we could command more than a thousand fighting soldiers. Now, with that number . . ."

"And come summer, Captain Parry, the Egyptian army will have landed to assist the Turks. Where will your thousand men be then? Besides, it is *now* that we must accomplish something. For what is the very greatest factor in war, Captain? It is not men or guns. It is morale. Do you not suppose that at this moment the news of Lord Byron's death is winging its way the length and breadth of Greece? The Turks will be celebrating, and our people will be utterly cast down. It is now that we must raise their spirits once again by some act of derring-do, some brilliant stroke which might have been devised by Byron himself."

Parry sighed, and scratched his head. "Undoubtedly there is a great deal of sense in what you are saying, Mr. Haggard. Then why not let me accompany you?"

"Because you are needed here, Captain, to command the garrison."

And because, he thought, I have a hidden advantage which you do not, my dear Parry. I am Johnnie Haggard, the scum of the earth. God is in no hurry to collect my worthless soul. He showed that on Haggard's Penn. The odds are less now; there are only a thousand Turkish soldiers encamped outside Lepanto. But you, Parry, you are a good man and a good soldier. You would certainly fall. And Missolonghi needs you.

He got up, put on his burnished helmet, fastened the buttons on his red jacket, for Byron had decreed that they should fight in British colors, and stepped into the other room. The box was the plainest of wood. And should it be there at all? Would Byron not have preferred cremation, to allow his spirit to soar free into the air and go chasing after Shelley's? But there were no Byrons here, and no Trelawnys, to decide what must be done. An English milord was dead; therefore his body must be embalmed and returned to his home in England. And Johnnie Haggard had not felt strong enough to oppose them.

Because without Byron at his side, Johnnie Haggard did not feel strong enough for anything, save to risk his life in another madcap adventure. He might never have left Barbados.

Save that in Barbados he had never had men like these at his back. He went outside, Parry at his shoulder, gazed at the Suliotes. They were already mounted, glittering in all the splendor of their Albanian finery, long white kilts, gold-worked cloaks, crimson velvet gold-laced jackets and waistcoats, silver-mounted pistols and daggers; he felt quite drab beside them.

Parry shook his head. "Godspeed you, Mr. Haggard."

"I am sure he shall, in one direction or the other." Johnnie swung into the saddle, looked up at the other Europeans, gathered on the veranda above his head. They were a sadly bewildered lot, not understanding what he was about at all. But then, not even Parry truly knew that. There were sound military reasons for so daring a raid. But they were irrelevant beside the personal reasons, the certainty that if he remained here a moment longer, with Byron's body in the next room, he would go mad himself and fall writhing to the floor.

He looked back at the Suliotes, drew his sword, and pointed at the gate, which had already been opened. They gave a cheer and trotted behind him down the road. All of Missolonghi had turned out to watch the Albanians ride by, and cheer them, even if they no doubt hoped that the fierce mountaineers might be gone for good. But Johnnie's blood was already commencing to tingle. His brain went back all of those eight years to that never-to-be-forgotten evening when he had led twenty men through the canefields to regain his home and avenge his wife. Now he had a far greater motive, to avenge the death of the only human being he had ever loved.

The town disappeared into the trees as the horses picked their way over the causeways. Johnnie signaled Yiotes to ride beside him. "We will have out-flankers," he said. "And two men in advance. There may be a Turkish patrol."

"Of course, Excellency," Yiotes agreed, and gave the necessary orders. He had complete faith in their commander. Johnnie had not only drilled with them every day since his arrival, but he was the milord's friend. He spoke with the milord's voice and undoubtedly he thought with the milord's brain. How odd, Johnnie thought, if, after we have triumphed, these fellows were to offer *me* a crown. There would be a turn-up for the book. What would Meg Bold say then? Or was she Meg Haggard now?

They rode in silence. From Missolonghi to Lepanto is hardly more than twenty-five English miles, and it was only now beginning to grow light; they would reach their destination, as he intended, just as the town was coming to life, the bazaars beginning to trade, the people to settle down to another lazy day in the sun. Just as the guards were being changed and the ships were putting to sea.

Thus theory. Undoubtedly the Turks would know that a body of horse was passing through the mountains. He wondered what they would do about it. And he did not care. Not today.

The trees thinned as the track began to climb. Now the sun played games with them, sometimes glancing from a sheer clifftop to send shafts of brilliant light down the valley, sometimes disappearing altogether behind a craggy peak to plunge them into semidarkness. But ahead of them, and above them, he could see the brilliant red jackets of their two skirmishers. So long as those two men remained out there and up there, there was no risk of surprise.

After an hour he called a halt, allowed his men to dismount and stretch themselves, allowed the horses to drink from a rushing mountain stream. He himself took a sip of brandy, offered the flask to Yiotes, who shook his head; he was as devout a Muslim as the Turks, fought for the love of fighting rather than for freedom or religion.

"Where do you think they will oppose us?" Johnnie asked.

Yiotes shrugged. "Where the road comes down from the mountains, perhaps."

"That is good for cavalry. Good for us."

Another shrug. "They would have opposed us up here, had they known we were coming, Excellency. But there has been no time. Besides, they also have cavalry. You have orders for this?"

Johnnie nodded. "As soon as the enemy are seen, we charge," he said. "Straight for the center of their force."

"There will be very many of them," Yiotes pointed out. "More than us."

Johnnie smiled. "We will seem as many, strike as many,

Yiotes, because we will be charging. I have charged before, many men, with few at my back."

Yiotes looked him up and down. "And you have won," he said. "Or you would not be here now. We are proud to follow you, Excellency. You have but to point your sword."

They mounted again, followed the track. Soon it ceased climbing—the high mountains were away to their left and in front of them, behind the seaport—and they were descending again. And now one of the skirmishers spurred his horse back to them, spoke rapidly in Albanian to Yiotes.

"What does he say?"

"He has been to where he can oversee the town, Excellency. The Turks are coming out."

"That is to the good," Johnnie said. "Once we have scattered their cavalry, the town will be ours."

He could think of no alternatives, because he had no alternatives. He knew nothing of warfare save the possible advantage that could be gained by an immediate and tremendous shock. He could only put his faith in what he personally had experienced.

And he could not let himself be afraid. Besides, what was there to be afraid of? He was not afraid of death. He would have welcomed it on several occasions in the past, and he would welcome it now, because it would send him hurrying behind Byron.

But he was Johnnie Haggard. He was not going to die.

In front of them there stretched a brief plain, and beyond it, the roofs of the houses in the town. To their right they could again see the sparkling waters of the gulf. This was a famous place. Out there in the gulf was where the fleets of Turkey and the papacy had met in 1571, to the utter destruction of the Turks. The bed of that sea, Johnnie realized, must be littered with bones and weapons, with shattered hulks and shattered dreams.

Today should hardly be less famous; in front of them the Turkish cavalry was taking its position, the morning sun glinting from their weapons and their helmets.

Yiotes drew rein beside him. "There are a great number," he observed.

"It is of no matter." Johnnie drew his sword and pointed it. "We will charge them, Yiotes."

Yiotes gave a tremendous shout, and his voice was echoed by every one of the two hundred behind him. Johnnie kicked his horse into a trot, resting his sword on his shoulder for the moment, gazing at the confused mass in front of him. He could not believe it was actually happening, but the Turks seemed as alarmed as he had hoped they might be by the approaching mass of men. Speed, that was what they needed now. Speed, to reach their enemy before the officers he could see riding up and down the ranks could restore order. He rose in his stirrups, waved his sword around his head, urged his horse into a canter and then a gallop, listened to the drumming of hooves from behind him. Now he crouched low over his mount's neck, sword pointed in front of him, watched the Turks draw closer. How slowly they approached. They had been farther away than he had supposed. But now he was almost upon them, although his horse was beginning to falter. He stared at them, the dark faces, the mustaches and beards, the pointed helmets, the gleaming swords . . . no half-armed and frightened slaves here, for all that they had still not formed a proper line.

He rose in his stirrups again, gave a shriek, and was into them. He swung his sword and caught one man a blow on the shoulder, which sent him tumbling from the saddle. Someone else thrust at him and he felt a start of pain, but it in no way hampered him, and in bringing his sword back his fist crunched into his adversary's face and sent him too reeling away. By now he should be through the other side, he thought, marshaling his men for another charge. But there was no other side. He was completely surrounded by the dark mustachioed faces, striking at him, reaching for him, shouting at him. He gave a gasp of pure terror as he realized that he was not going to reach the other side, swung with utter desperation and so much force, as his target ducked, that his toes came out of his stirrup and he turned right round in the saddle, teetered there for a moment, and then plunged backward between two horses, losing his sword in the process.

He struck the ground with a thump that drove all the wind from his stomach, gazed up at the hooves and the swords and the faces. I am about to die, he thought. My God, I am about to die. But I am Johnnie Haggard. Remember that, O God. I am Johnnie Haggard.

The horses were pulled away, and men dismounted, to seize his arms and drag him to his feet. I am Johnnie Haggard, he thought, relief seeping through his body like a warm wind. And I am an English milord, so far as these fellows know. I am far too valuable as a prisoner.

He tossed hair from his eyes, only then realized that he had lost his helmet. The battle, if it could be called a battle, was already over. There were several of the Suliotes lying on the ground, obviously dead, and there were several more being herded together, battered and bleeding, by the victorious Turks. And plainly terrified at the fate which was about to overtake them. The rest had disappeared.

And he was still their commander. He attempted to square his shoulders and walk straight, but it was difficult as he was forced forward by his captors, and then pushed to his knees before *their* commanding officer. The victor. He sat his horse like a god, his uniform glittering with gold and silver, his helmet agleam in the morning sun, and stared at Johnnie Haggard. His face was thin, and his mustache drooped, but Johnnie did not suppose he was very old. His eyes were like polished stones. Johnnie wondered whether he should smile at him, decided that a salute would be more appropriate, and shrugged his shoulders at the men holding him. Their grips tightened, for their general was speaking.

And smiling as he spoke. A terrible smile. Which was echoed by the men around him, as the arms holding his shoulders suddenly jerked backward. Johnnie lost his balance and tumbled over onto his back, still held there by the fingers gripping his shoulders. He stared at the smiling general, and other men held his ankles. Oh, my God, he thought. Oh, Lindy.

A man knelt beside him, slashed away the fastenings for his breeches, and he felt the sun on his flesh. Then the man raised the knife, and smiled at him again.

Johnnie Haggard screamed.

Chapter 4

The Abolitionist

Letters, Roger Haggard thought. It occurred to him that the only knowledge he truly had of his brother had always been through letters. Letters from his father, when they had first become reconciled, at a distance of over a thousand miles, extolling the virtues of the young undergraduate. No doubt Father had even then been consciously deluding himself.

Then there had been letters from Johnnie himself, anxious to make the acquaintance of the elder brother he had supposed dead. They had been well written, poetic, but with a touch of flamboyance. Then letters from Johnnie in Barbados, bringing news of the revolt and of the problems of planting. Then the one from Ferguson. In all the thirty-odd years that Johnnie had existed on the face of the earth, the pair of them had actually exchanged only a few words, spent only a few weeks in each other's company.

And now there was a letter from this Captain Parry, to accompany the box. The last letter. And the most terrible he had ever received.

> You will of course be aware, Colonel Haggard [Parry had written], that the Turks have a different cultural ethic to ours, and thus behave in a manner which we would often consider barbaric. And then, sir, this is a barbaric war, like all civil war, in which atrocity is the normal rather than the exception. No doubt we all, certainly your brother and his great friend, would have hoped to bring some of the characteristics of the gentleman to this loath-

some business. Alas, it would seem that we are doomed to failure.

You may believe, sir, how much it grieves me to have to write in this vein, but I do so in the firm belief that it will be your intention to open the coffin, if only to convince yourself that this helpless cadaver is indeed the last remains of your only brother, and therefore I felt it my duty to warn you in advance of what you will find. You may believe me, sir, when I say that the return of Mr. Haggard's body to Missolonghi plunged us into the deepest grief, especially as we realized that the mutilation, the most shameful mutilation, took place *before* he was beheaded. One is forced to the opinion that the Turks merely sought to frighten us by this example of their inhumanity and dishonor. If that is the case, sir, I can assure you that they have failed, and that we shall continue the fight to the bitter end, as Lord Byron and your brother would certainly have wished.

And now, sir . . .

Roger laid down the letter, stared at the wall, and then at the other letter, heavily sealed, which lay on his desk. Johnnie's last will and testament, no doubt. What would it say about Lindy?

But Lindy would have to be told. How much? That her husband had been castrated while begging for mercy? Because that was how it would have happened.

He got up, went to the door, looked up the stairs. She stood there, Jane and Alice at her side. No one in Derleth doubted what was in that coffin. The second Haggard to be buried here, a tortured caricature of a man.

"May I read the letter?" Lindy asked. Her voice was composed.

Roger hesitated, then held it out. Slowly she came down the stairs.

"I think you should sit down," he said, and showed her into the study. Then he went on down the stairs to the parlor, where the box had been placed.

Trum waited in the doorway, like a sentry.

"I must look at him," Roger said.

Trum nodded, snapped his finger to summon the two grooms who also waited, farther down the corridor.

"He was taken by the Turks," Roger explained. "And executed."

"My God," Trum muttered.

"Aye," Roger said. He watched the wooden lid being unscrewed, inhaled the smell of the camphor which had been used in the embalming process. He stepped forward, looked inside. The body had been dressed in ordinary clothes, and there was no sign of what lay beneath, or even what had happened save that the head had fallen sideways, in a way no head could possibly do naturally.

"Is it your brother?" Trum asked at his shoulder.

Roger nodded. "It is he." He turned away, looked at Lindy, standing in the doorway, Parry's letter trailing from her fingers. "Don't come any nearer," he said.

She hesitated, bit her lip, and then sank to her knees.

"Give Mrs. Haggard a glass of brandy, Nugent," Roger said. "And, Trum, would you be so good as to summon Mr. Shotter. I wish the interment to take place this afternoon."

He stepped past Lindy, into the hall.

"Roger . . ." Trum said.

"There is another letter," Roger said. "I will not be long."

"My dear Haggard," Mina said. "How terrible. How very terrible." She pulled off her gloves, gave Jane a kiss on the cheek, then looked around her. "Where is the widow?"

"In the garden with her son."

"The Negro. Yes. How did she take it?"

Jane shrugged. "She is a strange girl. She never shows any emotion."

She did not weep, Haggard thought. Nothing more than a single tear. Because she is a strange girl who does not show any emotion. But when next they had been alone, her nails had bitten into his flesh. She could feel, even if she could no longer reveal.

"Well, from her point of view, it is all to the good," Mina decided, seating herself on the settee and smiling at the room in general. "Now, you will be able seriously to consider a husband for her. Although there are difficulties. My God, yes. Haggard, have you spoken with her?"

"On innumerable occasions."

"Roger is quite fond of his little Barbadian sister-in-law,"

Jane said, winking at her husband. "I think she reminds him of his youth."

"Yes," Mina said. "Well, she will have to come to her senses now. I mean to say, a half-caste bastard son . . . it is too ridiculous. You will have to be firm, Haggard. Oh, by all means educate the boy. Although I imagine you would be wasting your money. A Negro is a Negro, and that is the end of that."

"I'm not sure I follow you," Haggard said, sitting beside her.

"Well, my dear man, it stands to reason, does it not? If they were as intelligent as we, then we would be the slaves and they the masters."

"There are a great number of black people in Africa," Haggard pointed out, "who are not slaves."

"But living in conditions of the most utter superstition."

"Which is surely a point of view."

"A religious argument," Jane cried in delight. "How splendid. I shall adjudicate."

"I have no intention of arguing with anyone about religion," Mina announced. "There is nothing to argue about. Is there, Haggard?"

Haggard smiled at her. "I have no doubt at all that you're right. But there is something I would like to discuss with you."

"Nothing would suit me better. What is it?"

"Johnnie wrote me a letter. The day before he died. I have a suspicion that he almost wished to die, although hardly in so terrible a manner. But with Byron gone, I doubt he wished to live."

"Were they really lovers?"

"I have no idea. They were certainly very close friends."

"I find that incredible," Mina said. "Two men, and Byron, of all people. Why . . ." She gazed at her daughter with her mouth open.

"I did not know him as well as you, Mama," Jane said wickedly. "So I am in no position to judge."

"Well, I can tell you . . . Oh, go on, Haggard. What is in this famous letter?"

"I suggest you read it." Haggard took it from his pocket, opened it, smoothed the sheets, handed it to her.

"Mm." She read with obvious speed and great concentration, finished the first page, raised her head to look at Haggard. "The boy was mad."

"Or far saner than most of us."

"Oh, really, Haggard. I have never heard such nonsense."

"I wish someone would tell me what this is all about," Jane complained.

"It is simply that this deluded late brother-in-law of yours apparently became something of a Methodist missionary in his last years."

"Now, Mina," Haggard said. "There is no suggestion of any religious point of view in that letter. It is based on simple observation."

"He says," Mina said, "that there is no true difference between a white man and a black, save in the color of their skins. He says they are as capable of high feeling and sound reason as any of us. He says that the institution of slavery is the greatest crime ever perpetrated upon any people since the world began."

"And is that not true?" Haggard inquired. "Is it not part of our platform?"

"Every reforming party is afflicted by hangers-on paddling their own canoes," Mina insisted. "Now, God knows I adore dear Willy Wilberforce. Why, when he was a young man I even set my cap at him once." She sighed. "Even then he was more interested in puerile social theories than the realities of life. My dear Haggard, I entirely agree that slavery is iniquitous. But so, alas, is death. And old age. My God. Believe me, I am entirely of the opinion that were it possible, every single human being on the face of this earth should enjoy an income of ten thousand a year, have a face like Helen of Troy or Apollo, have the brain of a Leonardo, and the longevity of a Methuselah. Alas, it is just *not* possible. Nature has made it not possible, and God has set his seal upon the whole miserable business. It is a fact of life that ninety-five percent of the population must labor in order that the other five percent can concentrate upon the sciences and the arts and improving the quality of life."

"For themselves," Jane pointed out, with another wink.

"You are an incredibly tiresome child," Mina complained. "Why do you not beat her, Haggard? She is spoiled rotten entirely because Alderney never beat her."

"And you suppose that such a state of affairs can never change," Haggard said.

"Of course it can never change. Otherwise we would have mass starvation. How could you exist, how could this valley exist, how could all of England exist, without your people in the mill or down the mine?"

"They are not slaves," Haggard said.

"Are they not? They are certainly in bondage. The bondage of money, Haggard. In a sense, we are all slaves to that god. Their bonds are just a little tighter than ours, that's all."

"They have the right to move on," Haggard said. "I have no power to flog them nearly to death. Or *to* death, in some cases. I have no right to abuse them."

"What rubbish. By all accounts your father abused them all his life. And suppose you did decide to beat one of them? Who is going to grant a warrant for your arrest? Jim Hutchinson?"

"There is still a difference."

"Absolute balderdash. It has been tried, time and again, to secure labor for the West Indian plantations from some other source. Europeans have been tried. And they die like flies. The blacks can survive there. But of course they will never work unless driven to it. They have no culture, no civilization. They would cheerfully starve on a patch of sand so long as the sun was shining. Believe me, Haggard, I have studied the matter most carefully. It is not as if we were enslaving some civilized Christian people and forcing them into damnation. We are actually having a civilizing effect upon these people, raising their entire standards, introducing them to the glories of religion. No, no. Your brother is clearly an idealistic madman, rather like poor Byron. I suppose they contaminated each other, in every way."

"Nonetheless," Haggard said, "I think he is right. I have thought of nothing else since I read that letter. I suppose in many ways he put into words what I have ever lacked the courage to think."

"You, Haggard? Lacking courage?"

"There are many different sorts of courage, Mina. I grew up with these people, knew them and liked them. Whatever his other faults, my father was a humane master to his blacks. Perhaps I never thought deeply enough about it in the past. Certainly I have never really thought about it at all in recent years. But I have thought about nothing else this past week. You'll finish the letter, if you please, Mina."

Mina scanned the last two sheets. "A sacred charge," she

said contemptuously. "Has anyone the right to make such a charge?"

"I think he did, as he was prepared to die, having made it."

"Now you are being a sentimental fool. And I seem to remember you arguing with me *against* emancipation not so very long ago."

"I was arguing against hanging slaves for revolting and merely transporting English laborers for doing the same thing. Besides, I'll admit my thoughts on slavery have always been a trifle ambivalent. Johnnie's letter has made me think, has made me evaluate my own position, perhaps."

Mina stared at him, her brows slowly gathering together into a frown. "You are not serious? You will free the slaves on your plantation?"

"I am not that irresponsible. There cannot be one group of freed slaves in a slave society. But I intend to campaign with Wilberforce."

Mina leaned forward, took his hand. "My darling Roger, I know, I can imagine, how upset you are by the news of your brother's terrible fate. Why, I feel quite faint at the thought of it. But you must not let it upset your reason. Supposing, just supposing, there were no slaves, who would work Haggard's Penn for you?"

"I should offer to pay them a wage."

"And suppose they did not wish your wage?"

"Well . . . there is a problem to be solved when it arises."

"Indeed? Is not Haggard's Penn the main source of your wealth?"

"Well . . . I suppose it is."

"Do you make any sort of profit out of Derleth?"

"A small one. Things are going quite well."

"A small one, my God. And you would throw away the source of all your strength. Haggard, Haggard. You could not find a more liberal-minded woman than I. I believe that we should work toward an increased prosperity for all. I believe we should improve living conditions and working conditions and even criminal conditions. I believe we must broaden the base of parliamentary representation. I believe the magistrates have far too much power. I believe in all those things, and I expect this country to move in the direction of those things. But the country must be led, Haggard. It must be led and directed by men with sufficient wealth not to care if they make themselves unpopular with the government, men who do not have to worry where their next crust of bread is coming from, but can spare the time to allow their minds to wander free and far. Only with such men to direct its affairs did this country become great, and only with such men to direct its affairs in the future can this country remain great. Take away a wrestler's muscles, and he is no good to anyone. Take away, or give away, the source of your wealth, Haggard, and you also will be valueless to your fellowman."

Never had he heard her speak so passionately. And no doubt much of what she said made hard common sense. But not good moral sense. He was realizing that now. And eventually, he realized, a man must choose between pragmatism and ethics.

But in any event, Mina was, as usual, projecting an entirely apocalyptical view of the situation. In freeing his slaves, he might be discarding a certain percentage of his capital; it would hardly interfere with his income so long as sugar continued to be in demand. And even without Haggard's Penn, he would still be one of the wealthiest men in the kindgom; the years of careful investment of the plantation's excess profits in government stock by John Haggard and the first Roger Haggard had seen to that.

He smiled at her, and squeezed her hand. "Nevertheless, my darling Mina, I intend to work for emancipation. Johnnie died too well to have his last wish neglected."

"You are mad," Mina declared. "Stark, raving mad. I despair." She stared at her daughter.

She got up to kiss Haggard on the cheek.

"I think he is magnificent, Mama. He will always have *my* support."

Could any man ask for a more faithful wife? Or sister?

"I am so glad," Alice said. "So very glad." She frowned through her smile as she kissed him on the cheek. "But there will be difficult times ahead."

"There have always been difficult times ahead, Alice," he pointed out. "Where would life be without difficult times ahead?"

But in his heart their support counted for nothing.

"I must leave Derleth," Lindy said.

They walked together through the wood, Strolo having been left in the care of his nurse. It was a delightful summer's afternoon, and the sun shot shafts of the purest gold between the tree trunks, diffused by the leaf curtain which rustled gently to either side.

"That is absurd," Haggard argued.

"It is essential." Her fingers tightened on him. "I have lived here for seven years, and almost every day of the past five has been heavy with likely disaster."

"Having survived five years, my darling, we are not likely to be discovered now."

"We are more than ever likely to be discovered now. Besides . . ."

"Now that Johnnie is dead, you would like to marry again?"

She gave him a quick glance. "It would be the best thing."

"Do you wish it?"

She sighed. "No. No, I do not wish it. I can love only you. You taught me how to love. I do not suppose I will ever be able to transfer that love. But . . ."

"But I can never marry you."

"I would not ask it of you, even if you could. *I* would not bring calamity upon you."

"And you will not. I promise you."

She smiled, and stopped walking, turning to face him. "When it happens, it will sneak up on you before you know what it is. But there is more than that, Roger. We . . ." She bit her lip.

"Say it."

"We love," she said. "That is all we have in common. That is all we have needed, for five years. I have always prayed that we should never need anything more. But we are human beings. You are a man with things to do. I cannot, I dare not, interfere with that. But I am a woman who can only feel."

"Ah," he said.

"I'm sorry."

"Why should you be? Cannot we discuss it?"

She shrugged. "If you wish to do so."

"Emancipation is an inevitable process. It must happen someday. There is no nation in history has succeeded in keeping another enslaved forever."

"The outcome is usually bloody."

"Indeed it has always been so. Therefore would it not be sensible to attempt to avert that bloodshed?"

"By an abdication of responsibility? By giving freedom to . . ." She shivered.

"English soldiers, French soldiers, Russian soldiers, German soldiers, they have all committed rape."

"I told you, I can only feel." She forced a smile. "I am not a very good Whig, Roger. I do not think I am a Whig at all. Soldiers are at least subject to military discipline. You would make the blacks free. And then you, or the next generation of Whigs, would give them the right to vote, or perhaps even to be elected. And then the next generation will appear and say that they must have power. . . ." Another shiver. "That too is an inevitable process."

"And you would carry your hate to the third generation?"

She raised her head. "I will carry my hate to the grave, certainly."

"And Strolo?"

A sigh. "Perhaps I keep him by me to remind me of my hate."

"I'm not sure I care for the idea."

"Nor should you." She held his hands, squeezed them. "You are Roger Haggard. You are great and good and strong, and very honorably you feel that that greatness, that goodness, that strength, should be used for the benefit of mankind, all mankind. Believe me, Roger, I am proud to have known and loved such a man. I am proud to think that he can love me. But I am neither great nor good nor strong. I am a woman who knows only hate, whose only pleasure for five years has been adultery. Who daily breaks bread with the woman she is betraying. Listen to me, my darling. Johnnie's death is, I think, something we were both waiting for. Johnnie's death, or Johnnie's return. It has affected you most powerfully. Do you not suppose it has affected me as well? It has made me think. It has made me understand what I am doing. And what I am doing is wrong. Terribly, terribly wrong. I would beseech you, dear Roger, to grant me a cottage somewhere, that I may live in peace, and bring up my son in peace."

He gazed at her. But there could be no doubt she meant it.

"And will I be allowed to come and visit you?"

She hesitated, then shook her head. "If I were to permit that, I might as well stay here."

He sighed, and nodded. "You shall have what you want.

But, Lindy, it is to give you time to think. And me time to think as well. Nothing more definite than that."

She smiled, but a tear trickled out of her eye. "Time to think, Roger."

"A win, sir, a win," James Hutchinson bellowed with joy, leaving his seat to hurry out into the throng, for a goodly number of Benligh people, confident in their team's growing ability, had made the journey down to Derleth to support their men in the annual cricket match.

"The first ever," Roger Haggard said sadly. "Ah, well, it had to come."

"All because you wouldn't play, Trum," Jane pointed out.

"My dear Jane," Trumley protested. "I am forty-seven years old. Time for some of those younger fellows to show their ability."

"They *have* no ability," Jane pointed out.

"As Roger says, it has to happen," Alice argued. "After all, it would be boring if we beat them *every* year."

"Well done, lads, well done," Hutchinson was roaring, pushing his way into the crowd, slapping people on the back, and shaking them by the hand. "Oh, well done."

"It's at least pleasant to see the old chap happy," Roger said, and followed more slowly. And therefore, he supposed, no one could complain that the squire of Derleth might not be looking as happy as usual. The first defeat in eight years. But eight years ago, how different had things been. Then Lindy had been sitting next to Alice, clapping her hands in pleasure as Trum had made the winning hit. Now Lindy was living somewhere on the Isle of Wight. He had not even been allowed to help her choose her new home, but had been forced to leave the whole thing to Alice. By Lindy's decision. He knew where she was, of course, as he knew the address to which his bank sent her monthly allowance. Presumably he could visit her. He *could* do that.

But he had not done so. She had forbidden it, and besides, this last winter had been one of the busiest he had known, as he had thrown himself more vigorously than ever before into parliamentary business. He sometimes supposed that even his Whig friends felt that he was becoming a little too radical, a little too vehement. Their ambitions, for the moment, went no further than obtaining a majority in Parliament. As this apparently could only be done by a major redistribution of the seats, a reconstruction of the entire electoral system, this was the main plank of their platform, the Great Idea that they presented to the public, time and again. Russell's concept was that if they followed this course resolutely, soon enough Tory opposition would begin to waver, sufficiently at any rate for the Whigs to gain just a few more seats at the next election. He had followed this course ever since 1817, but his arithmetic had suffered a severe setback following the discovery of the Cato Street Conspiracy, a latter-day gunpowder plot, unearthed a couple of years before. In the general election following *that* fiasco, the electors, with the built-in conservatism of the average Englishman, had increased the Tory majority, and the whole process had had to start all over again.

Thus, in Russell's view, civil disorder had to be avoided at all costs. In this he was one with the government. The country had to be convinced of the moral necessity of parliamentary reform, not frightened away from it by the thought of some radical like Orator Hunt being elected to a seat. The unfortunate point was that Haggard could not bring himself to believe in parliamentary reform, at least on the scale projected by his Whig friends, at all. Some widening of the franchise was certainly necessary, but the thought of the English lower classes being given the vote filled him with apprehension. He supposed it was his upbringing, both as a slave owner and a Tory squire. He believed in improving the lot of the masses as far as was conceivably possible, just as he was determined to free his slaves, even at great economic cost, but the impetus had to come from people like himself, not be the result of some subterranean explosion of popular feeling. That way lay revolution, and he had spent the best years of his life fighting against the results of revolution.

It was impossible to bring Russell to his point of view. He believed in liberalism, certainly, but he was a politician first, last and foremost; he knew what could be done and what couldn't, and to him Whig control of Parliament was the first, and indeed the only, way toward the better world which he agreed with Haggard in desiring. And that meant parliamentary reform. He hated to see valuable parliamentary time taken up in discussing laws to restrict child labor—there were even some extremists in his party who would see child labor abolished altogether—and laws for compensation for work-

270   *Christopher Nicole*

men injured in mill or mining accidents, and most of all in discussing the moral question of slavery in the colonies.

"Of course the slaves should be free, my dear Haggard," he had said, "and of course the slaves shall be free, just as soon as we are in power. But we must get the power first. And do not forget, Haggard, that it is the people of Liverpool and Manchester and Bristol, those vast conglomerates which at present only return one member each, upon whom we must rely for support when the time comes. You know as well as I that the entire wealth of those cities is based on the slave trade."

"The slave trade ended seventeen years ago," Haggard had argued.

"Not even a generation. Believe me, Haggard, it is best to hurry slowly in these matters. It must be done. It will be done. I give you my word on that. But in God's good time. Besides," he had added with that singular smile of his, "I'd not have our supporters think that we are demented. You, Roger Haggard, of Haggard's Penn in Barbados, would stand up and declare yourself an abolitionist?"

"I have already done so."

"Well, do it privately for the time being, I beg of you."

And Roger had been forced to sigh, and submit, and ask, "So you would also have us vote against the repeal of the Combination Acts?"

"By no means. This is Tory legislation, and is eminently to be desired. To my mind it shows a definite shift in the direction we are aiming. No, no, Haggard. We shall support the repeal of the Combination Acts. Those of us who are fair to our laborers need have no fear of them uniting against us. Those of us who are not fair, well, they are Tories anyway."

So, not much time last winter and this spring to think of Lindy. And then much of his time in Derleth had been taken up with Jane's miscarriage and subsequent illness. For a while it had been touch and go. He had been so unsure of his feelings as to be consumed with guilt through the Christmas holiday. Useless to remind himself that Jane's death, if it ever were to happen, could make no difference to his secret desires. A man could not marry his brother's widow, and there was the end of it. The guilt was as regards Jane herself. Utterly beautiful, utterly desirable, the perfect aristocratic wife and mother, and, in her own fashion, utterly devoted to her husband, or at least to what he represented and what he stood for. And utterly confident of *his* devotion.

And now as well as ever again in her life, walking with Alice up the slight slope to the patio, already calling out to her children, playing there under the care of their nurses, a picture in her gaily ribboned bonnet and her flounced skirt. The sort of wife to make any man wish the day's festivities at an end so that he could carry her off to their tower suite and love her and love her and *love* her.

Instead of which he found himself thinking about Lindy.

"Well, Haggard, why so sad?" Hutchinson, having congratulated his team and dispatched them off to the inn, had rejoined his host. "Had to happen, eh? Had to happen. It's that new bowler of mine. Saw him playing over in Sheffield last autumn, and offered him a post as gamekeeper. Between you and me he cannot hit the side of a barn with a fowling piece, and finds it hard to distinguish a partridge from a pheasant. But he can pitch them, eh? Oh, aye, he can pitch them."

"Indeed he can," Roger agreed. "And do you suppose it would be a good idea for me to journey to Yorkshire, looking for cricketing talent?"

"Ha, ha," Hutchinson laughed, a trifle uncertainly. "Ha, ha. You're not sore about that, Haggard? I mean to say, Trumley Sparrow is hardly a Derleth man by birth."

"No more am I," Roger pointed out.

"Oh, quite, quite. Well, what's sauce for the goose, eh? Anyway, you know," he said seriously, as they left the crowd behind and approached the ladies and the tea spread across the patio tables, "I didn't visit Yorkshire looking for cricketing talent. No, no. Serious business. I'm told you voted with the government last month."

"Most of us did," Roger pointed out. "We are perfectly willing to support the government when they promote desirable legislation."

"Desirable legislation?" Hutchinson bellowed, his good humor disappearing. "By God, sir, we fought to have those acts passed in the first place."

"In time of war, sir," Roger said. "Perhaps there was some reason for it, then. It is always necessary to dragoon people in time of war. But the war has now been over ten years, and there is no immediate sign of another one."

"Dragoon people?" Hutchinson's voice rose an octave.

"Those people sir, those so-called Combinations, or Unions, sir, were nothing less than radical revolutionaries."

"Oh, come now." They had reached the steps leading up, and he waited for his guest to mount first, but Hutchinson preferred to stand on the bottom step and wave his arms. "What did they do, save appoint one of their number to act as spokesman?"

"And accompany him, sir. And threaten not to work. Why, sir, that is outrageous. A man must work for his master. I have never heard anything like it in my life before. Not work, sir? Why, I find it difficult to believe my ears."

"I find it difficult to become agitated over," Haggard said. "If a man, or even a group of men, choose not to work, then they will surely starve. There is sufficient labor in England to fill their places. Anyway, Hutchinson, this repeal of the Anti-Combination Act expressly omits the right to strike. So your fears are groundless. And you must understand their minds, sir. You think of a group of your people approaching you to petition for the redress of some grievance as intimidation. But consider the position of the elected spokesman, were he forced to approach you by himself, you, with your dogs and your grooms and your gamekeepers."

"Ha, ha," Hutchinson roared. "Ha, ha. They did, the fools. By God, they did. Twelve of them, but a week ago. And I set the dogs on them. Oh, aye. Petition to form a trades union, they called it. My people. Benligh people. Young, they were. Right radical layabouts. Oh, aye, I saw through their little game. More wages, shorter hours . . . by God, sir, but it was sport."

Roger stared at him. "Then it is you, sir, who have broken the law. Those men were within their rights."

"Rights?" Hutchinson roared. "Rights? Why, sir, was it not for me, and my father before me, those fellows would have starved long ago. Rights? Do not talk to me about rights. I know you, sir. You are a confounded Bible-thumping Methodist, so I've heard. By God, sir, your father must be turning in his grave at the thought of what is happening here. Freeing the slaves? Gad, sir, I do not know what the world is coming to. A slave, sir, is a slave, and there's an end to the matter."

"My opinions are my own, Hutchinson," Roger said, keeping his temper with an effort. "And I request you to respect them."

"Opinions, is it?" Hutchinson shrieked, oblivious of the

ladies, who were looking toward them with anxious expressions, or Trum, standing by, his face crimson with embarrassment. "Your opinions, sir, and those of your entire family, are the concern of the country. Your opinions? A madman who rushes around opposing the will of the magistrates, talks about freeing the slaves, betrays his father's principles, has a confounded sodomite for a brother—"

"You'll withdraw that remark, sir," Roger said.

"Withdraw, sir? Withdraw? Why—"

"You'll withdraw that remark, sir," Roger said. "Or I will shoot the words out of your mouth."

Hutchinson stared at him, mouth opening and shutting.

"Oh, my God," said Mrs. Hutchinson.

Jane said nothing, looked at her husband.

"Trum . . ." Alice begged.

"Roger," Trum said, touching his friend on the arm.

"By God, sir," Hutchinson said, having regained his breath. "My second will call upon you."

"As soon as possible, sir," Roger said.

"Gentlemen, gentlemen," Trum said, taking Hutchinson's arm as well. "Now do you both seek to break the law. Dueling is illegal."

"Defamation of the dead is hardly a reasonable act," Roger said.

"Defamation?" Hutchinson bellowed. "Defamation? Why, sir—"

"Say it, and I shall strike you," Roger warned.

"By God, sir—"

"I'm sure," Trum said, "that a glass of wine, and a handclasp . . ."

"Hutchinson has but to apologize," Roger said.

"Apologize, sir? Apologize? Why—"

"Then I must request you to leave my property."

Hutchinson appeared to be on the verge of apoplexy, and was rescued by his wife. "I am sure we shall, Mr. Haggard," she said, seizing her husband's arm.

"My dear Charlotte ... ." Jane hurried toward them.

"I am sure we shall be friends again, Jane," Mrs. Hutchinson said. "In the course of time. When these men have made fools of each other. But for the moment, you'll excuse us."

"Would you be so kind as to order up Mr. Hutchinson's carriage? Trum?" Jane asked.

"Of course." He hurried off.

"My second, sir, my second," Hutchinson bawled, once again able to breathe.

"Come along, Mr. Hutchinson," his wife said firmly, guiding him toward the house.

Jane watched them ushered through the door by an anxious Nugent, and then threw back her head and gave a peal of the most delighted laughter.

"Jane," Alice protested. "How can you?"

"I have never seen anything more ludicrous in my entire life," Jane said, flicking a tear from her eye. "My God, he reminded me of a bullfrog about to explode. And you . . . I have never known a man so devoted to defending lost causes."

Haggard flushed. "He insulted my brother."

"He told the absolute truth about your poor demented brother, my darling," she said, kissing him on the cheek. "But I love you for it."

"And you are not concerned that Hutchinson might blow Roger's head off?" Alice demanded.

"Hutchinson?" Jane's smile faded, and she peered at Haggard. "Is that a possibility?"

"I have no idea. I doubt it."

"But you have never fought a duel before," Alice pointed out.

"Indeed I have not. Has Hutchinson?"

"With that temper, I should think it is extremely likely," Alice said.

"Well, you must get your shot in first," Jane decided.

"I have no intention of killing the fellow," Roger protested.

"My dear, darling, delightful lunatic," Jane said. "You may be sure he will try to kill you. If you don't bring him down first, you will be committing suicide. I'm not suggesting you aim at his head. That would be too risky in any event, unless you are a crack shot. But hit him in the chest and bowl him over. Then whether or not he dies is up to fate."

"You seem very experienced," Alice said.

"For God's sake, two of my uncles lost their lives in duels. And Papa has fought several. But he has remained alive, by practicing the very reasoning I am suggesting to you, Roger." She squeezed his arm. "I really am too young to cope with the problems of ruling Derleth. I should have to marry again, and really, my darling, I am far too comfortable to wish to consider adapting myself to another man. Besides . . ." Another kiss. "I am quite fond of you, you silly old man. Now I must go and dress for dinner." A last squeeze, and she was entering the house, moving with those hurried strides which were her custom.

Alice gazed at her brother. "Do you suppose she really cares about anything?"

"I am sure she does. It is just her manner. Inherited from Mina, I may say. Laugh at everything. That way, you will never have to cry. I am quoting Mina. And who's to say it is not good common sense?"

Alice leaned against him, her arms round his waist. "If anything were to happen to you . . . do you realize I would be quite alone?"

"What nonsense. You have Trum."

"He feels as I do. We are both but extensions of your personality. Don't be hurt, Roger. Promise me that."

"I should think the odds are considerably in my favor, my sweet. I have at least spent most of my life soldiering. Well, Trum?"

Trum stood in the doorway. "His man is here now. His bailiff. He was in the team, you know."

Roger nodded. "And?"

"Pistols."

"I expected it. Well, I suggest an early night."

"He wishes the duel to take place immediately," Trum said. "This very evening."

"It cannot be," Alice protested.

"Well, he's concerned that the moment the news gets abroad there will be a move to prevent it taking place. He seems very anxious for your blood, Roger."

"Then we might as well have it over and done with," Roger said. "Where is it to take place?"

"He leaves the venue to you."

"I suggest this very park. At seven o'clock."

"Seven o'clock?" Alice cried. "But it is five now. One is supposed to consider the matter, to give time for tempers to cool, to enable a possible reconciliation to take place. Otherwise the whole thing is . . ."

"Illegal?" Roger smiled at her. "It is that, in any event. But I am sure neither Hutchinson nor I wishes to find himself in court on a murder charge. Seven o'clock it shall be. And after we have exchanged fire, why, he and his wife will have supper with us and spend the night as was always intended."

"You'd willingly shake hands now, wouldn't you?" Alice said.

Roger shrugged. "I lost my temper."

"Then you will offer an accommodation?"

"He has but to withdraw his remark about Johnnie," Roger promised. "Now there are one or two things to which I must attend."

He went to his office, sat at his desk, ran his eye down the account book. No problem there; Jane took an interest in the running of the estate, and read all of Ferguson's letters from Barbados, and Alice was equally capable. He read his will, could find no fault. Lindy and Alice were secured for life, and Jane would be the wealthiest widow in the kingdom.

He leaned back in his chair, tapped his teeth with his pen. Of all the singular and senseless occurrences. He wondered if he was afraid. And decided that he was not. Presumably it was possible to be hit . . . but that risk had occurred every time he had led his men into battle. It was a far more important decision whether to hit or not. He did not doubt he *could* shoot Hutchinson down, if he wished; he had always been regarded as a very fair shot. But he certainly did not wish to. And yet, he would have to hit the man to be sure he was not himself hit. There was a damnable decision to have to make.

He wondered how his father would have chosen. As if he did not already know. Father had fought Malcolm Bolton, and coldly brought him down with a bullet in the chest. That was what Jane would have him do. Because it was the sensible thing to do, and a Favering always did the sensible thing.

He raised his head, because there she was, standing in the doorway, a shawl about her shoulders.

"You did not tell me it is to be tonight," she said.

"I wanted to think."

She came into the room. "About what?"

He shrugged.

"I never supposed you a fool, Roger," she said. "Or I would not have married you. Bring him down. You must bring him down. It matters nothing who was right and who was wrong. We are talking about survival. You have a duty to live. A duty to me, to Harry and little Mina, to Alice and

Trum, to everyone on Derleth, to Lindy and Strolo, to the entire Whig party. My God, to the entire country, if we are going to save it from disaster. You *must* bring him down."

"Do you not suppose Hutchinson has duties? He has a family. And an estate. And a political party."

She gazed at him for some seconds. "Bring him down," she said at last. It occurred to Roger that she was giving a command, as an officer might instruct his men what he wanted done in an approaching battle. "Now come and kiss the children good night."

He followed her up the stairs, watched her skirt swaying in front of him, her shoes appearing and disappearing with each step. How simple it would be to sit back and let Jane manage his life for him. She was quite capable of doing that. And suddenly he was tired. Perhaps he had been tired for a very long while without being aware of it, and it had needed something of this nature to make him realize it.

She waited while he hugged Harry. "We'll go for a walk tomorrow," he promised, memory drifting back all of forty-five years to his father standing in the doorway of his bedroom at Haggard's Penn, looking at him, the night before he had killed Bolton.

A kiss and a cuddle for little Mina, and then he was back outside, and Jane was closing the door. "I shall watch," she said. "From the window."

The time was ten minutes to seven. He hesitated, then leaned forward and kissed her on the mouth. She never moved, and he went down the stairs, past the servants, all gathered in the downstairs hall, past Mary Prince, gazing at him with tragic dark eyes, past Nugent, waiting to hold his coat for him.

"Dark colors, Mr. Haggard," the old fellow said. "They do say it is best."

Haggard squeezed his hand, went toward the patio door, where Alice waited.

"Jane . . ."

"Is upstairs," he said. "Will you watch as well?"

"Like some Roman matron?" she asked bitterly. "No, my darling brother. I will not watch. Come to me when it is over."

"You may count on that."

Trum waited at the door, and beyond, at the foot of the steps to the patio, Hutchinson and Bragg, his bailiff, were also waiting. And the end of the park was as crowded as it had been for the cricket match. Derleth and Benligh people, waiting to see their masters jousting as they had done earlier with bat and ball. What a crazy world it was, to be sure, Roger thought.

"Now, gentlemen," Trum said. "It is my duty to require you to abandon this quarrel and shake hands, like true Christians."

"Mr. Hutchinson has but to withdraw his remarks concerning my brother," Roger said.

"I spoke the truth," Hutchinson declared. "No man can be expected to apologize for the truth."

They looked at each other, and Roger shrugged.

"Then let us be at it," Hutchinson said.

"You'll inspect these weapons, Colonel Haggard," Bragg said, opening the pistol case. "I loaded them myself."

Roger shrugged again, walked onto the lawn. Trum followed him, with one of the pistols.

"This is very irregular," he said, "I have sent for Dr. Maltby, but he has not yet come. Do you not suppose . . . ?"

"The whole thing is irregular, Trum," Roger said. "As long as he is coming. Although pray God we shall not need him. Let's get it over."

Hutchinson had taken his place, Trum now walked across to stand beside Bragg. "At the count of three, gentlemen," he said. "There is no need, I am sure, to remind either of you of the rules of proper conduct. At the count of three."

Roger waited, staring at Hutchinson. They were so close he could make out every wrinkle. And amazingly, all the anger seemed to have gone. Hutchinson's face was severely composed, concentrated. He was a man who was prepared to die, but was determined to do it well. A dear man, whatever his eccentricities and his faults and his misguided opinions.

"Three," Trum said.

Roger realized he had not heard the first two numbers, discovered he was already raising his weapon. And Hutchinson had hardly moved. For God's sake, he thought, at least aim, you silly old fool.

Slowly and very deliberately he leveled his pistol, gazed down the barrel, looked at Hutchinson. Still the other pistol was not up. My God, he thought, I could kill him like I'd shoot a stunned rabbit. The sensible thing to do. Indeed it was. But not until his adversary had at least sighted his own weapon.

He became aware of a flash of light. In a most curiously detached fashion he realized that it had not come from his own pistol, and almost immediately he knew a tremendous pain in his chest. I must shoot him now, he thought. I simply must.

But there was no strength left in his hand.

Chapter 5

The Turncoat

Dim lights, shooting across the ceiling. Because he knew instinctively that he was indoors.

In a coffin? Hardly. He was breathing, although each swelling of his lungs was agony. And he lay on soft sheets rather than in a wooden box.

And there was Jane, looking down at him.

"Oh, you fool, Haggard," she said. "Oh, you fool."

Later there was Alice, sitting by his bed, his hand resting in hers while she wept.

"I'm not dead," he said reassuringly, but she did not seem to hear him.

Then there was a whole succession of faces: Mary Prince, leaning over him as she straightened his sheets; Trum, looking down on him with huge sad eyes; Nugent, peering at him from the end of the bed; Dr. Maltby, prodding at his chest and making him twist in pain.

And Lindy. She stood at the end of the bed, like Nugent, because she was flanked by Jane and Alice. How splendid she looked. And how sad. But he was not going to die. She at least must be able to understand that.

He attempted to move his arm, and found that he could, holding it up. The women exchanged glances, and then came closer.

Lindy's cheeks were pink. "I could not let you die," she said. "Without seeing you."

"I am not going to die," he said.

Another quick exchange of glances, and then Jane bent over him. "What did you say, Haggard?"

Haggard decided to shout. "I am not going to die," he shouted.

Jane raised her head slowly, to suggest his voice had not especially hurt her eardrums. Then she smiled, and kissed him on the forehead. "I do believe that you may not," she agreed. "But you must not be agitated. Maltby says so." She ushered the others from the room. Lindy hesitated in the doorway, looked over her shoulder. But she could do no more, and by the time he could leave his bed and, with the aid of Corky and Trum, slowly make his way downstairs to sit in the sunshine, she was gone, back to the Isle of Wight.

In her place there was Mina.

"Oh, foolish Haggard," she said. "Foolish, foolish Haggard."

"I did not wish to kill him," Haggard said.

"And instead did not fire at all? Do you not suppose you have killed him just the same? He considers himself all but a murderer, because you did not shoot him down. Men! My God, if the world is in such a sorry state, it is that your sex has had the ruling of it for too long. Look at you. As weak as a babe. And fortunate. But how long do you suppose it will take that wound to heal? Those muscles to grow again?"

"Maltby says in a year's time I shall be as strong as ever I was."

"A year," she cried. "My God. In a year's time you will be fifty-one years old, Haggard. Fifty is no age to be wandering around with a great hole in your chest. A year's time. I shall be sixty-five," she brooded. It was difficult to accept. Undoubtedly she dyed her hair, but there were still not sufficient wrinkles in that magnificent face. Only a few at the neck, a few raised veins in her hands, a slight hesitation in those quick, determined movements, suggested that she was no longer a girl. He wondered if she could still perform miracles of athletic contortionism in bed; certainly her name was still linked with a succession of men.

"There is so much to be done," she complained. "So very much. Have you heard that Liverpool is unwell?"

"In what way?"

She shrugged. "It is just a rumor. That he was speaking in the Lords the other day, and suddenly stopped, and turned pale, and sat down abruptly. We made great sport of it, of course, suggesting port as a possible reason, but it seems likely that he had a spasm of some sort. Now, if Liverpool were to leave office, for whatever reason . . . what do you suppose would happen then?"

"Peel?"

"Far too young."

"Well, then . . . the duke?"

"There you have it. Can you imagine Wellington Prime Minister? There is a recipe for revolution."

"As the Tories know as well as we do, Mina. But there's someone you haven't thought of. Who has been the real leader of the Tories in the Commons since Castlereagh blew out his brains?"

"Canning?" She stared at him for a moment, then threw back her head and gave a peal of laughter. "*Canning*? He's almost a Whig."

"Well, then? He commands support."

"But he isn't a Whig," she said fiercely. "He follows his own peculiar politics. He's confused and he's dangerous. No, no, they'll go for the butcher! And that means we shall need every man we have, to oppose him, so get well, Haggard, get well."

Oh, indeed, get well. But it was a longer process than Maltby had anticipated. No doubt, he thought, Mina was, as always, right; fifty is no age to be shot in the chest. So he was forced to watch events from a distance. To read of the Egyptian armies of Mehemet Ali, commanded by his brilliant son Ibrahim, landing in the Morea and beginning its reconquest for the sultan, eventually flooding north over the Isthmus of Corinth and taking Missolonghi itself, despite its swamps. How had Byron and Johnnie and all those other heroes died in vain? he thought.

He could only follow from afar the wrangling of Whig and Tory at Westminster, the tales of continued unrest throughout the country, rely for the truth upon Mina during her regular visits to Derleth.

And he could only dream of Lindy, standing at the foot of his bed. She wrote to him faithfully, but principally to keep him informed as to Strolo's health and his prowess as he reached the age of ten. He was to go to Eton the next year. Strolo. What would he make of Eton? And what, indeed, would Eton make of him? But he was being brought up as a very proper English gentleman.

Of herself Lindy wrote little. He understood she was in

the best of health, and that she spent a great deal of time walking the beaches of Sandown Bay or across the rolling hills to the old harbor of Bembridge. He could imagine her, with her long strides and her golden hair flowing behind her. How marvelous it would be to be there with her. And indeed Sandown was a recognized place for recuperating from illnesses, even if they be caused by flying lead. But that had to be a dream.

And there was never a word of what he most dreaded to hear. She was thirty years old, as lovely as ever she had been, and a wealthy widow, thanks to the share of the Haggard wealth which he had given her as Johnnie's relict. There must be suitors. But she never mentioned them.

It was a period when he necessarily drew closer to his children, simply because there was more time. At seven Henry was already a true Haggard, with the long nose and the cool gray eyes, and reaching for the height which would certainly be his. It was time, indeed, to think of the future. That *his* son would go to Harrow and then Cambridge, he never doubted. It was what followed that was important. Should he spend a while in Barbados, learning the intricacies of sugar planting? With the retirement of Ferguson, Roger promoted Beddoes to be manager, but Beddoes was slow to settle and seemed bemused by Roger's instructions that the whip was to be used only when absolutely necessary, and not at all on women. And what *of* the future of planting? At the moment he was unable to do more than lend Wilberforce his silent support, to the amazement of his friends and his enemies alike, but soon enough he would be able to take his place in the House. Then it was his decision to support the end of a way of life which had made his family what it was. How father and grandfather must be turning in their respective graves. But the fact was, as he sat on the patio on a cold winter's day and watched Fred Loon, as ever, breaking the ice on the distant trout stream, that the end of planting, in the sense that the Haggards had known it, was anyway in sight. Profits were falling every year as costs soared and markets dwindled under the impact of competition, not only from beet sugar, but from the great cane-sugar plantations of Louisiana, as the American nation grew and prospered.

So many things to be considered, to be estimated. His own marriage not least. After ten years, no one would expect the first flush of erotic fascination to remain, however Jane herself remained one of the great beauties of the day. But again the fact was that since the duel she acted the wife only as required. Her household she managed with an ever sterner grasp. Her husband she accommodated when he demanded it of her, saying, "Of course, Roger," removing her clothes and submitting her body to his caresses. No more transports of sexual delight. Easy to say that she knew he needed fully to recover his strength before they could resume their old pleasures. But he suspected they were gone forever. In not shooting down Hutchinson, he had broken her code, of always doing exactly what had to be done to achieve the best possible end for her. He watched her approach now, wrapped in her pelisse but with the hood thrown back to expose her hair, carrying a letter.

"From the Commons," she said. "And there is news. Liverpool has had a seizure and has resigned."

"At last," he said. "An election?"

She sat beside him. "I cannot say. Thus this letter is the more interesting. It is from George Canning."

Haggard glanced at the franking, slit the envelope with his thumb, scanned the two pages of neat handwriting inside.

" . . . the party is split . . . the old guard wish to go to the country . . . sufficient members wish to carry on and have invited me to form a government . . ." He raised his head, gazed at her, then went on reading. ". . . these troubled times . . . concept of a more broadly based administration . . . points of view sufficiently close . . . would ask no man to go against his conscience, but . . . good of the country . . ." He raised his head again. "My God, he wishes me to join the government."

"A Cabinet seat?"

Haggard shook his head. "He cannot go so far at the moment. An undersecretaryship at the War Office, to begin with, but it is a foot in the door."

"The Tory door. You'll not consider it, Roger."

He frowned at her. "I shall certainly *consider* it, my darling."

She bit her lip as she flushed. "Are you that ambitious?"

"I am ambitious to achieve the goal we have set ourselves. George is perfectly right when he points out that there is not that much difference of opinion between us. Almost every piece of liberal legislation that has been passed these past three years has been his doing. Don't you see, if he can form a middle-of-the-road party, then those goals have come that much closer."

She got up. "I can see that you will do what you wish, Mr. Haggard. It is a characteristic." Her smile was wintry. "Once I loved you for it."

George Canning was a short, heavy man with a long nose and receding hair. He had the appearance, from a distance, of tremendous strength and energy. Closer at hand Haggard was alarmed to see the change that had come over him in the two years he had been absent from the House. His cheeks had fallen in and his shoulders were bowed, while every few minutes he was convulsed by a racking cough. Yet his eyes were as bright as ever, his handshake firm.

"A damnable cold," he explained. "Caught in January, standing around waiting for the poor old Duke of York to be buried, would you believe. There is a sort of ghoulish satisfaction, I suppose, to see all of one's boyhood contemporaries dwindling. I do not suppose our gracious sovereign is very long for this world."

"Is he ill?" Haggard found it difficult to envisage an England without Prinny's bloated body drifting across its consciousness. Not that they saw much of each other; following the quarrel with his father, when George had been regent, the name of Haggard was not mentioned in court circles.

"Was he ever well?" Canning asked. "But sit down, Haggard, sit down. You'll understand that what I propose does not meet with universal approval."

Haggard nodded.

"There is a hard core of Toryism, led by men like Goderich and Wellington, who refuse to accept change in any shape or form. Great Britain was the greatest country in the world fifty years ago, therefore she will only remain so by practicing the methods of fifty years ago. They forget the industrial and economic changes that have happened since then. They forget, indeed, the *ca ira*. The entire world can never be the same again. Do you agree with me?"

"So far."

"Well, it would be simple enough to go to the country. But the result, I very much fear, would be faction. You will know as well as I how all England seethes, just below the surface."

"Would not an election be the answer, to let off some of that steam?"

"If it were to produce a result, perhaps. But consider the situation. The right wing of my part would certainly hive off and oppose me, whether openly or clandestinely, I cannot say. But you will not deny that under our present electoral system the Tories would again receive a majority."

"Now, there's a subject I'd like to discuss," Haggard said.

"In a moment. The result I foresee, if an election were to be held, say this summer, would be an increased Whig representation, to be sure, but yet not one which would command a majority. On the other hand, I can see a Tory party itself split, sometimes voting together, sometimes not. In short, I see a recipe for disaster. The country must not be under any misapprehension that it is being *governed*, Haggard."

"As it has been governed for the past twenty years?"

"If you truly thought that you would not be here," Canning pointed out. "I know all the evils that beset us. I believe I can put them right. But I need time, and above all, I need support."

"May I inquire?"

"Of course."

"Foreign policy?"

"Nonintervention."

"Eh?"

"The problem with huge wars such as the last is that every nation becomes every other nation's problem. Now, we have had too many years of the Russians and the Prussians and the French saying what can and what cannot be done inside other nations. My policy has always been that people should find their own level and their own governments. That is what I set out to do in America, you'll remember." He shrugged. "Well, the Yankees didn't care for it. I suspect they felt it was a way of claiming all of South America for Great Britain, and in view of our history, I cannot blame them. So Monroe has made his own declaration. Well, that suits me perfectly. I can see a day when even the Royal Navy cannot police the entire world. If the Americans will look after their own, that is one less headache for us."

"What of Greece?"

"I know how emotive that word is. And not only to you. There is an entire generation in this country whose parents hardly knew where the place was, and who now regard it as sacred as Westminster Abbey. Your friend Byron, and people like your brother, accomplished that. I am not belittling their achievements. And the way the war is being fought sickens any right-thinking man. We are urging peace on the Turks. The Russians are doing a great deal more than that, but between you and me, they are a little afraid of a bloody nose if they go in alone."

"And you have no intention of going in?"

"Only as a very last resort. I support Greek aspirations. But I cannot see that these aspirations would be served by plunging all Europe into another twenty years of war, and turning their land into a desert. You'll know my brother is minister at the Porte?"

Haggard nodded.

"Well, he has the ear of the sultan, and is doing what he can. I think that problem will be solved. But we must have patience."

"What about the situation here at home?"

"It is dreadful. But Bobby Peel is working on a possible solution." Canning smiled. "He and I do not see eye to eye on a lot, but he is brilliant, and he will work with me. Our concept is a change in the corn laws."

Haggard frowned at him. "You'd repeal them?"

"And bankrupt the farmers? No, no. But there must be some relief for the poor. When corn is plentiful in this country, by all means let us have protective tariffs. But when the harvest is poor, and God knows we have had sufficient poor harvests in the past few years, then it seems to me that it is right to allow sufficient European corn into the country to make up the difference. Stability, Haggard, stability. That is what we must make our first concern. I want the laboring man, the miner, the millworker, to know, first, that there will always be sufficient food for his family, and second, to have some idea of what it is going to cost him. If we can achieve that, we have removed a good deal of his misery, and thus his anger, at a stroke. And there is another cause I would promote, in the same direction. Catholic disability must go."

Haggard frowned at him. "You'd attempt to carry the Tories with you on *that*?"

"My Tories. And a few friends."

"Did not Pitt founder on that very rock?"

"George IV, for all his faults, is not George III, thank

God. Don't forget, Mrs. Fitzherbert is a Catholic. He'll go along with us. Have you strong feelings on the matter?"

"I'm inclined to agree with you, if it can be done without a revolution."

"It can and it must. There are too many of our best brains and our most loyal subjects existing in a wilderness just because they worship God in a slightly different manner from the rest of us. That is both absurd and iniquitous. And think of Ireland. Remove Catholic disability and you have solved the Irish question at a stroke." He leaned across the desk. "Will you join me?"

Here was honesty, and fair play, and a grasp of affairs comparable with anything to be found in the Whig ranks. And here too was the power to make his ideas work.

But he stood for certain principles.

"And reform? And emancipation?"

Canning leaned back in his chair. "My God, man, but you look far ahead. Surely emancipation is a great and desirable object. But a very involved subject. It will mean bankruptcy for a great many planters. It will hardly do *your* finances any great good."

"I am prepared for it. As for the rest, you will of course pay them compensation.

"Indeed? And who will settle that? Who will persuade the planters, indeed, to accept the situation? There have been rumblings enough as it is. Would you have me dispatching a British army to the West Indies, to die of yellow fever as so many brave fellows did during the war? My duty, my main duty, is to the people of England. I conceive that the people of England may have a moral obligation to the black people in the West Indies, but we *must* put our own house in order first." Once again he leaned forward. "Will you support me, Haggard?"

Haggard hesitated. But there was one inescapable fact about the situation. This man was a second Pitt. He was about to wrench the leadership of England from the hands of the hidebound Tory aristocrats who had practiced repression with such success for so long. And the country would follow him. There could be no doubt about that, either. So perhaps they did not altogether agree on their order of priorities. The goal for both of them was the same. Jane's anger would have to be tempered by common sense.

He held out his hand.

* * *

"You amaze me, Haggard," Mina Favering remarked. "Is there no limit to your ambition?"

"Why, that is exactly the remark Jane made," Haggard said.

"So she is not pleased at your decision?"

"I think not. But I also think that it is a poor man who makes his political decisions on the advice of his wife."

"Save that wives can often see a great deal more of the surrounding country than their husbands, who are wrestling with the problem of getting the coach over the next hill."

"Anyway," Haggard pointed out, "talk of ambition is absurd. I have never had the least political ambitions. In fact, in our further discussions I told Canning that I did not want his undersecretaryship."

"Yet you have promised him your vote?"

"Indeed I have."

"Without even a say in how he uses it, on the smallest possible scale. There is a peculiar streak of utter absurdity in you, Haggard. You contract yourself into marriage with some farmgirl. You go away from your inheritance and spend three years fighting when you could have bought yourself out without even noticing the money spent. You take in some colonial waif discarded by your brother and treat her like your very own sister—oh, Jane has told me how much you cared for her. You allow your interests to be swayed by the ramblings of a crazy sodomite about to commit suicide. You stand there like a tree and allow some squit of a Tory squire to shoot you down. And now you attach your star to one that is surely shooting across the heavens and about to burn itself up in its own velocity."

"Canning will be the greatest Prime Minister this country has had since Billy Pitt."

"For God's sake," Mina retorted. "What was so great about Billy Pitt? He involved us in the biggest war we have ever had to fight, and he invented income tax. God save us from any more Billy Pitts."

"We need one now," Haggard insisted. "The country needs one. And George Canning is the man. Thus he will have some support."

"They will hate you for it."

"Whom do you suggest?"

"The Tories, for a start."

"And the Whigs?"

"Oh, indeed. Most of them."

"I suppose you do not remember that I have never actually given allegiance to either party. My determination was to end the Tory rule of gentlemen like Liverpool."

"Oh, they'll remember. They'll also consider whether you are ever capable of giving allegiance to *any* party."

"That depends on the party's program. And now, Mina, I should love a glass of wine and something to eat. I am quite exhausted. I have told Corky to put my things in the crimson room."

"Have you, indeed. Well, you must tell him to move them back out again. A glass of wine I can provide, but supper also you will have to obtain elsewhere."

He frowned at her. "Elsewhere?"

"I cannot entertain you this weekend, Haggard," she said with great patience. "I cannot even entertain you for the night."

"Because you also hate me?"

She smiled at him. "Silly boy. No, I do not hate you, Haggard. I despair of you. But then, I have despaired of you often enough in the past." She leaned forward, rested her hand on his cheek. "You are not a political animal. You are an absurdly honorable man. They usually die young. That you have survived to the ripe old age of fifty is a total miracle to me. God knows you haven't tried. No, no, Haggard, my dear, dear Haggard, I do not hate you." Her mouth twisted. "But I have a guest coming to see me. And he will be here in the hour."

"You'll find yourself a hostelry, here in Southampton," Haggard told Corcoran.

"But, Colonel Haggard, sir," Corky protested, "you can't go riding off on your own."

"I have campaigned often enough on my own, old fellow," Haggard said. "I shall be gone for three days. Meet the packet on Monday morning."

"I will do that, sir." Corcoran hesitated. "It's not for me to speak, sir . . ."

"No, Corky, it is not for you to speak," Haggard agreed. Then smiled, and clapped his faithful friend on the shoulder. "A man may visit his widowed sister-in-law, surely."

"Indeed he may, sir. I but wished to be sure . . . whether this journey is to be mentioned in Derleth."

"No, Corky. This journey is not to be mentioned in Der-leth We visited Midlook, found that we could not obtain hospitality there, and returned to London for the weekend."

"Yes, sir. And visited none of your friends."

"I have no friends, Corky. So I am reliably informed. We took lodgings in an inn and gave ourselves up to three days of drunken debauchery. I suggest in fact that you do just that, here in Southampton."

"Very good, sir. And supposing you encounter an acquaintance?"

"In Southampton? Now, that would be an unlikely possibility. You worry too much, Corky. Find some accommodating young woman and enjoy yourself."

As I intend to do? he wondered, as the packet was towed away from the dock and the sails set for the short journey across the sheltered waters of the Solent toward the green hills of the Isle of Wight. Or am I committing an act of madness? What had Mina meant when she had reminded him that Jane was aware of his interest in his sister-in-law? He had never hidden it, to be sure. And he was certainly entitled to visit her, even if it would be for the best if Jane never knew of it.

He needed her. There was the point. That he loved her, that his life had been empty for the past three years, was less important at this moment than his feeling of utter isolation. In England a man had to have a party, or a club, or a regiment, and he was required to live his life by the codes of conduct laid down for any of those absurd institutions. Englishmen did not understand those who preferred to follow their own inclinations, their own goals; and like primitive aboriginals, what they did not understand, they did not trust. It had never overly concerned him. He had been a good soldier because he had submitted entirely to the dictates of regimental morale and regimental discipline, but he had never, because of the circumstances in which he had gone to war, been a part of the social organization of the regiment. Undoubtedly this had been resented by his fellow soldiers, in the beginning. He had needed his size and his ability with his fists to survive. But it had been simple enough in wartime. His courage and his efficiency had very rapidly taken him from the ranks into the sergeants' mess, and then even higher. He had not proposed to change his ways following his reinstatement as Haggard of Derleth, and had in fact drifted into the political orbit entirely through his love for Mina. Even then he had always reserved his position, sure in the security of his wealth, and eventually, sure too in the love of his wife. But of course she had never loved him, as he had never loved her. They had both, even without knowing it entirely, been obeying the dictates of Mina herself. It had been the match of the century, Haggard's wealth allied with Jane Favering's beauty and social position. It remained the match of the century, to all who observed it. Only the principals knew how empty that splendid facade had become.

And Mina?

But all that mattered today was Lindy's reaction to seeing him. He had given her no promises, merely acquiesced in her decision, because he had known how she felt, and because too he had known how dangerous their liaison was becoming. He had played the coward there. For the first time in his life. He had not been proud of it.

He walked his horse over the last hill, looked once again at the sea. The English Channel here, with France a scant sixty miles away to the south. Below him and to the right clustered the houses of Sandown, and before the town stretched the golden sands which were fast attracting the wealthy to this surprisingly large island for their summer holidays. Perhaps, he thought, it is time for me to create a holiday home. Save that the summers in Derleth were as beautiful as any here, and there was always so much more to be done.

On the other hand, save for his wound and the enforced rest, he had not had a holiday in thirteen years, and before then his only vacation had been that one in 1812, again caused by a wound.

But to build a holiday home on the Isle of Wight would mean that Jane would accompany him, and the children.

The cottage nestled amid the trees above the town, with a surprisingly large and pleasant garden, and well-maintained too, with a small stable for a gig and horses, with chickens out the back, and with a puff of smoke drifting away from the chimney to guarantee habitation, as well as warmth on a chill March day. He walked his horse through the open gate, drew rein as a large mongrel dog rose from beneath the apple tree beside the front door, shook itself, and then sat down to stare at him.

"Holloa," he shouted. "Is anyone at home?"

A face appeared at a window, and then in the doorway. A

tall, angular woman with very pink cheeks, drying her hands on her apron.

"You've business?" she inquired.

"With Mistress Haggard, to be sure."

"Who is it, Polly?"

Haggard's heartbeat quickened, and he dismounted. The dog gave a low growl, and he remained standing by his mount's head, his crop in his hand.

"Colonel Haggard?" Lindy pushed yellow hair from her forehead in a gesture he remembered so very well. "But . . ."

"I happened to be in Hampshire on business," Haggard lied. "And decided to pay you a visit."

"Colonel Haggard?" the woman Polly muttered, and made a hasty curtsy. "You'll forgive me, sir."

"I like the way you seek to protect your mistress," Haggard said. "May I come in, or will it be necessary to shoot the dog?"

Lindy smiled, and came outside to ruffle the hound's head. "His name is Caliban, and he is an even better watchkeeper than Polly."

Haggard stood beside her. "And am I welcome here, Mrs. Haggard?"

She raised her head to look at him, little pink spots gathering in her cheeks. "You are welcome here, Colonel Haggard," she said. "Oh, you are welcome here."

When you are very young, Haggard thought, to hold *any* woman in your arms is at once an achievement and an adventure. When you are older, and the world is suddenly full of women, the sense of adventure remains, in the variety, in the mental comparing of one with the other. Until one day you meet the woman who fits into your arms as if especially created for that purpose, whose mind and body and smell and movements are the best of all the others rolled into one. Such a woman, once found, makes all others meaningless, and certainly unnecessary.

You can only hope and pray that when that moment occurs, you are both unmarried. But he did not suppose he was less fortunate than most.

She stirred, her head moving on his shoulder. "How long can you stay?"

They had not spoken over supper, had merely looked at

each other across the table while Polly, the maid, had served the fresh-caught fish. Here was a simplicity he had not known since he had been a private soldier in the army, and all too seldom even then. He would not have supposed that Rosalind Campkin, or Rosalind Haggard, had enjoyed much simplicity either. Yet there was a tranquillity she was projecting, and which he found the most marvelous sensation in the world.

And they had not spoken since dinner either, for a long while. They had very little need of words, to express love, and understanding, and desire.

"I must catch Monday's packet to Southampton."

She sighed, and kissed his arm. The candle had burned low, and the fire was nothing more than a glow in the grate. He could see nothing of her, could only smell and feel, his arm under the blanket to stroke the small of her back, slide down to cup her buttocks, her leg thrown across his thighs, to possess him for this brief moment.

"And will you come again?"

"Whenever I can. If you will permit me."

They walked on the beach, the breeze flicking at the skirts of her pelisse, his beaver pulled well down to resist its force. Their gloved fingers were tightly intertwined. In March the beach was empty, their footprints the only marks on the pale yellow expanse.

"It will not be very often."

"I know. You should not come at all."

"There's a change of mood." He squeezed her fingers.

"I meant, you will be found out."

"I doubt that. I shall be spending a good deal more time than before in London over the next few years. No one will know, or care, that I occasionally slip away for a weekend."

"Oh, my darling," she said. "If only . . ."

"Yes," he said. "But one would have to set back the clock fourteen years."

She sighed and rested her head on his shoulder as they walked.

With the afternoon sun free of cloud, the leeward wall of her cottage was a tropical paradise, where they could sit for their tea, still well wrapped up, to be sure, but able to enjoy the lazy pleasure of the light and the heat.

"Strolo is enjoying Eton," she confided. "I think he needed a certain amount of aggressiveness at first, but he is big and strong, and now he has settled down. I am so very grateful."

"For what?"

"That you should have given him this chance. I sometimes shudder to think what I risked for him. Had you thrown us out, I mean."

"Was that likely?"

She kissed him on the ear. "It would have been the most obvious, as well as probably the best, thing to do."

"Do you ever hear from your mother?"

"I am dead to Mama." She sighed. "I do not even know if she is dead or alive. She will be seventy this year."

"Would you like to go back, ever?"

"No," she said with sudden vehemence. "Never."

"What would you like? I mean, if all the world were yours to command."

She raised her head to look at him, and he saw the tears trickling out of the corners of her eyes.

"You *could* come back, you know," he said.

"To Derleth? Once again to be the poor relation? To know your love only in snatched moments in the middle of the afternoon? To feel guilty all the time?"

Because she was, after all, Rosalind Campkin who had been Rosalind Haggard, mistress of Haggard's Penn. It was not something ever to be forgotten.

She sighed. "Here at least, if I cannot see her, I cannot feel guilty about her. And as all the world is not mine, Roger, dear Roger, then here is the happiest part of it I will ever know. I dreamed of you following me, and prayed for it. When you were shot down, I thought my world had come to an end, and even when I knew you would not die, I thought I would never see you again. Now . . ." Her shoulders rose and fell. "I am happy. This moment, I am happy."

"Even if I must tell you that I continue to support emancipation?"

For a moment her face closed; then she smiled. "My mind tells me you are right. It is only my heart opposes. But I love you with that heart, Roger Haggard. All my other feelings must be subjected to that."

"Yet I must love you and leave you again?"

She put up her hand to stroke his cheek. "Even if you told me you could never come again, I would still be happy, this moment, to have you here."

"But I will come again," he said. "Just as soon as I can."

•   •   •

Whenever possible. Whenever time could be spared from the requirements of supporting the new government.

"Now, sir," Lord John Russell said, standing in front of the eager Liberals, hands grasping the lapels of his coat, looking from the Speaker to the government front bench immediately opposite. "This treaty, this famous treaty, this Treaty of *London* to make sure of our place in history . . ." He paused, while his followers chuckled their pleasure. "Would it not be possible for the Right Honorable Gentleman to tell us what it *means*? For, Mr. Speaker, as I understand the situation, we have a treaty, a treaty subscribed by Great Britain, by Russia, and by France. May I say, Mr. Speaker, that there is an array of might against which no nation could stand with any hope of success. And these three mighty powers have agreed to recognize the independence of Greece, as they should, and they have called upon the Turks to do the same. And what, Mr. Speaker, has been the Turkish response? First of all they advanced upon Athens, took the Acropolis, and then sacked the city with all of the horrors and excesses we have come to expect from the Janisseries when they are on the march. Having done this, they have informed the powers, the three greatest powers in the world, that they do not intend to accede to the Treaty of London. So I must ask the Right Honorable Gentleman, what is this treaty? It is certainly a piece of paper on which a great many words are written. I have many such at home in my library, neatly bound in leather, and called romances. When I read them, Mr. Speaker, I am in search of rest from the dull cares of the world. I do not expect to believe a word they contain, only to be amused and distracted by their extravagances. But this treaty, Mr. Speaker, this famous Treaty of London, this immortal Treaty of London, subscribed by the three greatest powers in the world, if I do not believe that, what is there left in life *for* me to believe? I must know, sir, the nation must know, now, whether an English fleet is at this moment bombarding Constantinople, surely the only language the Turk will ever understand, whether a Russian army is at this moment crossing the Dobruja, whether a French army is at this moment embarking at Marseilles. I must either know these things, Mr. Speaker, or the Right Honorable Gentleman must explain that this treaty too is a work of fiction, created by hack writers for the amusement of people even less educated than themselves."

He sat down to the cheers of his party, and heads turned to look at the Prime Minister. Canning was slumped, his head on his chest. He had sat thus all morning, and there was no one in the Commons who was not aware this was no posture of contempt; it was the exhausted slouch of a sick man. Now he raised his head, and a moment later pushed himself to his feet. His right fist clenched, and the papers it held were crackled into disarray. His left hand rested on the dispatch box in front of him, and he gazed at his tormentor.

"Mr. Speaker," he said, and then began to cough. The agonizing retches seeped through his system as he bent double, and the packed house shifted uneasily.

"I think the Prime Minister should sit down," the Speaker said, and glanced over the ranks of the Tories. "Perhaps there is another Right Honorable Gentleman prepared to answer the Leader of the Opposition."

Canning sank back into his seat, and the other members of his Cabinet exchanged glances. The Prime Minister preferred to act as his own Foreign Secretary, permitted no one to answer for him on that subject, and especially on the subject of Greece. Yet had Russell's question been damning enough as it was.

Roger, seated two rows behind Canning, raised his order paper.

"The Right Honorable member for Derleth," the Speaker said.

Roger stood, to the accompaniment of a chorus of boos and hisses from the Liberal side. But he waited patiently until they had subsided, before facing his erstwhile friend.

"Mr. Speaker," he said. "I cannot hope to know what answer the Prime Minister will make, although I am confident that it will be complete and a total rebuttal of the Right Honorable Gentleman's implied criticism. But I would hope that the Right Honorable Gentleman's facts are not entirely as inaccurate as it would appear. The Janissaries, Mr. Speaker, no longer exist. They were disbanded sixteen years ago."

Russell's retort was lost in the uproar of cheering from the Tory benches, to which was added a fresh burst of booing from the Opposition. But Roger's attention was already returned to Canning; the Prime Minister had fainted.

They waited in a group in the corridor outside the office. There was nothing to say. Apart from being a mixed bag, for the Whig leaders had also come up to pay their respects, there was no comment to be made until they knew more about the situation.

But now at last the door was opening.

"Well?" demanded Sir Robert Peel.

"He is resting peacefully," the doctor said. "If you gentlemen will stand back, I will have him taken downstairs to his carriage. Mr. Canning needs rest, gentlemen."

"But will he be able to resume his seat?" someone asked.

The doctor glanced over the crowd. "Parliament soon breaks for the summer recess, gentlemen. We have everything to hope for from the autumn."

They stood against the walls, making a corridor through which the stretcher could be carried. Canning's eyes were shut, and he breathed irregularly. Slowly the bearers took him to the end of the corridor, and then down the stairs, the doctor walking behind.

"That man is dying," someone said.

Peel raised his head.

"And what will happen then, d'you suppose?" asked someone else.

Peel shouldered his way through the throng, went down the stairs.

"He's gone to Wellington," someone said.

"Now there will be a change of direction, by God."

"Aye," said someone else. "There'll be a few place seekers cast into the wilderness then."

Haggard looked across the heads at Russell, who returned his gaze for a moment without any change of expression, then turned and followed Peel down the stairs. Haggard went behind him, more slowly, but Russell had not waited in the lobby, had gone straight from the building for his carriage.

So, then, Haggard thought, himself going outside into the warm July air, a dream shattered by the whim of fate. In place of a sensible, decent, middle-of-the-road government, dedicated to slow but steady progress, to reform in the course of time, to creating an England which would shed none of its greatness while searching for new heights to conquer, there would be a return to two sets of ideas at quite opposing ends of the political spectrum, to vicious party infighting, to a refusal of all suggestion of reform from the Tories, to a frantic and disruptive clamoring from the Liberals.

Once again the country would be split. And Roger Haggard, like everyone else, would have to make a choice. Even if nobody wanted him.

He went down the steps, and his carriage rolled forward. He got in, sat back in his seat as the vehicle rumbled through the gates and was forced to stop in the throng which had gathered outside at the news that the second time in a year a Prime Minister had been struck down in the House.

"That's Haggard," he heard voices saying. "Led the charge at Peterloo."

He raised his head to look at them, heard his name again.

"Haggard, Mr. Haggard. Colonel Roger."

He leaned forward, gazed at Emma Bold.

Chapter 6

The Gossip

"Emma?" Roger found himself opening the carriage door without really meaning to. "Emma?"

She scrambled up beside him, and he held her shoulders the better to look at her. It was certainly Emma. There were streaks of gray in that magnificent auburn hair, and lines of suffering creased those gaminelike brown cheeks. But the almost febrile pleasure she had always been able to express had not disappeared; nor, he realized the pleasure she had always been able to convey to him.

"Oh, Emma," he said, and held her close.

The crowd applauded, and Doughty, the coachman, prudently got down to close the door before driving on.

"Where are you taking me?" she asked.

"Wherever you wish to go, my dearest Emma," he said, releasing her to look at her. Her clothes were threadbare but had recently been washed, and her hair was also clean.

And now she was flushing. "Meg is with me."

"And?"

"Tim." The flush deepened. "And the boy."

He frowned at her. "What boy?"

"You'd not know about him. Meg's boy."

"By Woodsmith?"

She nodded.

"And where is that scoundrel?"

"In Australia."

The coach had pulled clear of the crowd, and had now come to a stop, awaiting instructions.

"Where are they?" Roger asked.

"We've . . . we've a lodging in Wapping. But, Roger . . .

they don't know I've come to see you. They . . . well, they'd not impose."

"On me?"

"Well . . ."

Roger opened the hatch. "Wapping," he said. The coach started to move again. "You'd best tell me."

"Harry's dead."

"How?"

She shrugged. "Overwork. Heat. God knows. He was an angry man, Roger. Maybe he just died of anger."

"And you hold me responsible."

She shook her head. "Whatever happened to him, he brought on himself. You fought for him once, Roger. And you held out the hand of friendship more than once. And in reply he shot down your friend. He brought it on himself."

"Aye, well . . ." Roger sighed. "And Woodsmith?"

"He's not dead," she said fiercely. "He's served his time, but he's not dead."

"Tell me about him."

"He's a terrible man, Roger. Sometimes I think he's your father walking this earth again, but with none of John Haggard's nobility. Your father may have done some terrible things, Roger, but he never acted from anything less than arrogance. Jerry Woodsmith is a mean and vicious brute. Christ, the things he did to Meg."

"So she's run away from her husband. They *were* married?"

"Oh, aye. But, Roger . . ." She clung to his arm. "You'll not condemn her for that?"

Meg Bold. No, no. Meg Woodsmith. To all intents and purposes, Meg Haggard, come back to haunt him. But Meg was heaviest of all on his conscience. And she possessed his nephew. Haggards, scattered from end to end of the globe, he had once thought. But coming home to roost.

" 'Tis down that street," Emma said.

Roger tapped on the hatch, and followed the direction of her pointing finger. Here were overflowing gutters and despondent, half-clad children, stewing in the summer heat, while their mothers gossiped on unswept doorsteps, gin bottles close to hand. Their fathers were absent, but it was unlikely any of them was pursuing a useful occupation, or even an honest one. Here, he realized, was all the misery and injustice and incipient revolution of the country gathered on a single street, while the one man who might have relieved it lay gasping for breath in an attempt to live.

Perhaps not the *one* man, he thought. But the one man with both the power and the will, at this moment.

"We've no money," Emma explained. "We worked our passage back, and the captain still took all we had. 'Tis prison for us, the boy and all, Roger, by tomorrow morning."

"So you sought me out." He squeezed her hand and looked out of the window at Tim Bold. Tim had grown a beard, and looked very like his father, save that he was an altogether larger man than Harry had ever been. Now he stood in a doorway and stared at the carriage in amazement.

Roger tapped on the hatch, and the coach came to a stop. Doughty got down to open the door, and Emma hesitated.

"Out you get," Roger said, and followed her to the pavement. Instantly they were surrounded by a crowd of grubby, shrieking children.

"Roger Haggard," Tim said. "Have you come to send us back, then?"

"Timmy!" his mother cried.

"Where's Meg?" Roger demanded.

Tim barred the doorway. "You've no business with her, Haggard. You threw her out, just as your father threw my mother out. You've no business with her."

"Meg left my house of her own free will, Tim," Roger said, meeting his gaze. "And you know that."

"Roger's here to help us, Timmy," Emma said. "I know he is."

"Don't be a fool, man," Roger said. "Stand aside."

Tim hesitated, and then stepped to one side, and Roger entered the house, holding his handkerchief to his nostrils as he did so. No fresh air, not even any perfume, had entered this house for too long, and little had been allowed to leave it.

"To the left," Emma said, at his elbow.

Roger turned the handle, opened the door, stepped inside. Meg lay on the bed, half turned toward him. She appeared to be fully dressed, but was covered with a shawl.

"She's poorly," Emma explained.

Roger stood beside the bed, looked down on the girl. Because she was, still only a girl, even when approaching thirty. A very lovely red-haired, thin-cheeked fugitive from life, breathing heavily as she fought her way through the mucus, brows slowly gathering together as she stared at him.

"Roger?" she whispered. "Roger?" Her voice rose an octave. "Roger?" She rose onto her elbow, stared at her mother. "You didn't, Ma. You couldn't."

"I had to, Meggie," Emma said. "Or you'd die."

Meg slowly lay back on the straw-filled pillow, still staring at him.

"You've a child," Roger said, his voice equally thick.

Her eyes moved, and his head turned. One of the children had followed them into the house and now into the room. He was not very tall, but it was simple enough to identify the straight nose, so unlike his mother's or his grandmother's, the wide, flat mouth, the thrusting chin. The wonder was, Roger realized, that he had not immediately recognized him, even in the crowd outside.

"Will you help us, Roger?" Meg whispered. "Will you?"

Roger squeezed her shoulder. "I'll help you, Meg. Oh, I'll help you. That's my nephew standing there."

"I'm afraid I don't really understand." Jane Haggard's voice was cold. "Aren't these people convicted criminals?"

"Meg and her mother were never convicted of anything more than being poor," Roger pointed out. "Tim was sentenced to ten years for rioting, to be sure, but that is over with now. He has served his sentence."

"And this girl was once your betrothed," Jane remarked. "No doubt your mistress as well. Mama told me of it."

"A long time ago, my darling."

"Indeed? Just what do you propose to do with her now?"

"You must understand that we are almost brother and sister," Roger said. "Her mother was all the mother I had, for a considerable period of my life."

"Which to my mind is positively disgusting," Jane said. "But I had forgotten that you were such a good friend of Lord Byron."

"Now *you* are being disgusting," Roger said. He found himself beginning to be angry. After all, this was his house, in his village, in his valley. But of course his anger was prodded by his own conscience.

"Yes," she surprisingly agreed. "We make a good pair, do we not, Colonel Haggard? And should we not, as we are husband and wife? What do you propose to do with this Australian family you have so suddenly decided to accumulate?"

"Now, Jane . . ."

"Because I must tell you frankly, if they move in, then I move out."

She stood before him, her hands clasped in front of her, her hair all but concealed by her white mobcap, her features more beautiful than ever; like her mother, he realized, she would only improve in looks with the passing of time. But also like her mother, she presented to life an utterly inflexible set of assumptions. Which he was afraid to challenge? He no longer loved her, as she no longer loved him. Then why not take a stand now, and let events take their course? Because with Jane gone . . . But he was allowing his thoughts to stray into very dangerous paths. Into the world in which his father had made his way, the world of lonely ostracism, of universal rejection. The world of George Byron. And Johnnie Haggard?

Would it be so bad a world, at that, in such company? But such company was not available until he was dead. And for the living, there were too many complications, Harry and little Mina, the plain business of conducting a separation when there was so much to be done. He realized that the hardest thing in life is to break up a comfortable marriage, however definitely it may have ceased to exist.

"I had not thought of moving Meg and Emma into Derleth House, my sweet," he said. "But neither can I permit them to starve. Emma is Alice's mother, remember. I shall give them a house in the village. The one left vacant by the Laceys." One of the few Derleth families to join the prevailing exodus of the lower classes—all who could raise the necessary money—to the promised land of the United States and Canada.

"And support them for the rest of their lives?"

"Do you suppose you would suffer if I did decide to do that? But I'd ask no man to live forever off charity. I have already spoken with Emma. Tim will be blacksmith."

"We already have a blacksmith."

"Horrocks is past sixty, and ready to retire. He shall have a pension, and Tim shall take his place. It will all work out very well."

"Save that every time I walk down the street I will risk encountering a woman who has shared your bed."

He smiled at her. "Do you not suppose, my darling, that there are others of those on Derleth?"

"None that I know of." Then she smiled in turn, that delicious flash of utter pleasure which could dispel his anger in seconds. "I am being feminine, which cannot be so surprising, Colonel Haggard. Of course you must do what you can for these poor people. Where are they now?"

"In the servants' pantry, awaiting your pleasure."

She gave him a quick glance, then accepted the compliment, however false it might be.

"Then I shall go down to meet them." She gathered her skirt in her left hand, went to the door, and there hesitated, looking over her shoulder. "I should like to be sure that *this* girl, at the least, no longer holds any place in your esteem." She shrugged. "Once again, I am being femininely jealous, but I trust you will humor me in that."

Simple to lie. But then, simpler not to. Meg no longer attracted him in the way she once had. Now he thought back on it, he wondered if she had ever been anything more than a tug on his conscience? He was more interested in the boy, Dirk. In the Haggards of the future. In an odd way he felt as paternally ambitious for Dirk as he did for Strolo, surely the strangest Haggard of them all, as he did for his own Harry. That Harry would lead the way, he never doubted for an instant. But he would always be sure of the support of the others at his shoulder, much as he himself was always confident of the support of Trum, and gained in strength thereby.

Suddenly the future, which only a few months earlier had seemed fraught with imponderables and indeed looming crisis, was filled with nothing but interest.

"I love Meg," he said. "But as the sister she so nearly was to me. I hope you will believe that."

"Should I not, Colonel Haggard? You have never lied to me, to my knowledge." She went down the stairs, and he followed her. Nugent was waiting to open the door for her, and the people in the pantry leapt to their feet, except for Trum, who was already standing.

"Alice," Jane said, extending both her hands. "This must be a great day for you."

Alice's cheeks were wet. "One of the best in my life, Jane. I'd have you meet my mother."

Emma gave a quick curtsy.

"Roger has told me sufficient about you, Mistress Bold," Jane said. "And this is Meg."

Meg was wrapped in her shawl, for the persistent cold,

which had now deepened into a hacking cough, would not let her go. But she too curtsied.

"We must have a physician to see to you, my dear," Jane said. "And Dirk? Why, what a handsome boy. A true Haggard. You must permit him to visit the manor occasionally, Mistress Woodsmith, and play with his . . ." She rested her forefinger on her lower lip. "I shall have to decipher the true relationship. I suppose half-cousin would be most accurate."

"I'd like to visit the manor, mum," Dirk said.

"Hush, boy," Emma said.

"Visit the manor?" Meg asked, and looked at Roger.

"Colonel Haggard is allowing you the use of a cottage in the village," Jane said. "It is in need of some repair, I'm afraid, but I'm sure you will find that congenial work. And is this Mr. Bold?"

Tim gave a brief nod. Unlike his mother and his sister, he had not yet apparently been able to reconcile himself to returning to Derleth.

"Indeed, sir, you look like a blacksmith already," Jane observed. "You will prosper, Bold. All it takes is hard work." She smiled at him, then at the assembled company, lastly at Alice. "You must indeed be pleased, my dear," she said again. "Major Sparrow, I wonder if you'd accompany me? There are one of two matters I'd like to discuss about the harvest festival."

"Of course." Trum hesitated, then held out his hand to Tim Bold. "We'll talk later. But for the moment, here's my hand on it."

Tim hesitated in turn, then squeezed the proffered fingers, and Trum hurried from the room. Alice was biting her lip, and Roger squeezed her hand.

"Sometimes I wonder who is squire here," Alice said.

"It is a difficult thing for her to do," Emma said. "And she did it well. You're fortunate, Roger Haggard. More than just in your wealth. But Tim will be your blacksmith. I promise you."

The two men stared at each other.

"I'll work for you, Squire," Tim said at last. "But I'm no friend of yours. I'll not pretend to that."

"I never expected you to," Roger said. "But you'll find that Mistress Haggard is a most pleasant person, when she gets to know you." He stooped before the boy. "And I endorse that invitation. You and Harry are much the same age, and he lacks for a playmate. I'll expect to see you up here as often as you can."

"We'd not expected to be so well received, Roger," Emma said. "Or would you rather I also called you Colonel Haggard?"

He put his arm round her shoulders, squeezed her against him. "To you I'm always Roger. To all of you." He sighed. "I wish things might have been different. But they'll be different from now on."

"And if Jerry follows me home?" Meg asked in a low voice.

"Will he?"

She shrugged. "When he hears I've fallen on my feet, he might."

"He's entitled to," Tim said. "He's served his sentence, same as me."

"Well, we'll cross that bridge when we come to it," Roger said. "News takes a long while to travel from here to Australia."

"A great man," remarked the Duke of Wellington, leading the black-clad procession from the church. "A great man. 'Tis a pity he was not spared."

The gentlemen walking beside and behind him exchanged glances; even the Iron Duke was becoming given to politically untrue statements, at least by his own lights, as he grew older. But then, it was becoming too commonplace for a Prime Minister to die in harness; the last, poor Spencer Perceval, had been shot down by a madman in the House of Commons, and before then Billy Pitt had succumbed, from sheer overwork and concern, so it was said. But what else had killed George Canning?

The duke paused on the step, surveyed the guardsmen standing rigidly to attention beneath him, the carriages waiting in a line, his at the head. Everyone present knew that he had already been summoned to the palace, including the members of the crowd gathered on the far side of the street and restrained by more armed soldiers. There were even a few cheers. The duke was the long-nosed bugger who had beaten the French, and not a few of his old soldiers were present today. But they more than any would have cause to fear the prospect of such a disciplinarian becoming ruler of the country. So the cheers were muted.

Wellington did not seem to notice them at all. He waited for those on whom he would have to call as members of his government to draw abreast of him; Sir Robert Peel headed this group. Then there were the others, Canning's men, but surely certain to follow the traditional Tory line now that the flaming star which had led them astray was finally laid to rest.

But there were still others again, itinerants whom Canning had gathered into his net with his promise of a brand of Toryism which would seek progress rather than the stagnant preservation of existing orders. Would such passersby interest the duke? Certainly he was waiting, while the church slowly emptied, the dark coats of the civilians mingling with the red jackets of the military.

"Colonel Haggard," the duke said.

Haggard, walking by himself, shunned by Whig and liberal Tory alike as his reason for being had so suddenly been removed, raised his hat.

"Your Grace." They had not spoken since the morning after Waterloo.

"Do you mourn a friend, or a leader?"

"Both, your Grace."

"Ha, ha. You're a professional soldier, Haggard. How long did we fight together?"

"More than twenty years, your Grace."

"And you led the charge at Manchester." A ghost of a smile crossed those iron features. "Peterloo."

"I did, sir, to my everlasting shame."

"Come now, Haggard, you're a soldier, and the son of a Tory landowner. You'd not see the country go to rack and ruin."

"I'd not see it go to a Neapolitan dictatorship either, your Grace."

The duke's brows drew together. " 'Tis your vote I am interested in, Colonel, not your opinions. You've talent. Talent for leadership, sir. I've a mind this country needs to be led. Well, sir?"

"I am flattered, your Grace. Could I but be sure you seek to lead a country and not an army, then I would follow you without hesitation."

Wellington stared at him for some seconds. "You're an outspoken man, Colonel. I've no quarrel with any man who is prepared to speak his mind. I claim to be one myself. I shall lead this country, sir, and it had best follow, else will it find me a hard man. For I will tell you frankly, sir, that those who do not follow me, I shall regard as my enemies. Good day to you, sir."

He went down the steps to the waiting carriage. Peel drew level with Haggard for a moment. "You're a fool, Haggard," he said. "The duke was offering you a ministry."

"And I was refusing it," Haggard said.

Peel's turn to stare at him for some seconds; then he too went to his carriage.

John Russell came up. "You change your colors so often, Roger, a man never knows where he stands with you."

"From anyone else but you, John, I'd take offense," Roger admitted.

"To anyone but you I'd not have said it. What now?"

"I backed Canning because he could do what I would like to see done, John. I'd back the duke if I thought he'd follow the same course. But he won't."

"So you'll be voting Whig again."

"I'll be voting as my conscience tells me to, John. Will you support an abolitionist plank?"

"I'll have to consult about it. It will follow. Even Canning could promise you nothing more than that."

"Of course," Haggard agreed. "Well, then, consult." He walked down the steps to where Corcoran waited to hold the door of his carriage. "I'm for a ride in the country." South, to the Isle of Wight, and the arms of Lindy. Nothing really mattered besides that.

"Haggard?" Mina Favering raised her hand, allowed him to brush her knuckles with his lips. "I'm not sure I should receive you."

"Am I that much of an outcast?"

"You are that much of an uncertain quality, to be sure. At least, so I am told. But I was thinking more that you have not called here recently."

Haggard sat beside her, and her butler hastily presented him with a glass of port. "It is a considerable time since you have visited Derleth."

Her mouth twisted in that so-well-remembered gesture. "I do not travel well anymore, Haggard. Even to visit London is an ordeal." She gave a little shiver. "I am sixty-six years old, Haggard. There is an unfortunate experience for a woman who can remember."

"Who wishes to remember, my darling Mina," he said. "Instead of looking forward."

"To what?" She held both his hands, looked into his eyes. "What have I to look forward to, Haggard?"

"You are still the most beautiful woman I have ever known."

This time the twisted mouth was a smile. "You are not seeing me first thing in the morning, when I am lacking powder and paint, and my hair is not set—then you would see my scalp, my dear."

"You can see my scalp now, if you wish."

"Oh, bah." She leaned away from him. "I can pass for fifty, as when I was fifty, when I first encountered you, my darling boy, I could have passed for thirty. But looks no longer enter into it. I am old, Haggard. I have a stiffness in my bones which cannot be alleviated either by perfume or by passion. I still *feel*. Perhaps more acutely than ever before in my life. But to feel, with me, is to wish to do, and when I have done, I am a total wreck for the following week." She sighed. "But that tale of woe hardly interests you, hotfoot as you are from the arms of your mistress."

"Eh?" Haggard nearly spilled his port.

"Oh, come now. You attend Parliament with a regularity you have never even suggested before. . . ."

"Well, there are great issues at stake."

"Issues which you insist upon confounding with your absurd inconsistency. Is it true you made a speech in favor of emancipation, not a fortnight ago?"

"It is. Wilberforce was good enough to invite me."

"And you accepted. After your promise to me."

"I promised to consider the matter, and having done so . . ."

"You then decided to commit political suicide. And perhaps more than that."

"Mina, the only reason I joined Canning's party was because he promised me that emancipation would be undertaken by the government."

"In due course. And you discussed the matter privately. Oh, I know you have also discussed it with Russell privately. But now you have shouted your feelings to the world, nailed your colors to the mast, by God."

"Should a man not do so?"

"Not if he has any ambition, any common sense at all. For heaven's sake, Haggard, there is no hope of achieving emancipation under Wellington's administration. Now, is there?"

"Probably not."

"Yet you voted *with* the government on the Catholic issue."

"I did."

Mina threw up her hands. "For heaven's sake. Are they not your bitterest enemies?"

"The Catholics?"

"Wellington, and Peel, and their ilk, you idiot."

"No doubt they are. Or at least they consider themselves so."

"Well, then . . ."

"They put forward an entirely just and reasonable bill. A bill Canning himself intended to introduce, had he been spared. A bill which should have been passed a generation ago. A bill sponsored by Pitt himself. Indeed, the farmers' opposition was what brought about Pitt's resignation, you may remember."

"Pitt?" she shouted. "In the name of God, why should I wish to remember Pitt? He was the most detestable Tory who ever lived."

"He had sound ideas. You are a Liberal, so you say. How can you even envisage an England which calls itself free on the one hand and restrains a quarter of its population from holding any office, any military command, even from attending university, on the other, simply because they worship God in a different manner from ourselves?"

"It is because they will always worship God, in front of king and country, that sensible people object to them."

"Do you know, I have a suspicion that is blasphemy."

"So I blaspheme. Constantly. And you are misinterpreting my words, deliberately. It is the pope we have to concern ourselves with. To a Catholic the pope is greater than a king."

"Which is not a difficult concept, in this day and age."

Mina smiled. "And that, my darling, is uncomfortably close to treason."

"You are being utterly archaic, Mina. In everything. Perhaps it made sense to exclude Catholics from power a century ago, when we spent our time fighting France and Spain, nations which could always call on papal support. But now that the French have repudiated the papal link, and Spain is bankrupt . . ."

"And do you suppose those states of affairs are going to be permanent? Have you examined French affairs recently? Do you not suppose Charles X is hell-bent on restoring exactly the situation of fifty years ago? Who's to say he will not succeed?"

Haggard sighed. "I did not come here to quarrel with you, Mina. I came to visit you. I voted as my conscience dictated. As I shall always vote."

"As your conscience dictated you speak in support of emancipation. Do you know, they are saying you are mad?"

"Indeed? Did I froth at the mouth?"

"You may as well have done. You are proposing to give away half of your estate, perhaps more, I don't know. And to the very people who raped your brother's widow. If that is not some form of dementia, I do not know what is. Tell me what Rosalind thinks of it."

Haggard drank some port. He had known Mina Favering long enough to be sure it was not intended as an offhand question.

"As you well know, my darling, I have not seen Lindy in some time. We exchange letters, but it is merely to do with mundane matters."

Mina gazed at him for some seconds, then smiled. "I am sure you *should* discuss it with her, at least once. I can tell you that Jane does not approve in the slightest."

"Jane approves of very little that I do."

"With reason. My God, allowing that silly little man to shoot you down, taking up these absurd political positions, and now foisting upon her all your father's dreadful back-stairs progeny . . ."

"Now Mina, that is quite untrue. And if that is how Jane has represented the matter, I shall be very angry with her."

Mina sniffed. "It is how *I* see the matter, certainly. I think Jane is being very patient with you, I'm sure. And now, this mistress . . ."

Haggard frowned at her. "What mistress?"

"My dear Haggard, as I was saying just now, you attend Parliament, and then you go riding off for a few days, always south of London."

"Are you having me followed, Mina?"

"Me? Of course not." But she had the grace to flush.

"Because where I go, and who I see, is surely my business."

She leaned forward, held his hand. "Is it, Haggard? Is it?"

"Provided nothing I do can harm Jane, then it is."

She stared into his eyes for several seconds. "Pray God it is so," she said. "Oh, pray God. Because I still love you, my dear darling, foolish, romantic idiot. I still love you." Her fingers closed on his, with a strength he had forgotten she possessed. "But I love Jane more."

"There are some gentlemen to see you, Colonel Roger." Corcoran stood in the doorway of the room Haggard used as an office when in town, the silver tray with the visiting cards held in front of him like a weapon.

Haggard leaned back in his chair. He had been looking out of the window, across the square at the houses opposite. Behind them he could see the towers of the Palace of Westminster; his London flat was only a short walk from the Commons. But now the session was finished, and tomorrow he would be starting home. For another Derleth summer. And another lengthy separation from Lindy.

And another time to think. And not only about her. Because in fact he was concerned with where he was going, if anywhere. Although he would hardly admit it even to himself, he had not yet recovered from Johnnie's death. Here again it was a compound of guilt, both that he had never understood, or wished to try to understand, the boy, and that he should have seduced his wife, however she might have been rejected by her husband. And then, to die, at once gloriously and hideously, to have had to look death in the face and know that it was coming closer, in the most ghastly manner imaginable . . . His brain seemed to race every time he thought of it. To free the slaves, because Johnnie had wanted it so, had seemed like a duty. But a peculiarly appealing duty. Again, conscience, no doubt. He could never forget the way his father had treated those of his servants who had accompanied him back to England, turning them out into the snow when he had learned that in England they could no longer be used as slaves. Emma had gone with them. All conscience, as Meg had been conscience.

Just as conscience, uncertainty as to how right he was, had made him wait for Hutchinson's shot. But was all his life to be spent atoning for the mistakes of his father or his brother? At the end of it all, John Haggard had lived the role for which he had been born, as had Johnnie. Roger Haggard was the one playing false to his caste, and compounding guilt upon guilt by the demands of his own desires.

While life must continue to be lived, as Haggard of Derleth, England's most-talked-about squire.

"Well, Corky, you'd best pour some port," he said, and got up. There were three cards, and he turned the first one over idly enough, but frowned as he came to the second, and then the third. Not altogether unexpected, of course. But he was surprised they'd choose to come to him.

Corcoran held the door for him, and he went into the sitting room. The three gentlemen were gathered in a group by the window; now they turned, their own expressions guilty enough.

"Good day to you," Haggard said. "Blakeney. How are things in Jamaica?"

"Poor enough, to be sure," Blakeney remarked. "You've not met Harry Beamish."

Haggard shook hands. "From Antigua, is it? Another tale of woe?"

"By God, Haggard," said the third man. "You know as well as I that sugar is in a damnedly depressed state."

"Indeed I do, Crowther. Even in Barbados. Well, gentlemen, sit down. A glass of port?"

Corcoran presented the tray.

Blakeney, clearly the spokesman, sipped. "You'll understand why we're here, Haggard."

"I have no idea at all," Haggard lied. "If you are proposing a lobby to raise the price of sugar, why, I'll support you, to be sure, but I doubt there's much chance of success."

"Dammit, man, you are prevaricating," Crowther snapped.

"Now, now, James," Beamish said. "We agreed there's to be no temper."

"I'll say amen to that," Haggard agreed. "If I am mistaken, no doubt you'll correct me. Blakeney?"

Blakeney took another sip of port. "I may say, Haggard, that we represent not only the West India lobby, but every right-thinking man of property in the Commons. You'll not deny, sir, that we planters have had a great deal to put up with over the past twenty years."

"A great deal to answer for, I think you meant to say," Haggard said.

Blakeney stared at him, glanced at his companions.

"Has no slave ever been flogged on Haggard's Penn?" Crowther demanded.

"Indeed they have been, and probably still are," Haggard said. "Just as private soldiers are most cruelly flogged in the army."

"And how else would you propose to keep discipline, Colonel Haggard?" Beamish inquired. "Does not the duke himself describe the British soldier as the scum of the earth?"

Blakeney produced a silk handkerchief to wipe his brow. But Haggard continued to smile. "Indeed he does, sir. I was one of them for near twenty years."

Beamish's mouth opened, and then closed again. And then opened again, as he looked at each of his companions in turn. "Then I must apologize, sir. I was not informed." He frowned. "A private soldier, sir? You?"

"Life contains many strange quirks, Beamish," Haggard said. "But in my case I regard it as a stroke of fortune that I have been able to regard the subject from several diverse angles."

"May we discuss the subject for which we are here?" Blakeney asked.

"By all means, if you'd be good enough to tell me what it is. Not the price of sugar, but something to do with the treatment of our slaves, which I readily agree is abominable and should be ameliorated as soon as is possible."

"We are here to talk about emancipation, sir," Blakeney shouted.

"Yes?"

"Your speech," Crowther said.

"Yes?"

"For God's sake, man," Blakeney said. "What in the name of God are you about? You must know that there is no British government in its right mind that will support such a point of view. The West Indies, as you should know better than anyone, sir, are the most precious possessions of the British crown. Why, sir, consider the number of lives of British soldiers, your comrades-in-arms, sir, which were sacrificed during the war just to keep those islands under the Union Jack."

"A misguided and foolish waste of life, sir," Haggard said.

Blakeney stared at him for several seconds.

"Nonetheless, sir," Crowther said, "those lives were considered necessary, by the British government, and therefore by the British people. Now, sir, do you seriously suppose that these same British people, whose brothers and fathers and sons gave their lives so freely and so generously to preserve our islands, are going simply to give them away?"

"I was not aware that that was our intention," Haggard remarked.

"It will come to the same thing. Take away the sugar crop, and what have we left? Lumps of rock. We might as well hand them back to the Indians."

"Were there any Indians left," Haggard observed.

"Sir, you are persisting in treating this entire matter as a comedy. Well, sir, it is far from that. Now, sir, you know as well as we do that Mr. Wilberforce is a crank, and has been a crank for the past thirty years. He is one of those men with more money than brains"—he paused and wiped his brow again—"who decide to seize upon some one aspect of human existence and worry it, like a dog with a bone, regardless of the distress they may cause to others in so doing. That is a fact, sir, and it is one of which our nation's leaders, thank God, are well aware, just as the people of this nation are well aware of that fact. Mr. Wilberforce is a source of entertainment, sir, to the crowds who gather to hear him speak, to those of us who have to listen to him in the Commons. Now, sir, this is a great and glorious and free country, and woe betide that any one of us should wish to compel Mr. Wilberforce to cease his diatribes. They are harmless. But they cease to be harmless, sir, when they are suddenly supported by the wealthiest planter in the islands. You may be too modest to understand the situation, sir, but your voice carries weight, and nowhere does it carry more weight than in matters appertaining to the West Indies. Why, sir, there cannot be a man who heard your recent speech, or who has read of it in the newspapers, who has not paused to think, and say to himself and to his friends, there must be some point to the emancipation question, where Roger Haggard himself espouses it."

"That was certainly the effect I was hoping my speech would have," Roger agreed.

"You . . ." Blakeney leaned back, finished his port.

"Some more wine, Corcoran," Roger said, and leaned forward in turn. "Now, you gentlemen listen to me. I am the son and the grandson and the great-grandson of slave owners, and I am one myself. I inherited my position in life. That does not mean I have to be proud of it. I have considered the matter at length, and I have reached the conclusion that there is no possible justification, whether it be social, or religious, or ethical, or even economical, for the continuance of so abominable a system of labor. As I am against slavery, and as I am also a member of Parliament, it follows that I consider it my duty to speak against it."

"By God," Crowther said.

"Even if it means your own bankruptcy?" Beamish inquired.

"I am not anticipating such a misfortune," Haggard said.

"By God, you're not," Crowther said. "But there are those of us not so fortunate."

"Well, then, sir, let me relieve your mind, so far as I can. I included economics in my remarks just now. You may well go bankrupt; that I cannot say. But if it is going to happen, it is going to happen, and, sir, it will happen even quicker without emancipation." He held up his hand as there was clearly about to be a chorus of protest. "I think you should consider some facts, gentlemen. You came in here bewailing the poor prices we are obtaining for our sugar, the lack of the great markets we remember from our youth. Well, sir, that cause is beet. Great Britain may have won the war against Bonaparte, but we lost the sugar war. As the continent could not obtain our sugar, and they could not grow their own cane, they turned to beet instead. Those markets, gentlemen, will never be regained. You may take my word for that. But in addition, if you will pause to consider, you'll realize that there is more and more *cane* sugar coming on the market every year. Have you ever considered the size of Louisiana? Well, gentlemen, within twenty years from now Louisiana alone will be producing more sugar than all of the West Indies put together, and they too will be competing for the markets of the world. Sugar is done, in the sense that we were once fortunate to consider it. It will have its place in the commodity markets, but it never will again be worth its weight in gold."

"Balderdash," Crowther said. "For one hundred and fifty years sugar has steadily been appreciating in price. And you now say that it is in imminent danger of collapse?"

"I would say it has already collapsed," Haggard said.

They stared at him.

"Now, neither Wilberforce nor I am proposing emancipation without compensation. You'll be paid, and handsomely, for the slaves you let go. Heaven knows I'm sufficiently concerned about the poor devils anyway, but at least they will be the concern of the government rather than of the planters. Those of us who choose to continue planting, why, we must accept the fact that it will become a low-profit industry, but at least we will have received sufficient cash to pay off our debts and start again. Those of us who wish to abandon planting will be able to do so without bankruptcy."

"Pay off our debts," Blakeney scoffed. "Have you debts, Haggard?"

"My forebears used their money wisely," Haggard said. "I cannot answer for yours."

"Balderdash," Crowther said again. "All balderdash. You are being specious, Haggard. Oh, specious."

"I have to tell you this," Haggard said, speaking very evenly. "If you do not mind your tongue, I propose to take offense."

"You, sir?"

Haggard smiled at him. "I once conceded a duel, sir. You may have my assurance that I shall never do so again."

They stared at him. Then Blakeney put down his glass and got up. "We came here, Colonel Haggard, to ascertain your true frame of mind, and if possible to persuade you to our views. We did not mean to fight with you. But I am bound to tell you, sir, that as you appear determined to continue to oppose us, then we do propose to fight you, not with pistols, as that is illegal, but by any other means we may discover."

Haggard nodded. "I had assumed that."

"And we shall bring you down, sir," Crowther said, also getting up. "We shall bring you down."

"Corcoran," Haggard said. "These gentlemen are just leaving."

How tired he was. Haggard walked his horse up the drive to the manor, Corcoran, as ever, at his heels. Tired from attempting too much, or at least from attempting to see too many sides of the same question. Of course he could sympathize with Blakeney and Beamish and Crowther. They were not planters in the true sense of the word. Not one of them had set foot in the West Indies in his life. Their plantations had been created by their fathers and grandfathers and were managed by attorneys, exactly as Haggard's Penn was now managed. They knew nothing of the human misery of slavery, of the pent-up fury of grinding, of the hates and fears and horrors that can accumulate beneath the tropical sun. They knew only that the source of their wealth and indeed their livelihood was in danger, from people they considered as ill-informed cranks. So naturally they would react violently to one who could not be so considered.

But what did they propose to do about him? What could they do about him? He was Haggard. He could give away his plantation, as indeed he intended to as soon as it was practical, and yet remain among the wealthiest men in England. They could not harm him, however they tried. At the end of it all, he was not afraid of ostracism.

But as he *could* see their point of view, he was tired. He wished only his bed. With Jane in his arms? She would be there, certainly, should he wish it.

He dismounted, and the grooms held his bridle. The door was open, and Nugent waited with a stirrup cup.

"A fine night, Colonel Haggard. A fine night."

"Indeed it is, Nugent. But it is good to be home. Are the children in bed?"

"Oh, indeed, sir. Indeed. But Mrs. Haggard asked if you'd attend her."

Haggard nodded, took the stairs three at a time. A footman held the doors for him, and he entered the drawing room. Jane was by herself, seated, as she liked best, in the huge window seat overlooking the park.

"The bad penny, back again." He stooped over her, but she did not turn up her face, so he kissed her forehead. "Is all well with the children?"

"All is well with the children."

"The mine? The factory?"

"I believe so. You will have to ask Trumley."

"Where is he? He and Alice are usually here to greet me."

"I asked them to wait until tomorrow," Jane said. "I wished to greet you by myself."

"Ah." Warning signals started to flicker in Haggard's brain. "Well, it is very pleasant, to be sure."

"I hope it will be," Jane said, speaking very evenly. "I wish to discuss with you a letter I have received, informing me that you are maintaining Rosalind as a mistress, and have been doing so for some time."

Chapter 7

The Wife

Haggard was so taken by surprise he was quite unable to answer for a moment, and after gazing at him for that moment, Jane nodded and stood up. "I see."

"May I look at this letter?"

"No," she said. "It is a letter to me." She walked away from him, across the room.

"Then I assume it is from your mother."

Jane had reached the far side of the room. Now she turned to face him. Her face remained composed, but there were pink spots in her cheeks and her eyes were like twin darts of steel. "Does it matter, if it is true? And it is true, is it not?"

"I do not suppose I should make a very convincing liar."

She stared at him, and then without warning screamed. He had never before heard her raise her voice other than in pleasure. Now the room, and indeed the entire house, filled with this single high-pitched yet controlled note of frustrated anger and outrage, maintained for several seconds, causing the blood to rush to her face and the veins to stand out on her neck.

"Now, Jane . . ." He stook a step forward.

"Colonel Haggard? Mrs. Haggard . . . ?"

Nugent was in the doorway, Mary Prince at his elbow.

"Leave us, Nugent," Roger commanded. "Close the doors."

Nugent gazed at his mistress, just regaining her breath, then pushed Mary back into the hallway and closed the doors.

"Now, Jane," Haggard said again, taking another step.

"If you come any closer, I shall scream again," she said.

321

"You have yourself more than once recommended I take a mistress. You cannot suppose I have never done so."

"A mistress? My God."

"And I'm sure you will agree," Haggard went on, desperately trying to keep calm, "that over the past few years, since the duel with Hutchinson, indeed, our marriage has . . . well, not been what it once was."

"You behaved with an incredible stupidity I did not believe you to possess," she pointed out. "But it seems to have been only a facet of your personality. I doubt I have ever known you at all." She stepped to a table on which was one of her favorite vases, picked it up, and dropped it to the floor with a splintering crash which had pieces of china scattering in every direction.

"For God's sake, Jane," Haggard protested.

"Why should I not break it?" she demanded. "You have never cared for it, and I have no more use for it." Carefully she placed her foot on the largest remaining unbroken piece, and pressed down.

"Well, if it will serve to calm your nerves . . ."

"My nerves are perfectly calm, thank you," Jane said, stepping on another piece of china.

Haggard sat down, crossed his knees. He had no means of knowing what was going to happen next; he could not decide, at this moment, what he *wanted* to happen next.

"So you . . . began this liaison after the duel," Jane said, speaking quietly, but walking across the room in the direction of another vase.

"I went to see Lindy on the Isle of Wight, yes."

"You never slept with her while she was here?" Jane had reached her objective.

"Well, I . . ."

"You did." She turned to face him, the vase in her hands. "I know you did. My God, the number of times I have seen you looking at her like a lover, and refused to believe it. I have even seen you leaving her room, and supposed you had been visiting that black bastard. You wretch." She hurled the vase, but without sufficient strength to throw it right across the huge room; it struck the floor in front of him and shattered.

"It was one of those things," Haggard said, still attempting to be reasonable.

"One of those things," Jane said. "One of those things,"

she shouted, picking up a brass ornament from an incidental table and hurling it at a closed window; once again glass shattered as the ornament disappeared into the garden. "Am I not good enough for your bed?"

"You were pregnant."

"With Harry?" She turned to face him again. "Eleven years ago. My God, she has been your mistress for eleven years? Your own sister-in-law? My God." She sat down on a straight chair by the window; the draft seeping through the broken glass wisped her hair.

Haggard got up. "Yes," he said. "Eleven years. I was sorry for her, you were unavailable, and, well, it just happened." He crossed the room, stood above her. "And then we discovered we were in love."

She raised her head, to stare at him.

"In love, Jane. It was not a matter of money, or position, or ambition, because there could be none between us. It was not even a matter of sex, entirely. We fell in love. And then we decided to end it, and she went down to the Isle of Wight, but I could not stay away from her."

"I see," Jane said.

"And up to this minute it has made absolutely no difference to our marriage. You and I have never been in love, and you know that as well as I. But we are very well suited, and we have made a fine home here, and my feelings for Lindy have never interfered with our relations, up to now. Up to this cowardly attempt to harm me. Because it is just that, you know, Jane. I am upsetting too many people by refusing to run with the hares or the hounds. And now I am frightening my own compatriots by speaking in favor of emancipation. This is nothing less than an attempt to bring me down."

"Indeed it is," she said, and stood up. "Because there is no man in all the world who cannot be brought down, unless he be a saint. Is that not true, Colonel Haggard?"

"I'm not sure I understand you. Is having a mistress such a heinous crime?"

"A mistress?" Her voice was low, but every word seemed to drop from her lips like molten lead. "An incestuous affair with your own sister-in-law?"

"Oh, come now."

"In the eyes of the church, and therefore in the eyes of every right-thinking person, a sister-in-law is within the limits of consanguinity," she said. "You have committed a terrible crime, Roger Haggard. You have humiliated me. And you have betrayed me. As of this moment you may count me in the ranks of those enemies."

"Papa?" Harry Haggard scratched his head. "Why are we going away now, Papa?"

Haggard held Mina in his arms, gave her a last squeeze and a kiss.

"You are going to visit Grandma for a while," he said. "Won't that be fun?"

"I'd rather stay in Derleth," Mina whispered.

"Me, too," Harry confided.

Haggard raised his head to look at Alice, standing in the doorway, then past her, at Jane, just coming down the stairs. She wore a dark purple redingote with three capes, and a silk bonnet with matching ostrich plumes. She was quite the most beautiful creature he had ever seen, this day, in her composed anger, even putting his memory of her mother to shame. He wondered why he did not seize her and carry her back upstairs and put her to bed and love her into submission; there was no one on Derleth going to try to stop him. But then, he had had the same thoughts several times within the past twenty-four hours, and rejected them. For all her beauty, he did not love her. It was as simple as that. Deep in his heart he had always anticipated something like this happening, had always known it would eventually happen, had perhaps always willed it to happen. Now he was as incapable of moving toward her as if his feet had been anchored in stone.

"Is the carriage ready, Trumley?" Her voice was quiet.

"It is." Trum was hovering behind Alice.

Jane stood in the doorway, gazed at Haggard. He set Mina on the floor.

"I assume you have no objection to my taking the children?" she inquired.

"Pending a settlement, none at all."

"Of course," she said. "There will have to be a settlement. I shall have to talk with Mama."

"It would make more sense to talk with your attorney, and then he can contact mine."

"I'm sure Mama will know what is best to be done. Come along, children, nurse is waiting."

Harry hesitated, and Haggard rumpled his hair.

"Off you go, old fellow. Do as Mother says."

Jane stared at him again, then turned and went down the stairs. The two nurses each took one of the children's hands.

"Will you not see them off?" Alice asked.

"I doubt Jane wishes it." He snapped his fingers. "I think I would like a glass of port. Nugent."

"Immediately, sir."

Trum came into the room. "I don't really know what to say."

"Then I suggest you say nothing." Haggard took the glass from Nugent's tray, drained it at a gulp; he had never drunk port at nine in the morning before.

"It . . . it is all so unexpected," Alice confessed, standing beside her husband.

"Aye, well, perhaps not so unexpected to either Jane or myself." He took another glass, listened to the rumble of the carriage wheels, drank.

"You may be sure of our support," Trum said.

"Despite my heinous crimes?"

"Well . . ." Alice chewed her lip. "We can understand how these things happen. There will be a scandal, of course, unless Jane can be persuaded to hush it up. We shall just have to ride it out. Mr. Shotter may be a problem, but he has been here a long time, and is happy here. Presumably . . ." She gazed at her brother, and flushed.

"Go on."

"Well, in all the circumstances, I assume the . . . the liaison is over?"

"Why should it be?"

"Well . . ."

Haggard found himself becoming angry, and he could not ever remember being angry with Alice before.

"Because *I* feel, in the circumstances, that it is time to bring the liaison into the open."

"Roger . . ."

"Otherwise Lindy is at the mercy of whatever revenge Jane and her mother may cook up. The Isle of Wight is too far away."

"Roger, you couldn't," Alice said.

"I'm bound to say, old man, that I think that to pursue the matter would but add fuel to the flames," Trum said.

"Pursue the matter?" Haggard demanded. "Fuel to the

flames? I had thought better of you, Trum. Whose fire am I adding flames to? Jane needs no kindling from me. In the eyes of the world, I have apparently sinned most grievously. I do not agree with that point of view at all."

"Therefore you will challenge the world?" Alice cried. "Why, it could be Father standing there."

"And was everything Father did so very wrong?"

She met his gaze. "He had courage. I would never deny that."

"You must do as you think fit, Roger," Trum said.

"I intend to. I am leaving Derleth today, for the Isle of Wight."

Trum looked at his wife. "I do not see any alternative. Rosalind will have to be told what has happened. But if you would prefer me to act for you, Roger, I should be happy to do so."

"I shall be my own messenger," Roger said. "Besides, what I intend to do may well be beyond your powers of persuasion."

Alice's mouth sagged open. "You cannot mean . . ."

"In *all* the circumstances, my dear, I intend to invite Lindy to accompany me back here and take up her permanent residence in Derleth." He gazed at her. "As my mistress, as she cannot be my wife."

"Derleth?" Lindy asked. "Back to Derleth?" She stopped walking, and turned to face him, the sea at her back. As it was still September, the beach was no longer empty, as it had been the first time they had walked on it, eighteen months before. Now there were children digging sand castles, indulgent parents seated behind, and even one or two hardy souls with their shoes and stockings off, their breeches rolled up to their knees, or their skirts held at a similar immodest height, testing the temperature of the waters.

"Wouldn't you like to?"

"Oh, Roger, but . . ."

"Not as my mistress, to all the world?" He sighed. "I can never marry you, Lindy. You know that."

There were tears in her eyes. "I would be yours, dear Roger, no matter what the circumstances. I was but thinking of these people you oppose. Aren't they very powerful?"

"They think they are."

"And are you not afraid of them?"

"I don't think so. I do not imagine a great deal will happen. There are too many scandals for ours to last very long. As for Jane, well, I suspect that when she considers the matter, she will decide that she is well out of it. I intend to see that she does not suffer financially, and whatever affection she had for me ended with that duel."

"You make her sound very hard."

"I think she is very hard."

"And are you also hard?"

He smiled at her. "Every man likes to believe that he can be as hard as the next, if pushed to it."

"But do you want this to happen? I mean, did you want it to happen before the letter?"

He looked into her eyes. Of course I wanted it to happen, he thought, and realized that he was thinking the truth. And not just for the sake of being able to take Lindy back to Derleth. He realized that for too long there had been a simmering anger within him at the hypocrisies of English life, at least as lived by the gentry, at the compromises and behind-the-scenes dealing that went into politics, at the absurdity of people who all wanted the same thing, a greater and more prosperous Britain, becoming deadly enemies because their methods were different, at the narrow-mindedness of men like the Earl of Winchelsea, who would even challenge his Prime Minister to a duel because of his hatred for Roman Catholicism . . . and perhaps more than any other, at the double standards set by people like Mina Favering, who lived her life like the most profligate of Roman empresses, and yet considered it her God-given right to arbitrate the social scene as if it were her own drawing room.

And at himself, for sitting comfortably in England while Byron and Johnnie had gone out to fight for Greek independence, and died, on that heroic mission. He could not upturn the laws of England in his favor, any more than he could entirely negate the law of the Church, but to stand foursquare against everything that he disliked, to be his own man, and to place Lindy at his side where she belonged, regardless of the consequences—was this not what he had always wanted, and lacked the courage to risk?

He put his arm round her shoulders, held her against him. "Yes," he said. "I wanted it to happen. Long before the letter."

•   •   •

The Reverend Shotter stood on the hearth rug and twisted his hat in his hands. "Upon my soul, Colonel Haggard," he said. "But it is a hard thing. Derleth is my home. I know and love these parishioners, sir. I'd not thought ever to leave them."

Haggard leaned back in his chair. "Then why do so, Mr. Shotter?"

"Well, sir, my bishop . . ."

"Is obeying instructions issued to him from London. I am the sinner, Mr. Shotter. Not the people of Derleth. Would you visit the sins of one man upon an entire community? I doubt that is truly Christian."

Shotter shifted from foot to foot. "Well, sir . . ."

"Does this whole thing not remind you of what happened in my father's time? Litteridge was the parson's name, as I recall."

"Yes, sir. Mr. Litteridge was opposed to your father's stance as a slaveowner."

"Well, pray God you at the least will soon not be able to oppose me on those grounds. Then there was Malling. He opposed me because I insisted upon burying Father in consecrated ground. I've a notion that being vicar of Derleth is no sinecure."

"That is true enough, sir," Shotter said fervently.

"Yet I'd not have you shut up shop and steal away. What would my people do? No, no, Mr. Shotter, you must stay."

"My bishop . . ."

"Has condemned me for incest. And has said that no church should admit me. I had no idea that excommunication still obtains in the Anglican church."

"You have not been excommunicated, Colonel Haggard. It is just that no man, or woman, for that matter, not in a state of grace, can take communion. And you, sir . . ."

"Am not in a state of grace. Oh, quite. I still refuse to have my people suffer for my misdeeds. What will you require to make you stay?"

Shotter sighed. "I must obey the directive of my bishop."

Haggard nodded. "Very well, then. I shall not attend your services."

Shotter frowned at him; he was so surprised he stopped twisting his hat. "You will voluntarily withdraw from church?"

"If that is your requirement."

"But, sir . . . that is to condemn yourself to everlasting hell."

"Oh, come now, Mr. Shotter, you are not in the pulpit now. You know as well as I that this condemnation of marriage with a relative by affinity is English law, and has no meaning elsewhere. In fact, I seem to remember that a pope once specifically declared that marriage with a relative by affinity rather than blood was perfectly permissible."

"Roman Catholicism," Shotter muttered.

"A judgment given at a time when the Church of Rome was also the Church of England."

Shotter's frown deepened. "You intend to declare yourself a Roman Catholic, sir?"

Haggard laughed. "I do not think I would be any further ahead, Mr. Shotter, as they would have me on a second score, that of being already married. Oh, I am quite damned, for adultery on the one hand, and incest on the other, and God knows how many more things besides."

"It is no matter to be lightly dismissed, if I may be so bold, sir."

"It is no matter to be taken very seriously, either, where so many learned men, and holy men into the bargain, have placed so many completely different interpretations on what they assume were the thoughts of God on the matter."

"Sir, you are about to commit blasphemy."

"God forbid. But I meant what I said. I will stay away from church, shall utter my prayers, as I consider them necessary, here in the privacy of my own house. And hope for better times."

"I see, sir. There will be talk."

"Indeed there will. And I hope you will always see your way to telling the truth of the matter."

Shotter nodded. "As you well know, the majority of the people here in Derleth will consider you hardly done by. Oh, indeed, sir, I hope you will not take offense if I say that you approach all of life as if it were a political campaign, or a military exercise, or nothing more than a game which must be won."

"I like the last simile, Mr. Shotter. And who is to say it isn't?"

"There are rules, sir, even for games." He placed his hands on the desk, leaned forward. "Abjure this woman, sir. Send her back where she belongs. There can be no glory to be found in a woman's arms compared with the risk of everlasting damnation."

"Mr. Shotter, that remark convinces me that Mrs. Shotter is hardly done by. I have made my decision. Now you must make yours."

"Nor did I doubt for a moment what that decision would be," he told Lindy.

"Yet is it wrong to poke fun at the poor man. Everything we do is wrong. And I am the worst sinner of all. Coming back here was a terrible thing to do."

"Now, my darling . . ."

She sat up in bed to look at the snow clouding past the windowpane. In the tower suite it was possible, with the dressing room and the bathroom doors open, to be completely surrounded by falling snow. "How I wish there could only be this valley in the entire world. And perhaps just you and me in it. But that too is wrong, even to think it."

He ran his finger up the serrations of her spine to her neck, parting her hair to do so. Even in February she slept naked, because she preferred it and because Corcoran had damped down the huge fire to make sure the room remained warm throughout the night. And approaching thirty-three, she remained as slenderly lovely as on the night she had first come to his house seeking his protection. His hands slipped under her armpits to cup her breasts and slowly bring her back into his arms.

"You'd call happiness a sin?"

"Stolen goods can never be truly appreciated."

"Can't they?" He laid her on her back, his leg across her thighs, rising against her. " 'Tis commonly held they are the sweeter." His mouth sought hers, slowly and carefully, as his penis sought her slit, but with increasing passion. She slept every night in his arms, and every night he was as eager for her love as if he had been a boy, or had not known a woman in a year. It was as if his body had been rejuvenated, for all the thickening at his waist, the gray in his thinning hair.

"Oh, Roger," she whispered, moving against him. "Oh, my darling, darling Roger. Oh, how I love you. But, oh, my sweet, what are we to *do*?"

He lay on her breast, passion spent, mouth against her ear. "What we are doing now, for the rest of our lives."

"Roger . . ." She pushed against him, ineffectively, but he pushed himself up in turn, to smile at her. "There isn't just this valley," she said. "Not just this house, and this tower. Not just you and me. There's all the world, condemning us."

"Who, for example? Has Strolo suffered at Eton?"

"Of course not."

"And Harry is going to Harrow, so they are unlikely to meet. Does Alice condemn you, or Trum?"

"Of course not. But they are uncommonly sad."

"They are uncommonly *good* people. But they will support us."

"They will support *you*, because they owe everything to you."

"For no other reason than that?"

"Oh, they love you, Roger. But they know you are doing wrong."

"Aye, well, necessity is a good enough master for me. Then what of Derleth? Does it upset you to walk abroad? Is any man or woman rude to you?"

"They could not be more courteous. But this is Derleth, Roger. These people owe you their livelihoods. And anyway, country folk . . ."

"Practice incest as a matter of course."

She sighed. "So I have heard."

"And correctly. Well, then? Here at least you have nothing to worry about."

"But the rest. Out there, beyond the snow. Derleth has become as it was in your father's day. A place isolated, to be shunned."

"It prospered in Father's day, as it is prospering now."

"And all the while they are plotting against you."

"Who, do you suppose?"

"Well, Jane's family, and the politicians, and . . ."

"Everyone you can think of. Do you fear them?"

"For you."

"Well, in my opinion, there is nothing to fear. They sought to frighten me, because they are the sort of people who exist by frightening those weaker than themselves. I am not weaker than they."

"And if they bring moral charges?"

"I doubt their advisers will let them carry things that far. Burdett I know to be a sensible man, and one with an eye to the future, too. They'll do nothing until they discover the composition of the new Parliament. And that cannot happen until after dear George finally lays himself to rest. So sleep easy, Lindy, my love. There are more important things in the world than our happiness, to everyone save us."

Because he was Haggard, and he could do anything. But not *anything*, apparently.

"You may be sure," Wilberforce wrote, "that my colleagues and I value both your experience on this most important subject and the support you have decided to lend to our cause. However, I am bound to say that it is our unanimous opinion that at this present juncture it would be unwise of you to attend the House and speak in our support. Believe me, Colonel Haggard, it grieves me to have to give this advice, but the fact is that all too often a cause is judged by the people who espouse it and less for its intrinsic value, or importance. You find yourself, sir, at the center of a storm of scandal, which you have elected to aggravate in a remarkable fashion. Believe me when I say I would not so address you did I not know you both as a friend and as a man of great personal courage and determination, but these very strengths, so essential to the soldier and the man of action, sometimes tend to lead us astray. . . ."

Haggard handed the sheet to Trum, sitting before the desk, glanced at the remainder of the letter. "The trouble with dear old Willy is that he just cannot resist the temptation to preach. And to assume that the great British public, and its representatives, are as sanctimonious as himself."

"Then you mean to attend the next session?"

"I do not see why I shouldn't."

Trum chewed his lip. "It's possible that he may be right."

"Because you agree with him?"

"I'll not go against you, Roger. You know that. But I must give you advice, both as a friend and as a brother-in-law, and even more as your man of affairs."

"I'm quite prepared to listen."

"Well . . . it seems to have escaped your notice that you are not the best-beloved politician in the country. The Whigs distrust you because you went in with George Canning. The moderate Tories distrust you because you would not continue with them in their reconciliation with Wellington, and the Tories loathe you for your liberalism. While the antiemancipationists, and they *are* in a majority in the House, you know, go screaming mad with rage whenever they hear your name. But to this moment none of that has had the slightest meaning, because you and Wilberforce sat shoulder to shoulder, because you were seen as a man of unquestioned probity, and most of all, because you were married to a Favering, with all the might of the Whig aristocracy behind you. Now all that had been swept away."

"Oh, come now. Wilberforce is pussyfooting, as he has been pussyfooting these last ten years, or we should have had emancipation before now. Jane is angry, and I do not blame her. But she and her mother are entirely reasonable people. In due course she will request a divorce, and I shall give her one. And I am not aware that I have committed any civil crime."

"People in your position are more often condemned for their moral crimes than their civil ones. I know and respect your love for Lindy, but bringing her back here in open defiance of convention and society . . ."

Haggard leaned across the desk. "Trum, had I not done that, then would my moral probity have been shattered into too many pieces ever to be recovered. Can you not see that?"

"In an ideal world, perhaps."

"But you'd still not have me go to Westminster."

"For a while, Roger. Just for a while. People have short memories. Stay here. Here you are loved and respected. Here you are absolutely safe, from either insult or contumely. Stay here, and love Lindy, and let memories fade. By the autumn, as you say, Jane will have got over her anger, you will have arrived at a mutual settlement, or divorce, and the world will be more prepared to look upon you as an eccentric and less on her as a grossly injured party."

Haggard leaned back in his chair. How history tended to repeat itself, in the most absurd fashion. His father had also been ostracized on Derleth, but for exactly opposite reasons, for sending away his mistress, and for being too public about his belief in slavery. But of course Trum was right. He was himself acting from anger, and his anger was at this moment inspired entirely by guilt. He *had* treated Jane abominably. Easy to say that a man cannot overcome the promptings of his own heart. Easy to say that it had been an arranged marriage. Easy to convince himself that she would be better off without him, as she no longer loved him. The fact was that she was his wife, and he had fallen in love with another woman. When he could explain all of those things to Jane, when she was prepared to listen to him, then would be the time again to take his place on the national stage. Certainly, so long as Wellington held power, there was no chance of any emancipation bill being got through the Commons, so he was not truly backsliding on that issue.

He smiled. "Very good, Trum. You must be about the most sensible fellow I have ever known. I shall spend the summer here in Derleth, and wait for Jane to cool her temper. I do not suppose it shall be too long before she decides what she wants from me."

Nugent opened the study door, gave a brief bow. "Sir Francis Burdett, Colonel Haggard."

Roger stood behind his desk. "Well, Francis, a long ride in bad weather. We should have arranged a meeting in London."

Burdett stamped water from his boots; the April rain continued to cloud down outside. "On your own ground, Roger. That's the way it should be, in a business like this." He held out his hand. "You'll know I have the best respect for you."

"I have never doubted it." Haggard squeezed the proffered fingers. "Sit down, man. You'll take a glass of port?"

"Afterward, perhaps." Burdett sat down.

"I must say, I'm glad to see you. I had anticipated a solicitor."

"I volunteered my services, as I am friends to both," Burdett explained. "I was hoping that the law might be excluded until after you and I had scouted the ground, so to speak. And hopefully come to an agreement."

"I'll say amen to that," Haggard said, also sitting. "Well, I've drawn up my idea of a settlement. No doubt you'll want to read it at your leisure, and pick holes in it. There's nothing there which cannot be negotiated. I'll go along with anything reasonable."

Burdett picked up the sheet of paper, glanced at it, put it down again. Then he polished his monocle, put it back in his pocket. And sighed. "The Faverings are not exactly paupers."

"I had never supposed they were."

"Therefore they are not interested in money. They expect you to provide for Harry's education, and for little Mina's dowry. And I am sure you have done nothing less than that."

Haggard nodded.

"Jane's financial provision they do not regard as important."

"Nonetheless, it is covered," Haggard said.

"Quite." Burdett indulged in another long stare at the wall, another polish of his monocle. "They're a proud race, the Faverings. And a hard one. I know you've had the best of Mina. So did I, once. You'll agree she's not a woman to be slighted."

"I'd agree."

"And Jane is a chip off a slightly harder block, in my estimation. But you'll have allowed for that."

"Perhaps you'd better say what you have in mind," Haggard suggested.

"Jane wishes a divorce, on the grounds of your adultery."

"I have no objection to that. For God's sake, man, why did you not just say so from the beginning?"

Burdett sighed. "She wishes the divorce to be uncontested, the adultery admitted, Lindy named."

"I suppose that will be inevitable, in any event. Very well."

"Jane also feels that in all the circumstances, it would be best if you were to leave England. Perhaps return to your plantation in Barbados, whence, as they say, you came. Or if you prefer it, the continent. Italy, like your late friend Byron. Even Greece, now that it has been declared independent."

Haggard stared at him, felt the anger starting to surge. "Do they seriously suppose I will agree to that?"

"Well . . ."

"Really, Frank, I'm ashamed of you, lending your voice to such an infamous proposal. Go back to Barbados? You know that Lindy can never do that. Run off to Italy? They are trying to have me confess to the world that I am guilty and prepared to steal away into the night."

"Would you seriously contend that you are not guilty?"

"Before my own conscience, no. Call me an atheist, if you will. There is some difference between the God who controls my heart and mind and the Deity as interpreted by a bunch of second-rate priests and lawyers. Derleth is my home. Nobody is going to drive me out."

"That is your last word?"

"Absolutely."

Burdett sighed again. "I thought it might be. I also think that a compromise is possible. I've an idea that Mina wants you out of the way for a political as much as an emotional reason."

"She wishes the member for Derleth to vote Whig, come hell or high water."

"That is a part of it, to be sure. You've heard that Prinny is none too well?"

"Rumors."

"Well, there's talk he may not recover, this time. I suppose forty years of flogging your gut must have its effect in the end. And brother Bill is no Tory. There's more than a possibility he'll send for Grey."

"Without an election?"

"It makes no odds. Grey will certainly *wish* an election rather than govern with a minority, and the Whigs will win."

"You've been saying that for ten years."

"This time it's on, Roger. There's been a big swing in our favor in the country over the past year or so. All of our speechifying in favor of reform is beginning to bear. fruit. You'd do well to cast your mind a year or so in the future, with Grey as Prime Minister, Russell as leader of the Commons, and Mina Favering as the most important woman in the kingdom."

Haggard leaned back. The anger was growing. "Are you suggesting I should be afraid of Mina Favering?"

"Well, she's a proud woman. Proud. When you make a contract with a Favering you make something that's not readily to be broken."

"Jane's decision," Haggard pointed out.

"That's got nothing to do with it. Your guilt."

"Every man has a mistress. It was her choice to take it so hard."

"Her own sister-in-law? And coming on top of your bringing that Gypsy back here and giving her somewhere to live?"

Haggard shrugged. "Were I entirely ruled by my head, I'd wind up a carbon copy of my father, and probably blow my own brains out in the end as well."

"And then, bringing Mrs. Haggard back here to live with you. Why, man, that's adding insult to injury. Is she still here?"

"Frank, I love you like a brother. Therefore I'll take no offense. But you are getting close to impertinence. Who I maintain in my own house is my business, and mine alone."

"You think so," Burdett said. "I wish to God it was so

simple. Mrs. Haggard is your sister-in-law. That is within the bounds of consanguinity as recognized by the church."

"I know I can never marry her, by the laws of the Church of England. And regret it. But there is an end to the matter. Incest is not a civil crime. You may believe that I have studied the matter. It has not been a civil crime since the Restoration."

"It is certainly a moral crime, and Mina is taking the point of view that anyone so morally guilty should not be sitting in Westminster at all." He held up his hand. "Hear me out. It is, as we have agreed, a political matter. And it is simple enough for her to gain backing in political terms. People remember your irregular voting record, and especially your association with Canning. They regard you as unreliable, and should Grey take office, he will need all the reliable help he can get. The party feels that were you to be absent and unable to stand, they could secure a candidate, perhaps your brother-in-law, who would back them to the hilt." He gazed at Haggard's face. "On the other hand, an undertaking from you that you would not stand at the next election . . ."

"I'll see them damned first."

Burdett wiped his brow again. "Well, then, an undertaking from you that you *will* support the Whig whip. It would be no great thing. You have sat with us before. I have often thought that you would do so again. Would it not be possible for you to support the Reform Bill?"

"I have grave reservations concerning the future of this country if it is ever passed. But I too am prepared to compromise. I'll support the bill if Russell will give priority to emancipation once you are in power."

"You go too fast. There is a great deal about emancipation still to be considered."

"Then there is nothing more to be discussed."

"You'll give nothing."

"I'll give Jane her divorce."

"They want your seat as well."

"Then let them put a candidate up against me."

"They'll bring you down, Roger."

Haggard smiled at him. "By moral criticism? I doubt that, especially coming from Mina Favering."

"I am to tell you they are prepared to go the limit."

"You'll be good enough to specify?"

Burdett raised his hand, held up the fingers, ticked them

off. "Jane intends, if you will not cooperate, to cite incest as well as adultery in her petition."

"Will she not have to prove it?"

"You've given them sufficient proof in bringing Mrs. Haggard back here within a month of Jane leaving you. Proof of incest is surely the same as proof of adultery; no one expects to catch the guilty parties in bed. It is sufficient to prove that they love each other and that there has been an opportunity for cohabitation. Besides, what if you're put into the witness box and asked a direct question? Jane and her mother know you'll not perjure yourself, no matter what."

"I still cannot see where this is leading," Haggard said. "So they're out to blacken Lindy's reputation as well as mine. I had not really expected anything better."

"A reputation blackened is difficult to whiten again. Where a man confesses to stealing a loaf, it is easier to believe he may also have stolen the beer to go with it, even if he is innocent in that direction."

Haggard frowned at him. "Go on."

"Mina remembers that you were a close friend of George Byron."

"Will that poor devil never be laid to rest?"

Burdett shrugged.

"Go on."

"And there seems to be fairly common agreement that Byron and your brother were lovers, from time to time."

"I've never denied that."

"It's a pity you didn't. As I've just said, where people will believe one thing of a man, they'll believe much more. It is being recalled that you entertained Byron here, on more than one occasion, and also spent some time in his rooms in London."

"Now you *are* being impertinent."

"I'm speaking for the Faverings. But as your friend."

"Who knows it is not true."

"To my knowledge, certainly. Yet it can be suggested, and more than that. Jane intends to cite sodomy as the third reason for demanding a divorce."

Chapter 8

The Trial

Mr. Sergeant Roeham was a tall, thin man with gray hair who wore a pince-nez and had an unfortunate habit of twisting his hands together as he spoke. Or perhaps, Haggard thought, it was merely the nature of the case he was called upon to defend.

"Upon my soul, Colonel Haggard," he said. "It is a pleasure to be here, and I wish the circumstances could be happier. But yet it is an honor, sir. My father had the privilege of defending your father, sir, in that famous lawsuit, oh, forty years ago it was."

"A lawsuit which was lost, as I remember it, Mr. Roeham."

"Ah, well, sir, it was a historic judgment, to be sure." He seated himself before Haggard's desk, spread his papers. "Now, here we have an entirely different kettle of fish, if you'll pardon the expression." He peered at Haggard over the top of his pince-nez. "Let me make it perfectly clear, sir, that I am proud to be asked to act for you. Proud, sir. But I feel called upon, as I *am* acting for you, to offer certain advice."

"Which is the reason I asked you to undertake this journey, Mr. Roeham," Haggard said patiently.

"Yes, sir. Well, sir, as I understand the situation, you were in the beginning quite agreeable to granting your, ah, wife a divorce, allowing her to cite you for adultery with, ah, Mrs. Haggard."

"I am still perfectly agreeable to grant her a divorce on those grounds, Mr. Roeham. It is the additional demands that she has made which I refuse to accept."

"Quite so, sir. The demand that you leave the country?"

Haggard nodded.

"There is no, ah, prospect of your changing your mind on that score, Colonel Haggard?"

Haggard frowned at him. "Are you representing me or Mrs. Haggard?"

"It is my, ah, duty, sir, to place the facts of the situation, as well as the possible, ah, alternatives, before you in a straight-up manner, sir. Mrs. Haggard has intimated that should you not accede to her, ah, request, then she will name additional causes for divorce in her petition. Is that correct, sir?"

"That is why you are here, Mr. Roeham."

"Quite so, sir. Well, it is my, ah, painful duty to tell you that it will be a, ah, nasty business."

"I'm sure it will."

"Incest is an, ah, emotive word, Colonel Haggard."

"And no doubt provides ample cause for divorce. But it is not a crime for which I can be condemned in law."

"Indeed not, sir. That law has been a dead letter these hundred and fifty years. But your wife also intends to bring charges of, ah . . . well . . ."

"Sodomy, Mr. Roeham."

"Quite so, sir. And that is a vastly different kettle of fish. Sodomy, Colonel Haggard, if proven, is an indictable offense. Why, sir, as you may know, down to a very few years ago it was punishable by death. And even now, sir, why, it carries a lengthy term of imprisonment."

"If proved, Mr. Roeham. As I have never committed the offense, how can it be proved against me?"

Roeham peered over the top of his pince-nez, shuffled his papers together. "Quite so, sir. But you do intend to permit your, ah, wife to go ahead with these charges?"

"My father only ever gave me one piece of advice, Mr. Roeham, and it was repeated when I joined the army as a private soldier. Look to the front. The only trouble I've ever got into in this life of mine is when I've turned my head to either side. If my wife and her mother wish a fight, by God they'll have one. But I'll not turn my head aside."

"Quite so, sir. A very, ah, laudable sentiment. But in view of the, ah, possible gravity of the consequences, it behoves us to approach this matter with caution, would you not say?"

"My wife, Mr. Roeham, or more probably my wife's mother, is trying to frighten me, much as the establishment frightened poor old George Byron into fleeing the country. I do not intend them to succeed."

"Of course, sir, of course," Roeham said soothingly. "Yet must we prepare for whatever may be hurled against us. Witnesses, and, ah, that sort of thing."

"Witnesses?" Haggard cried. "How can there be witnesses to something I have not done?" He frowned. "Are you questioning my probity?"

"Heaven forbid, sir. Heaven forbid. Yet must there be witnesses. To that fact of the adultery, sir. You will understand, Colonel Haggard, that it is quite against the tenets of English law that a husband may be permitted to stand up in court and say: My wife accuses me of adultery and I admit the offense, so there is an end of the matter, please may we have our decree. No, no, sir, that would be to negate the entire principle of marriage, that whosoever God has joined together, let no man, or no conspiracy, put asunder. Save of course in *proved* cases of adultery, or cruelty. But I was of the impression that, as you are willing to grant the divorce on the grounds of adultery, you would have no objection to witnesses being called?"

"Of course I do not," Haggard said. "Who are these witnesses to be?"

"Ah, sir, there is the point. Mrs. Haggard's solicitors intend to call two from your own establishment. Does that meet with your approval, sir?"

"Perhaps if you'd tell me their names."

"Well, sir . . ." Roeham consulted his notes. "A Miss Mary Prince, described as housekeeper . . ." He raised his head.

"Mary is my housekeeper, yes."

"And a Mr. Thomas Corcoran, described as valet."

"Corky. By God." Haggard smiled. "These are the witnesses she would call to prove my adultery?"

"As I understand it, sir."

"Then she is welcome, more than welcome. They will prove my adultery, all right. And in the same breath they will also prove my innocence of the other accusation."

"Well, of course, sir, that would be admirable. But it shall be my intention, if I can, to prevent the court from proceeding along those lines in any event."

"It is of no matter to me, Mr. Roeham," Haggard said. "For I tell you this. If my wife accuses me of sodomy in open court, I intend to bring an action of criminal slander against her. It will be your province, so you had best study the matter."

"Quite so, sir, quite so." Roeham polished his pince-nez. "Yet perhaps it would be best for all parties were the subject avoided altogether. If, as you have suggested, it is the intention of Mrs. Haggard to frighten you"—Roeham allowed himself a deprecatory smile—"well, once she discovers that she has failed in that objective, you may be sure she will settle for as rapid and painless a divorce as can be managed. Now, sir, with your permission, I will just serve the necessary subpoenas on Miss Prince and Mr. Corcoran."

"You're sure you do not wish me to accompany you?" Trum asked for the tenth time.

"Your business is here, looking after Derleth for me," Haggard insisted. "Looking after Alice. Besides, I do not suppose I shall be away very long."

"Pray God that it be so," Alice said, weeping unashamedly. "Oh, pray God."

Haggard took her in his arms, squeezed her against him. "*You* know, at the least, that it cannot take longer than that. A week at the outside. I cannot imagine why you are all so agitated. Come along, Mary. Corkey."

For the two servants were in a complete state of nerves at the idea of having to appear in court, Corky more so even than the housekeeper.

"I am sure I shall not know what to say, Colonel Haggard," he confessed.

"You have to say nothing. You have but to answer questions, and truthfully. Speak the truth, always, Corky, and you have nothing to fear."

Then it was time to find Lindy, sitting alone in the sewing room, her tapestry on her lap, by the window from where she could overlook the park.

"I sometimes think I am damned," she said. "And thus also damn those I love."

"A divorce case," he said. "They are not so uncommon, my love. We knew it would come to this."

"But all this unpleasantness . . ."

"Will soon be over. And then, why, I have been consulting. There is no such stigma on affinity on the continent as there is here. Once I am divorced, we shall go abroad, to France, and there we shall be married. The marriage will never be recognized here, perhaps, but we shall be legally bound together."

She squeezed his hand. "But . . . why do we not concede Jane's terms and do that anyway?"

"I said we shall go abroad. We shall not be exiled. To flee now would mean that I am conceding every charge that is being brought against me. We could never return. Derleth is our home and will remain so. Trust me."

"I do. I but wish we could be certain of *what* may be brought against you."

"Nothing can be brought against me, my love, save what I have admitted. Because there is nothing to bring. I shall be back in a week."

It seemed the entire village had turned out to see him go, as they all knew why he was leaving them. He walked his horse down the street, Corcoran at his heels, Mary Prince following in the carriage, drew abreast of the blacksmith's shop, where, early as it was, Tim Bold was hard at work, stripped to the waist, muscles rippling in the morning sunlight.

"Godspeed you, Colonel Haggard." Meg, leaning from an upstairs window. With the coming of spring her cold had dried, and she looked almost healthy on her diet of fresh air and good food. "Godspeed you."

Godspeed you, Colonel Haggard, he thought. And bring you safe back home again. Because Derleth is the place to be.

The courtroom was small and uncrowded; the general public were not admitted to divorce hearings. Apart from the officials, there were only Jane and Mina Favering, both heavily veiled, an embarrassed Burdett sitting with them, and their advocate with his clerk. On Roger's side there was only himself, Roeham, and *his* clerk. Corcoran and Mary were of course in the witnesses' room, waiting to be called, but there were three other men present, quietly dressed but obviously not gentlemen, seated in the far corner.

"I thought no newspapermen were allowed at divorce proceedings?" Haggard whispered.

"Bless you, Colonel Haggard, they aren't reporters," Roeham said, anxiously polishing his pince-nez. But there was no time to pursue the matter, as the court was called to order. The presiding judge, Haggard discovered, was Prebble Strode, an old friend of the Faverings. He wondered if that could be coincidence.

"If it please your Honor," said Mr. Althorpe, appearing for the plaintiff, "it was hoped that today's session may have been a brief one, but it now appears that the proceedings may take longer than we had first anticipated. My client, your Honor, Mrs. Haggard, late of Derleth Hall in the county of Derbyshire, but now of Midlook House in the county of Surrey, is seeking to terminate her marriage with Colonel Haggard, of Derleth Hall in the county of Derbyshire, on the grounds of"—Mr. Althorpe appeared to read his notes very carefully—"of his incestuous adultery with his sister-in-law, Mrs. John Haggard, and also his indecency with various male friends and acquaintances."

Haggard sat up and stared at Jane. Various? But she was hidden behind her veil and he could not see her face.

"Indecency? Mr. Althorpe?" inquired Mr. Justice Strode.

"Gross indecency, your Honor."

"*Gross* indecency, Mr. Althorpe?"

"Sodomy, your Honor."

Mr. Justice Strode stared at Althorpe for some seconds, while the court was absolutely quiet; then he looked at Roeham.

"Mr. Roeham, have you anything to say?"

Roeham stood up. "My client is prepared to admit the charges of adultery, your Honor. And with the lady named."

"And the other?"

"Is denied, of course, your Honor, as it is untrue. However, my client's denial or otherwise appears to me to be irrelevant as regards this court. As he is admitting adultery, the purposes for which Mrs. Haggard had brought this action can be served without proceeding further."

"Yet is the second charge the more serious one, Mr. Roeham. And in denying it your client is accusing Mrs. Haggard of perjury."

"I submit, your Honor, that that is also irrelevant to *this* court. My client has admitted misconduct sufficient to justify the petition of his wife, and my learned friend has, I have no doubt, at his beck and call sufficient witnesses to attest to the fact of the adultery actually having taken place. Surely nothing else is necessary."

Haggard found himself drumming his fingers on the desk in front of him. Roeham's determination to sidestep the question of whether or not he had committed sodomy was becoming embarrassing.

And Mr. Justice Strode had decided to ignore him for the moment. He was looking at Mr. Althorpe.

"How now, Mr. Althorpe, here's a fine to-do. I'll not have perjury in my court, sir. Is there evidence to support your second charge?"

"There is evidence, your Honor."

"Bless my soul." Mr. Justice Strode allowed his gaze slowly to sweep round the room, resting for a moment on the men in the corner, before coming back to Roeham, who was vigorously polishing his pince-nez. "Mr. Roeham?"

Roeham's face was pale, and he was sweating profusely, but his voice was steady enough. "I must repeat, your Honor, and with great respect, that this further charge has no bearing on the matter to be decided here today. Indeed, your Honor, I am at a loss to understand why such an additional charge was made at all, where my client has signified his readiness to admit adultery."

Strode stared at him for a moment and then nodded emphatically. "Of course. Of course you are right, Mr. Roeham. Mr. Althorpe, I quite fail to see why it was necessary to advance additional causes, of such an unpleasant nature, however substantiated they may be. No, indeed, sir."

"Then I apologize to the court, your Honor," Mr. Althorpe said. "My client was unsure whether or not Colonel Haggard would withdraw his admission of guilt, and was merely prepared to substantiate her charges."

"Quite so. Quite so. But still unnecessary, as it turned out. Perjury in my court. By gad, sir, I'll not have it." He regarded the blank sheet of paper before him, picked up a pen and made one or two little notes, then sat back and cleared his throat. "We will concentrate on the matter of adultery. Mr. Althorpe?"

Mary Prince was first on the stand. But Haggard was not interested in what she had to say; he knew that already. He leaned close to Roeham. "Well done," he whispered.

"Well done?" Roeham was mopping sweat. "We are lost."

"Eh?"

"We have been done, Colonel Haggard. By God, sir, we have been diddled. A put-up job. Oh, indeed, sir, a put-up job."

"Your witness, Mr. Roeham," Mr. Althorpe was saying.

Roeham stood up, gazed at Mary, who had flushed scarlet
and seemed on the verge of tears.

"You have testified that you have several times observed
Colonel Haggard leaving the room of Mrs. John Haggard
when she first lived at Derleth Hall. Can you tell the court
what time of night this would have been?"

"Not at night, sir. In the afternoon." She gazed at Haggard.

"Afternoon? Good heavens," remarked Mr. Roeham.
"What time in the afternoon?"

"All sorts of times, sir."

"I see. But you have no true idea of why Colonel Haggard
should, or should not, have visited his sister-in-law in the
middle of the afternoon. They might have been discussing
family or financial affairs, for all you are aware."

"Oh, yes, sir."

"You never actually entered the bedchamber to discover
what they were about?"

"Oh, *no*, sir," Mary protested. "I never even thought about
it."

Roeham nodded. "Thank you, Miss Prince."

"Was all that necessary?" Haggard whispered.

"Well, sir, I cannot just sit here like a dummy," Roeham
pointed out. "Believe me, my questions will have no bearing
on the outcome of the hearing."

"Call Thomas Corcoran," the clerk said.

"This is a total farce," Haggard muttered.

"Of course it is, Colonel Haggard. Yet must the requirements of the law be fulfilled. Or divorce would be too easy,
eh? I only wish the entire proceedings were similarly
amusing."

Haggard leaned back, watched Jane and her mother, also
with their heads together, conferring. Well, as Roeham had
indicated, they had got the judge to bring the other charges
out into the open, but as divorce proceedings were held *in
camera*, he did not see how much further they could hope to
take it, or what Roeham was so terrified of. Anyway, he reflected it will soon be over.

Corcoran duly appeared in the witness box, took the oath.
He was clearly more nervous than ever, nor was he reassured
by Althorpe's manner, which was aggressive and bullying.
But he admitted having accompanied his master to the Isle of

Wight ferry while Mrs. John Haggard was living in Sandown, also to having overseen certain indiscretions at Derleth.

"I see," remarked Mr. Althorpe, consulting his notes. "Yes, that would seem to be all, Corcoran. Ah, wait a moment, though. Will you tell his Honor what you did with yourself while your master was on the Isle of Wight?"

Corcoran goggled at him.

"Come now, man," Mr. Althorpe said. "You have told this court that you saw your master onto the ferry, but did not accompany him, and that he returned the following Monday afternoon. You did not spend the three days that elapsed standing on the quay, did you?" Mr. Althorpe permitted himself a smile.

Corcoran seemed to be gulping for air. "No, sir."

"No doubt you found lodgings," Mr. Althorpe said helpfully. "Would you tell the court where?"

Mr. Roeham stood up. "If your Honor pleases, I am at a loss to understand the reasoning behind my learned friend's questions. What Mr. Corcoran did, or did not do, while my client was on the Isle of Wight, can hardly have any bearing upon the issue before you today."

"Indeed it may have, your Honor, if I may be permitted to elicit an answer," Mr. Althorpe said.

"Well," decided Mr. Strode, "I think I will require an answer to Mr. Althorpe's question, Mr. Roeham. Answer the question, Corcoran."

But Corcoran was apparently still having trouble with his breathing.

"You sought accommodation for the nights that your master was absent, Corcoran," Mr. Althorpe said. "Would it have been at number seventeen Green Gables Road, Southampton?"

Corcoran's mouth opened and shut.

"Answer the question, man," snapped Mr. Strode.

"Number seventeen Green Gables Road," Mr. Althorpe repeated. "Is that where you spent your time when your master was on the Isle of Wight?"

Corcoran sighed. "Yes, sir." He gave a quick glance in Haggard's direction, flushed, and looked away again. But whatever, Haggard wondered, would he be afraid of?

"And you went there every night that your master was on the Isle of Wight? On each of six separate visits, for three nights a time, to be exact?"

Another sigh. "Yes, sir."

Clearly, Haggard supposed, this mysterious address was a brothel, which indeed was where he had suggested Corky spend his time. But for the life of him he could not see where there was any connection between that and his affair with Lindy.

Mr. Althorpe was allowing himself another smile. "Thank you, Corcoran. I have no further questions. Mr. Roeham?"

"I have no questions," Roeham said, twisting his fingers together and carefully refraining from looking at Haggard at all.

"Then I will call the plaintiff, Mrs. Roger Haggard," said Mr. Althorpe.

Jane took the stand and the oath, and then in a low clear voice, looking neither to left nor right, testified to her shock and horror when she had discovered what was going on. Roeham did not wish to cross-examine her either—his sole objective now seemed to be to get the hearing over as rapidly as possible—but Mr. Strode was not so uninterested. He leaned across his desk, using an arch whisper.

"And at no time during the twelve years you and Colonel Haggard have been married did you ever suspect that your husband was having these, ah, peccadilloes, with men as well as women?"

Roeham jumped to his feet. "Your honor, I must protest. No proof has been offered against my client with respect to the second charge."

"Indeed you are right, Mr. Roeham. Yet I see no harm in asking Mrs. Haggard to answer me, in general terms."

"I never suspected my husband of anything, your Honor," Jane said. "I trusted him."

"Quite, oh, quite," agreed Mr. Strode. "Oh, please step down, Mrs. Haggard." He looked at Mr. Althrope. "Well, sir?"

"My case rests, your Honor."

"Mr. Roeham?"

"We have no evidence to offer, your Honor, as my client admits his guilt with respect to adultery."

"Quite so. Quite so. Well, it seems to me to be a proved case, certainly as there may be other aspects involved. I think this court can with a clear conscience grant Mrs. Haggard a decree *nisi* against her husband." He stood up and the court rose with him, swept from the room.

"I will submit the relevant papers in due course, Roeham," Althorpe said.

Roeham nodded coldly. "We'd best be on our way, Colonel Haggard. There may be—"

"Colonel Roger Haggard, of Derleth Hall in the county of Derbyshire?" The three men from the corner had moved forward.

"I am Roger Haggard," Roger agreed. "And who may you be?"

"We are police officers, sir, and we have a warrant here for your arrest on a charge of sodomy."

Haggard stared at them for a moment, then turned to look at Jane and her mother. Mina had lifted her veil for just a moment; her eyes gleamed at him like twin shafts of steel.

"Five hundred pounds," Roeham grumbled. "That is iniquitous, Colonel Haggard. Utterly iniquitous. That kind of bail, sir, is set only in cases of a most serious nature."

"And do you not suppose these charges are of a serious nature?"

Haggard unlocked the door of his rooms in the Albany, ushered the lawyer in. He still could not believe what had happened. "But the bail isn't very relevant, you know. I'm far more interested in this evidence they are claiming to possess. You'll get to work on that, right away."

"Indeed I will, Colonel Haggard. You may be sure of that." He took off his hat and coat, looked longingly at the decanters on the sideboard. "Although there is little I can do until the preliminary hearing."

Haggard opened the inner doors to the pantry and kitchen. "Corky? Corky? Where the devil has he got to? I do believe he has retired to some inn or other to drink himself insensible. He really did not like this morning's business at all." He himself poured two glasses of port, gave one to the lawyer.

"Indeed he did not, sir. Tell me, sir, have you *no* idea as to the nature of this evidence?"

"You know, Roeham," Haggard said, "it occurs to me that you don't really believe that I am innocent."

"Well, sir . . ."

"Because if you don't, then there is not much point in your continuing as my advocate, would you not agree?"

"Now, sir, don't take it so hard. It is not my place to inquire into your guilt or your innocence, but to do the best I can for you. And if that means asking embarrassing questions, then it must be done. Althorpe is neither a rogue nor a fool, sir. If he says there is evidence, then evidence there must be. And if there *is* evidence, then it is not unreasonable for me to suppose that you may know of it. If you'll forgive me, sir."

Haggard stared at him. He had not been spoken to so sharply in a long while. For the first time he realized that the lawyer was genuinely fearful for him.

"Be as blunt as you like," he agreed. "And I'll be blunt back. There is no evidence, Roeham, because there cannot *be* any evidence. What sort of evidence can they have?"

"Well . . ." Roeham got to work on his pince-nez. "The most conclusive evidence would of course be a confession by someone whom you had . . . ah . . . well . . ."

"Seduced," Haggard suggested. "You promised to be blunt."

"But of course such evidence would hardly ever be forthcoming, as the fellow would be condemning himself as well. Saving of course he was promised immunity by the courts."

"However, as *he* does not exist," Haggard pointed out, "such evidence can *never* be forthcoming. What else could there be?"

"Well, sir, it would have to be witnesses."

"To the act?"

"Oh, dear me, sir, that would be tantamount to a confession of participation. No, no, sir, I imagine the evidence would consist of much the same thing as in adultery, opportunity and known affection and that sort of thing." He mopped his brow. "I must confess, sir, that I have never defended a case of this nature before."

"That seems apparent, Mr. Roeham. But all of this evidence you are suggesting would still have to be perjured."

"Oh, indeed, sir, as you say."

"And even if it weren't, could be contested by a simple denial."

"Indeed, sir. It will be a case for the jury, you see. Whether they believe you or the witness."

"And if you *know* a man or a woman is lying, can you not expose them?"

"Well, sir, I can try. But it is no simple matter. And we have to weigh the certainty that this other matter, the adultery and the incest, will be brought up."

Haggard allowed himself a smile. "I would have supposed that would go a long way toward winning our case for us."

Roeham stared at him for a moment, then also smiled, but it was a bleak performance. "Oh, indeed, sir, I see what you mean. On the other hand, the element of incest will also establish you as a gentleman who cares nothing for propriety or convention. Will it not, sir? And indeed, sir, one who, like the late Lord Byron, might believe in sampling every, ah, pleasure that life has to offer."

They gazed at each other, Roeham's mouth slightly open with the enormity of what he had just said. A gentle knock sounded on the outer door.

"Damnation," Haggard said, but he got up, opened the door. "Why, Francis. Have you come to gloat? But you'll take a glass of port, anyway. You've met my solicitor, Roeham? Sir Francis Burdett."

Burdett nodded, drank. "This is a damnable business."

"Indeed it is. From your side of the fence."

"I've told them, I want nothing more to do with it, whatever the truth of the matter."

"Oh, come now, don't tell me *you* think I've been chasing some young fellow's ass?"

"I prefer not to think about it at all. But they do have evidence, Roger. It's going to be damned unpleasant. As everyone knows. I've an idea that if you were to slip across to the continent, no questions would be asked."

"Are you sure you haven't been sent by the Faverings again?"

Burdett flushed. "As a matter of fact, I have. I agreed to come, Roger, because they say they have you dead to rights. And yet they have no real desire to push it to the end. No one wants to do that. And it makes sense."

"They are still trying to frighten me, Frank. They are committing perjury to frighten me."

Burdett glanced at him, sat down. "They do not see it that way. Look, Roger, they have even asked me to tell you that they'll forfeit the bail, if you choose to leave."

"Francis!"

"They asked me to tell you that, Roger. I have done it, and I have washed my hands of them."

"Not yet. You'll go back and tell them I'll see them in court. By God I will. In their stupid rage they have started something they don't know how to finish. Well, they must abide by the consequences."

"Aye, well, that seems fair. But, Roger . . . you're positive they cannot do you?"

"I'm sure of my innocence, and therefore of the perjury of anyone they set against me, Frank. What evidence they may have, I cannot say."

"Hm." Burdett picked up his empty glass, looked into it, set it down again. "It consists in the main of your association, your very intimate association, I may say, with a confessed sodomite. Your valet, Thomas Corcoran."

"The scoundrel," Trum said. "The utter, dastardly scoundrel." He squeezed Alice's hand, standing beside where she sat on the sofa by the window in the drawing room of Darleth Hall.

"I still find it difficult to believe," Haggard said, taking a long drink of port.

"And you mean Corky stood there in court and accused you of . . ." Lindy flushed.

"No, he didn't," Haggard said. "You have to be fair to him. You even have to be fair to Jane and Mina, I suppose. Corky was caught out. It seems this was an old acquaintance of his from the army days. A man called Spart. Well, I knew the fellow too; he was in our regiment. And apparently he and Corky had, well, I suppose you would have to call it a brief affair back then, and lo and behold, they met again when I turned Corky loose in Southampton, and he went back to this house with Spart to have a drink, found himself in what the prosecution described as a male brothel—and I imagine they are quite accurate—and succumbed. My fault, really."

"*Your* fault?" Alice cried. "How could it be your fault?"

"In leaving him alone in Southampton in the first place. And then in underestimating Mina. She must have had me followed to Southampton and even across on the ferry. So obviously she had Corky followed as well. And it never occurred to me even to consider it."

"What *reason* could you have had for considering it?" Lindy cried. "Oh, my God, my God. How *could* he?"

"Aye. Well, you see, once information was given against Spart, he was arrested, and promptly turned king's evidence to implicate as many other people as he could. He even claims I stopped there on my way back from the Isle of Wight, more than once."

"My God, the devil," Trum said. "And Corky supported this?"

"Corky denied it like a man, just as he denied that he and I had, well . . . one really doesn't have the words to describe it before ladies. But of course the charge was made, and Corky's guilt being indisputable—would you believe the poor fool actually left a watch I gave him there as security? And the magistrate took the view, not unreasonably, I suppose, that Corky, being my servant, would in any event deny my implication. After all, you see, the magistrate doesn't have to decide guilt or innocence. Only whether or not there is a case to be answered. And he so decided."

"The shame of it," Alice moaned.

"That's the least of it," Trum pointed out. "What do you mean to do, Roger?"

"Aye, well, to be sure, I mean to have Spart convicted of perjury, for a start. And then I mean to settle with Mina Favering. By God I will."

Lindy had been standing at the window, watching the two boys, Strolo and Dirk, playing at cricket on the practice pitch. Dirk was bowling, and Strolo was using the bat with that remarkable skill of his which had so eased his way at Eton. Now she turned to face them. "Supposing she loses her case," she said. "You have been committed for trial, Roger. You, Roger Haggard, have been committed for trial upon a charge of sodomy. That is what *I* find unbelievable."

"Aye, well, I've explained, there was not much else the magistrate could do, in the face of the evidence offered. Roeham asked for the case to be dismissed, of course. He gave in reply to the prosecution my sworn statement that everything Spart said or claimed with regard to me was an utter lie."

"And you were still committed," Lindy insisted. "Because no one believed you. Because of me. Oh, my God, because of me."

"Now, sweetheart." Haggard put his arm round her shoulders. "It will be different when we have a jury to listen to us. I promise you."

"Which is?" Alice asked.

"Well, it should have been the autumn assizes, but there is some question that it may have to be delayed on account of the King's death. It makes very little odds."

"And they have subpoenaed Nugent," Alice said. "My God, who else?"

"Well, we have a few strings to our bows. Well, you know, Trum here, and Rowland Hill. Let them top the commander-in-chief."

"Do you still intend to stand in the election?" Trum asked.

"Indeed I do. I'll not concede that point to the Faverings. Besides, were I to withdraw now, it would be taken as an indication of guilt."

"But you'll not attend the King's funeral," Alice begged.

Roger shook his head. "Roeham and I are both of the opinion that it would be unwise. No, no, I shall remain here in Derbyshire until after I am acquitted."

"If," Lindy said gloomily.

"Now, sweetheart . . ."

"I had forgot the election," she said. "Is it not supposed the Whigs will obtain a majority?"

"Indeed it is."

"And then Earl Grey will be Prime Minister, and Lord Russell will be his right-hand man, with people like Burdett and Brougham, all friends of Mina Favering."

"But honest men. It is out of Mina's hands now, my darling. And I can believe that not even she really intended it to go this far. Had I been frightened away, as she hoped, then everything would have been all right. Now . . . I'm told even her closest friends are appalled at the way she and Jane are pursuing their vendetta against me. Burdett has washed his hands of them, and so has Russell. Why, do you know, I understand the Faverings have gone abroad, and at the height of the London season, mind you." He smiled. "I have no doubt that that is a greater penance than any the law could impose."

"They may also have it in mind," Trum suggested, "that it would be a good idea not to be in England should charges of perjury be preferred against the man Spart."

"And still, at the end of it," Lindy said bitterly, "you will be left known as the man who was tried for sodomy." She lay her head on his shoulder. He tightened his arm round her, thinking that now, at least, she was able to sleep with him in the tower suite instead of a guest apartment, and their love was not a matter of stolen moments, but of whole long, splendid nights.

"And was acquitted," he murmured, nuzzling her hair. "And was acquitted, my own sweet love."

Because he was Haggard, and he was indestructible. Those who challenged him and overreached themselves, be they the greatest in the land, must suffer the consequences in the end.

Did he feel any real desire for vengeance against Jane and Mina? He honestly did not think so. Undoubtedly he was guilty as regards Jane, and Mina was just Mina, a fascinating creature who acted from her heart rather than her mind, however she pretended the opposite. Yet he would not have been human, he supposed, had he not felt a certain ironic amusement that after it all they should be the ones forced into exile, ostracized by their friends. For their sakes he hoped they had the sense to stay abroad.

Because Spart had to be destroyed, and in his fall, the Faverings had to be implicated. It was not revenge he sought. But they had set out to bring him down, to interfere with the Haggard dream and the Haggard legend, and even more, with the Haggard future, as he conceived it for Harry, and for Strolo and Dirk as well. The whole world must be made to know that Haggards would live their own lives, would not be interfered with or brought down by those they angered or even outraged. He supposed in many ways he was just as arrogant as his father had been. But at the least, he thought, his arrogance was tempered by love, by being loved. And not only by Lindy, or by Alice and Trum as well. By all the people of Derleth. It was not necessary for him to campaign, as the twenty-odd electors in the borough were all employed by him. Yet campaign he did, as he had in the past, making a speech to the entire village, basking in their affection and their support, walking among them to shake their hands and listen to their congratulations and their blessings on a successful outcome to his trial. This was what the Whigs would destroy. Well, he supposed, no doubt in the theoretical world in which most of his liberal friends existed, pocket and rotten boroughs were indeed social and political horrors. And he could admit that were he a Manchester or Liverpool merchant, with no parliamentary representation at all although belonging to one or another of England's greatest provincial cities, he would undoubtedly be as vehement as ever Burdett had been in his demands for reform. And yet, however iniquitous in theory, the system *worked*. The old hidebound Tories, the men who had led the resistance to the French Revolution and still lived, mentally, in 1793, were fast disappearing. They were dying and they were losing their seats to younger, more forward-looking men. And if it had taken a little longer than the radicals might have wished, it had been accomplished in the main without bloodshed or destruction of property, the dreadful episode of Peterloo alone excepted. It would be his business to attempt to influence Grey and Russell, with all the force that his acquittal in the assizes would lend to his moral strength. Reform, yes. But a modulated reform, granting representation to the large urban areas, but on a carefully restricted franchise so that only those who truly possessed a stake in their communities would have any say in how those communities should be run.

Why, even Frank Burdett would have to admit that to grant a vote to someone like Spart would be an utter disaster.

But his first duty was to prove to the world that he was innocent of anything more than love for the one woman who might have especially been intended by fate as his wife. He stood in the dock and surveyed the courtroom, the packed public galleries—he recognized Hutchinson and several other of his neighboring squires—the black-robed clerks, Roeham leaning forward to whisper in the ear of Brooke, the barrister briefed for the defense, and Askham, the prosecutor, leaning back in his chair and regarding the ceiling with a benevolent expression while his junior made copious notes. And then the jury. Twelve good men and true, and not a gentleman among them, so far as Haggard could decide from their clothes. Honest farmers and businessmen whose knowledge of sexual practices and habits went no further than the duty they paid to their wives perhaps once a week and the tumble they enjoyed with the serving maid in an upstairs loft perhaps once a month. Because he was in no doubt that he was at least as much on trial for incest here today as for the graver offense.

"The court will rise."

Mr. Justice Lawton entered, surveyed the crowded gallery, and frowned. Slowly he lowered himself into his seat, cleared his throat. He gave Roger but a single quick glance, then nodded to the jury, before concentrating on his papers for a moment. Then he raised his head again. "Will you approach the bench, Mr. Brooke, Sergeant Askham."

The two counsel stood before his desk and an animated conversation was carried on for some minutes. While Haggard continued to look at the jury, and they continued to avoid his gaze. Suddenly it occurred to him that he was nervous. He had not expected to be. But only those twelve mattered. They had to believe *him*.

The two barristers were returning to their places, and Mr. Lawton was striking his desk with his gavel to subdue the hum of whispers that was filling the court.

"The court will be cleared."

There was a moment of astonished silence; then the hubbub broke out in earnest. Mr. Lawton went to work with his gavel, at the same time calling on the sergeants-at-arms to do their duty. Slowly the spectators were ushered from the room.

"I have no intention," Mr. Lawton remarked at large, "of permitting my court to become a circus of depravity. Mr. Boles."

The clerk of the court stood up. "Prisoner at the bar," he said, "you are charged with having committed the lewd and disgusting act of sodomy, with one Thomas Corcoran and others, specifically on March 21, 1827, on September 3, 1827, on April 4, 1828, on August 31, 1828, on February 17, 1829, and on July 4, 1829, at the house known as number seventeen Green Gables Road, Southampton, and on other occasions, too numerous to mention, at Derleth Hall in the village of Derleth in the county of Derbyshire. How do you plead?"

Haggard drew a long breath. "Not guilty."

The plea was recorded, and then Mr. Askham rose.

"May it please your Worship, gentlemen of the jury," he said, his hands resting lightly on the desk in front of him, his back turned to Haggard, at the rear of the room. "I must begin today by confessing to you that this is one of the most unfortunate, the most distasteful cases I have ever been called upon to prosecute. The prisoner at the bar is no ordinary criminal. He is a member of Parliament, a landowner, and a colonial planter, a man of wealth and education, and even of power, a man, moreover, with a distinguished record of military service, which carried him from the lowest rank in the army to that of major in a regiment of foot. This last you may think a strange career for one so well-born and endowed, so fitted for command from an early age. But that, gentlemen, is but a facet of the case I intend to put before you today. For Roger Haggard, for all his birth and upbringing, his wealth and his position, is possessed of an unhappy flaw, a tragic flaw, an *unnatural* flaw. I shall produce witnesses today to prove to you, beyond a shadow of a doubt, that Roger Haggard, when a young man and already commissioned into the Royal Horse Artillery, suddenly threw up that commission and disappeared, leaving no trace of his whereabouts, or even of his existence, to his grieving family and friends. I will leave it to you to decide what event, what emotional upheaval—for he was accused of no crime at that time—could have caused a young man with the world at his feet to throw it all away so abruptly. What *relationship*, gentlemen, so strong but so terrible in its nature, could have caused such a disastrous act."

Mr. Askham sipped some water. "But Roger Haggard was a talented man. No one can deny that. And even, one may say, a gallant and patriotic man. Having deserted his regiment and his commission, he rejoined the army as a private soldier, under the somewhat prosaic name of Smith, and conducted himself so well in the face of the enemy, that he rose, after seventeen long years, to be sergeant major of his regiment. Let no man detract from Roger Haggard's courage or achievements, gentlemen. But let no man either attempt to disguise this fatal flaw which I have already discribed, and which accompanied him like a terrible disease throughout his life. For I shall produce witnesses to show that Sergeant Major Smith, and before then, Sergeant Smith and Corporal Smith and Private Smith, although a good and efficient and brave soldier, revealed none of the vices common to our soldiery. For when they, as soldiers will, made free with the ladies of the towns they entered, this Private Smith, and then this Corporal Smith, and so on up to this Sergeant Major Smith, preferred not to accompany them. He remained in his tent or his billet, for *his* vices were of the solitary and secret variety. It was toward the end of his years in the ranks of his majesty's forces that Sergeant Major Smith made the acquaintance of a young recruit, fresh from England, and unused alike to campaigning in a foreign land or to the ways of those tainted members of mankind. It was in 1809 that Thomas Corcoran drifted into the orbit of Sergeant Major Smith, young and fresh and innocent, and willing."

Askham took another sip of water. "Roger Haggard exerted an unholy influence over young Thomas Corcoran. More than twenty years later, he still exerts that influence. For on regaining his name and his rank, following, let us be frank about this, an act of heroism at the Battle of Talavera, Captain Haggard, as he became, chose Thomas Corcoran, who else, to be his batman, and when he left the army following the Battle of Waterloo, Corcoran once again accompanied him, as his valet. They were more than master and servant, they were more than friends, they were more even than lovers, with the result that to this day, and despite the very grave charges brought against him, and of which he has already been convicted, Corcoran still refuses to admit the truth about his relationship with his master. Yet are the facts, as I shall present them to you, inescapable, for I shall prove to you not only that one of Major Haggard's very first acts on regaining England was to make a friend of the notorious Lord George Byron, whose homosexual tendencies have been widely recognized, but also that this taint pervades the entire Haggard family, in that Roger Haggard's own brother, John Haggard, was also widely known for his unnatural desires. This too I shall prove by means of witnesses."

Another sip, and now Mr. Askham was leaning forward, both hands on the rail before him. "Now, gentlemen of the jury, I have to tell you, and you have to know, that Colonel Haggard is a married man, and the father of two children. But you must not be deluded by this apparent evidence of orthodoxy and true manhood in the prisoner. Colonel Haggard's marriage to Miss Favering was an arranged affair, as so many marriages are, and no doubt he fulfilled his duties as a husband to the best of his abilities. But his tastes ever lay in the direction of the bizarre and the unlawful. Mistress Haggard has only recently won herself a divorce from the man she was once proud to call husband. Certainly the knowledge of his sodomy played a part in this terrible decision for any woman to have to make. But there was more. For Colonel Haggard's earliest female 'love,' if I may use the term, was the daughter of his father's mistress, virtually a half-sister, and the woman with whom he is now living in incestuous domesticity is the widow of his deceased brother. It may well be, and you may well consider, gentlemen of the jury, that here we have a man larger than life, for whom the constraints of polite society are too narrow, who is perhaps unfortunate to have been born an English gentleman instead of a Turkish sultan, able to indulge his every whim at a snap of his fingers. But such reflections are irrelevant to the facts of this case. For the facts of this case are that Colonel

Haggard *is* an English gentleman, and as such is bound and restricted by the laws of this land. In committing sodomy he has broken those laws, and if, as I intend to do, I prove that he has broken those laws, then, gentlemen of the jury, I expect you to pronounce him guilty, and require him to suffer the just punishment ordained by these laws. I will now call my first witness."

Roger felt like mopping his brow; he had never considered how almost every action during a lifetime could be misconstrued to suit the interpretation of another point of view. And Askham's list of witnesses for the prosecution was impressive. Two sergeants from the Worcesters, whom he scarce remembered, but who apparently remembered him, to testify to his failure ever to attend brothel parade.

"Do you seriously contend," asked Brooke in cross-examination, "that a reluctance to expose himself to the risks of venereal disease or the insults of a pack of depraved women stamps Colonel Haggard as a pervert?"

"It was unusual, begging your pardon, sir," said the second sergeant, now apparently a publican. "Unusual."

Then there was Nugent, bowing apologetically toward the dock, peering miasmically at Askham.

"There is naught to fear, Nugent," Askham said. "You are under oath and are bound to tell the truth. Do you understand that?"

"Yes, sir," Nugent said.

"Because I am sure Colonel Haggard understands that also. You were the butler at Derleth Hall when Captain Haggard, as he then was, returned from the wars for the first time?"

"Oh, yes, sir."

"Was Thomas Corcoran with him?"

"Oh, yes, sir. Mr. Corcoran was Captain Roger's batman."

"Quite. Can you tell me who else visited the hall during that summer of 1812?"

"Well, sir, it were a long time ago."

"Indeed it was, Nugent. But you can remember if you try. Was Mr. John Haggard in residence that summer?"

"Oh, aye, sir. Mr. John was in residence every summer. He were at Cambridge then."

"Tell us about Mr. John Haggard. What sort of a man was he?"

"Oh, a fine lad, sir. A fine lad."

Askham sighed. "Did he ever bring any guests back to the hall? Any female guests?"

Nugent frowned. "Well, sir, no, sir. Not to my recollection."

"Indeed, is it not true to say that when on one occasion Mr. John Haggard Senior, the late squire of Derleth, made up a house party which included at least one very attractive young woman, Mr. John Haggard scarce spoke to her?"

Brooke stood up. "I must protest against this irrelevant line of questioning, your Honor. Mr. John Haggard is not on trial here today. He is in fact dead, having died a hero's death in defending the freedom of the Greeks against the Turks. I can see no reason for his name to be tossed about a courtroom."

"Mr. Askham?" asked Mr. Lawton.

"By the very nature of the charges against the accused, your Honor, and with a principal witness who is prepared, apparently, to perjure himself in favor of the defense, it is very necessary to fill in completely the accused's background, establish his friendships and his habits, your Honor. There is direct evidence of the accused's guilt. But there is also a great deal of circumstantial evidence which also points in that direction, and I consider I would be failing in my duty if I did not present such evidence to the jury."

"Hm," remarked Mr. Lawton. "Hm. Yes. I think in the circumstances I will overrule your objection, Mr. Brooke. You will answer the question, Nugent."

"Well, sir," Nugent said, "I can't rightly remember what happened at the house parties back in 1812."

Brooke smiled, and Askham glared at Nugent for a moment; then he said, "But you can tell me this: did Mr. John Haggard Junior entertain any *male* guests at Derleth Hall?"

"No, sir," Nugent said. "Not that I remembers. Except . . ." He frowned.

"Go on," Askham invited.

"Well, sir, he had one particular friend who came to stay, more than once."

"Would that have been Lord Byron, the late poet?"

Nugent gave Roger a quick glance, and then sighed. "Yes, sir."

"Did they spend a lot of time together? I mean, alone together?"

"They were friends," Nugent pointed out.

"Quite so. Now, tell the court, Nugent, was Lord Byron in

residence at Derleth Hall when Captain Haggard came home for the first time?"

"I think so, sir."

"I'm sure you can remember more accurately than that, Nugent. Because Lord Byron *was* resident at Derleth Hall when Captain Haggard came home. Now, tell me, what was Captain Haggard's relationship with Lord Byron, as you remember?"

"Sir?"

Askham snapped his fingers. "Did they spend a lot of time together?"

"Well, sir, they spent some time together."

"After supper, for example, did you often leave the gentlemen alone, with their cigars and their port?"

"Oh, aye, sir, that I did."

"And they remained alone together, until the small hours?"

"Oh, aye, sir, that was common enough."

"To your knowledge, drinking and smoking and talking?"

"Yes, sir."

"But completely private from any interruption from the servants?"

"Oh, yes, sir. We would never interrupt the gentlemen, sir."

"Thank you, Nugent. Your witness, Mr. Brooke."

Brooke scratched his ear. "Obviously other gentlemen visited Derleth Hall from time to time, Nugent."

"Well, sir, not many. Old Mr. John Haggard, well, sir, he never entertained. Only when Mr. Johnnie or Captain Roger were home."

Brooke scratched his other ear. "Yet there were others, after Mr. John Haggard died, and Captain Haggard had inherited?"

"Not immediately, sir. Captain Haggard went off to the wars straightaway after the funeral."

"Well, when he returned from the wars. After 1815."

"Oh, aye, sir. After Captain Haggard came home, why, we entertained regular."

"People like Lord Alderney, Sir Francis Burdett, Lord John Russell?"

"Aye, sir, as I recall."

"And after supper, when the ladies had retired, did not the men sit late over their cigars and their port, talking?"

"Why, yes, sir. Of course."

"Thank you, Nugent."

"Saving, sir, that in those days the ladies never retired, sir. They sat up with the gentlemen."

Brooke opened his mouth, and then closed it again. But Askham was now smiling. It was difficult to say who had won the point.

"Call William Fletcher," said the clerk.

Haggard stood straighter. He had not seen Fletcher since Byron had fled England.

"You were Lord Byron's servant?" asked Askham.

"I was, sir."

"When were you first taken into his lordship's employ?"

"I worked at Newstead Abbey since I was a lad, sir," Fletcher explained. "I was there when his lordship first took up residence, oh, back at the turn of the century."

"But when did you actually become his servant?"

"Well, sir, it would have been in the spring of 1809, sir. He was going on his travels, sir, and he needed a personal manservant."

"Quite. So you accompanied him on his journeys through Albania and Greece and to Constantinople."

"I did, sir."

"Now, Fletcher, you are under oath. Will you tell this court what was the purpose of Lord Byron's journey to these Eastern places?"

"He was always interested in Turkey, sir."

"In Turkey? Or in Turkish habits?"

"Well, sir, I would say the two went together."

"Fletcher," Mr. Askham said, leaning forward and speaking slowly and distinctly, "you are in a court of law, and must answer the questions truthfully and accurately, or you may be held in contempt. Is it not a fact that Lord Byron undertook the journey to the East only in order to study Eastern sexual practices, and particularly their homosexual practices?"

"I wouldn't know about that, sir," Fletcher said, his mouth setting into a determined line. "His lordship never discussed things like that with me, sir. You'd do better to ask Mr. Hobhouse. He was Lord Byron's friend, and went with him, sir."

"But Mr. Hobhouse did not remain with Lord Byron for the entire journey," Askham said, refusing to be deflected. "After the three of you had been to Constantinople and returned to Athens, Mr. Hobhouse went home, did he not?"

"Yes, sir, he did."

"Why?"

"I believe it was a question of funds, sir."

"Not that Mr. Hobhouse became disgusted with the way of life Lord Byron was then proposing to adopt?"

"Your Honor," Mr. Brooke said. "The answer to that question can only be supposition."

"Quite so, Mr. Brooke," Mr. Lawton agreed. "Mr. Askham?"

Askham ticked something on his notepad. "Now, Fletcher, after Mr. Hobhouse took ship back for England, you and Lord Byron were alone in Athens. Is it not true to say that his lordship at that time contracted a relationship with a young man named Nicolo Giraud?"

"Relationship, sir?"

Askham sighed. "Were they friends, Fletcher?"

"Oh, well, sir, yes, they were friends."

"More than that?"

"I cannot say, sir." Fletcher looked properly prim, as if to suggest he had no idea what the lawyer was talking about.

"Did Lord Byron move into a male convent in Athens soon after Mr. Hobhouse left for home?"

"Yes, sir. He quarreled with his landlady, sir, and was asked to leave. The convent was very reasonable."

"Oh, quite," Askham agreed sarcastically. "There was no other reason?"

"His lordship was always concerned about money, sir."

"I'm sure he was," Askham said. "But was not this lad named Nicolo Giraud a resident of this convent?"

"Why, yes, sir, so he was," Fletcher agreed in surprise.

"So he was," Askham said, making another tick. "Can you recall the sleeping arrangements at this convent?"

"Primitive, sir. Primitive. Nothing more than cells, they were, with a cot. Nothing more."

"And Lord Byron had one of these cells to himself?"

"Oh, yes, sir."

"Where did you sleep?"

"In the cell next to his lordship."

"Quite so. And no doubt you could hear if his lordship were to call out for you in the middle of the night?"

"Oh, yes, sir. Those walls were like paper."

"Quite so." Mr. Askham smiled. "Therefore you would have known if his lordship was ever visited in the night?"

"Sir?"

"You would have known, Fletcher, indeed, you did know, whenever his lordship received a visitor after the convent had retired. In fact, you would have known who the visitor was."

"Well, sir, as to that . . ."

"Fletcher, you are under oath. Did Nicolo Giraud ever visit Lord Byron in his cell in the middle of the night?"

"Well, sir . . ."

"Did he, Fletcher? Yes or no."

"Well, sir, yes, he did."

"More than once?"

"Perhaps, sir."

"Many times?"

Fletcher had flushed scarlet. "Well, sir . . ."

"Thank you, Fletcher. Now tell the court how long this relationship lasted."

Fletcher drew a long breath of relief. "I do not know, sir. Soon after we went into the convent, his lordship sent me home as well."

"As well," Askham remarked, half to himself. "So, Lord Byron, a young man of taste and upbringing if ever there was one, elected to send his personal servant away, and remain by himself in a foreign city in a foreign country. Did you not suppose that was a singular decision?"

"His lordship was short of funds, sir," Fletcher explained. "And letters were unreliable. He sent letters by me to request assistance."

"I see. As he was sending you home because he was short of funds, would it not have been easier to accompany you? He apparently had sufficient funds for your passage?"

"Well, sir, that I cannot say."

"He preferred not to accompany you. He preferred to remain in Athens in the company of this Nicolo Giraud, safe from even the criticism of a faithful servant. Is that not the truth, Fletcher?"

"I cannot say about that, sir."

"But you can tell this court whether or not it is true that when Lord Byron himself finally left Athens he took Nicolo Giraud with him, to Malta, where he put the lad to school. Is that not true. Fletcher?"

"Well, sir . . ."

"Yes or no, Fletcher."

"Well, sir, yes, as I understand it."

"Thank you, Fletcher. Now, let us hurry home to England, with his lordship. Can you tell this court when Lord Byron first made the acquaintance of Mr. John Haggard Junior?"

"They was at Cambridge together, sir."

"Quite so. But Lord Byron was several years older than Mr. Haggard. Yet they became friends. Did John Haggard ever visit Lord Byron at Newstead Abbey?"

"Oh, yes, sir. In company with several other gentlemen."

"Several other gentlemen," Askham said happily. "And then, after his return from his travels, Lord Byron visited Mr. Haggard at Derleth Hall."

"Yes, sir."

"Several times?"

"Well, sir, more than once, as I remember."

"As you remember. And it was during one of these visits that Lord Byron made the acquaintance of Captain Haggard?"

"Yes, sir."

"And they became friends?"

"Well, sir . . ."

"Fletcher, when Lord Byron, Captain Haggard, and Mr. John Haggard all left Derleth together, in the autumn of 1812, did they not journey to London together, and did not the Haggard brothers stay with Lord Byron at his rooms in the Albany?"

"Why, yes, sir, they did."

"Can you tell this court how many beds there were in that flat?"

"Why, sir, only the one. But it was a large one."

Mr. Askham smiled. "Quite so. A large bed."

"There was a settee as well, sir," Fletcher said. "And I got the impression that one of the gentlemen slept on a mattress on the floor."

"You got the impression," Askham said. "Thank you, Fletcher. That will be all."

Mr. Brooke stood up. "Tell us, Fletcher. You continued in service with Lord Byron for the rest of his life, did you not?"

"Oh, yes, sir. I was with him when he died."

"Indeed you were. Now, correct me if I am wrong, but Lord Byron was married, was he not?"

"Oh, yes, sir."

"And had a child by that marriage?"

"Oh, yes, sir."

"But the marriage, most unfortunately, ended in a separation and Lord Byron took himself to Italy, where you accompanied him?"

"Oh, yes, sir."

"And where he lived for a period of some seven years. Now, Fletcher, no one wishes to speak evil of the dead, but would it not be true to say that throughout those seven years Lord Byron had a succession of mistresses?"

"Well, sir . . ."

"By one of whom he had another child?"

"Well, sir, he did have another child, yes, sir."

"Thank you, Fletcher. I have but one more question. You have testified that Captain Haggard, as he then was, spent a few days staying with Lord Byron in London in 1812, before taking ship back to Lisbon and the army. But he did not spend the whole time left to him in England with Lord Byron, did he?"

"Ah, no, sir. I don't think he did."

"Can you remember where Captain Haggard went to stay when he left Lord Byron's rooms?"

"Well, sir . . ."

"You are under oath, Fletcher."

"Well, sir . . ." Fletcher glanced at Haggard. "I do believe he went down to stay at Midlook House, sir."

"The residence of Lord and Lady Alderney, in fact."

"Yes, sir."

"Thank you, Fletcher. I have no further questions."

But Mr. Askham was again on his feet. "There is just one more question I have to ask, Fletcher. It is a matter of clarification. You have testified that after his disastrous marriage and his return to Italy Lord Byron lived the life of a roue."

"Well, sir . . ."

"But I would like you to tell the court whether or not it is true that while Lord Byron was apparently living this orthodox, if disreputable life, he was rejoined by Mr. John Haggard."

"Well, sir, yes. Mr. Haggard did come to stay with us."

"And in fact Mr. Haggard even accompanied Lord Byron to Greece."

"Yes, sir, he did."

"And he also was with Lord Byron when he died?"

"Yes, sir."

"Thank you, Fletcher."

The court seemed to give a collective sigh of relief. But everyone knew that what had happened so far was just preliminary to the true crisis of the case. For Mr. Askham was again on his feet.

"I call Thomas Corcoran."

Corcoran looked pale but defiant. Mr. Askham treated him to several moments of a stare, which he turned aside by gazing at Haggard, his lips tightly pressed together.

"Would you state your full name, Corcoran?" invited Mr. Askham.

"Thomas John Corcoran, sir."

"And your address?"

"Derleth Hall, sir, Derleth Village, Derbyshire."

"Oh, come now, Corcoran. You are no longer at Derleth Hall, and you know that. What is your present address?"

Corcoran looked dumbfounded, as if the true gravity of his situation had not up to this moment occurred to him.

"Well?" asked Mr. Askham.

"Well, sir, I suppose it is this building."

"And where do you suppose it is going to be for the next few years?"

Corcoran sighed. "Walton jail, sir."

"Quite so," Mr. Askham agreed. "What is the nature of the crime of which you have been convicted?"

"Sodomy, sir."

"Quite so." Mr. Askham consulted his notes. "With a Mr. Horace Spart, and others. Am I correct?"

"Yes, sir." Corcoran's voice was hardly audible.

"Now, Corcoran, will you tell this court when you first met Colonel Haggard?"

Corcoran looked at the ceiling. "It would have been spring of 1809, sir."

"Where?"

"In Lisbon, sir. The regiment was resting, the whole army was resting, and we was new recruits from England."

"And there you met Colonel Haggard for the first time. Only he was not then known as Colonel Haggard. How was he known, Corcoran?"

"We knew him as Sergeant Major Smith, sir."

"And you became friends, you and this Sergeant Major Smith?"

"Oh, no, sir."

"Corcoran, you are under oath."

"Sergeant Major Smith didn't have friends, sir. But he was fair. Hard, but fair."

"Well, tell us when the friendship between you began. Because you are Colonel Haggard's friend, aren't you, Corcoran?"

Corcoran shot Roger a quick glance. "Yes, sir."

"Well, when was it?"

"It . . . I reckon it was after Talavera, sir. Sergeant Major Smith was wounded when trying to save a Frenchman, sir. A very brave act it was, sir. And when he was wounded, the truth about him came out, sir. So he was made an officer, like he always should have been. And he chose me as his batman, sir."

"Why did he do that?"

Corcoran sighed. "Maybe I polished the leather proper, sir."

"Polished the leather," Mr. Askham remarked, looking at the jury. "However, to cut a long story short, you became Captain Haggard's batman, and you accompanied him back to Derleth when he was again wounded, at the siege of Badajoz, in 1812. When, in fact, he was reconciled with his father."

"Yes, sir."

"But they had been reconciled earlier, had they not, by letter?"

"I believe so, sir."

"This meeting in 1812, however, was the first time they had met in some twenty years. It must have been a memorable occasion."

"Oh, yes, sir."

"Yet only a couple of months afterward, and while Captain Haggard was still in residence at Derleth Hall, Mr. Haggard Senior committed suicide."

"Sad it was, sir," Corcoran said. "Sad."

"Now, Corcoran, why do you suppose that Mr. Haggard, reunited with his long-lost son after twenty years, and discovering, into the bargain, that his son was a hero, should then blow out his own brains?"

"Well, sir, there was this court case, with Mr. Johnnie being condemned for frame-breaking and murder . . . mind you, sir, it was never proved that Mr. Johnnie done no murder."

370. *Christopher Nicole*

"Yet was he condemned and sentenced, by his own father. But Mr. Haggard Senior did not commit suicide on learning that his younger son was a criminal, in perhaps more ways than one. He did his duty as a magistrate and sentenced him to the penalty prescribed by law. It was only after this that he killed himself. Do you not suppose, Corcoran, that Mr. Haggard was able to console himself, after discovering that his younger son was a wretch who did not deserve to live, with the thought that at the least he retained his son and heir, Roger Haggard, a man's man if ever there was one, a famous soldier, in fact, everything a Haggard should be, and that his spirit only broke when he discovered that Roger too was tainted with the awful disease of sodomy?"

"I must protest, your Honor," Mr. Brooke said. "This is asking the witness to draw conclusions."

"Of course it is," agreed Mr. Lawton.

"Then I withdraw the question, your Honor," Askham agreed.

"The jury will disregard it," Mr. Lawton said.

But Askham could afford to smile as he resumed. "Whatever the reason behind Mr. Haggard Senior's so strange suicide, Corcoran, Captain Haggard inherited, and gallantly fought his way throughout the rest of the war, rising to the rank of major, and taking part in the Battle of Waterloo before returning to Derleth to take up his inheritance. You were at his side throughout those years?"

"Oh, yes, sir."

"And ever since?"

"Oh, yes, sir."

"So, now will you tell the court when it was that you and Sergeant Major Smith, or Captain Haggard, first became intimate."

Corcoran stared at him.

"You know what I mean, Corcoran. But if I must put it more bluntly, when did Captain Haggard become your lover?"

"Never, sir."

"Corcoran, you are under oath, and therefore if you have been proved to be lying, that is, if Captain Haggard is convicted of this charge, you will be liable to prosecution for perjury, and when convicted, that sentence will be added to the one you are already serving. In your interest I would ask you to tell the truth in this matter. When did Captain Haggard become your lover?"

"Captain Haggard ain't never been my lover, sir," Corcoran said. "Captain Haggard is a straight-up gentleman."

Mr. Askham stared at him for some seconds. Then he said, "Corcoran, you have pleaded guilty to sodomy. Have you not?"

"Yes, sir."

"Then answer me this, Corcoran. Are you a sodomite?"

Corcoran hesitated.

"Have you ever been to bed with a woman, Corcoran?"

"Oh, yes, sir."

"Did you enjoy it?"

"Well, sir . . ."

"You would rather make love to a man. If that is how you feel, then you are a sodomite. So now, tell the court, are you a sodomite?"

"Well, sir, if you puts it that way . . ."

"Have you never felt like making love to Captain Haggard?"

"Well, sir . . ."

"Of course you have. And you *have* made love to Captain Haggard. Now tell this court when it first happened."

Corcoran's jaw set at a truculent angle. "It ain't never happened, sir. Never. Mr. Haggard is the master, sir. It ain't never happened."

Another long stare from Mr. Askham. Then he said, "Corcoran, the acts of sodomy to which you have pleaded guilty took place at the house of Horace Spart in Southampton. Is that correct?"

"Yes, sir."

"A house you visited while Captain Haggard was on the Isle of Wight?"

"Yes, sir."

"Now, do you know that Mr. Spart is going to tell this court that on his return from the Isle of Wight Colonel Haggard came to his establishment, in your company, to enjoy what he and his minions had to offer?"

"He will be lying, sir."

"Corcoran, like you, Spart has been convicted. He has been given a reduced sentence for turning king's evidence, but that has nothing to do with the accusation against Colonel Haggard. What has he got to gain by lying at this stage? It will not mean any further reduction in his sentence. Is it not obvious that it is you who are lying, entirely out of midguided loyalty?"

"No, sir."

Mr. Askham indulged in another stare. Then he leaned forward. "Then may God have mercy on your soul, Corcoran," he said. "Because the laws of this realm are not to be lightly tampered with." He sat down.

"I have but one question to ask you, Corcoran," Mr. Brooke said. "As Mr. Askham has reminded you, you are under oath, and you have already been sentenced to a lengthy jail term for sodomy. To add perjury to that sentence would be a grave and terrible decision. Therefore I will ask you again what my learned friend has asked you: have you, at any time in your life, had sexual relations with Colonel Haggard?"

Corcoran stared at him. "Never, sir."

"Have you at any time in your life had *any* relations with Colonel Haggard other than those to be expected between master and loyal servant?"

"No, sir."

"Thank you, Corcoran," Mr. Brooke said, and sat down.

"I call Horace Spart," said Mr. Askham.

Horace Spart turned out to be a tall, remarkably good-looking man with graying brown hair. Haggard in fact remembered him as a good soldier, if one, like himself, who had shunned the fleshpots. Now he presented a blandly smiling face to Mr. Askham, as the prosecutor went through the obvious questions, elicited the information that he was about to commence a six-year prison sentence at hard labor for maintaining a male brothel. Mr. Askham then invited him to identify Colonel Haggard as being one of his customers, and Mr. Spart duly obliged. Which seemed to content Mr. Askham.

"Now, Spart," said Mr. Brooke. "You are aware of the penalties for perjury, are you not?"

"Yes, sir," Spart said.

"And you are aware that Colonel Haggard totally denies having ever visited your house, or indeed having see you, since he was wounded in 1812?"

"Well, the gentleman would, wouldn't he?" Spart pointed out.

"You are here to answer questions, Spart, not to make comments. You are aware, therefore, that when Colonel Haggard is acquitted of this charge, you will be charged with perjury?"

"He can't be acquitted," Spart said. "He was there." He looked at the jury. "I ought to know."

Brooke decided to attack from a more technical angle. "You have testified that Colonel Haggard visited your house on six occasions." He listed the dates. "Now, are you aware that on each of those occasions he was on his way back from the Isle of Wight?"

"It may have come out," Spart agreed.

"Do you know what he was doing on the Isle of Wight?"

"No, sir."

"Well, I can tell you. Colonel Haggard was visiting his mistress. There is no dispute about this fact. On every occasion he is supposed to have visited you, he had just returned from a weekend with a woman with whom it is accepted he is deeply, passionately, sexually in love, but whom he was only at that time able to visit but twice a year. Yet you are asking this court to believe that immediately on leaving her arms, on every occasion he rushed into yours? Is that possibly credible?"

"I don't know what Colonel Haggard was doing before he came to my house, sir," Spart said.

"But you persist in perjuring yourself by claiming that he *did* come to your home?"

"Yes, sir," Spart said. And grinned. "I mean, sir, I am telling the truth."

Brooke's fingers curled into fists. But there was obviously nothing more he could do.

"The crown rests, your Honor," said Mr. Askham.

"I think we should adjourn for luncheon," said Mr. Lawton.

"The crux of the matter," said Mr. Brooke, "is the fact that Corcoran is a self-confessed homosexual. If it were a straightforward matter of your word against Spart's, Colonel, there would be no contest. Did you *never*, sir, suspect it of your man?"

"It never crossed my mind," Haggard said.

"Did it never strike you as strange that he never dallied with any of the serving girls at Derleth?"

"I have never inquired very deeply into what went on be-lowstairs at my house," Haggard pointed out. "He certainly never indulged in anything odd in Derleth."

"Apparently not. He seems, indeed, not to have a very pro-nounced sexual drive, and in fact, sir, had you not made that first fatal visit to the Isle of Wight, he might never have been found out."

"I do not regard that visit as fatal, Mr. Brooke," Roger said. "It was the cause of my greatest happiness."

"Nonetheless, sir, it could be fatal to your freedom and your reputation. You see, sir, sheer belief in either you or Spart aside, the evidence, as it must always be in cases of this kind, is circumstantial. But there is a great deal of it. Now, I have been thinking very deeply about our best course, and I think the whole thing hinges on your reasons for throwing up your commission in the first place, and rejoining the army as a private soldier. Askham as good as said that you did that because of a homosexual affair, and if the jury get that into their minds, then obviously all the other hints and allusions, your solitary life in the army, your friendship with Lord By-ron, the fact of your brother having apparently been recog-nized as a homosexual, and of course, your employment of Corcoran, seem to fall into place. So, sir, however painful it may be, I am going to have to ask you to tell the jury the reasons for that very strange act of yours. And whatever you tell them, sir, it is going to have to convince them that it is the truth."

"I am not going to tell them anything," Haggard said.

Brooke leaned back in his chair, his mouth open.

"I really feel that Mr. Brooke is accurate in his summing-up of the situation, Colonel Haggard," Roeham said.

"He may well be," Roger said. "But I am not discussing my actions thirty-eight years ago, with anyone. There has been enough mud thrown at my family during this trial. I'll not have it increased."

"Not even to save yourself from prison, sir?"

"I think you are being pessimistic, Mr. Brooke. It is my word against Spart's, when you come down to it. I cannot be-lieve any jury will accept a lie over the truth."

Brooke sighed. "A jury will, can, only consider the facts as presented to it, sir. I do beg you to consider."

"I have considered."

Another sigh. Then Brooke stood up. "Well, sir, will you

answer me yes or no to this single question: did you throw up your commission because of a homosexual affair?"

"I did not," Haggard said.

"Gentlemen of the jury," said Mr. Brooke. "This may have begun as a trial for sodomy, but it has come down very simply to a trial of honesty. It is a matter of whom you choose to believe. On the one hand you have Horace Spart, a convicted sodomite, who claims, for whatever reasons, that Colonel Haggard visited his house on six separate occasions for the purposes of illegal and unnatural sexual acts. On the other hand, you have Colonel Haggard, a gentleman and a member of Parliament, a distinguished soldier, a husband and a father and one of this country's leading businessmen, who utterly denies that he has ever visited Spart's house in his life. You have heard Colonel Haggard in the witness box, and you have observed the straightforward and manly fashion in which he has answered both my questions and those of my learned friend for the prosecution. Now, Colonel Haggard has refused to answer my learned friend's probings into his reasons for giving up his commission thirty-eight years ago. But he has stated, under oath, that it had nothing to do with any homosexual relationship. I believe him. More than that, those who know him best also believe him. You have heard the testimony of Major Sparrow, who has served and lived with Colonel Haggard for the past eighteen years, and knows him probably better than any other man alive. And you have heard the evidence of General Sir Rowland Hill, commander-in-chief of the British army, and twenty years ago and more Colonel Haggard's own commanding officer, both when he was known as Sergeant Major Smith and later when he was reinstated in his rightful rank and position. Both of these distinguished gentlemen have testified to his probity, to his honor, to his sense of duty. And you have heard, because Colonel Haggard has himself told you, how he has recently been divorced by his wife, because he has fallen deeply, passionately in love with another woman. Now, gentlemen of the jury, to have an affair with another woman, and have your wife discover it, and demand a divorce, is a misfortune. One, I may say, which could overtake any gentleman." He paused, looking for smiles, and got but one in return. "It may be, gentlemen, that this is a moral issue of which not all of us can approve. But, gentlemen, it hardly suggests the picture of a rampant homosexual. As for the circumstance of his having employed Thomas Corcoran for the past eighteen years, without being aware that Corcoran was a homosexual, well, gentlemen, how many of us really know the secret desires of our servants? And let me remind you that Corcoran, if now convicted of this unhappy crime, did not indulge it during the main part of his time with Colonel Haggard. Not one shred of evidence has been produced to suggest that. It was only after, by a most unhappy chance, Corcoran once again fell in with the man Spart that he was led into resuming his old ways. Gentlemen of the jury, there was no *reason* for Colonel Haggard ever to suspect his servant of any unnatural leanings."

"My learned friend," said Mr. Askham, "has made much of Colonel Haggard's distinguished war record, of his distinguished place in the community. And who am I to argue with such a record, which is there for all to see, and is supported by testimony from so distinguished a soldier as Sir Rowland Hill? Gentlemen of the jury, Roger Haggard was born to be distinguished. His father was reputed to be the wealthiest man in the kingdom, and Colonel Haggard himself certainly ranks *among* the wealthiest men in the kingdom. That he would be brave and upright and honest was expected of him. But that he might suppose himself to be different from other men, superior to other men, perhaps, may also be expected of him. And how often have we heard, have we indeed known, men of public position and public acclaim, who at bottom have been made rotten by the twisted skeins of their own desires? The evidence suggests, gentlemen, that Colonel Haggard has been at the mercy of such desires all of his life. Why *did* he abandon his commission, at a time when his regiment had just been ordered off to war? It certainly was not cowardice, for he immediately reenlisted as a common soldier under an assumed name. But for a young man to prefer to do that, deliberately placing himself beneath the heel of the harsh discipline of a private soldier, when he could have enjoyed the privileges of his rank, gone to war in comparative comfort and in the company of his friends, is indeed remarkable. From what was Colonel Haggard fleeing? He will not tell us. It is a question of honor, he says. Indeed it probably is, gentlemen. His honor. And then, more recently, this mistress of his, of whom such play has been made by my learned friend. She has not been named, gentlemen of the jury. But you know as well as I who she is. She is his own brother's widow. To a man like Roger Haggard, incest is nothing more than a nuisance, or a joke. It means nothing should it appear to stand in the way of his desires. But there is more. Mrs. Rosalind Haggard is the wife of his deceased brother. The wife of an acknowledged homosexual. And now the mistress of a man accused of homosexuality." He glanced at Haggard, saw the anger in his face, the whiteness of his knuckles as he gripped the rail of the dock, and flushed. But he would not be diverted from his duty as prosecutor. "You may well choose to consider that more than just coincidence."

"This is as sad a case as it has ever been my misfortune to hear," said Mr. Justice Lawton. "But I agree with counsel for the defense. It really is a question of whom you choose to believe. There has been a great deal of circumstantial evidence produced by the crown to show that Colonel Haggard *could* have indulged in homosexual practices, that he had the opportunity, and that he did not always behave as the common herd. But circumstantial evidence is never truly satisfactory, except where it supports facts. The crown has produced no independent witness to testify that he or she *saw* Colonel Haggard entering this infamous house in Southampton. Had they done so, that would be circumstantial evidence of great importance. But they have merely proved that he was in Southampton on the relevant dates. They have made great play of the fact that he was a friend of Lord Byron's, that his own brother apparently indulged in these disgusting practices. But, gentlemen of the jury, I would ask you to consider how often we have had friends, and to our misfortune, even brothers, who have turned out to be frauds or cheats or criminals in some fashion. And even more may the same be said about servants. So I would say to you, the circumstantial evidence can only be considered as a support to the main fact at issue here. Horace Spart has stated that Colonel Haggard attended his house for unnatural sexual purposes. Colonel Haggard has denied under oath that he has ever done so, and in this denial he is supported by his servant, Thomas Corcoran. It is a simple matter of whom you believe."

"As plain a directive to acquit as I have ever heard," Mr. Brooke declared. "Oh, Askham was angry."

"Not half so angry as I am," Haggard said. "There was no

call to drag Lindy's name into it at all, much less to drag it through the dust. When I get out of here . . ."

"He was but doing his job, Colonel Haggard," Roeham said. "Just doing his job. Your triumph, and his humiliation, comes in his defeat."

"He shall apologize," Haggard said. "By God, he shall."

"They are back," Brooke said. "We must go in."

"Gentlemen of the jury," asked the clerk. "Have you reached a verdict?"

"We have," said the foreman.

"And how say you, do you find the prisoner at the bar, Colonel Roger John Haggard, guilty or not guilty of the crime of sodomy?"

"We find the prisoner guilty, sir," said the foreman.

Chapter 9

The Victory

"A year," Lindy moaned. "Oh, my God, a year at hard labor."

"Only a year," Haggard said.

Alice said nothing, just sat in a corner of the interview room and wept.

"It is a very lenient sentence, Mrs. Haggard," Roeham pointed out. "The more usual sentence for the crime of which Colonel Haggard was convicted is seven years hard labor. To my mind this proves beyond a shadow of a doubt that Mr. Lawton considered you innocent, sir. I wonder we do not have reasons for launching an appeal."

"On what grounds?" Haggard inquired. "Our only hope is to prove that Spart has perjured himself. I'll leave that in your hands."

"You may rely on that, Colonel Haggard. You may rely on that."

"I'll visit you every month," Lindy said.

"No," Haggard said, "not you. I don't think I could stand that. Trum will visit me. No one else. Trum will do everything. I shall apply for the Chilterns, and resign my seat. You will stand in my place."

"And honor your principles, I swear it."

"I never doubted that for an instant. You'll also manage Derleth for me, as you have been doing for so many years. And you'll take care of Alice and Lindy, and Strolo."

"You've my word on that."

"But who is to take care of you, my darling?" Lindy cried, seizing his hand. "A year at hard labor. And on such a conviction . . . You are nearly fifty-five years old."

"And as fit as at any time in my life," Haggard pointed out.

"Still," Trum said, "to be at once a gentleman and a convicted homosexual, thrown into such surroundings . . ."

"Oh, my God, my God," Alice whispered. "You'll not survive."

"I'll survive," Haggard said. "I have things to do when I come out again."

Was he afraid? He did not think he was. He was too angry. He was aware only of a slow, consuming rage bubbling in his belly. Perhaps the fear would come later. For the moment, it was a fear of hurting others, in his own fury.

Thus he could ignore the comments made both by his fellow prisoners in the wagon taking him to the prison and by the guards. He sat at the end of the line, feeling the weight of the manacles on his wrists and ankles, looking down at the arrows which marked his rough blouse and trousers, feeling the arrow-marked forage cap on his head. Roger Haggard, squire of Derleth. But he had worn uniform before. A better uniform, to be sure, but still one subject to a savage and irregular discipline. What a blessing those years in the ranks had turned out to be.

And at the end of it, he would once again be Roger Haggard, squire of Derleth. No one could take that away from him. It was only necessary to keep that promise firmly in front of him, all the time.

"You'll understand, Haggard," said the governor, "there can be no special privileges for gentlemen. You were sentenced to hard labor, and it'll be the quarry for you."

"I understand that," Haggard said.

The crack of the stick across his shoulders made his head jerk.

"You'll address his excellency as 'sir,' " said the guard.

Haggard turned his head to stare at the man, and the guard took an involuntary step backward.

"That is the rule in here," the governor said. "Of course, we do not mean to be unnecessarily harsh. If it were to be discovered that you were unfit for quarry work, well, then, I am sure we could find you something more congenial."

His hand, which had lain on the desk, fingers down, turned over in a peculiar gesture, and remained there for some seconds. Haggard gazed at it.

The governor sighed. "And of course this prison is overcrowded. All of our prisons are overcrowded, Haggard. It is a pity you never thought of fighting *that* cause when you were in the Commons, eh? But there it is. Most of our cells have at least four inmates. There are, of course, one or two with less, and there is actually one cell with but a single inmate. It is occupied at the moment, but we could make a change in our arrangements for a man we felt deserved it."

Once again the gesture with the hand.

"I'll not bribe you, sir," Haggard said.

The governor raised his head.

"I'll but suggest you remember that when I leave here, I'll be Roger Haggard of Derleth Hall once again. And I've a long memory."

"We've never taken a year yet to break a man, Haggard," the governor said. "As you make your bed, so you must lie on it. He's for number twenty-seven."

"Twenty-seven, sir?" queried the guard.

"Twenty-seven," said the governor. "And may God have mercy on his soul."

The door of the cell clanged shut, and went on clanging, endlessly, along the entire floor. Haggard moved quickly to the far wall, and stood there, beneath the tiny grated hole which acted for a window, inhaling the dreadful stench of unwashed bodies and untreated sewage which filled the prison, surveying both his home for the next year, and his companions.

They were the more important. And one at the least was even bigger than himself both in height and breadth. But not, he estimated, the most dangerous. This man had lank black hair and a somewhat vacant expression, stood by the door, and picked his nose.

The two smaller men were the more alert. One was yellow-haired and young, hardly more than twenty, Haggard estimated. His mouth was slack and his face lacked any feature to redeem its vicious cast. But he would clearly follow the lead of the older man, who was about his own age, Haggard estimated, with a sharp nose and a stubbled chin, and hooded brown eyes which were never still.

"Good evening to you," Haggard said.

They stared at him, and the clanging of doors ceased. There were no candles in the cell; the lanterns which gave the night guards the light necessary for their inspections did not reach through the solid doors, and in another half hour it would be dark. Half an hour.

"Hey, Sam," came a call from outside. "You got that sodomite in there?"

"Mr. Haggard," called someone else.

"*Colonel* Haggard."

"Hey, Sam, we want to hear him scream."

"Come on, Sam. We ain't never heard a squire scream."

Still they stared at him. Less than half an hour now. Haggard suddenly felt curiously light-headed. It was a feeling he had known before, immediately prior to going into battle. Because that was what he was going to have to do now. There could be no question of waiting for them to make the first move, of waiting for darkness. This business had to be settled in the next twenty minutes, once and for all. There was no furniture in the room save for the four bunk beds, a pair of uppers and lowers. Apparently if one needed to relieve oneself during the night one did it on the floor, which was officially washed out come morning. Not that this one appeared to have been scrubbed in some time. But there was no weapon available to him save his fists and his mind, and his fists, as he had been reminded too often, were very nearly fifty-five years old. As was the capacity of his body to take punishment in return.

The man called Sam, the older of the pair, slowly pushed himself from the bunk on which he had been sitting. "Sodomite scum," he said.

But the prison was old too, Haggard realized. In places the bare stone of the walls was crumbled and even loose, and there was a crack running over one piece, perhaps six inches long.

"Bust his ass, Peter," Sam said. "You bust his ass. Then we'll see what kind of a sod he really is."

The big man left the doorway, moving slowly. Haggard stepped to his right, struck the wall with the edge of his hand. The crack widened and he could dig in his fingers, pull the wedge of stone out, close his fingers around it.

"I'm going to bugger you," Peter said, and reached for him.

Haggard ducked the bear hug, stepped free, turned, and drove his right fist at Peter's chin with all the power he could command. The pain was frightful. It started in his splitting knuckles, which sent blood flying across the cell, traveled up his arm, and seemed to dislocate his shoulder. But the fist had connected, and the knuckles, clamped against the stone, could not give. Peter might have been hit on the jaw by a bag tightly filled with sand. He made not a sound as he went back against the wall, hit that too with his head, and collapsed in a heap beneath the window.

Both the others were on their feet. Haggard spun on his toes, opening his hand to allow the stone to drop to the floor, reached forward to seize their ears. Their hands came up, but too slowly, and a moment later their heads clashed as he pulled them in. The young man gave a wail of pain and fell to his knees. The other also screamed, and half turned away. Instantly Haggard thrust both arms round his chest and up to seize his throat, squeezing with all his strength for a moment, while Sam's scream gave way into a strangled gasp.

Haggard forced him to the ground, still kneeling behind him, knees grinding into Sam's back, while he allowed his fingers to relax just a little. "Now, you listen to me," he said, loading his voice with the authority he had used as Sergeant Major Smith to bring recalcitrant recruits into line. "If you, or anyone else, ever addresses me again, you'll use the word 'sir,' or by God I'll kill you, even if I swing for it."

He released Sam, stood up. The boy made an abortive grab for his ankle, and Haggard kicked him smartly in the cheek, bringing blood and another wail of pain. Behind him Peter was slowly regaining consciousness, groaning and holding his face, but it was the opening door that was more important. Because his task was only half done. Sheer physical dominance was not practical, for a whole year, where he was so outnumbered. He had to dominate their minds as well.

The door swung inward; three guards stood there.

"What's happening here?" asked the first.

"These men attack you, Haggard?" asked the second.

"No, sir, they did not," Haggard said politely. "I attacked them."

"Eh?"

He had spoken loudly enough to be heard outside. The hubbub died as if someone had turned a switch. From the floor Sam gasped his incredulity.

"You expect me to believe that?" asked the guard.

"Why?" asked the other.

"I felt like it," Haggard said. "I like to beat a man, now

and then. Or maybe two. Or even three." Blood dripped from his shattered fingers to the floor.

"You're a madman," said the guard, holding his stick ready to repel an assault.

"It'll be solitary for you," said the other guard. "Bread and water and the rats. We know how to deal with nutters in here."

Pain, seeming to envelop him like a shroud. Pain in his hand, where the blood had coagulated, in his arm and his shoulder; pain in his head where the guards had clubbed him to the floor; pain in his back where they had kicked him and stepped on him; pain in his legs where they had bumped as he had been dragged down to the black hole of the solitary cell. He supposed he really was too old for this sort of thing. And over the past fifteen years he had drunk too much port. Now, despite the deathly chill, for he was several feet beneath the earth, he estimated, and it was November, he sweated.

He did not know if his plan had succeeded. It had been born of desperation, because he could think of no other. He had been in sufficient barrack-room brawls to know the law of the jungle. Dominate, but never betray. This jungle could be no different from any other.

Slowly he pushed himself up. There was a grating, but it was set in the roof, and was several feet out of his reach; there was no glass up there, and the rain dripped damply onto his upturned face; it was the rain which had wakened him, in fact, brought him back to the pain of being alive. But at least it was relatively clean water. He opened his mouth to catch each drip as it came in. But the water kept landing on his head and shoulders, making him shiver. It was no part of his plan to die of pneumonia. He heaved himself into the corner, sat against the wall, watched the square of light. It was important to know when it was day and when it was night, to keep a grip on sanity, to think, and to plan. He could do no more for his safety while in prison. He must look to the future, to proving his innocence. It had to be possible. It would be possible, could he manage only half an hour with Horace Spart.

And to regaining Derleth, and Lindy. But there could be no thoughts of Lindy while lying here in solitary confinement. That way did lie madness.

A scrabbling sound, from above him. He raised his head, stared at the tiny aperture of light.

"Colonel Haggard," someone said. "Colonel Haggard, sir. Are you there?"

"I'm here," Haggard said, pushing himself to his feet.

A hand slid through the grating, closed in a fist. The fist opened, and a square of tobacco fell from the fingers.

"Chew, Colonel Haggard, sir," said the man. "You chew. It keeps the marbles in place. You chew, Colonel Haggard, sir."

The hand was withdrawn, the scrabbling ceased. Slowly Haggard sank back into a sitting position. He had won his first battle, at any rate.

"My God." Trumley Sparrow peered through the bars. "But what have they done to you?"

"Very little," Haggard said.

Trum frowned at him. "I came last month, and was not allowed to see you."

"Ah," Haggard said. "I was in solitary."

"In solitary? But . . ." Trum glanced to left and right, at the other men lined up against the fence, speaking with their loved ones. "You?"

"It was a necessary and successful exercise."

"And these people . . ."

"Are my friends. Now, tell me of the family."

"Well. And loving you. And dreaming of your return. Can you really have been in here two months already?"

"Believe me, I count the days too. What of Westminster? Are you elected?"

"I am. Holding the seat only in trust for you, Roger. As I told your people. They welcomed the news."

"And what else? Has Wellington gone?"

"Just after your sentence. He realized he could carry on no longer. Grey is Prime Minister, as we supposed, and Lord Russell is now preparing his reform bill. Have no fear, I shall vote against it. And I have a sizable block in support of me. There is a growing feeling that you were hardly done by. When we manage to *prove* your innocence, why, I'll wager there'll be a move afoot to make you Prime Minister."

Haggard smiled at his enthusiasm. "Then would I believe in miracles. Now, tell me about Spart. Has Roeham made

any progress?" He stared at his brother-in-law's expression.
"None?"

"None," Trum said. "And . . ."

"Well, out with it."

Trum sighed. "The man's dead."

"Dead?" Haggard cried, causing heads to turn, and one of
the guards to rap his stick warningly on the table at the end of
the room.

"A prison brawl," Trum said. "Within a week of his arrival
there."

"But . . ."

"Oh, aye, it was murder, no doubt about that. And deliberate, even if they have no idea of the actual killer. But it was
paid for from outside. So there it is," he said miserably.
"There is no hope of proving your innocence now."

No hope, Roger thought. No hope. But there has to be
hope. Once he was out of here, only ten months from now
. . . Oh, there had to be hope. It was only necessary to contain himself for ten months. Ten months, he thought. Surely
a man can survive ten months.

"There's no reason," Sam said. "Twelve of us, Colonel
Haggard, sir? Twelve of us."

"Then I would make thirteen," Haggard said with a smile.
"An unlucky number."

"Bah," Sam said. "We wouldn't feel it was right, going off
without you, sir. You're the innocent one. There's nobody in
this jail doubts that now. Not even the governor, I'll stake my
life. Come with us, sir."

"And be a fugitive for the rest of my life?"

"Better than rotting in here," Peter growled.

"You'll not stop us, Colonel Haggard, sir," Sam said.

"I'll wish you good fortune," Haggard said. "But I'll not
come with you. When I leave this place, I mean to be able to
go where I choose, do what I choose, say what I choose. But
I'd suggest you wait for better weather."

"Oh, aye," Sam agreed. "Beginning of April. We can wait
until then. No freezing on the moors for us."

April, Haggard thought. By April I will have served half
my sentence. By April the sun would begin to shine. And by
April his enemies would have changed from gnashing their
teeth in impotent anger to beginning to tremble.

By April, working in the quarry was almost a pleasure, and

by April his muscles were again hardened to the condition they had enjoyed in the army. He swung his pick with more than usual force, delighted in watching the rock splinter before him, was alerted by a shout and the explosion of the fowling piece carried by the guard. But his pellets had gone wild, and he was lying on his back, gasping for breath, while the other twelve men in the work party scaled the craggy sides of the quarry toward the fence and then the freedom that lay beyond.

"Stop, there, stop," bawled the guard, rising on his elbow and regaining his breath. Then he blew his whistle to summon assistance, but Sam and his friends were already at the top. "We'll be thinking about you, Colonel Haggard, sir," Sam shouted, and climbed the fence.

Haggard waved, went across to help the guard to his feet. "You're mad, Haggard," said the guard. "Mad. I've told the governor one man wasn't enough for this section. There's a clean break." He watched another six men doubling into the quarry, armed with rifles and supported by two dogs. "A clean break. And you chose to stay here."

"I have things to do," Haggard said.

"So it's back to square one," Trum explained.

"Tell me exactly what happened," Haggard said.

"Well, they got the bill through, thanks to the gains they made in the election. But the majority was only one, which you'll agree was the next best thing to a defeat. And that is exactly what happened when it went into committee."

"So what will happen now?" Haggard asked.

"Well, Grey is dissolving. He is sure he will get a true majority this time. And he could well be right. The country is seething with discontent. And of course most of the people who are doing the seething haven't even read the bill, have no idea what it truly contains. They are merely convinced it is some universal panacea which will end all of their misfortunes at a stroke. But there can be little doubt that the Whigs will get their majority, this time."

"Aye, well," Haggard said, "maybe it'll be no bad thing."

"Eh? But you . . ."

"Have had time to think. These men in here are criminals, Trum. The very lowest of the low. Yet are they true men, and true Englishmen. Perhaps they would thrive on the responsibility of having the vote. Who knows?"

"And if you are wrong? As I still believe you and Russell and Grey are. Then you have a recipe for revolution. Anyway, I doubt the Lords will ever accept it. The Tories are still in a majority there."

"Aye, well, there's naught I can do until my own affairs are settled. Have you information for me?"

"There has been a revolt in Jamaica."

"The slaves? My God, the fools. If they'd only wait . . ."

"Well, they won't," Trum said. "There's been some loss of life and property. And the island is being filled with troops. I don't know much more than that. The Faverings are back in England. But, Roger, you understand, there is nothing proved against them, nor has Roeham been able to discover anything. You'll have to go easy when you come out."

Haggard nodded. "I have no intention of ever coming in here again, Trum. I give you my word on that."

But yet there had to be proof, somewhere. The man who had been paid to stab Spart during the riot. He had never been discovered or betrayed. But yet, proof. Proof of the guilt of Mina and Jane, and Favering himself. People who ruled the country, and the nation, by virtue of their control of Parliament. People who would fight to retain that rule until kingdom come, however much they might pay lip service to reform.

And he was one of them. There was no pride to be found in that. And meanwhile the country was going to rack and ruin, from Trum's reports. The election was one of the most viciously fought ever, and yet the Whigs increased their majority to a hundred and more. There had been only one issue, the bill. So that it would now become law was inevitable, unless the Lords threw it out. And what would happen then, no man would tell. And all the while he languished in jail, unable to lift a finger, either for or against the cause of progress.

At least Trum was able to reassure him about Jamaica, as it was clearly established that the revolt there had been provoked by the planters, seeing the dread finger of abolition coming closer with the Whig victories in the elections.

But slowly the summer came to an end. An oddly happy summer, Haggard realized. It was incredible, but it was true. He was healthier than ever before in his life, and he had accumulated the strangest complement of friends. Presumably any one of them would slit his throat for his wallet the moment he was once again dressed as a gentleman, but as long as he was one of them he was a member of a strange, desperate fellowship, far more closely knit than ever the army had been. The majority of them had been driven to crime by sheer poverty, that was certain; even the harshness of prison life, the agony of separation from their wives and families, was more acceptable than starvation. Save that for their wives and families there remained starvation. Would the bill, when passed, make any great change in that?

But for Haggard there were no such problems. His family did not starve. Nor did he even have to endure any harshness. His refusal to join Sam's escape had convinced even the guards that he was, truly, a man apart, a man most likely innocent of the crime for which he had been convicted. Especially as they knew their charges intimately, knew that there was a good deal of homosexuality within the prison, and knew that he took no part in it. Even the governor nodded apologetically whenever their paths crossed. In one or two ways, he thought, he would even be sorry to leave this place when the time came.

But only one or two. The last week was the longest he could remember in his entire life. Five more days, four more days . . . He paused in his daily perambulation around the yard to stare at an incoming batch of prisoners. Sam? "Sam," he shouted. "In the name of God, what brings you back?"

The guards waited patiently. They were neglecting their duty, but no one was going to take a stick to Colonel Haggard.

"Gave meself up, Colonel," Sam said.

"Gave yourself up? After six months of freedom? But why?"

"Had to see you, Colonel. Had to warn you," Sam explained.

Haggard frowned at him. "Warn me? Warn me of what?"

"They're out to get you, sir. When you leave prison."

Haggard gripped his arm. "Who? Who is out to get me?"

"Now, that I couldn't rightly say, sir. But there's been a recruitment, sir, mostly from Lowden, where you're not remembered any too happily. Six men, I'm told, sir. Why, they asked me to join with them."

"And where will this ambush take place?"

"Well, sir, they know the road you'll take back for Derleth. Past Benligh and then over the hill by Lowden. They'll be waiting for you between Lowden and Plowding. That's what the word is, Colonel Haggard."

"By God," Haggard said. "By God. And you gave yourself up, Sam, to tell me this?"

"Aye, well, sir, you're a proper straight-up gentleman, and hardly done by. I'd not see you shot down on a lonely road on top of everything else. But you take the long way round, Colonel, and you'll be all right." He grinned. "They'll sit there the night."

"Aye," Haggard said. "They'll sit there the night. Six, you say?"

"The long way home, Colonel Haggard," Sam insisted. "The long way home."

"Well, Colonel Haggard," said the governor. "The great day."

Haggard shrugged his shoulders to make the coat sit better; he had lost weight and his clothes hung on him. Even his hat did not properly fit his close-cropped hair. "As you say, Governor."

The governor held out his hand. "I did my duty, Colonel Haggard. You'll not hold a grudge."

"Your duty, sir, will have to be changed," Haggard said. "I'm of the opinion that men are sent here to be punished, certainly, but not to be broken. Yet I'll not hold a grudge." He shook hands, hesitated as Trum held the door for him. "Who's with you?"

"They'd not stay away."

Haggard drew a long breath, filled his lungs, stepped through the door into the November sunlight. The carriage door was opened, and inside he could see the ladies' skirts. After a year. He was not sure how he would react. And with so much else on his mind. Slowly he crossed the ground, and Tim Bold jumped down to hold the step for him.

"Tim?"

The blacksmith flushed. He had put on weight, and was a mountain of a man now, his beard full and black, his teeth gleaming. "I wanted to tell you, sir, how sorry we are you were done up. How sorry we all are. All Derleth. They kind of elected me to come, sir." He grinned. "Besides, you needed a coachman."

Haggard shook hands. A tremendous feeling of well-being

and warmth spread over him. And a moment later he was in Lindy's arms, with Alice smiling through her tears and Strolo jumping up and down on the seat opposite.

"You should be at school," Haggard said.

"Mama kept me home," Strolo explained. "To meet you, Uncle Roger."

"And you grow bigger every day," Haggard said, his face still pressed against Lindy's cheek, feeling her tears dribbling down his chin. "How old are you now?"

"Fourteen, sir."

"And the most promising cricketer at Eton," Trum said, getting in behind them and shutting the door. He opened the trap. "Home, Tim. Home to Derleth."

"There's a happy thought." At last he could release her, look at her face, into her eyes, take in the threads of gray which were appearing in her hair; there had been none a year ago. But she was still Lindy, always Lindy. He kissed her on the lips.

"Oh, Roger," she whispered. "Oh, Roger. To have you home at last. To have you home."

"For the very last time," he said. "But there's something I must do first." He opened the hatch. "You'll drive to Benligh, Tim."

"To Benligh, it shall be, Colonel."

"Benligh?" Alice cried. "But . . ."

"I doubt Hutchinson will be pleased to see you," Trum said.

"Benligh?" Lindy asked.

"You don't mean to quarrel with him again?" Alice begged.

"I do not. I mean to ask for his help."

"His help?" Trum was incredulous. "Hutchinson?"

"I wish to ask him to give Alice and Lindy and Strolo a bed for the night," Haggard explained. "And I wish the loan of some weapons. You've none with you, have you, Trum?"

"There's a shotgun up on the roof," Trum said, frowning. "But I must confess I do not understand."

Lindy clutched Haggard's arm. "Weapons, Roger? And us stay the night at Benligh?"

"Aye," Haggard said. "I think darling Mina has over-reached herself at last."

●　　●　　●

Squire Hutchinson bristled. "Six men," he shouted. "Lying in wait? By gad, sir, but that is infamous. Infamous. You'll take a glass of port?"

"I think that would be very acceptable," Haggard said. "Well, Hutchinson, will you lend an old lag a pistol or two?"

"An old lag? An old lag, sir? Why, sir, I'll call out the yeomanry."

"No, no," Haggard said patiently. "Don't you see, if a body of horse comes down the road, my would-be assassins will merely run away and arrange some better moment for my demise. It must be my carriage, traveling by itself."

"But six men, Haggard, armed and determined . . ."

"As shall we be armed and determined," Haggard said. "We will be three . . . you'll ride with me, Tim?"

"That I will, Colonel." Tim touched his forehead as Hutchinson, staring at him, obviously recognized him.

"By gad," he said. "By gad. Whenever I am in your company, Haggard, I feel the earth trembling beneath my feet."

"And we shall have the element of surprise, not them," Trum pointed out.

"I still think it is unnecessarily dangerous," Alice said.

"It is necessarily dangerous, my love," Haggard said. "Don't you see, with Spart dead, there is no hope of ever proving my innocence of the charges brought against me. Believe me, I was in despair, could think only of manhandling Mina herself, which would surely land me back in jail. But now, an open act of violence against me, clearly with the intent of preventing me from pursuing the matter further . . . if we can capture but one of those thugs, I will have the proof I need."

"But still," Lindy said, "the odds are great."

"Not so great, Mama," Strolo said. "I will go with Uncle Roger."

"You?" Roger demanded.

"Well, sir, I can fire a pistol. And I am as big as most men."

"Now, that's true enough," Trum observed.

"I don't really think . . ." Haggard looked at Lindy.

Who hesitated, and then shrugged. "If you fall, Roger, we all fall. And if you are confident of success . . ."

"More confident with five," Hutchinson decided.

"You, sir?" Haggard demanded.

"And why not, sir? You claim these rascals are to waylay

you within Nottinghamshire. Why, sir, that is my own parish. I'd be failing in my duty did I not see to them personally. If you'll not let me turn out the yeomanry, then the least I can do is swear you all in as special constables. That way it has a legal smack to it, eh? And that way I can command you."

"You?" Trum demanded.

"Do you doubt my ability, sir?" Hutchinson roared.

"On the contrary, sir," Haggard said. "If you will take command of this expedition, I shall be eternally grateful, and once again your friend. I have but one request to make of you."

"Then ask it," Hutchinson shouted, shaking hands. "Just ask it."

"That you take your orders from me, as after all it is my business we are about."

Hutchinson, fingers still locked, stared at him for some seconds, then smiled. "I'll not do business with you, Haggard. By God, I won't. But I'll ride with you tonight. Come along. Haste. Haste."

Raison, the butler, was summoned, fowling pieces and pistols and stout cudgels were passed out, powder and shot given to each of them, while Mrs. Hutchinson and her daughter prepared a punch and some bandages, just in case, and the servants stood and gawped, and Alice patted perspiration from her neck, and Lindy waited, and watched, and gazed at Haggard.

"We should be back by midnight," he promised, taking her in his arms. "With my innocence and the Faverings' guilt proved."

"Just come back," she said. "For God's sake, Haggard, just come back."

He had not been so elated since leaving the army. For the last time, he was going to war, and on his own behalf. It was incredible that someone like Mina, who thought so deeply and calculated so carefully, and whose friends were now the government of the country, should be so stupid as to take overt action of this kind. It could only be because she knew there was proof for the finding, of her guilt, and therefore of Jane's guilt as well. But she would fail. With such men beside him and behind him, there could be no doubt about that.

The day was already far advanced, the sun dropping toward the horizon, already hidden by the heavy blanket of dark cloud which obscured the November sky. And the turn-pike was empty, as one would have expected, on such an afternoon in such threatening weather. The carriage traveled slowly, for this far north the roads had not yet been subjected to the new macadamized process, and the potholes were numerous. Tim drove, and the four gentlemen stayed inside, the blinds drawn to conceal their true identities.

"But you'll keep a careful lookout, Tim," Haggard commanded. "We don't want you tumbled from there by a stray shot."

"They'll not find me so easy to bring down, Colonel," Tim promised. "No, indeed."

"Six men," fumed Hutchinson. He glared at Strolo, sitting opposite, and also nursing a fowling piece. "Careful you don't shoot yourself, sonny. Or me, for that matter."

"He can bring down a partridge with the best of them," Trum promised, and moved the blind just an inch. "We are about two miles from Lowden, I'd estimate. And there are some trees ahead."

"So check your priming," Roger suggested, and himself did the same.

The carriage continued on its way for some time longer, and Roger began to wonder if they were not close enough to the village to relax for a while, when there came a sudden exclamation from Tim, and immediately the brakes squealed as he applied them, while from the lead horse there came a wild neigh.

"Are they upon us?" Trum shouted.

"A wagon, blocking the road," Tim gasped.

"Stay down," Haggard snapped at Hutchinson, about to throw open the blinds. "They must make the first move."

"Stand, there," shouted a voice, and an educated one at that. Haggard's heart gave a mighty leap as he thought he recognized it. "You'll see we're armed, driver. Turn out your people." There was a thump, and the carriage heaved as Tim jumped down.

"Now," Haggard said. "You, Hutchinson, and you, Strolo, out the other door."

"But that's—"

"That's my order, Hutchinson," Haggard said. "You'll have your share of it. Trum, are you ready?"

Tim's fingers touched the door. "There's some men here wanting you out, Colonel Haggard," he said loudly.

He knew what to do. Haggard gave him a second, felt the coach move again as Tim dived beneath it, then threw open the door and jumped out, a cocked pistol in each hand. Before him were the trees and six men, waiting with pistols and muskets, for the moment taken by surprise.

"There he is," shouted their leader, who stood a little to one side, a handkerchief tied across the lower part of his face to leave only his eyes showing between it and his beaver. "Shoot him down. Shoot them all. There must be no survivors."

Haggard's hands came up, and he fired, right and left. Neither bullet struck home, such was his haste, but at his shoulder Trum had taken aim, and one of the men gave a howl and half-turned around before falling to his hands and knees, while from beneath the coach came the explosion of Tim's shotgun and from the other side the crack of Hutchinson's pistol and the roar of Strolo's blunderbuss. Another of the assailants fell, tumbling over backward without a sound, and yet another gave a howl of pain and commenced hopping up and down. Only one shot was fired in return, and this smacked into the wood of the coach harmlessly enough.

The three remaining would-be footpads immediately threw away their weapons and fled for the trees, followed by the second shot from Tim's double barrel, which urged them on their way. The gentleman, for such he certainly was, who had overseen the affray, gazed at Haggard for a moment in impotent rage, and then pulled a pistol from his greatcoat pocket and leveled it. Haggard hurled his empty weapon with all his strength, at the same time running forward as fast as he could, his muscles surging with the power restored by a year on the quarry face. He heard the shot, and knew therefore that he had not been hit, at the same time as he was surrounded by the shouts of his friends, hurrying behind him.

The masked man muttered a curse, and turned to run for his horse, but Haggard, throwing himself full length, caught his ankle and brought him to the ground. He turned and kicked himself free, but before he could regain his feet, Trum and Tim were upon him, dragging him up. Haggard also got up, stepped forward, gazed into the hate-filled eyes.

"Now, let us see just who you are, my friend," he said, and pulled away the handkerchief, to gaze at James Crowther, of Barbados.

"Haggard, Haggard, Haggard." The noise was tremendous,

as the concourse was immense. They filled the turnpike, thronged the road down to the village, packed the fields beyond, shouting their greetings to the coach which came rumbling slowly down the road.

"Your people, Roger," Lindy said. "They love you."

"There are more than Derleth people there," he said.

"Aye," Hutchinson grumbled. "From all over Derby. We should have called out the yeomanry."

"I sometimes suppose you do not attend the privy without an escort of yeomanry," Haggard remarked.

"Why, sir, by gad—"

"Gentlemen, please," begged Mrs. Hutchinson. "Alice, restrain your brother. This is a great occasion."

"Roger," Alice said.

He smiled at her. "I meant no offense. But it would be a sad thing if I needed a mounted escort to restore me to my people."

"Haggard," they chanted. "Haggard. The bill. The bill. Haggard and the bill."

"What did I tell you?" Hutchinson snorted. "This is a political gathering."

"They have identified you with their cause, Roger," Trum said.

"So they have," Haggard agreed.

"Without knowing the truth of the matter," Hutchinson pointed out.

Haggard bit his lip, rapped on the trap. "You'd best pull to a halt, Tim."

They had reached the top of the rise, where the old gallows had stood in the past, and from where the entire village was displayed below them. The crowd surged up the slopes to surround them, and Hutchinson began to prime his pistol. Haggard opened the door, and stood on the step.

"Haggard," they screamed, surrounding the coach.

"Depend upon it," Hutchinson growled. "Our last moment has come. But I will save my bullet for you, my sweet," he said to his wife.

Lindy put her arm around Strolo, and Alice held Trum's hand, but the noise outside was already dying as Haggard held up his hands.

"Colonel Haggard, sir." Truff, from the mine. "We had heard you had been rearrested, sir, after an affray on the Lowden road, and returned to Benligh."

"It was I did the arresting, Mr. Truff," Haggard said. "I'm back, and my name will be cleared. Derleth's name will be cleared."

"Three cheers for Mr. Haggard," Tim shouted from the box, and the afternoon rang.

"And the bill, sir," someone shouted as the cheering died down.

"They'll not let us have the bill, sir."

"The bill, Colonel Haggard."

"You'll stand for the bill, Colonel."

The noise welled up around them.

"By gad," Hutchinson. "Murdered in our seats we'll be. Murdered in our seats."

Haggard held up his hands again, and slowly the noise died down. "I am no longer a member of Parliament," he shouted.

There was a howl of anger and outrage, and Trum's fingers tightened on Alice's.

Once again Haggard waved for silence. "But I know sufficient of those who are," he said. "I do not know this bill, as yet. Where I have been this last year, it was not published." This brought a shout of laughter. "But study it I will. And if it is a good and just bill, then will I speak with my friends."

There was a howl of anger. Haggard waited patiently, while Hutchinson cocked his pistol.

The noise died slowly. "I am Haggard," Haggard shouted. "You all know me. I'll not be coerced, by you or by the government. You must trust me to do what I think is best, for you and for the country. If you are not prepared to do that, then stand aside and let me through. I can do nothing for you."

There were several moments of a quite deathly silence, broken inside the coach only by the sound of breathing. Then Truff waved his arms.

"I trust Squire Haggard," he shouted. "If he says he'll study the bill, then let him study the bill. He'll not do us down. Squire Haggard has never done us down. He's the one been done down, by the Whigs as much as the Tories. But he's back. He'll not do us down. Three cheers for Squire Haggard."

Once again the afternoon cascaded into sound. Haggard got back into the coach, wiped his brow. "Hot work."

"I thought we might be in for a rough-and-tumble," Trum confessed.

"By gad, sir, so did I," Hutchinson said. "But you blunted their anger most skillfully. Yet, sir, if I may suggest, when you tell them the truth of the matter, you had best surround yourself with the yeomanry. Indeed you had best."

"The truth of the matter?" Haggard inquired.

"Well, sir, you will hardly choose to vote with the Whigs now, even if you were not against the bill by choice, as is any sensible man. What, give the vote to that bunch of savages?"

The carriage was rolling down the hill, and before him was Derleth Hall. And a soft bed. And Lindy's arms, after a whole year. Haggard smiled at Hutchinson. "I think, if we try, we can probably discover some cause to commit you to prison for a brief while, Mr. Hutchinson," he said. "It does wonders for a point of view."

"Sir Francis Burdett," said Nugent.

Haggard stood up, waited behind his desk. "How good to see you, Frank. Always the ambassador."

"Aye, well, they regard me as your friend," he admitted.

"And so you are. But looking old. Too old."

"I'm feeling old. I gather I cannot say the same thing for you."

"Ah, well, you see, I've spent a year in training. Sit down, man, sit down. Port?"

Burdett nodded. "I'm here to tell you that the government intends to make amends."

"I never doubted that."

"Crowther is going to be charged with perjury, attempted murder, and murder, in that he procured the murder of the man Spart in prison. Blakeney and Beamish will also be tried, but their involvement is not yet established. It will be, I have no doubt."

Haggard nodded.

"And your name will be publicly cleared by a statement in the Commons. You've John Russell's word on that. I'm afraid we cannot immediately give you back your parliamentary seat, but no doubt that is a matter for you to settle with Trum."

"He can represent Derleth as well as I. And Corcoran?"

"His sentence for perjury will be quashed. There is nothing we can do about the other."

"I'd not expected that. Well, Frank, I'm satisfied with the

government's attitude. But you're not here just on behalf of the government."

"No," Burdett said. "You'll know Mina and Jane are back in England?"

"I had heard so."

"Staying at Midlook, and keeping very quiet."

"And my children?"

"Are with them. You'll understand that the divorce is now final."

"Indeed I do."

"And you'd not choose to change that, I presume."

"I would not choose to change that, no," Haggard said. "But I would like to see my children."

"That right will certainly be established," Burdett agreed. "You do understand that Crowther's confession clears them as well."

"Not of bringing the charges in the first place."

"Well, man, what would you? The facts were there, supplied to them by the planters, and they were very angry." He sighed. "And now you are very angry."

Haggard made no reply.

Burdett sighed. "Aye, well, it may turn out to your advantage. This whole business has caused some thinking to be done. It is Russell's intention to introduce a bill restoring the criminal aspect of incest, and especially incestuous marriages."

"*That* is to my advantage?"

"It will obviously take some time. This reform business must be completed first. So nothing is likely to get onto the statute books for at least three years. And then it is not going to be retroactive. It is felt that would be iniquitous."

Haggard stared at him.

"So," Burdett said. "If you were to get married on the continent, or even by a noncomformist priest over here, well, no one will ever interfere with Lindy's rights as your wife. Or those of her child."

"Russell told you to offer me this?" Haggard felt his heart begin to pound.

"He did."

"And in exchange?"

Burdett finished his port, got up. "The country is on the verge of revolution, you know. The army has just yesterday regained Bristol from the hands of a mob. They held it for two days. What will happen next is anyone's guess."

"I've seen some of it," Haggard said.

"Have you read the bill?"

"I have."

"And?"

"It is considerably less radical than I had supposed it would be. Or has it been watered down?"

"A little. It is sometimes necessary to bend with the wind."

"Indeed it is. As I understand it, you will just about double the number of voters, from half a million to a million. What is the population of this country?"

Burdett shrugged. "Fourteen million, I suppose. Give or take a thousand."

"There's a franchise."

Burdett stared at him. "You were against a broad-based franchise."

"I still am. I think perhaps you've got it right, this time."

Burdett gave a sigh of relief. "Then you'll support it?"

"I am a simple country squire, Frank. What difference does my support mean?"

Burdett placed his hands on the desk, leaned forward. "You're the man whose name is on everyone's lips at this moment. And in a unique way you straddle both the squire-archy and the people, here in the Midlands. And it's here that there is most resentment and unrest. We intend to bring the bill back, in the spring. The country will wait until then, I am sure. And we will get it through the Commons, with our majority. But the Lords have said they will throw it out again, and when that happens, we are going to be at war, Roger. Make no mistake about that."

"I agree with you."

Burdett straightened. "We have two possible courses. One is to confront the King with the situation, and demand he create sufficient Whig peers to command a majority in the House. We *can* do that. But not only would that estrange relations with the crown, but it would virtually end the House of Lords as we know it. Its purpose as a senate would be useless. We might as well disband it altogether and have a single-chamber Parliament. Yet we *will* do it, if we have to."

"And the other?"

"Is obviously to persuade the Tory lords to withhold their objections."

"How do you propose to go about doing that? Not by means of me, I hope. Those gentlemen have apoplexy every time my name is mentioned."

"They are also honorable men, Roger. Who believe that it is their duty to stand in the way of radical reform in this country. They rest that belief on the vast support they are sure they have, among all the sober right-thinking people in the land, support which is revealed by the still-large and solid block of Tory opinion in the Commons, a block which gains its greatest strength here in the Midlands, from people like Trum, and Jimmy Hutchinson, and Richardson, and the like. If the Midlands squirearchy were to support the bill, then the Lords would have to accept the fact that the country as a whole wants it."

"And you think I can persuade Hutchinson, and Richardson, and the like, to vote Whig?"

"To abstain, perhaps. And tacitly show that they no longer oppose it. You can do that, Roger. They'll listen to you, right now."

"Hutchinson?"

"Even Hutchinson. He loves you like a brother, for all your quarrels. And they know it is your personality alone stands between them and real bloodshed, here in Derbyshire."

Haggard bit his lip, got up, walked to the window, looked out at the park. The first snow was falling, and in a fortnight it would be Christmas. A Christmas full of promise, for Lindy and himself, for Strolo, for everything Haggard. And for Derleth as well. Even for all of England. Even for gallant Sam. Could a man that faithful to his idea of friendship misuse the right to vote?

He turned. "You suggest a great responsibility. But then, perhaps it is a great cause. Yet do I know of a greater."

Burdett poured himself a fresh glass of port, sat down. "Russell supposed you would make that point."

"And?"

"We can do it now. The Jamaican planters have discredited themselves by provoking that rebellion in the spring, and Crowther's crime has discredited the West Indies lobby here in England. A bill for the abolition of slavery in his majesty's dominions will be brought in as part of the government's first program, once the bill is through."

Haggard smiled. "Bribery and corruption, double-dealing and deception."

Burdett also smiled, held out his hands. "Politics, dear Rogger. It is the lifeblood of democracy."

Haggard walked his horse up the front drive of Midlook House, brought it to a halt before the great columned portico, was immediately surrounded by grooms. While at the top of the steps stood Hargreaves, an old and bent Hargreaves, but nonetheless very much the man Haggard remembered.

"Her ladyship is not at home, sir," he said.

"Papa." Harry Haggard brushed past the butler and ran down the steps, little Mina at his heels. "Oh, Papa."

Haggard dismounted, hugged each of them in turn. Harry was thirteen! Mina twelve. Both Haggards, he thought. But tempered with the Favering beauty, which made them unique. He looked over their heads at the butler. "I shall come in, nonetheless, old fellow."

Hargreaves hesitated.

"I think you may, Roger," Jane said from the doorway. She wore a house gown, and had her hair in a mobcap, but she was not diminished in beauty.

Roger climbed the steps, still holding the children's hands. "A happy Easter to you."

"And to you. Frank warned us that you might be coming. To enjoy your triumph and our humiliation?"

He released Harry, kissed Jane's hand. "To congratulate you on the passage of the bill. Is it not what you always wanted to happen?"

"Politics," she said contemptuously.

"It is what *I* always wanted to happen," Mina said from inside the house. "Come in, Haggard. Come in. I do not enjoy the light."

He stepped inside, gazed at her. She was sixty-eight years old, and in the gloom of the hallway hardly looked a day older than when he had first met her.

"I am told you played your part in that also," she said.

"In return for a promise of emancipation, yes."

"And other promises as well, I understand." She held out her hand and he kissed her knuckles. "So the world is once again at your feet, Roger. As it was in 1812, and again in 1815. You must be careful you do not throw it away again."

He smiled at her. "I am for domesticity. And forgiveness. I wronged you, Jane."

Her mouth twisted in the way he remembered so well. "As I endeavored to wrong you in reply. Will you marry Lindy?"

"We leave for France the day after tomorrow. She awaits me in Dover."

"Then I will wish you joy. We never shared joy, did we, Haggard? Only ecstasy, and that is not an emotion to be sustained."

"And will you not also marry again?" he asked.

"After being Mrs. Roger Haggard?" Another twist of the lips. "I have never been able to settle for anything less than the best. Besides, there are the children to be cared for. Like you, I shall settle for domesticity. Godspeed you, Haggard. Common sense tells me it would have been better had we never met. But as we did, Godspeed you."

"And never change, Haggard," Mina said. "The world is too poor a place to afford such waste. Do not ever change."

ABOUT THE AUTHOR

Christopher Nicole, who currently lives in the Channel Islands, has traveled widely in Europe, the Orient, and the Americas. Other Christopher Nicole novels available in Signet are the best-selling CARIBEE, THE DEVIL'S OWN, MISTRESS OF DARKNESS, BLACK DAWN, and SUNSET, his five-book historical saga of the Caribbean, as well as *Haggard,* which began the story of the Haggard family.

Recommended Reading from SIGNET

Big Bestsellers from SIGNET

Buy them at your local
bookstore or use coupon
on back page to order.

Recommended Reading from SIGNET

- [ ] **ONE FLEW OVER THE CUCKOO'S NEST by Ken Kesey.**
  (#E8867—$2.25)
- [ ] **THE GRADUATE by Charles Webb.** (#W8633—$1.50)
- [ ] **'SALEM'S LOT by Stephen King.** (#E9827—$3.50)
- [ ] **THE STAND by Stephen King.** (#E9828—$3.95)
- [ ] **THE SHINING by Stephen King.** (#E9216—$2.95)
- [ ] **CARRIE by Stephen King.** (#E9544—$2.50)
- [ ] **THE DEAD ZONE by Stephen King.** (#E9338—$3.50)
- [ ] **NIGHT SHIFT by Stephen King.** (#E9746—$2.95)
- [ ] **SAVAGE RANSOM by David Lippincott.** (#E8749—$2.25)*
- [ ] **SALT MINE by David Lippincott.** (#E9158—$2.25)*
- [ ] **TWINS by Bari Wood and Jack Geasland.** (#E9094—$2.75)
- [ ] **THE KILLING GIFT by Bari Wood.** (#J7350—$1.95)
- [ ] **SPHINX by Robin Cook.** (#E9194—$2.95)
- [ ] **COMA by Robin Cook.** (#E9756—$2.75)
- [ ] **BLOOD RITES by Barry Nazarian.** (#E9203—$2.25)*

* Price slightly higher in Canada
